the
greatest
risk

the
greatest
risk

KRISTEN
ASHLEY

ST. MARTIN'S GRIFFIN ✳ NEW YORK

For Liz Berry
A Champion of Writers
A Champion of Sisters
My Beautiful Friend
And one of the most beautiful hearts on the planet

THE GREATEST RISK. Copyright © 2018 by Kristen Ashley. All rights reserved. Printed in the United States of America. For information, address St. Martin's Press, 175 Fifth Avenue, New York, N.Y. 10010.

www.stmartins.com

The Library of Congress Cataloging-in-Publication Data is available upon request.

ISBN 978-1-250-17710-0 (trade paperback)
ISBN 978-1-250-17711-7 (ebook)

Our books may be purchased in bulk for promotional, educational, or business use. Please contact your local bookseller or the Macmillan Corporate and Premium Sales Department at 1-800-221-7945, extension 5442, or by email at MacmillanSpecialMarkets@macmillan.com.

First Edition: May 2018

10 9 8 7 6 5 4 3 2 1

acknowledgments

As ever and always, thank you to my agent, and my friend, Emily Sylvan Kim, who is so many things, it'd take another book to acknowledge them all. And gratitude to Alexandra Sehulster, who took on my Honey at the finale, and allowed me to release the breath I'd been holding after she fell for Stellan and Sixx (almost) as hard as I did.

prologue

Opposites Attract

SIXX

Two years ago ...

Sixx sat in the booth at the Bee's Honey and watched.

She watched what she'd seen time and again.

She watched what set a heavy weight to taking residence in her stomach.

Mistress Amélie had selected her toy for the evening and was going back to the playrooms.

And Master Stellan was sitting in his booth, watching her go, a look of disappointment on his usually remote but always extortionately handsome face that he did not hide fast enough.

Thus Sixx caught it.

"Not gonna go anywhere, sweetheart."

She turned her eyes to the man sitting across the semi-circular booth with her. A booth he owned because he owned the Honey, a luxurious, exclusive BDSM sex club in Phoenix that had sister clubs in cities across the West.

Aryas Weathers was a very large black man with a bald head, a thick beard and a beautiful soul.

"Pardon?" Sixx asked.

"Leigh and Stellan," he answered. "It's not gonna happen."

"I don't know what—" she began.

"Yes you do," he said softly.

She spoke no more because Aryas was a handsome black man with a beautiful soul and a number of sex clubs he owned and operated. He was also a Dom, and a good one, thus keenly observant and empathic. Last, he was a friend and an excellent one.

In other words, with his friends that empathy hit extremes.

"She's into him and he's into her," Sixx replied.

"They'd never make it. He needs a challenge and so does she," Aryas told her.

Sixx looked down at her glass of red wine, something she'd ordered wishing it was a cocktail with gin involved, but that wouldn't work with the rep she had going at the Honey, doing this thinking that two Doms finding their way together in life when sexually they didn't quite fit would be one hell of a challenge.

"Opposites attract."

Those quiet words from Aryas had her head coming up again and her eyes finding his.

"Can't say how I know, outside what you know only I know, just will say that I know, you wanted in there, you could turn his eye," Aryas shared.

She was not going to put herself out there like that.

She couldn't.

She was strong. A female Goliath, a superhero with a vagina in a five-seven, trim-but-nice-ass, though not-so-much-in-the-breast-department, long-legged frame.

Straight up.

Fuckin' A.

But not with something like that.

Not that.

"I've got an assignment taking me out of town," she reminded him, and watched his lips form into a frown. "I don't know when I'll return."

Or . . . *if.*

Phoenix was awesome. There were good restaurants. There were palm trees. There were hiking trails. Sedona and Prescott were just hours away if you wanted spiritual enlightenment in a place that proved God existed or a break from the pounding sun in a place that proved God didn't mind flexing his creativity over a matter of mere miles. There was every sport you could want including hockey even though you could usually count the overnight freezes of a year on one hand. And everyone was so damned happy that the summer heat had broken that from October to June it was one huge-ass party, people taking to the streets, malls, outdoor dining, hiking trails and city-wide events like it was a slow-roll Mardi Gras.

And if it snowed, the residents acted like the world was coming to an end because it seemed like it was, but the panic didn't last because what would only amount to a dusting of that white shit was gone by noon.

But it also had Stellan.

Stellan who got what he wanted.

Always.

And he wanted Amélie.

And Stellan was what Sixx wanted.

But she rarely got what she wanted (as in, *never*).

Thus Stellan would end up with Amélie.

"You gotta quit that shit," Aryas replied, his sweet, soft tone turning biting.

Sixx pulled herself out of dismal thoughts and reacted to his tone, shooting back, "And how would I pay for my leather if I stopped that shit?"

"You'll not have a body to put that leather on if it's buried in the ground," he retorted.

"I know what I'm doing, and I'm good at it," she returned.

"You've done work for me, that's how I met you; you settled that shit like the pro you are, so that's not in question. But now you're not a contractor, you're a friend, and I'm not feelin' as cheery about your present occupation."

Sixx quirked a brow. "So, say, a friend of yours who's in my business is sitting opposite you in this booth and he happens to have a dick, would this conversation have taken this turn?"

Aryas's full lips thinned as he looked to the hunting ground, the expanse of space situated in the middle of the room surrounded by a classed-up bar on one wall, the other three walls lined with posh horseshoe booths in order that the Doms in those booths could look over the subs in the hunting ground.

She gave it time, and he did not answer.

So she had her answer.

Eventually, Aryas broke the silence, looked back to Sixx and said, "Leigh will find someone."

"Or they'll find each other," she rejoined.

Aryas kept going like she'd said nothing. "And if you take off, he'll find someone too."

"Yes," she agreed. "When one or the other of them quits circling and goes in for the kill, that will happen for both of them."

"Is there a reason you're allergic to happy?" he asked irritably.

That had Sixx snapping her mouth shut and looking at the hunting ground.

"You think he's too good for you?" Aryas pressed.

She stared at a male sub who she had not yet had.

He was not her type.

Her type was a tall, lean, lethal, sexy, rich-as-fuck, handsome-as-all-hell Dom who, she flicked her glance his way, was right then calling over a beautiful, willowy sub to his booth.

She was not beautiful.

Though she could be described as willowy, at a push.

Damn.

"You think he's got it all together and won't want to put up with a mess like you?" Aryas kept pushing.

Her eyes slanted back to him, and they were slits.

But she couldn't argue the fact she was a mess. A big one.

And Aryas knew that.

He did not know because she'd told him anything.

She hadn't told him anything.

Not a thing.

But he was Aryas, he read it on her like she had her story tattooed all over her skin.

Which, with how much that story didn't feel too good living, it was a wonder she didn't.

"You haven't cornered the market on demons, Sixx. Stellan's got his own, just like you. And he might also want someone in his life to help him beat them back."

"I suddenly feel the need to crack a whip," she retorted.

"Of course you do," he muttered, looking frustrated.

"I leave in a few weeks," she declared.

His eyes narrowed angrily.

"Of course you do," he repeated.

"I might not be back," she spoke the decision she'd right then made.

"You'll be missed and not only by me. You might not have taken this in, but your prolonged stay here, my sweet, means I'm not the only one in Phoenix who's pleased he can call you a friend."

She couldn't handle that so she didn't.

She slid her tight, black-leather-pants-covered ass out of the booth and took her feet on the stiletto heels of her black boots.

"He'll go all in for you."

Aryas throwing that out there got her attention again, and she twisted toward him.

He kept at her.

"Stellan finds the one that's worth it, he'll break his back, sell his soul, work his fingers to the bone to win her and keep her."

"And you can't tell me why you know that about him, of course," she remarked.

"I can tell you you're gold in one of my playrooms, and the amount of subs out there whose mouths just set to drooling just 'cause you slid your ass out of a booth lays testimony to that. But you got a long way to go to earn the premiere status of Domme that every-one thinks you have. You rock at the practical, but if you can't read that on Lange, you might have it all in practice, Sixx, but you're not hiding from me you don't have a lock on the most important part of the scene. Theory."

"How disappointing that I have to strike off my to-do list start-ing my Dominatrix Academy," she returned sarcastically. "And here I was, had the curriculum all set and everything."

She knew she'd pushed Aryas too far when he spoke again.

"Lived most my life watching the two most important people in it, my mother and my brother, do without," he fired back. "She did the best she could for her boys. Gave it her all. And we still had dick. Think it was daily growing up I told myself I'd do something about that. And I did. So now she's good. He's good. But if you got that in you from the moment you learned how to breathe, wanting the best for the people in your heart, you can't get away from it. So get pissed. Put up your shields. Go play with some sub who means dick to you when the man who's taken hold of a piece of your heart is sitting thirty feet away. But don't expect me to like it. And don't expect me to keep my mouth shut about it."

"You know, you're intensely annoying when you're being all that's you, especially the good parts," she retorted sharply.

He shrugged. "It is what it is."

"Can I go force some orgasms now?" she requested. "Or are you still feeling the lecture?"

"You can if you promise to think about it," he replied.

"Think about what?" she asked.

"Being happy."

Sixx stared at Aryas Weathers's face.

Years ago, he'd had a nasty problem, and she'd been referred to him to assist in solving it.

When she had, she'd found out what he did, and he found out who she was and guided her to being all she could be with that.

During that time, she'd kept taking jobs, but she'd made Phoenix her base, coming home there.

Coming home to him.

Because he was her friend.

The only one she had.

Also because she owed him huge chunks of her sanity.

And right then, she owed him reining in her smart mouth as well as giving him that promise.

Just doing that her way.

"How about I won't actively avoid it?"

He shook his head but did it with his lips curling up.

"Go," he ordered. "Play."

Sixx turned from him, took a step away, and turned back.

"I love everything about you," she whispered. "I'd break my back, sell my soul, work my fingers to the bone for you. There is precisely one human being on this planet that has that from me. You."

With that, in order not to give him a shot at replying the way the beauty of his face told her he was going to, she immediately strolled away on her four-and-a-half-inch, pencil-slim heels, pointing at two male subs as she went but not breaking stride to the door that led to the playrooms, knowing with no doubts they'd follow her.

They did.

And she did this also knowing she had one pair of male eyes on her and only one.

Aryas's.

But Sixx's awareness was unusually incorrect.

She had two pairs of male eyes on her.

And that second set stayed on her all the way through the room and didn't move, even after she disappeared behind the door.

Seven months later ...

It was like a whisper of wind against her skin when the door opened, and Sixx knew to turn and look, not because she'd do that as a matter of course just to be aware of her surroundings and who was occupying them (something she would do).

But because something told her what was coming she could not miss.

And she was right as she sat at the bar at the swank restaurant in Washington, D.C., and watched with some surprise as Stellan Lange walked in the front door.

He looked magnificent, as he always did. Though she'd never seen him in the way she was seeing him now, with the black, cashmere overcoat covering his sleek, bespoke, dark gray suit.

The suit was *de rigueur* for Stellan.

But he lived in Phoenix where overcoats were entirely unnecessary.

Sleek, she thought, her eyes roaming him, consuming him, *devouring* him.

That was Stellan. Not slick, *sleek*.

From the top of his head that was covered in thick, dark brown, perfectly styled hair all the way down the six-plus feet that made him to the tips of his shining, custom-made, Italian leather shoes.

He was an Aquascutum ad. Cary Grant with a kick, all the polish, good looks and sophistication with a rugged, dangerous edge.

He was perfect.

She wasn't on the job at that very moment, so considering her heart started tripping a faster beat, her first inclination was to lift her hand, call his attention to her, take this surprising circumstance away from Phoenix, from the Honey, and turn it into a drink among friends all the way across a continent.

Turn it into time with Stellan.

Just time . . . with Stellan.

She didn't care what they did. She didn't care if he could only be in her presence for thirty seconds to give her one of his charming smiles, one of his head-to-toes that took every minute detail in and made her clit pulse, then touch his smooth cheek to hers and whisper a hello in his deep, silk voice as she smelled his amazing cologne.

Without bidding them to come, the words filled her head.

Think about what?

Being happy.

Yes, even if it was just thirty seconds with Stellan, that would make her happy.

But then he swung his head from the hostess he was looking at to sweep his gaze across the space toward the dining area, and she caught sight of the expression on his face.

A chill slid down her spine, and Sixx was not used to that kind of chill.

Murderous.

He looked like he wanted to kill somebody.

Perhaps not the time to ask him if he'd like to take this surprising opportunity to have a chat over a noontime Scotch with a friend from home.

He was nodding peremptorily, seeming impatient as well as homicidal, as the hostess spoke to him and moved from behind her station with a menu clutched under her arm.

"Ready to order?"

Sixx tore her eyes from Stellan prowling behind the hostess toward the dining room to look at the bartender.

"Filet, medium rare, and err on the side of rare. French fries," she ordered, beginning to turn her attention back to Stellan.

But the bartender said, "All we have are *pommes frites*."

Was he serious?

She held his gaze probably looking a little like Stellan did as he'd walked in and replied slowly, "As I said. Filet, medium rare, and *French fries*."

"Right," he muttered.

She glanced quickly to her left and then to the back of the bar to see the shelves holding liquor were framed in mirrors.

Mirrors she could now see Stellan through as he stood tall and straight, proud and arrogant in that oh-so-special way of his, at a table in the middle of the dining room with the hostess standing at his side.

"I'll be moving down to the end," she told the bartender. "Cool?"

"Sure," he replied. "I'll nab your Pellegrino."

Sixx grabbed her bag, he got her sparkling water, and with her gaze fixed to the mirror, she moved down six stools to the one at the end of the bar against the wall. A darker space, more removed, not as easy to see her.

But with that mirror, she had a view of the whole dining room.

She sat with her eyes glued to what was happening with Stellan in that room.

The hostess had disappeared, and an older man was standing with Stellan. Stellan who had not taken off his overcoat and also appeared like he had no intention to do so.

Sixx felt the fissures of tension opening up all the way across the space.

Stellan was regarding the man standing with him like he'd rather be dipped naked in a vat of slime with his eyes and mouth forced open than be in that man's presence.

And the man had to be a relative. The age difference was definite, as was the resemblance.

A close relative.

Uncle at least.

Or father.

The man was holding himself awkwardly, like he wanted to go in for a handshake, or even a hug, but Stellan's body language and facial expression were not only not inviting that, they were actively warning against it.

And then Stellan shifted, turning his back on Sixx.

That was when Sixx saw her.

A woman sitting at the table facing them, her eyes lifted, trained on Stellan, a look of astonishment and something else suffusing her features.

She was blonde. Very beautiful. Put together perfectly from head to waist, which was as far as Sixx could see, but that meant it went down further. Perfect hair. Perfect makeup. Perfect accessories. Perfect blouse. And all that perfect was the best money could buy.

She was either a professional stylist, a model or *had* a professional stylist because she was a model. She looked like she'd walked right off the location of a photo shoot to come have lunch.

She also looked like she wanted to eat every inch of Stellan up with a spoon.

Sixx's heart started tripping even faster.

And then it happened.

The blonde beauty's mouth went slack, and the fissure of tension splintering through the dining room split wide open.

Sixx stopped messing around with the mirror and turned on her stool to watch it in full view.

Scanning the scene with skilled attention, thus taking it all in within seconds, Sixx saw the older man now looked infuriated, his face flushed, his brows snapped taut, his slightly jowly jaw having tightened up.

The blonde appeared wounded.

And Stellan looked done.

He proved her assessment correct by turning on his expensive shoe and sauntering away.

Sixx watched him go, all the way out the door, noting that he no longer looked murderous.

He looked his usual.

Aloof.

What he'd come there to do, he'd done.

And now he was moving on.

She turned her attention back to the couple, and that was when she spotted the huge rock on the blonde's left ring finger. Massive. Ostentatious.

Sixx could see it now because the woman's hands were covering her face like she was hiding tears.

The older man sat and leaned immediately to her, putting a hand on her back to soothe her. Not in a fatherly way.

In a loverly way.

If Sixx had to call it, that man had to be at least in his sixties, the blonde in her twenties.

Sixx looked to the door to the restaurant Stellan had just disappeared through for a fleeting instant before she turned to her bag.

She pulled out her slim-line laptop and got the attention of the bartender.

When he jerked up his chin, she asked, "Do you have Wi-Fi?"

He nodded. "Password is BookerTMG. The 'TMG' in caps."

Well, whoever thought that up had good taste in music.

She thanked him, opened the laptop, started it up, hooked into the Wi-Fi, and as she sipped Pellegrino then, when it arrived, ate her filet and frigging *pommes frites*, it didn't take long for her to find it.

Andreas Lange, multimillionaire hotelier, father of multimillionaire developer Stellan Lange, had just last week announced his engagement to the woman who would become his fifth wife, Priscilla Newton.

Andreas Lange was sixty-nine years old.

Priscilla Newton was twenty-two.

Sixx didn't dig any deeper because she wasn't on the job then, but she was on a job, and she needed to eat and get back to business.

It wouldn't be until she was bone-weary but unable to sleep in her hotel room late that night (or more aptly, very early the next morning) that she'd go back to her laptop.

It didn't take long before she wished she hadn't.

She snapped the laptop closed and looked out the window across the night landscape of the purposefully-built-to-impress-and-intimidate capital of the nation.

"This is why I never do a deep dive into people I know," she told the window.

She said it, but her heart was far heavier than it should have been, or than she'd want it to be after doing a deep dive and discovering all she'd discovered about Stellan.

Sixx left her laptop to slide between the sheets (in a hotel, incidentally, that Andreas Lange owned, which meant she'd be moving to another one the next day), but she did not go to sleep.

She stared at the dark ceiling and did it until it lit with dawn, pissed as hell that Aryas had been right.

Everyone has demons.

Including Stellan Lange.

But not everyone knew the name of their demon.

But Stellan did.

Just like Sixx knew the name of every single one of hers.

Six months later . . .

Sixx was sucking in breath to handle the pain, driving, and hoping with everything she had she could make it to the doc Carlo had told her he had waiting for her without passing out when her phone rang.

When she saw in the dash who was calling, not thinking straight, she hit the button on the steering wheel to take the call.

"You've got impeccable timing," she said into the car, hearing that her voice sounded strung tight and hoping the caller wouldn't hear it too.

"How's that?" Aryas asked.

Just that, if I'm going to die, the last voice I want to hear is yours, she thought.

"I'm dead tired but completely unable to stop myself answering when you call," she answered, and all of that was true, she'd just left some things out.

Like a couple of fresh bullet wounds.

God, if she lived, it was going to be hell getting the blood out of the cognac leather of her beloved Cayenne.

Though, right then, that was the least of her worries.

"Just thought you'd want to know, that stallion I approved for Leigh..." He made her wait for it, but not long. "That shit took. He's the one, and if I'm not sittin' in a pew watching them walk down the aisle in twelve months or less, I'll let you spank me," Aryas told her.

At these words, but not entirely because of them, Sixx swerved, righted the car, and drew in another deep breath that wasn't exactly cutting it to dull the pain.

When she didn't answer, Aryas said, "So, what I'm sayin' is, clear shot for you."

"How'd Stellan take it?" she asked.

"He doesn't usually Oprah it up with me," Aryas answered.

Focusing on the conversation as well as the road, both doing wonders with keeping her conscious, she returned, "Come on. You've got your finger on every pulse of every player in every club you own. How'd he take it?"

"He's not speaking with Leigh right now."

Translation: He'd failed to make a play. Screwed the pooch.

Now he was licking his wounds.

God, but she'd love to lick Stellan Lange's wounds.

Kiss all his hurts away.

Including the ones she laid on him with him begging her for more.

"You know I want all my babies happy, Sixx. Come home. Get some happy and give some to my·boy," Aryas urged. "Stellan is due, and it goes without saying you are too."

Damn, it was starting to snow.

Just what she needed.

Driving, listening, talking, watching it come down, and trying to stay lucid, Sixx realized how much she hated snow.

Phoenix didn't have snow.

"Sixx?" Aryas called.

"I'm here but I gotta go."

"You cool?" he asked.

"Peachy," she lied.

There was silence before, far more alertly, she got, "Sixx, are you cool?"

"Awesome," she puffed out as an unexpected wave of pain hit her when she made a right turn and the movement didn't suit her gunshot wounds too much.

"What the fuck is going down?" Aryas rapped out.

"It's snowing," she said.

"Yeah?" he prompted.

"And I'm driving," she told him.

"All right," he replied.

"So I've got to concentrate," she pointed out.

He returned that favor, sharing out loud her earlier thought. "It doesn't snow in Phoenix."

Right then, Sixx made a decision.

That was, she made a decision if she lived to carry it through.

But mostly, she made the decision because she was realizing acutely in that moment that life was short.

Even so, that decision had conditions.

"You don't interfere," she stated.

"Say what?" Aryas asked.

"I'm coming home."

"Brilliant," he muttered, a lightness in his deep voice she hadn't heard since before she left, and they didn't talk all the time, but they talked frequently.

Or it was more like Aryas checked in frequently. Sixx wasn't one to stay in contact or give much away.

Ever.

"And you don't interfere," she demanded. "It happens naturally with Stellan if it happens at all without you sticking your big nose in it."

"I do not have a big nose," he huffed. Though he was pretending to sound hurt, even in her state she couldn't miss he was pleased.

"Now let me go so I don't crash this vehicle and end up in a body cast, not on my way to finishing this job and heading to the Valley of the Sun."

"The job going okay?"

Hell no.

"It's almost done," she answered.

And that was no lie.

"Then I'm letting you go," he said.

"Right."

"Sixx?"

"What?" she demanded impatiently, beginning to blink too much and knowing from past experience that wasn't good.

Maybe she should keep him on the line.

"I love everything about you. I'd break my back, sell my soul, work my fingers to the bone for you. And if you want me not to interfere, I'll do that too. But if you start fucking shit up, I'm in the game. Now finish this fucking job and come home. We miss you."

The call dropped before she could say a word.

But it was good Aryas got his words in.

They kept her going until she was safe.

Then, dragging herself through the back door of a clinic that through the powers of Carlo had been opened specifically for her, it was lights out.

one

Let's Go

SIXX

Present day...

Sixx wandered the halls of the Bee's Honey for absolutely no purpose except to make the boys in the booth watching the cameras that monitored the action in the club think she was taking in the scene.

Instead, she was biding time to go into the Dom Lounge to get what she'd stashed in her locker.

She was over it.

Over the scene.

Over the wait.

Done.

The Honey had now become a place she could hang and have a drink, connect with some friends if she was in the mood, get some of her kink by watching, and torture herself being around Stellan.

It was also where she stashed something if she had it to stash. This was because the Honey had surveillance and security that rivaled that of the White House. If a person wasn't supposed to be there, they didn't get in there. The end.

She'd been back in Phoenix now for a while.

Months.

And although she'd put on a variety of shows, bided her time, put herself out there, made herself available, Stellan hadn't thrown down the gauntlet.

She sure as hell wasn't making the first move.

Thus that first move wasn't going to be made.

So be it.

She hadn't expected much and she sure got that.

And she had to admit, part of her was relieved (a large part).

Because if he took a shot, what then?

Could she protect him from all that was her?

Doubtful.

More like impossible.

She never had with anyone who mattered, not that she'd had many in her life who mattered.

And Stellan absolutely did not deserve to have to deal with all that could befall anyone who got close to Sixx.

Tonight was different, though.

Tonight, she wanted done with the extracurricular activity she was engaged in.

Also tonight she roamed the halls knowing Stellan was there, he'd taken a room, and he'd gone off his normal *modus operandi*.

He'd selected a female sub.

He'd also selected a male.

If in a mood, though that mood was always rare, he'd pick more than one sub.

But they were always females.

Sixx had a feeling she knew why he'd done this. She had Google alerts set up, and she'd seen it.

That *it* being that it was announced to the media that day that the two-and-a-half-month marriage of Andreas Lange and his pretty-much-child bride Priscilla was done. Although the press was asked to leave the couple alone in this trying time, it was nevertheless reported that Andreas might often think with his dick and had apparent self-esteem issues that drove him to having a pretty young thing dripping off his arm, but when it counted, he used his other head. The one with an actual brain in it.

In other words, he had a reported ironclad prenuptial agreement, and the soon-to-be-again Ms. Newton would walk away with the engagement ring he gave her, any gifts she'd acquired during their relationship and nothing else.

Nothing else.

Not even a settlement.

She was young, and Sixx knew that young didn't make you stupid, it just made you young, naïve, and perhaps with the beauty that girl had, overconfident. Thus she probably thought her golden looks mingled with a twenty-two-year-old pussy would buy her a lot more time to get a lot more gifts.

Sadly, she'd been wrong.

Sixx could not know how this news affected Stellan. Although they had exchanged a variety of words since she'd been home, they'd both been at a few get-togethers where he didn't avoid her, but he didn't pursue her, they'd caught each other's eyes on a number of occasions; and she'd noted him watching her work with her submissives, as he'd noted her doing the same with his, they had not even resurrected the loose but friendly relationship they'd had before she'd left.

She put it down to him still smarting from Leigh's falling in love with another man.

That said, even if Leigh had, it appeared that not much had changed between Stellan and Amélie. Although chilly between them when Sixx got back, that had thawed, and they were as sociable and close as they ever had been. And it was clear Stellan liked Olly, Amélie's enormous, gorgeous stallion.

Then again, everyone liked Olly. It was impossible *not* to like the guy. He was just that guy who had it all and not simply the fact he was so easy to look at.

He adored Leigh, for one. Utterly. And he did not hide it in the slightest.

But he was outgoing, funny, solid. If you were moving house and you needed an extra pair of hands, he was there. If you had a nephew (or niece) who wanted to be a firefighter (which Olly was), he'd take the kid through his station and introduce him to all the guys. If you were at a cookout with him and running low on your drink, you found your glass slid out of your hand and another one put in it without even having to ask.

Even Stellan, wanting Amélie for as long as he did, couldn't dislike the guy.

So they'd become friends.

And Sixx had watched.

That was one of the two things she'd done since being back.

In a halfhearted attempt to get his attention (and keep Aryas off her back), she played.

And she watched.

Which was what she was on a mission to do now before she hit the Dom Lounge to prepare to complete her other mission.

As she wandered, Sixx didn't spend time watching Mira and Trey in their room.

It was tough watching Mira work now that she had a sub and they were *together* together. In other words, in love. Mira was good at what she did, and Trey liked what his Mistress gave him, but that look of adoration on her face while she was doing it . . .

Sixx just couldn't deal with it.

This was also why she avoided Leigh and Olly when they were at play (and more recently, also when they weren't because the connection they had between them just didn't stop).

Right then they weren't in a playroom. They were still in the bar, holding court, The Stallion Alpha Sub King and his Dominatrix Queen, as usual reigning supreme over the club and enjoying it before they moved to a room to enjoy each other.

They were actually worse to watch than Trey and Mira, they were so beautiful together. They were like watching dancers, so perfectly in sync, expressive, at one with each other and their own bodies.

The sequence practiced, even if it was always different, it was so graceful it was sublime.

Putting this out of her mind, Sixx moved on her black platform pumps to the back hall full of playrooms, noting, and not surprised, that Aryas's red room was shuttered away from view. The blackout blinds to that room were scarlet, not black like all the others, thus its name.

It was his own personal playroom if he was in town. And he was. And he had one of his babies in there, working her.

Sixx didn't need to watch that, although she would have. She'd not only seen Aryas at play, he'd worked her because he'd trained her. He showed her how to be who she was. He introduced her to other Dommes to teach her the things he could not. And he'd played with her in his sessions in which she was required to sub so she could understand the headspace her own subs had to get in to serve her.

She had been surprised she'd liked it.

She'd been freaked she'd liked it so much.

Too much.

Aryas had handled that too for her—amazingly. Which meant he'd helped her handle it.

And then she'd locked it away.

However as she bypassed his room, she felt her lips thin that he was back there with one of his babies and not with the woman he should be with.

At first when Sixx arrived back in Phoenix, he'd let things lie.

Now that months had passed, he was getting up in her face about making a move on Stellan.

Fortunately, she was able to fight back since he wouldn't make a move on Mistress Talia.

Which was where Sixx went and where she stopped to watch, also not surprised that Talia was working a sub mostly because those two circled each other just this way. If Talia took a sub and he caught it, Aryas wasn't too far from taking his own. If Aryas took one and Talia caught it, she hustled a sub into a playroom.

Retaliation.

As Sixx watched Talia work a sub named Bryan, definitely a favored and oft-used toy of hers, she got worried.

In a heartbeat, Bryan would take things further with his tall, slender, lithe, beautiful, mocha-skinned, tawny-fro'ed Mistress, and not just because he seriously got off on the way she worked him.

She wasn't just beautiful and had a serious style going on in and out of a playroom. She was funny, quick-witted, smart-mouthed, loyal and very sweet. And Sixx had witnessed her aftercare of Bryan when she got down to serious business with him, and even knowing Talia's heart was with Aryas, her head and attention was with Bryan in a way he could mistake the fact that he didn't have a place in that particular vital organ.

Sixx considered having a word with the Mistress.

She did that, and then she decided instead to have a word with Leigh so Leigh would have a word. Amélie was probably already thinking of doing it. She wasn't Queen Bee just because she rocked a playroom, and she took her unofficial role seriously.

But if Sixx had a word, she might light a fire, and perhaps if they double-teamed Aryas and Talia, they could get something going.

Before hitting the Dom Lounge, she found her feet taking her one last place.

At first, she positioned herself carefully in order to be able to process what she might see and at the same time be out of his line of sight because he always broke scene to catch her eyes if he saw her at the windows. And the possibility of seeing him working a male sub was something she wanted without him breaking scene.

This eye contact, at first, she'd found terrifying, because it was encouraging. It was rare a Dom working would do that unless he was working directly with another Dom.

When months passed and nothing came of it, Sixx stopped finding it terrifying or encouraging and just found it weird.

There was no invitation in his gaze. No challenge issued. No warmth or comradeship or humor or anything.

He'd just catch her gaze and hold it for as long as it took for her to break it. Even if he was physically inside one of his subs, he'd thrust while simply looking at Sixx, remote and disengaged, from her *and* his sub, until Sixx herself broke the contact and his attention went back to his sub.

But if he was working a male, especially inside one, this she'd want to see. Man-on-man was a thing of hers, and since she'd returned to Phoenix, she'd indulged in that, always taking multiple submissives, they were always male, and she'd call the shots to get that fix.

Seeing Stellan engaged in something like this would probably make her orgasm right there in the hall. Hell, just thinking about it got her wet.

Then again, although this would be an extraordinary sight to see, Sixx didn't figure it would take much to do that. In all her play since she'd come back, she had not once let a single sub touch her, she'd rarely touched them, and she hadn't had that first orgasm, not in play, not with some random partner she picked up out in the vanilla world (because she hadn't picked anyone up), not even at her own hand.

But as she hesitated at the edge of one of the rooms Stellan favored, the silhouette and blackout blinds up like he normally played it, she didn't even see Stellan.

The female was working the male, and that work was inspired, but there was no Stellan.

Sixx took one step along the hall.

Another.

And there he was, still in his trousers and dress shirt, but the suit jacket was thrown over the back of the leather club chair he was sitting in. He had his long legs crossed, and he was slanted to the side, elbow on the arm of the chair, head propped up in his hand where it held his square jaw at his knuckles with his forefinger extended along his chiseled cheek.

She drew in a breath at the bored expression on his arrestingly beautiful face, that expression running deep into his dark blue eyes.

He did not look annoyed, upset, or distracted, as news of his father acquiring then disposing of another wife in a matter of months might make him.

He didn't look anything, certainly not like he was in a room where sweet and dirty sex acts were being performed at his command by the slaves he'd chosen for the evening.

He looked like he was in a meeting that he couldn't wait to get out of.

Then suddenly, his gaze came to her.

He didn't move, didn't lift his head, just swept his eyes straight to her, not like he'd noticed her standing there, like he'd *sensed* she was there.

His expression didn't change. Neither did his position.

He stared her right in the eyes, pinning her to the spot, giving her nothing except his regard.

She wanted to scream, *Why? Why do you look at me like that? Why can't you give me something? Anything?*

She didn't do that.

Of course not.

She accepted the only challenge he gave her and stared straight at him in return for as long as she could stand it.

And Sixx could stand a lot, so this lasted a long time, perhaps full minutes, before, as ever (and as ever wanting to kick her own ass), she broke the contact and walked slowly, and as casually as she could fake it, away.

Once out of sight of Stellan, she didn't mess around going to the Dom Lounge.

There were cameras in there too, but she'd given herself a reason to return there after she had a drink in the hunting ground. This being so she could collect what she'd put there a week ago and be done with the job she was on so she could then collect the paycheck.

She did just this, going directly to her locker and grabbing the small, boxy, black python Alexander McQueen clutch with its four finger loops topped with various skulls or roses. A clutch she'd placed there after she'd arrived rather than giving it to reception, which was what most of the Dommes did.

Inside was a slim, business-card-sized wallet with her credit card, ID and a few banknotes, her phone, another phone that was hers-but-also-not, her lip liner and lipstick, her fabulous vintage compact with mother-of-pearl inlaid in black depicting cranes flying across a yellow moon, her Cayenne keyfob and nothing else.

With her back to the camera, she grabbed a random vibrator she had in her locker, twisted off the bottom where you'd put batteries, upended the flash drive she'd hidden there, and slid it in the lining of the clutch that she'd jimmied so she could open it, hide things behind it, and then press it back in place where it held.

She then went to the mirror.

At first, she didn't look at herself, but instead used it to take in the plush surroundings of the Dominants' Lounge.

Deep-seated, purple-velvet banquettes spanned the walls. They were covered in red-and-silver-velvet toss pillows. The patterned silver wallpaper behind them was bottom-lit with soft light.

There were attractive steel tables with scented candles glowing on top of them.

The lockers were made of the same steel as the tables and looked like a bank of cabinets with a variety of digital locks, not lockers.

The gleaming black basins had no faucets, just wide, lush waterfalls that activated by motion. There were no paper towels, instead thick, soft, purple, red or silver hand towels and washcloths.

There were showers around the side, as well as a Jacuzzi tub, a steam room and a sauna.

Available for use was anything you could need. Disposable razors (for men and women) and shaving cream, aftershave, a variety of colognes and perfumes, hairspray, lotions, oils, deodorants, tampons, condoms, face moisturizer, bath soap and scrub, shampoo and conditioner.

Submissives were specifically disallowed there. The lounge was for downtime and Dom time outside any scene. If a sub needed to be cared for or it was part of the scene, you requested a room that had those amenities, and the Dom took care of that.

And Sixx longed to stretch out on those banquettes and close her eyes to the D. L. & Co. candles that smelled like vanilla, balsam and pepper, soothing and spicy, so very Aryas. So very the Honey.

God, she loved it there. It was like her home. It was the only place, outside being on a job, where she could be . . .

What?

Not herself. She played a role there. No one knew who she was. Not really. (Except Aryas, or at least he knew more than everyone else.) Not even people she called friends.

So why did she love it there so much?

And why was her heart hurting that she wasn't getting out of it what she needed anymore?

She looked at herself in the mirror.

"Because it's safe," she whispered to her reflection.

That was it.

And now it no longer felt as safe.

Because Stellan was there, and wanting him and not having him—but more, knowing she should never expose him to what it would mean to have her . . . hurt.

That didn't make sense either. She'd wanted a lot in life.

And never got it.

But Stellan was different.

Stellan was . . .

Sixx shook off her thoughts and took herself in through the mirror.

She couldn't see the black pumps or her long legs she'd sleeked not only by giving them a close shave all the way up to her pubis but also with a subtle oil that made them shine.

What she could see was the black leather micro-mini that sat tight on her hips, cupped her ass and had a wide black belt with a bold silver buckle.

Up top she wore a white leather modified camisole that had a deep plunging neckline that went to her midriff and spread wide at the sides, showing the inside curves of her smallish breasts. The straps were very thin. There was a tight band across her ribs. It was cropped but not by much, showing only a hint of flesh at her belly between camisole and skirt, depending on how she moved.

Her hair was short, clipped in a graduated bob at the nape of her neck, the champagne highlights in her dark cinnamon hair looking (she thought) great in the sweeping, long bangs that fell well past her eye, the sides of her hair hanging below her jaw, all the ends in messy flips.

She had to style it, which was a minus. But it was short so it didn't take long, and it had a sex-bomb vibe, so that was a definite plus.

She looked into her wide, brown eyes and wondered, *What next?*

A weighty question because it wasn't about what was next for her at the Honey.

But what was next for her with everything.

At Aryas's appeal (which meant repeated demands), she'd given up "the job."

Ostensibly.

As far as he knew, Sixx had gone legit, working as the internal investigator for a large local law firm.

However, directly due to Aryas's interference in some of his other friend's lives, a need had arisen in Phoenix when Branch Dillinger stopped doing what he did out there and became the operations manager for all of the Bee's Honeys.

Nature abhorred a vacuum.

Cue Sixx stepping in because first, her pay at the law firm was good, if you weren't used to making a lot more doing a lot more dangerous shit for a lot more dangerous people. And second, if you were used to doing a lot more dangerous shit for a lot more dangerous people, as well as used to the adrenaline rush that got you, it wasn't an easy habit to break.

So she had a proper job, not a normal one, but one that included a 401K and a bi-weekly paycheck that gave her insurance benefits.

And on occasion, she moonlit on the side.

Aryas didn't know.

No one knew (except her friend and sometimes partner, Sylvie Creed, and her husband, Tucker, who she and Sylvie sometimes had to call in to help. But Sylvie wasn't in the life Sixx pretended to lead through her play and relationships at the Honey).

Even if Sixx got off on it, and the cash she accumulated doing it, not to mention the freedom that offered, she knew she couldn't do it forever. She had the scars to prove that particular story you told yourself to stay on the job was a lie.

But what would she have if she stopped?

The kink was getting boring. There were only so many orders you could give that led—perhaps in a lengthy way, but nonetheless the end was always the same—to someone else's orgasm.

It had lost its appeal.

Because she wasn't connecting.

She used to connect.

She used to stay mostly silent, watch, listen, open herself to being acutely aware of every expression or even twitch of the skin to sense what her sub wanted . . . then she'd find some elaborate or creative but always hard-earned way to give it to him.

Now she didn't even have that.

Anyone could give their own self an orgasm. It was her job as a Dominatrix, regardless if the emotion wasn't there, the attention and the respect and the motivation and the deliberation had to be there to *connect*. Somehow. Some way.

That was gone.

So what was the point?

To yank herself out of thoughts that were going nowhere, even though her long-lasting lipstick was doing its job, she still opened her clutch, pulled out the liner and lipstick, refreshed the ruby red, ended it with a nice coat of clear gloss, and dropped the stuff back in her bag.

She then grabbed her phone—not her actual phone, the other

one—before she clicked the clutch closed and made her way out of the lounge, deciding to have a drink while she dealt with the details of finishing up her final mission of the evening.

She wandered the halls, doing it avoiding having to walk past Stellan's room, and hit the hunting ground.

The back corner booth was open, so she went there, flipped open the burner phone in her hand, set it to silent and then used her thumb in the onerous task of hitting the numbers on the pad repeatedly to get to the letters she needed to send the short text.

Really, smartphones were a gift from God.

The drop happens tonight.

She tucked the phone by her thigh when a server came, and she decided cool-but-luxe Sixx, Mistress with the Mostest, was fucking dead.

It was over.

No rep to uphold.

No bullshit to convey.

She was over that too.

She wasn't going to sip from a glass of wine, withholding any personality, any hint of what made her, what defined her, that she might convey through the simple matter of ordering her preferred drink.

"Gordon's cup. Hendrick's," she ordered.

"Gotcha," the server said then moved away.

She looked to the hunting ground and saw subs avoiding her eyes but still preening in view, hoping she was there to make a selection.

God, she was dried up. Not even a tingle.

The only time she'd felt anything in—Lord, it had been days— was when Stellan's eyes met hers earlier through the windows to his playroom.

And those days had been the days since she was last at the Honey and Stellan had turned his attention to her.

She looked down to her thigh, flipping open the phone to see no return text, and muttered under her breath, "I'm a fucking mess."

"Sorry, didn't catch that."

Her head snapped up just in time to watch Stellan, back in his suit jacket and definitely out of his playroom, slide in the booth across from her.

God, he was gorgeous.

But . . .

What the fuck?

"You were saying?" he prompted.

She flipped the phone shut and tucked it against her thigh so she'd feel it vibrate when the text came in.

"I have something on my mind," she shared, not knowing what to make of this, him in the booth opposite her, making an approach, sitting there looking magnificent but still inaccessible, speaking directly to her with only her there to speak to.

"And that would be?" he asked.

"It's work," she told him.

"Ah," he murmured, glancing to the side and looking up when the server set her drink in front of her. An action he oddly watched with what appeared to be rather avid fascination as the old-fashioned glass came to rest on the burgundy cocktail napkin. "Scotch, please," he ordered before the guy could ask.

"On it," the server said and moved away.

Stellan didn't watch him go and it took a good deal, Sixx didn't look away when Stellan's attention came back to her.

"Not in the mood tonight?" he queried.

She shook her head, lifted her drink, and took a sip.

When she put it down, she verbalized that same response. "No."

"Hmm," he murmured, and there it was.

God.

There it was.

That "hmm" was almost like a purr, and that purr snaked right up her pussy, an area that instantly got wet.

"You're finished early," she noted.

He gave a one shoulder shrug that managed to be masculine and elegant at the same time, something only Stellan could pull off.

"I thought I'd try something new."

"And?" she asked.

"It wasn't as successful as I'd hoped."

"Too bad," she murmured, taking another sip of her drink.

"Is it?" he returned, and her gaze lifted to his, because he'd asked a question but mostly because that question was strange.

"For you, and them, of course it is," she replied.

"They got a good deal out of it, I assume, unless she faked it, which is doubtful. He, however, couldn't fake it as the evidence he left was physical."

Perhaps she shouldn't have left so soon. It would undoubtedly have been interesting to watch Stellan orchestrate something like that.

"Unusual for you to choose a male," she remarked.

He turned his head to the hunting ground and remarked, "An experiment I'm unlikely to repeat."

She gave it some time, and this was mostly because she was arrested in the act of taking in the beauty of his profile. The cut line of his strong jaw. The angle of his cheekbone. The shadowed hollow under it. The fine lines that fanned from the corner of his eye. The straight slope of his nose. And, Lord God . . . that remarkable swell of his lower lip.

When she realized another second and she'd start squirming in the booth, she spoke.

"It might be more enjoyable if you went hands on," she suggested.

He looked back to her and more wet surged between her legs at the expression on his face and what was emanating from his eyes.

"If I fancy ass, it comes with breasts and a vagina or not at all."

Sixx would take him up her ass, deep, hard, fast, soft, slow, gentle, any way he liked it.

She'd beg him for that.

On that thought, her salivary glands went into overdrive, and

she lifted her drink, tipping it to him in salute, before she brought
it to her mouth but didn't take a drink.

"Too bad," she murmured.

Then she sipped.

His lips, including that luscious bottom one, curled up slightly
at the ends.

"Mistress Sixx," he said softly. "If she had it her way, they'd be
lined up by the score and fucked raw, climaxing at her command at
the tip of her whip."

She stared at him, her stomach feeling like it was cramping, but
her voice sounded even when she asked, "You say that like there's
something wrong with it."

"Of course there isn't," he drawled, totally and openly lying.

I'd make you like it, she said in her head. *I'd make you beg for it. I'd
break my back, sell my soul, do anything I'd need to do to make you come harder
than you've ever come before, tying you to me, connecting you to me, making you
never want to leave.*

He held her gaze, his face arrogant and knowing.

Or I'd give it to you, her mind whispered. *Anything you wanted, anything you'd want to do to me to give you what you needed in a way that need could
never be eased and you'd always come back for more.*

He kept holding her gaze, but in the dim light of the bar of the
Bee's Honey, she could swear she saw something in his expression
grow soft, like he could read her thoughts.

Before she could get a lock on it, or better, turn from him so he
couldn't read anything further, for once he looked away first, but only
because the server was there, placing his lowball of Scotch over ice
in front of him.

Sixx picked up her drink, looked to the hunting ground, and
took a healthy sip.

"Are you staying?"

Stellan's question brought her attention again to him.

She put her drink down and asked, "Pardon?"

"In Phoenix," he explained. "I know you travel for work and it takes you away for long periods of time. But this time, you've been back for a while, so it seems like you're staying."

She had been intending to stay.

Now she didn't know.

"For a while," she replied.

He nodded, sipping his drink, and then stated, "I've been meaning to invite you, simply haven't had the chance. But I'm having a party next weekend. We've hit June, and the weather hasn't yet started baking. I'm taking advantage. We'll start with a pool party, then everyone can change and we'll move in for dinner. I'd be delighted if you'd come."

She hid her reaction to that by throwing back more gin.

"Leigh and Olly will be there," Stellan went on, back to his gaze set unwavering on her. "Mira and Trey. Felicia's bringing a couple of her toys. Penn and Shane will be there. Victor has a new slave he's enjoying so he's bringing her. In other words, it's a play party, just to make that clear. Though, depending on how it goes, we'll make things more sociable and less structured for dinner. That will be up to the Dom."

When he hesitated, she nodded, indicating she'd heard and taken this in, and he kept speaking.

"Belle's bringing Tiffany. Talia is bringing Bryan. Aryas will be out of town, as will Evangeline's partner, but Evangeline will be there in her usual capacity. Observation only."

It was an unwritten rule when referring to the Honey's Domme Evangeline's "partner"—who was really her boyfriend who was essentially living with her—at least in the confines of the walls of the club, people did not use his name.

But he was Branch Dillinger. Her partner. Her boyfriend. Her sub. But he was also the Honey's new top guy, since Aryas had taken a step back from operations in order to focus on opening his new club in Tahoe, and he needed someone he could trust to pick up the reins.

And if Branch played it that way, wishing things to be private, he got it that way, and would even if the man couldn't probably snap your neck with his bare hands then walk away and not give that kill a second thought.

It was just the life and everyone obeyed that rule.

Though the threat of having your neck snapped worked too.

Sixx was just relieved Evangeline was back, not to mention ecstatic she had a man in her life like Branch. Especially after what was done to her to make her take a prolonged break, all of this happening when Sixx was away.

It was good it happened when she was away. If she was close, retaliation would have been much different than what Aryas had ordered, and even much different than the vastly more thorough way in which Branch had handled it.

But it was handled. So at Aryas's firm request, she'd let it be.

She was relieved and ecstatic for Leenie . . . and also jealous.

Jealous because she wondered what it would feel like to have a miracle happen after the world as you knew it turned to complete shit and then one day . . . you might not be healed, but you were again whole.

"And if you like, I'll have a couple of male slaves available for your use. Fresh meat. I know a few who'd volunteer that I'm sure you'd like," Stellan continued.

And that stomach cramp got worse.

He'd provide her "a few volunteers."

Thoughtful.

And damned disappointing.

She wondered who he'd have there.

And how many.

"I'll think about it," she told him.

"Please do," he said before taking another sip of his Scotch.

She followed suit with her gin, practically willing her phone to vibrate against her leg to give her a reason to get away from him.

Stellan spoke again.

"So you're not in the mood, will you allow me to offer you something that might strike a different mood? One I'd wager you'd enjoy a great deal."

At this proposal that came out of nowhere, Sixx almost choked on her gin.

But of course she didn't, and again her voice was clear and cool when she asked, "What's that?"

He shook his head. "I'm afraid it has to be a surprise. But I will say it will be a surprise you'll like. I also have to say, you shouldn't wait to make your decision or things will culminate and we'll miss our chance."

Things will culminate?

Oh no.

She was intrigued.

Damn it!

"Can you give me a hint?" she pressed.

He made a tsking noise that she felt tap against her clit, and as was his usual, he didn't lose contact with her gaze.

But he wasn't looking aloof anymore.

This was both an invitation and a challenge.

She just didn't know to what.

And with Stellan—this sudden Stellan who was vastly different than the Stellan she'd been getting (or not, as the case was) for the last too-many-months—she wasn't sure how to handle it.

"Don't disappoint me, Sixx," he said quietly. "The Honey's Ice Princess, cool and composed in every situation, shying away from an adventure?"

"I simply need to know how long it would take," she lied. "I have something I need to do tonight," she didn't lie.

"As soon as you need to go, I'll bring you back."

He'd bring her back?

He was going to take her somewhere?

"What's it going to be, Sixx?" he pushed. "In truth, I should have asked you the minute I joined you in this booth. We risk missing the grand finale the longer we wait."

"Stellan—" she started, wondering how to get out of it at the same time how not to appear like she was jumping on it by accepting too quickly.

She needed time to assess this change, plan, strategize, prepare, fashion a brand-new Sixx. One who could deal with the likes of Stellan Lange and come out the other side of whatever became of whatever was happening unscathed.

And more importantly, make certain he did.

Or time to find a place to hide. Or escape, her mind taunted. *Coward.*

"I've bought you a present," he shocked her by announcing. "I did this some time ago. I've been wishing to give it to you but haven't had the opportunity. Now's the opportunity." The movement was almost not there, but yet it was when he leaned slightly her way and warned in a low voice, "Don't waste it."

Again, eye contact, unrelenting.

Challenge.

Invitation.

Finally.

And a gift?

She lifted her drink, took another healthy swallow, put it on the table and then dropped her hand to her thigh to curl her fingers around the phone there while grabbing her clutch off the table with her other hand.

She looked back to him and said, "Let's go."

When she did, all vestiges of her stomach cramps disappeared.

Because when she said that, Stellan Lange smiled a wicked, roguish, beautiful smile.

Right at her.

two

Bait and Switch

SIXX

Her damned burner vibrated in her clutch the minute Stellan maneuvered his midnight silver metallic Tesla Model S into a parking spot outside a large building so far east of Phoenix that there was nothing but the building, its expansive parking lot and a lot of desert around it.

The trip there had not been short.

But it had been silent.

Sixx found this incredibly uncomfortable, and that grew by the minute mostly because it seemed Stellan didn't.

Though it was more.

It seemed the edgier she got, the more he enjoyed it.

It was a Dom trick. She knew it. And because she did, she should have been able to handle it.

She should also have taken that time to get her head together, assess the risk she was taking, and prepare herself for all possible eventualities.

But not only was she Sixx, who prepared just enough not to get her ass handed to her (because what was the fun if you didn't get thrown a few curveballs?), she also was in his fabulous car in the middle of nowhere with *him*.

Stellan.

Stellan.

In other words, she was off her game.

She pulled the burner out of her purse, flipped it open and read the text.

When and where?

Tapping on the number pad to reply, she typed, *Wait for instructions and be ready.*

She sent the text just as Stellan asked, "You have a flip phone?"

She turned to him to see him definitely turned to her, hand behind her on her seat and all, filling the opulent, state-of-the-art interior with an authority and hauteur like it was he himself who designed it.

And she liked all of that.

A great deal.

Oh yes she was edgy.

"It's a work thing."

In the lights of the parking lot she saw his gaze drop to her lap where her clutch and her hand around the burner was, and she could swear she saw his mouth get tight.

His eyes cut back up to her. "Ready?"

"Of course," she replied.

That was when his face got lazy in a way she'd not once seen (and she'd been watching so she'd never have missed that).

Then he got out of the car.

She was out too, on her feet about to close her door when he got into her space.

In surprise, she twisted and looked up at him.

"A gentleman opens the door for a lady," he declared.

"I'm very capable of—"

As unexpectedly as he'd gotten close, he completely erased the space between them and she snapped her mouth shut.

"A gentleman," he took her elbow, "opens the door," he put pressure on his hold on her and guided her from the car, "for a lady."

He shut the door.

Okay then.

Sixx decided it was time to set some ground rules.

"It isn't necessary—"

"Is this my gift to you?" he asked.

"Apparently," she answered.

"My adventure on offer to you?" he went on.

"Yes," she said shortly.

"So we play this my way."

Her gaze slid to the large building. Having already noted there were quite a number of cars parked in that lot, it had been impossible to miss there was also a security guard at the entrance to it that Stellan had slowed to nod at before they'd driven in.

She looked back to him.

Well-guarded.

But why?

"Is this a new club?" she asked.

"No," he answered.

She drew her brows together. "This isn't a Pound, is it?"

"Fuck no," he growled, looking offended.

She'd never seen that on him either.

It was hot.

And damn . . .

It was also more than a little adorable.

Seeing that, experiencing it, not thinking Stellan had it in him to look even remotely adorable, she realized belatedly she should not have said at the Honey, "Let's go."

She should have slid out of the booth without a word, gone home, packed and written Aryas a snail mail note he would therefore get when she was long gone. This note explaining she was taking the stash of cash she'd already accumulated and moved to . . . she didn't know where. Bali maybe.

No, Samoa.

Samoan men were gorgeous.

It may seem insane, only maybe an hour after lamenting the fact Stellan had given nothing to her, now to be questioning him giving her something, whatever that something was going to be.

But it wasn't insane.

Because Sixx was used to taking risks. She did not calculate them. She did not move through them cautiously. She met them head on.

However now this was happening, and since it was, she knew innately this was the greatest risk of all.

It was a risk that could have consequences she might not survive in a way that survival wasn't the hoped for conclusion simply to keep breathing.

It was crucial simply to stay sane.

Though she could imagine Stellan would be offended at her guessing he'd brought her to a Pound. The traveling sex scene in Phoenix known as the Pound was not anywhere a snob like Stellan would ever be seen, and further what it had to offer he'd find revolting.

"Are we playing this my way, Sixx?" he pressed. "Or am I taking you back to the Honey?"

Another challenge.

She should apologize for wasting his time, ask him to take her back to the Honey, go home and decide what was next in her life. Whatever that next was would be considered ridiculously unsafe to normal individuals, but it wouldn't be something that would wreak havoc on Sixx.

Yes, that was absolutely what she should do.

She did not do that.

Because she was with Stellan.

Finally.

And apparently it didn't matter what she was risking, even if this time she knew it was heart, soul, body and mind, not to mention whatever may happen to Stellan through it all, Sixx was Sixx.

All in.

"We're playing it your way."

That earned her another one of his wicked smiles. It also earned her his taking her hand, curling her fingers into the crook of his arm, and walking her toward the building like he was escorting her up a red carpet.

Or down the aisle after a wedding.

Lord, she had to get her head together or this could go very bad, and that bad was her losing control of . . . well, *everything*.

Sixx needed control just as much as she needed chaos. She couldn't have one without the other because she was addicted to both, and her elaborate efforts to maintain a perfect balance kept the mess that was her from flying apart.

That night the balance had already shifted, though, so she knew she was in serious trouble.

So she had to get back on her game.

Pronto.

She caught sight of two security guards patrolling the parking lot, both wearing head-to-toe black, from unmarked baseball caps to combat boots.

And they were armed.

There was a similarly attired (but without the cap) guard at the set of double doors where Stellan guided her. One of four sets of doors along the side of the building, each separated by a goodly number of feet.

"Mr. Lange," the man muttered as he moved to open the door for them.

Stellan said nothing until the guard looked at Sixx.

"Eyes," he clipped so severely Sixx almost missed a step due to surprise at his tone.

The guard immediately looked to his boots.

Okay.

What was that?

Stellan ushered her through the door.

When it closed behind them, she looked to his profile. "I'm not exactly in the closet, Stellan."

He dipped his chin to catch her gaze. "That doesn't matter."

"I—" she began.

"We shouldn't delay."

And he set about making them not do that by moving her.

It was then she heard the noise.

Muted cheers.

Like at a sporting event.

Right.

What the hell was happening?

She saw they were in a long hall that curved on the interior wall at the ends like they were in the cement-floored, cinder-block-walled, currently deserted foyer of an auditorium.

There were also a number of doors along the inside wall, all closed, all staffed by guards, all just like what would lead into a theater.

Stellan walked her down to the third set, turned them toward the doors, nodded to the guard—this one catching Stellan's eyes, but not Sixx's—and the man moved to open the door.

When he did, a wave of sound came out.

Definitely a sporting event, and she could tell that not only by the roars of what had to be a large crowd, but also by the scaffold structure that held bleachers that were on either side of a passage-way. That wide walkway led to what appeared to be two throne-like, very-high-backed, clean-lined, attractive chairs at the end. The chairs were butted arm-to-arm, and each one had a small, but ornate, cir-cular table next to it at its free side.

Beyond that, the tall, wide, cream leather backs of the chairs obscured whatever was happening.

Stellan did not move them to the steps that led to the bleachers.

Of course not.

He led them around the side of one chair, and there she stopped so abruptly, Stellan stopped with her.

There was a sunken pit in front of her. Large. Oval. Lined at the sides and bottom in thick black mats that now shone in places.

With oil.

And probably sweat.

Good Lord.

It was a gladiator pit.

Quickly, her attention moved to the two men currently grappling in the pit not far away from where they stood, and she felt her legs start to tremble and they weren't the only things on her body experiencing that sensation.

The men were glistening, muscled, (mostly) naked, magnificent, savage brutes that were locked in combat with their only adornment—outside a full-body oiling—a black leather belt around their waists.

This had a small leather triangle above the pubis from which led snapped straps that rounded their erect cocks and high, tight balls with another strap coming from the behind the balls, separating each testicle, snapped to the cock strap.

From the back of the belt, shanks of leather curved around the sides of their asses and under them, cupping them and drawing the cheeks up, with another thick strap cutting through the crevice, opening it, a wide silver ring placed precisely, highlighting their anuses.

"I knew you'd like it," Stellan purred in her ear, and damn it all, her movement was jerky when she forced her head around and up to look at him.

He did not hide he was pleased.

Yes, he knew she liked it, he'd guessed how much, and he got off in a big way that she did.

Even so, she hid she liked how pleased he was.

Before she could say anything, he guided her to her chair, and before she fell down, she sat down as gracefully as she could, which fortunately was an effort that went smoothly.

He barely got his ass in the throne beside hers when, appearing at his side, there was a female server in nothing but another variety of black leather straps, clearly the theme, though hers covered her completely at strategic parts, leaving all the rest bare.

"Refreshments, Master Lange?" she asked.

"Scotch," he said and turned to Sixx, raising his brows and remarking, "They don't have a full bar, but they have most everything you might want."

"Gordon's cup," she said.

That got an amused look from Stellan, something she had seen, but not much, since she'd been home.

She'd missed it.

Horribly.

She knew it before, but she knew it keener then.

She was in a dangerous place.

Very dangerous.

Precarious.

He turned to the server. "Can you manage that?"

"If we can't, I'll return," she said, obviously having no idea what the drink was.

"A male slave serves this Mistress," Stellan ordered before she left.

She nodded, bowed, and took off.

Stellan turned back to Sixx.

"I didn't know there was a gladiator pit in Phoenix," she remarked.

"It's new," he replied.

"How new?" she asked.

He shrugged. "Around four months."

She turned her attention to the space, which had high bleachers going up behind a variety of double sets of thrones like the ones she and Stellan were in, all the thrones flanking the pit having the best views, sitting maybe only four feet from the edge.

She took it all in and noted there were a few thrones that were empty, not many, but most of the bleacher space was taken by bodies.

There had to be hundreds of people there.

Her eyes again caught Stellan's, noting something further.

He was watching her, not the warriors in the pit.

Her.

Closely.

"You didn't pay to get in," she stated.

"Tickets need to be purchased in advance."

"You didn't hand a ticket to anyone," she noted.

"No," he looked to the pit, "I didn't."

Okay.

Um.

Okay.

Shit.

"You run this, don't you?" she queried to his profile.

"I have a few other investors," he answered, not taking his attention from the action. "But yes."

But yes.

Trying not to appear dazed, she looked all around again.

This was a gift to her?

How?

Why?

She avoided the men in the pit, tuned out the cheering that was hitting extremes, and looked among the thrones.

All Doms, for certain, though she couldn't know if they were the other investors. If they were, there were a number of them.

Some had two people sitting on the two chairs, men and/or women.

Some had only one.

Some had a sub sitting on the floor by their chairs.

Two had what obviously were gladiators defeated earlier. The defeated were on all fours at their Doms' feet, still in their belts, but although one was too far away for her to see, another was just a few thrones down, and as it was pointed her way, she saw the raw red of his ass cheeks.

As well as the cream coming from it.

So there was a definite price to pay in losing.

My, my, my.

"Who gets the thrones?" Sixx inquired, turning back Stellan's way.

"Owners," he shared.

"Investors?" she pushed.

He looked to her again.

"No," he said slowly. "*Owners.*"

Owners.

Of the warriors.

He knew she caught on, and she must have given something away, something that pleased him, because he didn't hide it.

And she liked that she'd pleased him.

But again she hid it.

"They pay an impressive sum for their warriors to play, so they pay for their seat to be unobstructed," he shared. "But also, in the end, however way they wish to be, they're part of the show."

Obviously from her superior vantage point she could definitely see dipping into her painfully acquired and carefully attended stash of cash for such a show.

He turned back to the action.

Sixx did too.

The instant she did, the sexual savagery of it smacked her in the face, drove up between her thighs, throbbed through her nipples and shivered across her skin.

And once it caught her attention, she couldn't look away. The beauty of it was too extreme.

She was captivated.

She wanted one, and she didn't even know what it meant to own one.

But she wanted one.

She wanted her own gladiator to battle for her, earn the spoils of his victory for her, or take the punishment of defeat . . . for her.

Perhaps the only thing that could draw her attention did just that.

A tall, built, good-looking, well-endowed male slave appeared at her side. He had a black belt around his waist. Leading down from the center of the belt, his large cock was trapped in an upward position behind black leather laces surrounded by rivets, his impressive balls caged with it but bulging out the sides. He also had a cut crystal glass filled with ice and a slightly murky liquid with visible bits of pepper on a tray.

The bartender clearly knew what he was doing or had access to the Internet.

And Stellan clearly had someone who rocked in picking server attire.

The slave set the glass on the table by her side and backed away. After she lost sight of his attractive chastity cage and the meat it packed, she picked the glass up to take a drink before she set it aside, and she did all of this taking her attention from the pit as sparingly as she could.

And Sixx would discover all victory and defeat entailed when what appeared to be an unofficiated match ended at the loud sound of a gong reverberating through the space. This happened after the crowd grew frenzied when one combatant pinned the other to the mats on his stomach, reached between his legs, and they heard the pained grunt as the straps were ripped from around his privates.

Sixx sat back, tucked her clutch in her lap and crossed her legs.

She did this because she knew very well it gave the appearance of being calm and collected.

It had the added benefit of tightening her flesh around her misbehaving clit and ending the quivers quaking up her inner thighs.

She'd already exposed to Stellan she liked what she'd seen, though he'd watched her in playrooms so he could hardly be in question that she would.

How much it affected her, she felt it paramount *not* to expose.

She felt heat in her legs that had nothing to do with the winner dragging the loser up to his knees by his hair, and she slanted her eyes sideways to find Stellan was not interested in the pit any longer (if he was at all—this was her scene, it was not his).

He was studying her legs.

Sixx instantly looked back to the pit.

The winner had thrown the straps in the loser's face and was working the crowd, squatting and shouting, pumping his bent elbows into his body with fists clenched, circling the loser who was still on his knees, head bent, strapping himself back up.

The winner stopped in front of a man seated in one of the cream chairs who looked easily like he could be given his own belt, take his place in the pit, and win. The victor dropped to his knees, ripping his straps off his cock and balls and lifting them, head bowed, toward his Master.

She couldn't hear what the Master said since he was on the curve of the oval, several sets of thrones down from her and Stellan. But whatever he said allowed the winning warrior to toss his straps up to the floor in front of his Master's seat then take his feet and stalk to the loser.

Catching the losing warrior by the hair again, he took him unresisting to his back with a moist, resounding thud of slickened flesh on mat, and the crowd lost their minds.

The winner dropped to his knees again, jerked the loser's legs up high, pressing them out. The loser held this position as the winner guided his cock where he intended it to be, dead center of that silver ring, and pounded in.

An answering pound rocked Sixx's body.

God.

Glorious.

She did her best not to press her legs together because she knew Stellan would not miss it.

She also did her best not to come right on the spot. She had on a lace thong that in no way would absorb the slick she'd leave if she allowed herself what she needed very, *very* badly watching the winner take his reward and the loser give it.

Instead, she endeavored to watch the action like it was mildly entertaining and knew she failed at this. But at least she wasn't staring in the open-mouthed, undoubtedly drooling awe she would have used if she'd let her true reaction free.

It became apparent that the triumphant warrior was gracious in victory when he started brutally fisting his opponent's cock.

The loser came first.

The winner bellowed his climax minutes later.

The crowd went wild.

Although her seat was equal to none, mid-oval on the wide side, she was going to ask Stellan how to buy tickets in the bleachers because she'd attend again. That was for certain.

She just wouldn't do it sitting beside Stellan.

After his recovery, the victorious warrior pulled out and took his feet, sauntering toward his master.

"There are female gladiators too," Stellan said as Sixx watched the gladiator use his beefy arms to pull himself out of the pit, the sides of which came up to his chest, and he was not a small man by any account. "They usually open the night."

"I'm sure they're quite popular," she murmured, still watching as the winner grabbed what appeared to be a wet towel from the table beside his Dom and roughly wiped his cock clean.

She kept watching, now with some surprise, when a dominant sneer rolled over the champion's face as he stared down at the man seated on the throne while that man stroked the back of his flank.

That was when she knew.

She knew who owned who.

And the crowd again lost their minds when the gladiator cupped the back of the man's head in one mighty hand, wrapping his fingers around his still-hard dick with the other, and forced the man in the chair to take him deep into his mouth.

Oh yes.

She was not only buying tickets. When she found out the number to the box office, she was inquiring after season passes.

This was a reason to remain in Phoenix.

For certain.

"They're both Doms," Stellan told her. "They trade off who competes. And if one wins, the other submits to him. If he loses, he takes the winning gladiator's cock, and then he submits to his partner.

It seems to work for them, and their ensuing antics make them popular with the crowd."

Pumping into his partner's face and openly enjoying it with the audience cheering him on, Sixx would tend to agree.

"They're bi," Stellan continued. "They each also have female subs. I hear they have very interesting parties and also give intriguing demonstrations. They're all for hire, but they cost a great deal."

As if the gladiator felt her gaze, had seen her or could simply sense her reaction to the show he'd given, his head turned, and his flashing eyes locked on Sixx's.

She felt her mouth get soft, her gaze open up, that dominant sneer shot her way, she accepted it, beginning to return his smile and then . . .

Her jaw was caught in a hard grip, and she saw nothing but Stellan's handsome, hard face.

She went completely still.

She'd seen that look before too.

It was the one he assumed when he had a slave who was being a brat, testing his patience, and he had a lesson to teach.

There was no way to control the soak that drenched between her legs or the lean that automatically began toward him at his touch, the firmness of his hold, the look on his face.

And his touch and the words he next spoke caused a warm, slow, gorgeous ripple to course throughout her body. An orgasm, to be sure, beautiful and nuanced in feeling, truly the most exquisite climax she'd ever had, but indistinguishable by sight except for the soft parting of her lips.

"You sit here as mine, Simone," he growled.

She started breathing heavily, feeling her eyes getting lazy in the languid throes of her silent orgasm, and worked hard to hide it, keeping her eyes wide and alert, forcing her breaths to steady.

He'd used her real name.

How did he know her real name?

And she sat there as *his*?

When?

How?

God.

"You can watch because I allow it," he stated.

"Stell—"

His face came right to hers.

"*Master*," he bit.

Oh God.

God.

God.

No hope for control, her breathing was now erratic, and her response was overpowering.

She eased in his grip, giving herself over.

Immediately.

Without thought.

Without hesitation.

Without a fight.

Good Lord.

What was happening?

"Soon, I'll be giving you your gift," he declared.

He'd be giving it to her?

Him bringing her here wasn't her gift?

"After I do, and you have your time to enjoy it," he went on, "I'll be taking you back to the Honey. As you were on the way here, you'll be silent on the return journey. You'll use that time to think about how inappropriate you've just been and the measures you'll take to make that up to me. In fact, you'll have the rest of the week to think on this, so I'll assume your apology, when I'm ready to accept it, will be creative. On Saturday, you'll be at my home. You'll enjoy the party. You'll enjoy being with your friends. You'll enjoy my attention. There, you can also look, but you can't touch, no matter what I have on offer for you. We'll entertain my guests, and when they leave, we're going to broker a deal."

"A deal?" she whispered.

"A deal," he announced.

"I—"

She said no more because he moved in further, slanting his head at the last minute, tipping her head the opposite way at the same time, and a pulse of sheer splendor coursed through her and detonated between her legs as he sunk his teeth into the side of her neck, right at her jugular.

Deep, sharp . . .

Not breaking the skin, but she knew, absolutely leaving a mark.

As fast as he moved in, he was back in her face.

"A response is not required," he shared.

She said nothing.

"This business you're doing later, do you need someone with you?" he asked.

Oh God.

Why was he asking that?

"Simone, I asked you a question and your response *is* required for that," he clipped.

"N-no," she answered, stammering.

Her!

Mistress Sixx!

Stammering!

"Is it dangerous?" he queried tersely.

Again, why?

Why was he asking that?

How did he even know to ask?

Had Aryas . . . ?

"Don't try my patience further, my darling, by making me repeat myself," he whispered silkily.

"It's not dangerous," she said quietly.

"If you're lying, there will be consequences," he told her.

How would he know if she was lying?

She didn't ask.

She sat there in his grip, staring into his heated blue eyes, trying very hard not to come again, and this time do it bigger, louder and far more noticeably.

His head tipped to the side as he slid his grip from her jaw to the back of her neck.

The hold was gentler, but it was just as relentless.

"Do you think I didn't catch it?" he asked, his tone gentler too.

"Catch—?"

"Don't be coy, Simone." He was back to his silken whisper. "Every time I make you come, I'll know it."

She decided again not to speak.

"Wise of you," he said softly, like he could read her mind. Then he brought her face closer to his, and since there were but inches between them, there wasn't far to go—but he took her there to the point she could almost feel the tip of her nose brushing his. "Until we have our negotiations Saturday evening, we'll get something perfectly clear."

He said no more, so she took a chance and gave a quick nod.

"Excellent, darling," he murmured. "Now, what we'll be clear on is that you can look, but you cannot touch. So obviously, you cannot play. Not anywhere. At the Honey, nor should some other opportunity cross your path. And if you need to look, you do it at my side. In other words, should you feel the need to watch, you contact me, and I'll attend you. Is that understood?"

"I won't—" she fought clearing her throat, fucking failed, had to do it, and hated that she loved the flash of satisfaction she caught in his eyes when she did, "need to do that."

"I'll leave you with my card just in case."

She again remained silent.

"Say, 'Thank you, Stellan,'" he ordered.

She stared in his eyes.

"You can say it," he began, giving her more silk, "or I'll carry you out to my car, bind you at ankles and wrists, gag you, take you to my home, cut your clothes off, tie you naked down to a bed and stripe you from the soles of your feet to your shoulders. To avoid that, I'd advise you now to say, 'Thank you, Stellan.'"

Different urges warring within her, battling it out in extremes that kept her body perfectly still, her mind a maelstrom of chaos unleashed, she stayed quiet.

"You may think you have the skills to best me," he whispered. "But I know you have the intelligence not to try. Last chance, Simone," he warned.

"Thank you, Stellan," she gritted between her teeth.

"Beautiful," he murmured reverently, his gaze dropping to her mouth.

She knew that reverence, having a headstrong sub offer obedience through clenched teeth.

It was transcendent.

Oh God.

Another orgasm loomed.

Fortunately, she was successful at beating it back.

He held her gaze, and she didn't know if she missed him being remote and detached or if she'd instantly become addicted to him being everything but.

Then he let her go, settled back in his chair, and reached for his Scotch.

Sixx had to take several deep breaths to steady herself before she reached for her own drink.

And when she took it to her lips, she sucked back half of it.

Stellan chuckled when she did.

Seriously.

What was happening?

She sat there, staring at the now empty mats before her, trying to understand what was going on, how things had changed so quickly, and how she'd let it get so out of hand.

Before she got close to getting anywhere with any of that, she found her fingers captured, and along with her arm, her hand was pulled Stellan's way. He rested it held in his on the arm of his chair, his fingers curled around the back of her hand, his thumb caressing the inside of her wrist.

As heavenly as that felt, in an effort to wrest some control over the situation, she started to remove it from his hold, but the instant she did, his grasp intensified, the pads of his fingers biting in.

She let her hand relax.

"You never pull away from me," he said softly, easing his hold and again caressing her wrist with his thumb.

She stared at the mats.

"Assure me I'm heard, Simone."

"How do you know my name?" she asked.

"I'll answer that when you assure me I'm heard, darling."

She turned her head to look at him, seeing she already had his attention, loving and hating having his beautiful eyes in his handsome face aimed her way with that kind of extreme focus where she knew he didn't miss anything.

Not a thing.

"You're heard."

"This once, I'll allow you to get away with not giving me the word that should conclude that statement," he murmured.

She knew how he expected it to conclude. He was a stickler with his slaves.

They referred to him only as Master.

However, she was not his slave.

She was a Mistress.

And yet she'd just become his slave.

Oh yes, most definitely yes, things were precarious.

Cataclysmically so.

"My name?" she prompted.

"I'm assuming, considering I went to the trouble of establishing a gladiator pit for your amusement, that you're aware of my interest in you. Taking that further, it wasn't very difficult to ascertain your name."

"So you looked into me," she stated blankly, not about to share that over a year earlier, she'd seen him in D.C., done the same, and had the skills to do that thoroughly.

Skills he probably knew she had.

And more chaos infested her brain.

"We'll talk more Saturday evening," he replied.

"And should I tell you to go fuck yourself, get up and walk out of here, and there is no Saturday evening?" she inquired.

"You have no intention of telling me to go fuck myself, sweetheart."

Her breath caught in an odd way, a way she'd never felt, this coming from his tone, the look on his face and his endearment.

All of a sudden this was not Master Stellan expending an overwhelming amount of effort to flip a certain kind of switch on Mistress Sixx.

This was Stellan talking to the woman at his side, a woman only two people in her life—him now being one of them, the other one appropriately rotting in prison—knew as Simone.

Okay, okay, okay.

What was happening?

"There are things—" she started on a rush.

"We'll speak Saturday."

"Stellan—"

Again he was in her face, his palm in hers, his fingers holding her hand steady and warm.

"Honey, I've waited a long time to give this to you, so please, enjoy this evening, and *we'll speak Saturday.*"

She knew this side of him too. The charmer who slides in after the tyrant, assessing the challenge he was facing with a recalcitrant sub and doing what he must to assure he got exactly what he wanted.

He could be affectionate, demonstrative, even tender and gallant with his subs.

Although she'd rarely heard him speak to them inside a playroom, she'd been in booths with him when he had one close, or booths around him where she could overhear, and she'd never heard him use a single endearment except softening the term "slave" with a "my" or an additional "beautiful" or something akin to that.

"Yes?" he prompted.

"Yes," she agreed.

Still facing her, he turned his head to look over his shoulder, and when he turned back to her, he was smiling.

Nope, not wanting the blank back.

Yep, instantly addicted.

And yep times two, her situation was cataclysmically precarious. In the extreme.

"Your gift arrives," he declared.

She stared.

He sat back.

And she saw that two men were walking in at the narrow part of the oval, and like the last two combatants, they were tall, large, powerfully built, and although one wasn't difficult to look at, the other, bald, taller than his opponent but leaner to his adversary's stocky, was very handsome in a harsh, rough, craggy way.

They hit the edge of the pit, jumped down, and the mildly attractive one moved in the opposite direction.

The bald, craggy, handsome one moved their way.

"His name, for the purpose of these proceedings, is Flamma."

"Flamma?" she asked as the man's gaze swung from Stellan to Sixx, back to Stellan, then settling on Sixx as he continued toward them.

"Considered second only to Spartacus as the fiercest gladiator in history," Stellan explained. "As the tale is told, he was apparently awarded his freedom four times due to his popularity, skill and success in the arena. He declined, continuing to fight until his death in the Colosseum at age thirty."

Whoa.

Choosing Spartacus was way too obvious.

So good choice in name.

The man stopped in front of them, dipped his head to Stellan, then looked to her.

"Your assumption is correct," Stellan said, and Sixx looked at him to see he was addressing the warrior. "You're finally meeting your Mistress."

Oh God.

Her gift.

She fought her eyes rounding as Flamma nodded to Stellan before he shifted only a foot to the side so he was positioned directly in front of her. He then dropped right to his knees, bowed his head, his hand going directly to his flaccid cock, and he started pumping.

She'd missed this part before.

She hoped she didn't miss it again.

Stellan's thumb was back to stroking the inside of her wrist, undoubtedly feeling her response through her pulse.

At the sight before her, she was way beyond caring.

"Do you like your gift, my darling?"

Sixx tore her eyes from the masturbating gladiator in front of her and aimed them at Stellan.

"He trains for you. He fights for you. He fucks for you," he carried on.

And yet again, she couldn't stop herself from squirming in her throne.

Stellan smiled. "I see I don't need an answer to my question."

She looked back to the gladiator who was now hard but still stroking, and what he was stroking had grown highly impressive.

"He never loses, so when he wins, he'll come to you, give you his harness, and you'll tell him how you wish him to celebrate his victory," Stellan explained. "You also need to tell him when he's ready to fight, Simone. Or he'll come on the mat at your feet."

She was very good at sensing when enough was enough with a sub. It was integral for every Domme to have a precise handle on sensing just that.

But she'd never met this man, was not all that close to him in terms of proximity. She couldn't see his face, hear his breath, and he was so built she couldn't tell if the tension in his body was due to excitement at what was happening between his legs or he was just made that way.

However, he had a physical battle on his hands, and that was imminent.

She couldn't have him making an offering prior to that.

"Should I tell him to stop now?" she asked Stellan.

"I would."

"Stop," she called.

He stopped, took his feet, and glanced under his thick, dark lashes at her. Otherwise, he didn't move.

Stellan leaned into her and said in her ear. "He fights for you, sweetheart. So you might want to tell him to get on with that."

Good Lord.

The man called Flamma was entirely at her command.

She had a frigging sexual gladiator *at her command*.

This was . . .

It was . . .

Fucking *spectacular*.

"You may fight," she ordered.

He dipped his head to her and turned toward the pit.

Stellan stayed leaned into her, lifting their hands and rubbing her knuckles against his jaw as he shared, "Although gladiator battles are held the first and third Tuesday of every month, gladiators only fight once a month. It can get extreme, no rules except no blows to the groin area, so they need plenty of recuperation time in between bouts. All the fighters are different, and we have new ones approaching to sign on regularly, which is excellent as the audience enjoys fresh meat. They train different ways. Boxing. Various disciplines of martial arts. MMA. Wrestling. But in the end, stamina, strength, strategy and a good grasp on a combination of disciplines takes the win."

Flamma's opponent was in a crouch, hands up, circling him,

but Flamma was simply standing straight, eyes locked on his adversary, pivoting as his challenger moved.

"Flamma is retired Mossad," Stellan went on to share.

Uh.

Mossad?

"God, really?" she whispered, impressed.

"Really," Stellan answered. "Now he owns a gym where he teaches krav maga. His real name is Ami. He is not bi, and he's also not homosexual. He's a combatant and an alpha-submissive who has yet to be claimed by a permanent Mistress. When we were recruiting, he came forward without that requirement, which normally would mean we could not use him. I met with him, thought you'd like him, so he's been battling under my command, and not liking it due to my gender, though I assured him he'd eventually be owned by a female. Now that he's doing this for you, although he hasn't disappointed in the past, I've no doubt tonight he'll put on quite a show."

Stellan was not wrong.

Within seconds after Stellan stopped talking, Flamma's opponent decided to strike.

He clearly knew who he was taking on.

But he was no match.

It wasn't over quickly. But Flamma managed to keep himself almost entirely protected. In fact, she could count on one hand how many blows he sustained, at the same time moving lightning quick to land devastating strikes that had pained noises exploding from his challenger and awed "oos" and "ahs" emanating from his audience.

It was a dance, and he was the expert faced with a beginner. It was grace and power and patience and perception. He knew where he was at every second and could predict his opponent's moves before his challenger had even gotten into the stance to attempt to deliver them.

Flamma never lost the upper hand and seemed to only pounce

on his adversary with a hammering succession of destructive moves
to end the match after he felt he gave a good enough show but was
beginning to get bored with the effort.

This might have been the case, but he clearly wanted to offer
his Mistress a grand finale because he did just that.

Sixx sat motionless, her hand still held in Stellan's, and as he
remained leaned her way, it was tucked to his neck where she could
feel his pulse, Flamma picked up his now bleeding, and also flail-
ing, opponent upside down. He stomped toward her and held him,
with one arm at his hips, displayed full-frontal to her while he ripped
the straps off his genitals with the other hand. He tossed them aside,
pounded the man facedown to the mat and landed on top of him
with a booming thud.

The crowd shouted their approval, and the gong sounded.

Yes, a stunning finale.

Well done, Flamma.

Like the loser was part of the mat, Flamma got up, stepped over
him and walked to her.

He ripped his straps off and tossed them to the floor at her feet.

Oh yes.

Well done, Flamma.

He waited, perfectly inert.

Damn.

Now what did she do?

"Whatever you want him to do," Stellan said into her ear, again
like he read her mind.

She gave a short nod and called, "We're learning each other, so
why don't you show me the kind of offering you wish to give your
Mistress?"

He nodded just as short, stomped back to the man who'd brought
himself to his knees and took hold of his hair.

Sixx made a note to give more detailed instructions next time
as he dragged the man across the mats by his hair, something she
wasn't keen on, though fortunately it wasn't far.

Then he bent, and she jumped in her seat, hearing Stellan's chuckle come again, when he lifted him bodily and dumped him face-down right at her feet.

He bounded up out of the pit, kicked the man's legs apart, sank to his knees between them, jerked up the man's hips and leaned over him, shoving his face down next to her pump.

Okay, yes.

One hundred and fifty percent yes.

Best.

Gift.

Ever.

His voice was a grating rumble when he asked, "My Mistress, do you want him to offer his cum?"

Seeing as he wasn't bi, or gay, she wondered what he wanted.

But in her position, she couldn't ask.

"No," she told him.

Another curt nod but then nothing else.

"Darling." Stellan's voice was trembling with humor. "You've done this before. He's yours. *Command him.*"

Oh.

Right.

"Carry on," she ordered.

His eyes locked to hers, he positioned his cock to the ringed ass before him and drove deep.

She watched his jaw flex, heard the grunt float up from the mouth at her feet and heard more as the loser took the winner's cock.

"You don't come until I say," she demanded, her gaze also locked to Flamma.

Another curt nod, more tension in his face, a flash of excitement in his eyes (alpha-sub indeed), and a rumbled, "Yes, Mistress."

She sat motionless, feeling Stellan now stroking her knuckles with his thumb, and she alternately watched her gladiator's face and his shaft sinking in and out of the flesh of the defeated, thinking again this was by far the best present she'd ever received.

The truth was none of the few she'd gotten were any good.

But it would take quite something to be better than this.

"Faster," she whispered.

He went faster.

Fabulous.

"Harder," she ordered.

He pounded harder, the grunts got louder and started coming from two throats.

And then the tension wasn't only in Flamma's face, but beating from the cords of his neck, into his chest, down to his boxed abs.

She knew what that meant.

"Pull him into you," she commanded.

The slapping flesh got louder as Flamma followed her command.

Sixx saw the pain mingle with devotion on his face, devotion for a Mistress he did not know, but who he did know was serving his needs, and she knew it was time.

"Let go."

His head jerked back, the veins and muscles in his neck along with the column of his throat standing out as his fucking turned savage.

He roared loud and long when he came.

The crowd roared with him.

Sixx wanted to roar too.

Roar and turn and straddle Stellan in his seat, begging him to fuck her harder than they'd just witnessed and not simply as a thank you for her gift.

Panting, his head righted, and his eyes again locked to hers.

Stellan's hand gave hers a squeeze, reminding her he wasn't gay. He'd fuck male ass on command because he was submissive.

But the deed was done.

"You're relieved, warrior," she said softly.

He pulled out by shoving the man to his stomach at her feet.

"You've served me well," she shared.

"Thank you, Mistress. It's been my honor."

"You may go."

He nodded more than once that time, got up but bent over, pulling the loser by his ankle and sending him crashing back into the pit.

The crowd loudly shared their approval of this act as Flamma bent again to nab his straps, stood before her and bowed his head, looked to Stellan for another brief bow, then he stalked off. Shifting behind the thrones, he lumbered toward the doorway where he'd entered with his opponent, doing this with an ovation following in his wake but looking like he didn't give that first shit.

He'd served his Mistress.

She'd met his needs by allowing him to serve.

It was time for a Budweiser.

"Regardless of the result of our negotiations," Stellan began, and Sixx looked to him just as he lifted her knuckles to his lips.

She watched with great fascination as he rubbed them along his lower one once, twice, again, and again.

Four times before he stopped.

Four times she wouldn't forget of that gentle touch, how soft his lip felt, and the different feel she got in her belly that he'd even do it.

"They know you now," he continued. "He's yours. This chair is yours. The first Tuesday every month, you command Flamma from this seat until you release him from his duties."

"And I'll have to do that when?" she asked.

"When he finds a Mistress who doesn't like sharing. He'll inform you if this happens. We'll discuss your uses for him in alternate ways later. However, this seat is always yours if you have a fighter in the arena or not."

She didn't have the mental capacity at that point to consider Flamma's alternate uses.

At that point, she had to stay on target.

"And your seat?" she queried.

"Is always mine."

She started to pull back, but his hold on her tightened so she stopped.

But she did begin, "Stellan—"

"Trust me."

She felt her lips part.

She trusted no one.

No one but herself.

And Aryas.

And sometimes Carlo, but he could be a prankster, and it chapped her ass whenever he was.

But maybe two hours ago Stellan was a remote Dom who shared an acquaintance with her as well as membership at the same sex club.

That was all.

And now he was . . .

What?

Stellan's face changed.

And she stopped breathing.

Good Lord.

How could he get more handsome?

She had no idea.

But she'd just witnessed it happening.

"Just trust me, Simone," he urged gently. "And if you do, I swear to fuck I'll make you happy that you did."

The night bore down on her, crushing her, a warm, exciting, welcoming weight the likes she'd never felt, not once.

She wondered if that feeling was what kids felt the night before Christmas. The day before a trip to Disneyland. Sitting at a dining room table and facing the lit candles on their birthday cake.

But she wouldn't know because she'd never had any of that.

"Did you build this building?" she asked.

A soft look entered his eyes when he replied, "No. It was owned by an online shopping company who tried to rival Amazon and failed. I just bought it, dug the pit, reconditioned it to serve as an auditorium, and hired a talent recruiter, a promoter and an event manager."

"So the building sits vacant when there aren't gladiators in the pit?"

"No."

He didn't elaborate.

"And you did this for me," she went on.

"Yes."

He did it for her.

God.

All of this . . .

For her.

He didn't say anything more on that either.

"You've barely spoken to me since I came back," she pointed out.

"When a man prepares to broker a deal he very much wants to swing his way, he's certain to prepare thoroughly before discussions begin."

God.

This was unbelievable.

"Perhaps we should have our talk tonight," she suggested.

"Oh no," he replied. "That wouldn't be fair, darling. You've had no time to prepare. And I might have been thorough, and obviously I'll be entering the negotiations knowing what I want. But if I come out with the deal I'm hoping for, it won't be as sweet if I get it taking advantage."

"This is a lot," she admitted.

Though that was an understatement of epic proportions.

And Stellan knew it if the amused smile he gave her was any indication.

"You have four days to become accustomed to it."

The sounds of the milling of the crowd filtered through the intensity of their discussion, and she realized Flamma's victory heralded the end of the night.

She also had a flash drive to deliver.

And a mind-boggling number of things to assess and consider.

You can if you promise to think about it.

Think about what?

Being happy.

Was happiness sitting in a chair right by her side holding her hand?

Or was it just another path—one that might prove to be far more painful than the not-so-fun ones that came before—leading to everything ending up just plain shit?

"Sixx?"

The name she gave herself coming from his lips brought her back into an auditorium retrofitted to offer her something she enjoyed greatly and receiving a gift a woman like her could only cherish.

It meant everything, and it was then Sixx learned that everything was just that.

Everything.

And everything was way too much.

Suddenly that crushing weight wasn't warm and welcoming.

It was just crushing.

"Sixx," Stellan whispered, his hold on her hand tightening, again like he sensed the turn of her thoughts.

"Bait with an exceptionally elaborate switch, and you reeled me right in," she whispered back.

"Did I?" he asked.

She stared into his eyes, and she did it for a beat, two, three, four.

How about I won't actively avoid it?

Damn, she'd promised.

Sixx was capable of a lot of things.

Breaking a promise wasn't one of them.

Definitely not one she'd made Aryas.

So she had no choice but to answer, "We'll see."

three

The Ones I Love

STELLAN

Stellan prowled down the hall toward his office in a foul mood.

He was just back from a lunch meeting that went on far too long, especially for the large amount of nothing that came of it, and he was not a man who appreciated having his time wasted.

However, this was not why he was in a vile mood.

It was Friday afternoon.

The next day, he was having a party. The kind of party he always thoroughly enjoyed.

However, this particular party was one he'd expended no small degree of effort in making meticulous plans to *significantly* enjoy.

And in the early hours of Wednesday morning, when he stood with Simone at the driver's side door to her Cayenne and handed her his card—a card that had his office phone and address engraved on the front, his cell phone and home address written on the back—he'd ordered her to phone him prior to Saturday to get details of when she was to arrive and what she was to bring with her when she did.

She had not phoned.

She'd had some "business" to attend to, and that, as well as all Stellan had bombarded her with that night, was on her mind.

And although Stellan had contacted Aryas to make certain he'd heard from Sixx (he had), Stellan had decided in future, if she did not cease these antics that were foolish at best, could be deadly at worst, he'd put a man on her to make certain she was safe until he could talk her out of continuing to do the incredibly stupid things she did.

In the meantime, if she did not arrive at his home the next day like she'd been told to do, it would be the shortest party he'd ever thrown, considering the fact that he'd leave it, find her, and toss all the rest of the meticulous plans he'd made out the window while he communicated to her precisely what he wanted her to know.

And he'd do this until she submitted to it.

In fact, the only thing that kept him from taking his mood out on anyone in his path were the new elaborate plans he was making, detailing how he'd be certain to teach Simone some very important lessons.

They were varied. They were imaginative. And if there came a time when they were carried out, both of them would enjoy them. It was just that Stellan would do this throughout and Simone would only do it eventually.

He was considering this when he walked into his assistant's office. An office that was the bastion of defense protecting him from the tedious minutiae of office politics, gossip, petty grievances, weak excuses for poor performance and false claims of illness that people used to get out of the work he paid them to do.

An office that was outside his own.

The minute he walked in, her eyes came direct to him.

They were wary.

His assistant Susan had been with him for over seven years. Outside of her honeymoon and bi-yearly vacations, during the work week (and the not-rare weekend), she'd only not been at her desk for seven months, six of those being the amount of maternity leave he gave his staff as policy, the last one he gave to her because she was Susan.

He was godfather to that child.

And considering Susan's own father was an extreme asshole, in their time together she'd given Stellan one other honor.

That being dancing with him, just the two of them, on the dancefloor at her wedding reception to the song that played after the first she'd danced with her then brand-new husband, and before the song that played when her husband danced with his mother.

Stellan didn't often take his foul moods out on his team, definitely not Susan, but that didn't mean they didn't sense them.

Especially Susan.

And the wary in her gaze shared his current mood had been sensed.

"Stellan, there's been—" she began.

"You can brief me later," he interrupted her, not breaking stride on his way to the gleaming wood double doors to his office, finishing, "I've some calls to make."

He opened one of the doors, strode inside, swung the door shut behind him and stopped dead when his eyes hit his desk.

On the corner was a large cream pottery vase, and spiking out of it was a profuse spray of palm fronds mingled with copious dripping orchids the extraordinary color of azure blue.

From business associates to women in his life, he'd been given bottles of Scotch or vodka, Belgian chocolates, Cuban cigars, Tiffany cufflinks, Robert Talbott ties, and the like.

Not ever had he been sent flowers.

He walked to the arrangement, removed the small envelope from what appeared to be a holder made of a notched stick of bamboo, and saw on the outside it had a handwritten "S."

He opened it and pulled out the card.

Inside, also handwritten, and not, he was certain, by a florist, it said:

S~

Flamma is magnificent.

~S

PS: Spoke with Amélie. See you tomorrow at 1:00.

Staring at the card, Stellan took in a deep breath, let it out slowly, and then for the first time in two and a half days, he allowed his lips to curve up.

He dropped the card on his blotter and circumnavigated his

desk, shrugging off his suit jacket. He took his phone out of the inside pocket before he rounded the jacket to rest on the back of his chair.

He sat and twisted his chair to the side where there was a wall of windows that ran the length of his office that afforded the entirely *not* picturesque view of downtown Phoenix.

That view was one of many things Stellan loved about the city he'd chosen to make his home.

Phoenicians were living in a modern-day Wild West.

That was to say they didn't give a shit about anything but freedom to do and be whatever the fuck they wanted to do and be.

There were no airs in Arizona, unless you wanted to have them, and if you did and someone didn't like it, they could go fuck themselves.

Phoenicians needed no impressive skyscape to stamp their mark on a nation.

There were Cardinals games to go to.

Stellan had traveled widely. There were many places he'd been to that he'd enjoyed greatly.

However there was and always would be only one home.

He engaged his phone, went to the text screen, and entered a name that was attached to a number he'd acquired months ago but never used.

He then sent the text, **The flowers are beautiful.**

After he sent that to sweep through the global telecommunication system, he typed, **But you've ignored my instructions, darling.**

He sent that.

Finally he typed, **Consequences.**

And he sent that.

Knowing he'd receive no reply, he tossed the phone to his desk and looked out the window, his lips still turned up.

She was intrigued.

She was also afraid.

She was further titillated.

And completely terrified.

She saw the possibility of a future that included having something.

Anything.

A concept that was entirely foreign to her.

And that made her scared out of her fucking mind.

Therefore no.

He'd receive no reply.

But she would show the next day.

She might not have anything but a Cayenne and what appeared to be a death wish.

But she also had her pride.

It was an understatement to say he'd been stunned that the instant he'd claimed her, she'd orgasmed. Her eyes growing unfocused, her lips parting, she'd climaxed at his first touch as her Master, and she'd done it instantaneously.

Stellan sat turned from his desk, not seeing the view, allowing himself to start to grow hard remembering it.

He'd taken a risk, a hefty one, called the shot, took it, and found he'd been right.

She was a switch.

She needed power.

But she craved being powerless.

Months of precision planning to get her ass where it belonged, in her throne by his side, had culminated in her immediate submission the moment he'd claimed her as her Master.

It was more than he'd hoped for.

By far.

It couldn't have gone better.

Flawless.

"Christ," he whispered, swiveling in his chair back to his desk, his gaze moving to rest on the flowers.

Another surprise. That was not Sixx.

Mistress Sixx did not send flowers. If in the mood, she gave orgasms, but only if extremes were met and they were earned. To friends and acquaintances she gave time and attention, in a remote and seemingly surface-only way, not realizing that she poorly hid the fact that she gave a significant shit under layers of frost that only thawed with those she held in her heart.

But he'd seen her look at Leigh and Olly. Mira and Trey. Penn and Shane.

She was thrilled that they'd all found each other, fallen in love.

And she was envious.

And he'd seen how she was with Aryas.

Devoted.

Now Simone . . .

He studied a fragile bowed stem adorned with azure orchid petals.

Apparently Simone sent flowers.

This gracious act reminded him that it had taken huge amounts of effort not to follow up on all that had happened on their first night together and do it immediately. From leaving her at the driver's side door to her Cayenne instead of taking her directly to his home to finding an excuse to seek her out every moment in between.

But he knew.

Stellan knew.

He knew everything.

It was dangerous what he was doing, and that danger centered entirely on all that could be lost.

He'd played a game once where the stakes were the highest they could be.

He hadn't lost because you couldn't lose to someone who didn't know she was in the game.

He'd still lost.

With this . . .

With Sixx . . .

No.

With Simone . . .

It could be nothing but a game.

A game it was essential that he win.

Because if he didn't, it would still be Simone who'd be the loser.

As promised, when Stellan had asked Branch Dillinger to get him everything on Mistress Sixx, Dillinger had delivered.

So Stellan knew.

He knew Simone Marchesa was treading water, failing in her efforts not to go under, and not much caring if the current pulled her away.

So the game had to be played not only so Stellan could drag her to safety.

But so he could lift her up.

Then at his side he'd take her to the highest peak.

And once he got her there, she'd never, not fucking ever, look back down.

She'd been held down long enough.

The door to his office opened, his gaze went there, and he watched Susan walk in.

Blonde, petite, always impeccably dressed, and even though Crosby was eighteen months, she hadn't lost all of her baby weight.

She didn't care. She'd ended her pregnancy addicted to My Nana's tortilla chips and Baby Ruth bars, and since she wasn't finished reproducing, she wasn't bothering with the effort to kick those habits.

Stellan thought this was wise.

Then again, Susan was the opposite of dumb, and that was not the only reason he was as devoted to her as she was to him.

Within moments she assessed his mood had changed, tossed a hand toward the palm fronds and orchids, and remarked, "So I can now assume those aren't from your Ahsweepay in an all-new but never improved effort to apologize yet *again* for being a gargantuan *ahsweepay.*"

Ahsweepay was the name she'd given his father, a moniker that originated from a skit from *Saturday Night Live*, and although phonetically correct as per the skit, it was actually spelled much differently.

"I believe upon his announcement of his engagement to his latest there and gone, I made it clear how I felt about him continuing to consider me a part of his life," Stellan replied. "So no, the flowers are not from him."

She walked right up to his desk and leaned a thigh against it, not hesitating a second to reach out and grab the card.

Stellan's lips turned up.

"What's a Flamma?" she asked.

"A sexual gladiator," he answered.

Her hazel eyes shot to him and got wide.

When they did, his smile did the same.

There was nothing Susan did not know about him. Nothing he hid. Nothing that was not hers to have.

She reciprocated that gesture.

Which meant she was his assistant.

But although he paid her (handsomely) to be all she was to him in the office, missing only the blood ties, in his life she was something else entirely.

And she felt the same.

"A present for a woman I've started seeing," he explained.

"You gave her a . . . *person?*" she asked, her voice pitched high.

And an auditorium where she could command that . . . *person,* though he didn't sign over the deed.

"Yes," he answered.

She burst out laughing.

Stellan smiled at her indulgently as she did.

"Only you," she muttered toward the card, then looked to him and shook it in the air before she plopped it on his desk. "And who is 'S?' "

"Her name is Simone."

"Pretty," she murmured.

"She is," he replied.

Her gaze slid to the bouquet then back to him. "She's got class."

"Her father was a drug dealer."

Susan blinked.

"He was killed in a turf-war massacre that also killed her mother," Stellan continued. "A mother who shared the profession of distributing narcotics."

"Oh my God," she whispered.

"Unsurprisingly, this was not a loss, in either instance," he shared. "What was unfortunate was that she witnessed it. They brought her with them to meet their supplier. She was one of only two people in the room to survive. That room contained nine, four of those the rival foot soldiers of the supplier who instigated the incident. She was twelve."

He watched her pale.

"Stellan," she said softly.

"She was then raised by her uncle, who was also a drug dealer, and the succession of women in his life, all of whom were junkies, some of these underage junkies not much older or even the same age as Simone."

She shifted, moved slowly back, and lowered herself to the edge of one of the minimalist, backless, black leather chairs behind her.

His office was beautifully appointed.

But except for him, it was not meant to be comfortable.

He was there to work, not socialize, and that was the message he conveyed with the two chairs opposite his desk.

Susan, of course, could spend as much time as she liked with him, and if she needed to be comfortable doing that, she stretched out on the modern, white-leather-with-chrome-arms sweep of a lounge chair at the other end of the office. And she did . . . often.

Which was good, since he wouldn't own it if it wasn't to give it to her.

"She used her natural intelligence, firmly ingrained survival skills and familial criminal contacts to become what's known as a fixer," he told her.

"As in, what Olivia Pope does on *Scandal*?" she inquired.

Really, Susan needed to stop watching so much television.

"What does this person do on this show?" he asked.

"Fixes jams people get in, mostly politicians."

Stellan nodded and didn't lie, precisely, since Simone fixed "jams" people found themselves in, those people were just not politicians.

"Mostly, but not entirely."

"Do I want to know all that entails?" she queried.

He gave her the truth.

"No."

This answer didn't make her happy. She also didn't hide that.

"Are you . . . *unsafe* . . . being with her?"

"Not at all," he assured.

She fell silent, and did this examining him closely.

Then she said in an awed voice, "Oh my *God*, you're in love with her."

He shook his head. "I'm infatuated with her, Sue. She's fascinating."

"If she's like Olivia Pope, I can imagine."

He raised his brows. "Does this Olivia wear a lot of leather?"

She grinned. "Not unless you count her Prada handbags. And why am I not surprised your Simone wears leather?"

His Simone.

This made Stellan return her grin. "It cuts deep, honey, that I'm such an open book to you. I much prefer to be thought of as the brooding, mysterious boss."

"You can be broody, case in point, the last two days before these flowers showed. And just to make you feel better, I'm the only female in your offices that doesn't find you mysterious. The rest twitter about you around the staff room and in the john all the freaking time. And to further soothe your ego, all of them want to jump your bones. Even Darby."

"Darby?"

"She's one of your recorders. She's set to retire in August. She's sixty-seven."

It was Stellan bursting out in laughter at that.

When he was done, Susan's expression had changed.

She didn't make him ask after it.

"So this is just an infatuation?"

"We've known each other for years, but Tuesday evening was our first date."

Both her brows stretched high. "And you gave her a person . . . on your *first date*?"

"I like to make an impression."

She shot him a huge smile. "I've no doubt you did, but you probably would have done that even if you hadn't gifted her with a human being."

Stellan shrugged.

Her head tipped slightly to the side. "And she gave you all that history on a first date?"

"No. I had her investigated."

Her face shut down and her lips mumbled, "Uh-oh."

"It'll be fine," he assured.

She leaned toward him. "Stellan, she's a . . . a . . . *fixer*."

He felt his lips twitch before he said, "Sweetheart, you don't even know what that means."

Her shoulders straightened. "Well, I do know what it means to be a woman, and seriously, no joke this time, women don't want to seem broody, but we absolutely *do* like to be mysterious. We like to be the ones who share all our inner secrets and past histories. And I can only assume a woman who's also a fixer feels that more than just your average chick."

"I've already told her I looked into her."

"Looking into her and *investigating* her are two very different things."

Stellan made no reply to that because unfortunately, she was right.

Her gaze narrowed on him. "You're more than infatuated with her."

This was absolutely true.

"The week is winding down, but there's still work to get done," he noted, his message not vague, his hopes she'd read it also not high.

And as suspected, they were dashed.

"That trick done left the building, boss man," she declared. "My kid has spit up more on you than he has his own father."

"That's not true," Stellan murmured.

"Okay, than he has his own grandfather."

"That wouldn't be hard. You haven't spoken to your father since fruitlessly telling him the news Crosby was coming."

"I mean *Harry's* father, Stellan," she snapped, losing patience.

"Of course," he muttered.

"And he's a good guy," she went on.

"The man lives in Texas."

"He's still a good guy with his first grandson and he's retired, so the man's at my house more than he's in his fishing boat."

"Honey, please don't take out your frustrations that your in-laws are far too in your business on me. Especially Harry's mother, which is what this is really about. As I've said before, all you have to do is find a way to tell them to back off, or better, find a way just to let it go. Betty does not know better when it comes to Crosby. Let her speak her piece, then just do what you do. She's got no choice but to let you do what you do since you're the boy's mother. In the end he'll grow up to be the only thing you and Harry can make, a good man, and it'll all be fine."

"Stop manipulating the conversation around to my problems," she demanded. "Are you falling in love with this woman or not?"

He looked her directly in her eyes.

"Yes."

Those eyes he was looking into started getting wet.

So Stellan turned his to the ceiling.

"Oh my God, this is so *awesome*," she whispered.

He looked back at her.

"Sue," he said quietly, "we've had one date."

At a gladiator pit.

Where she climaxed on contact.

In other words, the perfect first date.

"But you've known her for years," she said.

"I have."

"And she's a fixer. She's not a dud, like, I don't know . . . a socialite or something. She's exciting. She's Olivia Pope in leather. I love that for you."

Jesus.

"If I see one bridal magazine anywhere near your desk, I'm sacking you," he warned.

"Can I pick out her engagement ring?" she requested.

He was offended she'd even ask.

"Yes," he agreed.

Her entire body twitched.

Then she burst into tears.

His eyes narrowed.

Susan was a crier, but this . . .

"Are you pregnant?" he demanded to know.

She was sniffling, her breath hitching, her eyes leaking, then her head started bobbing.

"Y-y-yes."

Stellan's chest grew light.

"You're expecting?" he whispered.

She nodded. "But I'm still, like, *super* happy you're falling in love."

"Who knows?" he asked.

"Well, Harry, obviously."

He smiled and murmured, "Obviously."

"And you."

Stellan had no reply to that.

He just held her watery gaze.

"That's all," she whispered.

And that was when Stellan's throat grew tight.

He also shoved his hand in his pocket and pulled out his handkerchief.

He tossed it across the desk, and she reached out, picked it up and dabbed her eyes.

She got herself together and focused on him.

"Just so you know, Harry's still not over the trust fund you set up for Crosby," she shared.

"How far along are you?" he queried.

"Almost three months."

"Then he has just over six months to get over it because another one is coming."

"Stellan—"

"I take care of the ones I love," he said softly.

She closed her mouth, and more wet hit her eyes.

"I'm happy for you," he shared. "You and Harry and Crosby. I'm so fucking happy for you, sweetheart."

She took in a broken breath and snapped, "Stop making me cry."

"If the last one was anything to go on, you have just over six months to cope with that because your pregnancy hormones run havoc with your tear ducts, and I have nothing to do with it."

"I know," she agreed. "Sucks. I burst into tears at the YouTube video of the 'Sad Cat Diaries.'"

"Christ, why would you watch something like that at all?" he asked.

She shook her head, a tremulous grin on her lips. "It's supposed to be hilarious. And it is. They just picked a bunch of cats who look sad to illustrate the hilarity. You totally have to watch it. If you're not pregnant, which you'll never be, it's a scream."

"And I totally am not going to do that."

She kept shaking her head. "Stell, my man, you need to enter the age of social media."

"On my gravestone it will say, 'His proudest achievement: He never tweeted.' And if I manage that colossal feat, it will indeed be my proudest."

She dissolved into laughter again.

And Stellan again looked on indulgently.

When she sobered, she said, "I suppose I should go back to work."

"That *is* why I pay you."

She shot him a fake annoyed look that didn't work due to the massive smile on her face.

She also got up and started the long walk to the door.

She stopped halfway there.

He braced.

She turned back to him.

"If you give it to her, she better be worth it," she declared.

"She is, or I wouldn't give it to her," he returned.

"One date and you're sure?"

"No, but I am sure I want to explore if I can be sure."

"You're handsome and you're rich and you're exciting and you're generous and you're kind and you're funny and she wears leather and has ugly history and is a fixer. I'm not trying to be offensive. What I'm trying to say is that you deserve the best, someone who gives all that, or something else worth just as much, right back to you."

"Sometimes, Susie," he said gently, "love is not about give and take. There are loves that are only about giving. And with Simone, who was born with nothing and to protect herself carried on keeping it that way, it might be high time she had the opportunity to take all she can get."

"Then she found the perfect man," she replied, suddenly not sounding happy about it.

"Perhaps," he allowed.

"Definitely," she retorted, slightly lifting her chin but absolutely straightening her shoulders. "Even with what you just said, I'll say it again. If you give it all, Stellan, she freaking better be worth it."

Delivering that, considering she was a last-word type of woman, something he and Harry had commiserated about over drinks on more than one occasion, he knew she needed it to be done.

So Stellan made no reply as she turned and walked the rest of the way to and through the door, closing it behind her.

four

Sangria

SIXX

Sixx drove up the wide semi-circular drive to the large, two-story, sprawling, southwestern-adobe home that could be defined as nothing other than a mansion.

Not a McMansion.

No, it was older. Unique. Settled. Refined. And time had made it at peace with the landscape around it.

It was also bigger.

There were a number of cars in the sweeping drive.

This was because she was late. Only by twenty minutes, but she was still late.

In normal circumstances, it was not rude to be late to what amounted to a pool party. People would come, they would go, and fun was to be had whoever was there, or not.

But she had a feeling Stellan would not be pleased she was late.

She reached to the passenger seat and nabbed the black handles of her white Henri Bendel weekend duffle.

She did not intend to spend the weekend, however pool time to dinnertime in a Phoenician mansion required sitting at a table for dinner in something other than the t-shirt dress you'd arrived in or the bathing suit and sarong you'd spent the afternoon in.

So she'd come prepared.

And although she was highly apprehensive about what was happening with Stellan—most especially imminently after not calling as he'd told her to and showing late—he *was* Stellan, and although she'd never in her life dressed to impress anyone but herself, it was worth a repeat.

He was *Stellan*.

She felt slightly ashamed, slightly elated about the fact that she'd even gone shopping.

Frigging *shopping*.

For Stellan.

This, she told herself, was why she didn't chicken out. If she did, and considering the fact she wasn't going to haunt the Honey anymore, where would she wear her new threads?

She also didn't chicken out for the sole reason that she was not a woman who chickened out.

In other words, she'd waged an internal battle up to and through the last minute.

And now she was late.

But she'd come prepared.

She also nabbed her Valentino Rockstud clutch and shoved it under her arm as she hopped out of her car.

She weaved her way through the other vehicles, taking in the copious barrel, saguaro and ocotillo cacti intermingled with olive and palo verde trees of the landscaping, the impressive three-tiered fountain the cars were parked around in the center of the drive, and the log-festooned veranda and recessed entryway decorated by brightly colored Mexican pots overflowing with healthy succulents.

That was, she took this all in until she realized in the shadowed entryway one side of the front double door was open.

And leaning against the jamb wearing faded jeans and a white linen, long-sleeved shirt, his feet bare, was Stellan.

God, God, *Gawd*.

The man could be adorable.

And he wore jeans.

She'd never seen him in jeans.

He looked . . .

Edible.

She hit the tile of the veranda, wondering why he couldn't be in board shorts, or something that made him look just normal (something she suspected was an impossibility), her sunglassed eyes adjusting from the bright sun to the shadows, and it was then she saw he also looked ticked.

Hmm.

"Stellan," she greeted.

"Sixx," he replied, unmoving from his place, essentially barring one half of the two ornately and exquisitely carved doors.

She stopped in front of him.

He swept her top to toe.

And when he did, the way he did, made one of the two sets of lips she had, the hidden ones, quiver.

She disguised her reaction by shoving her sunglasses on top of her head.

His gaze tracked her movement.

Another quiver.

Hell.

"Have I been uninvited?" she asked, quirking her eyebrows.

"No," he answered.

He still didn't move.

She held his gaze.

She also, as per the norm, lost the staring contest.

"Listen, I—"

He disengaged from the jamb, leaned into her, and she braced.

But he just took the duffle from her grip and ordered, "Come."

Then he disappeared into the cool dark, his disappearance sending a wave of frosty air-conditioning to chill her skin.

In Phoenician, that translated to, *Welcome to my home.*

"Shit," she whispered.

And followed.

His door weighed a ton, and she was no lightweight. She battled the monster and managed to get it closed.

She moved in and noted the beautiful, soft, sandy buff of the outside adobe was not carried through to the inside.

The ceilings were beamed with dark, shining timbers. The floors were covered in uneven, large, square, undulating blocks of shimmering, rich chocolate tile. And the adobe walls on the inside were a deep terra-cotta color that sucked out all the light.

With lots of rugs, comfortable but large and space-eating furniture, huge prints on the walls depicting epic Western scenes, and gluts of toss pillows, throws, furs and poofs, the dim, dark interior veritably screamed, *"Lie down and take a freaking nap, why don't you!"*

In fact, everywhere you turned there was nothing that didn't say, at the very least, *Relax, I got you.*

She'd been there before.

But she'd never been there as Simone.

She'd always been there as Sixx, a guest, removed, belonging and . . . not.

Now, she didn't know what she was.

She also didn't know where Stellan was.

"Hey there."

Her head came around, and in a large arch behind which was a huge, rustic dining room table with approximately fifty chairs (a shade over-exaggerated), she saw a Hispanic woman with a mass of gray-and-black hair, a petite, round body, gorgeous skin, sparkling brown eyes and a friendly smile.

"Sixx?" she asked.

Sixx nodded.

"The last one to arrive!" she cried, as if that won a prize.

"Sorry I'm a bit late," Sixx said.

"There is no late at Casa Lange," she replied on a smile, like she owned the joint. Though Sixx was relatively certain she was in error as to what she said, she wasn't going to correct her. "I'm Margarita. Stellan calls me 'M.' I'm his housekeeper, and cook, and the annoying woman who tells him to take his vitamins even though he's a grown man. I've got five kids. They're all grown too. And so far, two grandkids, who are not grown. Also one on the way. So you know . . . habit."

God, she was cute as all hell.

And she was Stellan's housekeeper.

Growing up, she'd known a couple of women who were kind of like housekeepers considering they were house cleaners.

But she knew not one person who *had* a housekeeper.

Not true.

She did.

Frigging Stellan.

Not knowing what to say, she stupidly said, "Hi."

"Hi," Margarita replied brightly, still smiling, friendly and big.

Sixx stood there with her clutch under her arm, feeling awkward.

"He went upstairs," Margarita shared, indicating to her right with a little tilt of her head. "With your bag."

"Oh, okay," she mumbled, but didn't move.

Margarita's eyes took in Sixx with her big gold hoops in her ears. The fall of a plethora of tiered, thin, gold chains hanging from her neck adorning her front from upper chest to below her breasts. The thin gold bangles at her wrist that were so profuse that although each was delicate, they crawled up five inches on her wrist. Her black t-shirt dress that looked just that at the top, but was tight and ruched at her hips. And her gold slides that were a series of straps from her toes to the tops of the bridges of her foot.

"You're to, uh . . . change in his room," Margarita explained.

"Oh, right," Sixx again mumbled, deciding to move, something she did.

"All is set for your fiesta, which means I'll be leaving soon," Margarita announced when Sixx came abreast of her. "So I'll say now it was nice meeting you."

"You too," she returned, spying the stairs that were around a wall.

A graceful curved design that included some log action as well as some fancy wrought iron.

He couldn't just have stairs.

No, his stairway had to be a showcase.

She took the first step realizing why she was out of sorts, and it didn't just have to do with the split-personality thing she'd been experiencing since Tuesday night.

She knew nothing about real estate.

But she didn't have to in order to know she was in a home that cost more than she'd make in her entire life, even if she still did for a living what she used to do for a living and now just did for the thrill (and so she could buy Valentino clutches).

"Master's at the far end!" Margarita called up as Sixx made it past the curve.

She could say that again, as Sixx was sure he was, though the woman was referring to his aptly named bedroom.

"Thanks! And again, nice to meet you!" Sixx called back, feeling like an idiot.

She hit the top hall, which was wide and also decorated with a heavy but handsome hand with paintings on walls, half-tables against them, candles, lamps, four-foot-high bronze statues, and she saw a variety of doors, most of them open, except one.

She headed down to the door at the far end.

She entered it and ceased moving.

Completely.

Good Christ.

She'd been to Stellan's home.

She'd never been in there.

There were chandeliers. There were French doors to furnished balconies. There were arches. There was stained glass. There was wrought iron. There were carved columns. There were arched doorways. There were tapestries. There were acres of wood floors. There was heavy, magnificent furniture. There were two levels, the bed one was to her left, up two steps.

And everything was in colors of . . . nothing . . . but beauty. Parchment. Linen. Ivory. Alabaster. Pearl. Cotton.

And on the smooth white comforter of the huge bed was her Henri Bendel duffle.

Stellan appeared through an arch that led to . . . she had no idea where. There was the bed platform, and the lower area was big enough to be a living room, and furnished as such (also in *Relax, I got you*, just lighter in shade). And then there was the desk area, like he was some French count and needed a desk in his chambers to write missives by candlelight, something he could do with the thick candles set in gorgeous candelabrum there.

It was insanely beautiful.

And just *insane*.

"Is it your goal to leave me waiting all weekend?" Stellan's question jerked her out of her amazed, inferiority-complex-steeped stupor.

She said nothing.

He came to a stop in order to lean one broad shoulder against a blond column, one of two that flanked the steps up to the bed area.

He also crossed his arms on his wide chest.

Man of the house.

Dear Lord.

"Bendel is nice, but we'll be getting you LV. Or perhaps more you, Bottega Veneta," he carried on.

What did she say to that?

Apparently nothing as he continued.

"The others will be using the pool house, or the guest bedrooms. But you change up here. You also shower up here before dinner. And you'll be sleeping in here too."

She stopped looking at him and started staring at him.

She also found her voice.

"Is this a sleepover?"

He started down the steps. "For you it is."

He halted in front of her as she asked, "I thought after the party we were having a conversation."

"We are," he confirmed. "Then we're going to fuck, and after that, we're going to sleep."

She locked her legs so they wouldn't visibly tremble.

"Stellan, I've had a lot of time to think . . ."

She didn't finish that because she had, she'd just come to no conclusions.

However, slapped right in the face with his immense . . . *everything* . . . conclusions were coming to her.

He didn't need her to finish.

"I hope so. And we'll discuss that after the others leave. Now, is your suit under that," he dipped his head to her dress, "or do you need to change?"

"It is, but I need to lose the dress and grab my sarong."

"Do that. I've got something to give you before we join the others."

Oh man.

His last gift was an entire auditorium and a human being.

Considering the fact he lived in the Saint Basil's of adobe mansions in Phoenix, who knew what would come next?

"Maybe we should take a—"

"Lose the dress, Sixx, and grab your wrap," he ordered.

"I—"

His hand snaked out, caught her at the back of her head, and she heard her Valentino thump on the floor when she found herself molded to his body with his gorgeous face inches from hers, his other hand clamped at the side of her neck, and his voice had gone low.

"Lose the fucking dress, Simone, and grab your wrap," he commanded.

Her hand had landed on his abs, and she'd seen them when he was working a sub.

But feeling them . . .

"Okay," she whispered.

He let her go.

She immediately missed his abs.

Lord God.

He bent to retrieve her clutch and put it on his French count desk.

She moved up to the bed quickly in order to hide she did it unsteadily, unzipped her bag, and yanked out her wrap. She pulled her sunglasses off her head, dropped them to the bed, and tugged her dress off, leaving all her jewelry where it was, acutely aware that Stellan was on the lower level, watching.

This should not concern her considering the fact he'd watched her work in a playroom in a sex club with some frequency.

However, for a variety of reasons, when in a playroom, she wore her leather, and except on occasion when she left her arms or legs bare, she was always covered. Usually, she wore full-body catsuits or jumpsuits.

But again, she'd been here before, at one of his parties, even been to one wearing a bathing suit.

So why did she feel weird?

Maybe it's those gunshot-wound scars you didn't have before when you could wear a bikini, which meant you also had to buy a one-piece when you were shopping? her mind suggested.

There was that.

There was also the fact he'd said they were going to fuck, and she doubted if that happened he'd let her keep her one-piece on to hide her bullet wounds.

Her mind was scrambling for answers to the question when the question got a different answer.

It got this answer at the same time her mistake was made plain. She'd turned her back on him.

Thus when she was standing in nothing but her swimming suit, earrings, necklace, bangles and slides, she suddenly found herself caged in his arms, one at her chest, one at her ribs, her back pressed to his front, his lips at her neck.

God, he smelled really good.

His body felt a whole lot better.

"My mark is fading," he said there.

It was.

She'd been right. She'd had a bite mark that was angry the first day but started fading the next.

She knew she'd miss it the minute it was gone.

She didn't reply to his comment.

She was too busy deep breathing and trying very hard to keep hold on a variety of different bodily reactions.

Though he wouldn't be able to miss what was happening at her nipples.

Damn.

"I told you to call me," he reminded her.

It was far more bluster than confidence that made her reply, "You're not the only one who gets to make the rules to this game."

"I'm not?" he asked.

She was beginning to wonder if she had the right answer to that.

"We'll talk about it later," she evaded.

"You're right, we will. Now, however, we'll be talking about how you not only didn't call, you arrived late."

"I had some thinking to do that was important to do before I showed," she explained.

"You also have my number to share that this was something you needed and therefore also share you'd be late."

This was true.

"In truth," he went on, "I'd wanted you to arrive earlier so you could meet Margarita and I could show you what I've arranged for you before the others arrived. The problem with that is you didn't call so I could share this with you. So actually, you're not twenty minutes late. You're an hour and twenty minutes late."

Even for a pool party, that was not good.

"The good news is, I met Margarita before I came upstairs," she informed him.

"Yes, while she was leaving."

Hmm . . .

His nose slid up her neck.

Nice.

She bit her lip.

"What would you do to one of your subs if they kept you waiting for over an hour?" he whispered in her ear.

"Stellan, I'm not . . ." she swallowed and started again. "I'm not one of your subs."

"No, you're correct. You're not. You're my Simone."

She had a feeling she knew precisely what that meant and loved the idea with every little piece of her heart.

At the same time it scared her senseless.

She closed her eyes. "Stellan."

"I'm not a man who's kept waiting."

"Just let's get through—"

She didn't finish.

She was cheek to the bed, ass in the air, his hand firm at the back of her neck.

She was also trembling and close to orgasming.

Damn, damn, *damn it all to hell.*

She was a goddamned Domme, for Christ's sake.

She should see this shit coming.

She bent her arms and put her hands to the bed to push up and attempt to get some control of the situation.

But she went completely still when he pulled the material of her suit covering her ass up tight so it was bunched between her cheeks.

Okay, no.

No pushing up.

She was just going to stay very, very still and hope whatever he did left her able to sit.

Her breaths came fast and shallow as her pussy saturated, which told her whatever he was going to do, the effects of it were not going to go unnoticed by Stellan.

"Feel free to come, darling," he murmured.

She was right.

It had not gone unnoticed.

Then he spanked her, five sharp smacks on one cheek, all precisely aimed to land one on top of the other to increase the heat through blood flow, as well as the pain, five of the same to the other.

Each blow was impeccable, elegant.

Delicious.

And then she was up, turned, pulled to his long, hard body and held with one arm across her shoulder blades and the other hand cradling the bunched material at her behind, which was good. If his arms weren't around her, her legs would buckle and she'd go down.

She stared dazedly up at him.

He gazed adoringly down at her.

"If I didn't have guests, I would have given you enough to take you there, Simone. Sadly, I do. So you'll have to wait," he murmured, his hand shifting, fingers carefully arranging the material of her swimsuit to cover her bottom. "Now, the rules. Today, for you, I'll hide how demonstrative I intend to be in the future. However, I won't hide where I intend us to be, who you are to me and your place at my side. Am I understood?"

No, he was not.

There was a lot of ground to go over, with *all* of that.

She nodded.

"Good," he said softly and let her go.

She tried out her pegs, fortunately found they stood strong, if a little wobbly, and watched him bend to the bed to nab her shades.

He did not give them to her.

He slid the arm of them in the opening of his shirt.

They were Chanel. They had rhinestones. They were huge and flashy and feminine.

And she shot right back to near orgasm seeing he did not give that first shit about any of that.

Because they were hers.

"Your wrap, sweetheart," he prompted when all she seemed to be able to do was stare at her sunnies in his shirt.

Distractedly, she twisted to where she'd dropped the wrap on the bed, reached, and took up the thin silk.

Stellan took her hand and used it to tug her across the bedroom space, down the stairs, through the living room space and out the door.

One thing this all explained. He was likely as fit as he was because if she was wearing a FitBit, she knew it would tell her that they'd walked their daily ten thousand steps simply traversing his bedroom.

He led her down the hall, but not to the stairs, to the one closed door.

He turned to her.

"Would you like to put that on?" he asked, indicating her sarong with another dip of his head.

Mutely, she looked down, let out the material, then positioned it at her hips where she tied it in a knot at her hipbone.

"Mm..." he purred.

Her clit buzzed at the sound, her head went back, and she saw his eyes at her hips.

They came to hers, and he gave her that wicked smile before he turned to the door, opened it, took up her hand again and led her in.

She again came to a dead halt.

Stellan closed the door.

"As I said," he started, sliding an arm around her waist, turning her so her front was pressed to his side, but her head stayed facing forward, her eyes riveted to what was displayed on the floor, "I'd get you some playthings for the party. I got you some playthings for the party. You know Ami. You also might remember Tip. The last is Jennifer. She can be used should you be feeling generous to the boys. She's on loan from Victor today for your amusement."

Well, that answered that.

The future uses for Flamma.

Because there he was, on his knees, thighs splayed, head bowed, arms held behind his back.

Next to him, in the same position, was the well-endowed waiter that brought her the drink at the gladiator pit.

She'd already noted Stellan noticed everything.

But apparently, Stellan missed absolutely *nothing*.

Both were wearing what the waiter had been wearing: the laced-up chastity cage attached to the black belt.

That was it.

She studied Ami's bald head.

She then studied Tip's dark one.

Finally, her gaze went to Jennifer, who was not on her knees, but on her hip, her legs curled in an "s" at her side, her upper body resting into a hand on the floor, but her blonde head was bowed. She wore nothing but what could loosely be termed as a black bathing suit, but it was only strips of material that ran up from a vee at her fully-waxed pubis, over her nipples, her shoulders, probably to disappear in the crevice of her ass.

Stellan again put his mouth to Sixx's ear, and when he spoke, it was low, only for her to hear.

"You look, you command, you watch, you enjoy . . . but again, Simone, you do not touch. They are yours to do with as you will. They have no hard limits that you could hit at this party. But they all share the safe word 'zebra' just in case you get creative. And you need to know, Tip is hetero as well. But that is not a hard limit, or he wouldn't have been chosen."

When she just stood there in his hold, staring down at the bounty she'd been offered, Stellan spoke again.

"Darling, is there a way you'd like to prepare them for the party?"

The better question was, was there a way she *wouldn't* like them prepared for the party?

"Boys, lean back on your hands," she ordered.

They did, almost in unison.

All that muscled meat.

A thing of beauty.

She drew in a delicate breath.

"Jennifer," she called on the exhale. "Unsnap the cages at the bottom and suck them hard. When you've done that, loosen the laces at the top, cinch them back in with their cockheads free, the rest of them caged. If I see them anything but rigid for the rest of the afternoon, this won't make me happy. And I want not only their shafts, but their balls shiny, and I don't mean oil."

"Yes, Mistress," she replied and moved, going first to Tip.

Sixx looked to Ami and found his attention to her.

The instant he got hers, his eyes lowered.

My, my, my.

He was going to make some Mistress very fortunate one day.

"Is she pleasing to you, Ami?" Sixx asked, her tone less commanding, more gentle.

"Yes, Mistress," he answered.

"Would you like to fuck her?" she went on.

"Yes, Mistress," he repeated.

"When you earn it, I'll enjoy watching that," she murmured.

"I'll enjoy pleasing you," he replied.

"I've no doubt you will," she said.

She looked to Jennifer, who was curled into a ball and bobbing on Tip's large and growing larger cock.

Her attention switched back to Ami to see his expression had grown slightly pained.

Her eyes dropped.

He was getting hard behind the confines of his cage.

"You're welcome to watch your partner get blown, Ami," she offered.

"Thank you, Mistress," he muttered, his eyes moving to the action.

Hers did the same.

As she watched, Stellan's hand shifted down to curl around a cheek of her heated behind.

Her eyes lifted to his profile to find his gaze aimed down at Jennifer.

That was when it struck her.

Now she was not Simone.

She was Sixx, he was Stellan, Mistress and Master, enjoying their subs. His hold was claiming, and sent a message, but it was not commanding. Not now.

In his bedroom, she was his.

Here, she was a different kind of his.

His message was he could give it all to her. Everything she needed.

And everything she wanted.

But she knew that by the look of his bedroom.

Hell, by the existence of Margarita.

No, by a frigging auditorium.

His head turned, and his beautiful blue eyes caught hers.

They flared.

Then they warmed.

"Believe in it," he whispered, pressing in with his hand, tightening her in his hold, again reading her thoughts. "It's right there, sweetheart."

"I can get this on my own," she told him the truth.

His fingers curled in, taking the fabric of her sarong and rubbing it against her still-stinging ass cheek under the tight material of her swimsuit.

She bit the inside of her lip.

He didn't miss it.

"No you can't," he returned.

"I need a drink," she replied.

He grinned and slid his fingers out, smoothing the silk over her swimsuit at her behind.

"I think Ami would be disappointed if you didn't let him serve you while in your presence," he shared.

"Since when did we allow subs to dictate the proceedings?" she asked.

"For my part, darling, the only slave I care about, she'll be dictating everything."

A cascade of tremors fluttered along the insides of her thighs.

Fortunately, he didn't seem to require a response to that.

"Tell me, how many blows would failing to call and being late have earned one of your playthings?" he asked curiously.

"None, by hand. I'd use a switch," she answered condescendingly, like he'd blown it.

Which he had not.

"Something to remember," he murmured, his lips twitching.

She decided to ignore the throb in her clit and instead simply sigh.

A low noise floated up from the floor, and they both looked that way.

Now Ami appeared to be in real pain, which wasn't a surprise, considering his huge dick was hard as a rock and trapped behind laces that had grown intensely confining.

But Tip was in a serious condition because he was liking what he was getting but he knew it couldn't culminate.

"Maybe it's time for her to trade off," Stellan suggested.

"Not quite, she hasn't done his balls," Sixx replied.

Tip groaned.

Sixx smiled.

"See to that," Stellan ordered Jennifer.

Sixx stopped smiling and snapped her eyes to Stellan.

"I thought you didn't want to hurry things," Sixx noted.

Stellan looked back to her. "Darling, Margarita makes exceptional sparkling sangria. And I'm dry. Ami's already hard. He can fuck her face by the pool. We've got guests that are right now guests without hosts."

She turned to Ami. "How does that sound, my gladiator?"

"Whatever you wish, my Mistress," he bit out.

"You'll have to stay trussed on the way to the pool," she warned.

"As I said, as you wish, Mistress," he returned.

"Cage Tip, Jennifer, and let's go," Sixx ordered.

She stopped laving Tip's balls, he let out a relieved breath, and she said, "Okay, Mistress," then sat back but reached for his cage.

Tip's thighs were trembling.

She'd pushed him to fighting the thrust.

Lovely.

"How are you, Tip?" Sixx asked.

"Ready for anything, Mistress Sixx," Tip answered roughly.

"Good answer," she murmured.

"Are we done?" Stellan asked impatiently.

She looked up at him. "*You* gave me these toys, Stellan. Did you not expect me to play with them?"

"Not in a guest room away from the sangria," he returned.

She sighed again.

He grinned again.

"You wet?" he asked.

Just the question made her wetter.

"Yes," she gritted.

"From this," he jerked his head to what was on the floor, "or me bending you over my bed?"

A noise came from Ami.

Indication Ami had a lock on visualization.

And a hard-on for his unattainable Mistress.

And there it was.

Wetter.

"You were mentioning sangria?" she prompted.

Stellan chuckled.

Sixx looked at the feast on the floor.

Tip was caged, except, well, his *tip*.

"Right, on your feet. Let's go," she ordered.

They got up.

Stellan moved his hand from her ass so he could hold her about the waist.

Thus he guided her out of the room, down the hall, down the stairs and into his massive open-plan kitchen/dining room/family room that spanned the back of the house, with its multiple sets of arched French doors beyond which was a pool, their friends and decadence.

Not a single thing she needed.

No.

Only everything she could ever have wanted.

five

Vital Understanding

SIXX

Sixx reclined on her hip atop a double-wide patio lounge beside Stellan's fabulous pool, torso propped up on her arm resting on the thick white pad on the tilted back of the lounge.

She had a refreshing glass of chilled, delicious sangria in her hand that tasted of champagne and peaches, her sunglasses over her eyes, and a slab of muscled meat on display on his back in front of her.

She was in retreat.

And she was this in an effort to regroup.

This was because, half an hour before, Stellan had led her out to the pool deck and taken her around, attached to his side, so she could greet his guests, making a point she was there not as Mistress Sixx, friend and fellow believer in the right to partake of your kink.

But instead she was there . . .

With him.

Obviously, this caused a ripple of intrigued surprise and in some cases (these cases being the people she was closest to, Amélie and Evangeline) out-and-out shock.

Stellan was as smooth as ever, acting like nothing was out of the ordinary.

Sixx went along with the game.

But the instant she could, she found her oasis, removed from the rest in this remote and unoccupied corner of Stellan's deck, close to the pool house. She walked the sangria Stellan poured for her there, set Jennifer lying on her back in a lounge close to the one Sixx settled in, with Tip on his stomach between her legs, ordered to keep his face in her crotch and nothing more.

Ami, she'd commanded to lay on his back in front of her. He was on a slant, as she was curved into him, but not touching him, his head close to her shins, his big cock released from the laces she'd ordered him to pull out, and he was lazily stroking it at her command.

She was not watching him.

Her eyes through her shades were all the way across the vast pool where Stellan was standing, now wearing his own sunglasses, aviator ones with blue lenses and gold trim, which of course looked ridiculously attractive on him.

Stellan's friend and fellow Dom, Victor, was standing with him, wearing a pair of loose swim trunks, his furred chest bare, his slightly pouching belly working for him considering the breadth of his shoulders, the bulge of his pecs, and the command of his sub, who was on her hip on a folded towel at his feet like Jennifer had been upstairs.

Clearly Victor's signature.

Sixx didn't know Victor very well. He'd come to the club after she'd left. He seemed okay enough and was popular with the female subs.

He was also, she'd heard, like Stellan (but perhaps not as much)—ludicrously wealthy.

But seeing him standing there beside Stellan, tall and built as he was, he seemed . . . dull. Almost a nonentity.

Because Stellan was matchless. He outshone everything around him. Even just wearing jeans and a linen shirt (and those freaking aviator glasses).

Including outshining her.

Like he knew she needed it, the same as he'd done from Tuesday night to that day, Stellan was where he was, away from her, giving her space.

As were the others.

A benefit to having friends who were in the life. They were far more aware of, in tune with and sensitive to things than people who were not.

Sixx refused to take in the opulence of Stellan's pool area, what that all meant along with all the rest, and instead looked down at Ami.

Another opulence.

From Stellan.

"Tell me, Ami," she murmured, "you've put on sunscreen, yes?"

"Yes, Mistress," he rumbled, eyes facing the sky, hand still moving on his cock.

"Do you know if the others have done the same?" she asked.

"Yes," he answered. "And they have."

This was good, but if they got into the thick of things, she'd have to remember to give them a break to reapply.

"Do you need sunglasses?" she went on.

"No, Mistress. Thank you. I'm good."

"All right," she muttered, her gaze gliding to his slow manipulation of his dick and her mind wondering what it would feel like, what it would look like, to have Stellan laid out before her like that.

Too good by half, she was sure. She knew this because it was that, even just in her head.

Not fair to Ami.

She couldn't touch him, but she needed to focus on him.

"We need to speak, you and me," she said quietly. "And when I ask what I'm going to ask, I want you to be honest when you answer."

"Of course," he replied.

"When you battle for me, I need to know where you are at the end. In other words, the other night you offered to provide me with your opponent's cum. Is that something you want to give to me?"

"If it's something you want."

The standard submissive reply.

She leaned slightly toward him, but not too close. When she'd looked, Stellan hadn't been watching her.

But she knew he would find times to turn his attention to her, and she further knew he'd just simply sense if she'd broken his rule.

So she held herself in check.

Why?

She had no idea.

Except for the fact that she'd been claimed at the side of a gladiator pit, and she could think on it all she wanted. Hours. Days. Weeks. Years.

But since she'd been claimed by Stellan Lange . . . that was that.

Considering how much these thoughts messed with it, and she didn't need that (ever, but especially not now), she forced her mind back to the conversation at hand.

"That's not being honest, Ami," she told him. "I'm asking what *you* want."

"May I look at you, Mistress?" he requested.

"Yes," she answered.

His gaze came to hers.

He had really beautiful eyes. No hair on his head but such insanely gorgeous lashes.

"I'm being honest," he declared. "I want what you want. If you get off on it, I get off on giving it to you."

"Pull your cock up harder with each stroke, Ami," she ordered quietly. "I want to see you stretch for me."

Those gorgeous eyes flashed, then grew sultry, his teeth sunk into his lower lip, and she switched the direction of her attention to his hand to watch him obey.

Another kind of gorgeous.

She looked back to his face and resumed their discussion.

"I do know how this game is played."

That made his face stiffen. "I know you do. What I'm saying is if *you* get off on it, I'll get off on giving it to you."

"I get what you're saying considering you just repeated yourself and I heard you the first time."

"With respect, Mistress, I'm not sure you do," he said.

"Then maybe it's best you expand on that," she suggested.

"Right," he began. "You want to call Tip over here, and you tell me to, I'll give him a handjob, make him come. For you. I'll do it fucking his ass, coming up there, if that's what you want. But also, if you order him to blow me, I'll take that, shoot down his throat, if that would please you." His voice changed when he finished, "And if you want him to fuck my ass, me to blow him, I'll do it. If *you* get off on it, that's what I'll do, and I'll get off on doing it for you."

She was beginning to understand.

"The inference is that you wouldn't do all that for another Mistress," she noted.

"You've read the inference right, my Mistress."

Surprising. Knowing how her play went with multiple male subs, she would have thought Stellan would have covered this before he offered Ami to her.

"Which parts wouldn't you do?" she asked with curiosity.

"Take a man's dick in my mouth, for one," he told her.

Hmm.

"I'll let my ass get fucked if I earn that by losing in the pit, or if my Mistress does the fucking. But by a pool with some random guy . . ." he let that lie.

"I'm sensing these are big concessions," Sixx remarked.

"You're sensing right too."

"Did you tell Master Stellan about these concessions before you arrived today?" she asked.

"Of course."

Very interesting.

"Such concessions, and I've only been with you once and not even in a scene," she pointed out.

"The first time you had command of me, you didn't make me jack him because you didn't know if I'd get off on that. You also made me pull out the second I got done shooting my cum, which was cool. Your Master, he knows how I play it, Tip too, so he made sure we had safe words just in case. But even if I didn't know all that when it comes to you, this time you asked me if I had on sunscreen and if I needed shades before you asked me if I'd get off on jacking a guy. I don't need much more to know what kind of Mistress you are, and because of that, the lengths I'd go to get you off."

Sixx found that very affecting.

Even moving.

She never chatted with her subs during a scene outside the necessary preliminaries, which would, of course, share such hard limits, which in this instance (of course), Stellan had ascertained for her.

When she was with subs, she just worked them.

And they always performed for her, even if she took things to extremes.

She really had no idea why they did, and she didn't care. A good motto: If it's not broke, don't fix it, and she lived a lot of things in life that way.

But if pressed, she would have thought it was the superior training Aryas had ingrained in her and the Dommes he'd included in giving her that.

And it actually was.

It was just that she did what she did as she was taught how to do it, adding her own style along the way.

The challenge she got off on was not diving into their minds and meeting needs outside reading what they wanted sexually, giving them that the way *she* wanted, which was what they needed, and making them like it.

That was not how some Doms played it, like Leigh. Or even Stellan.

But it was her style of play, which meant she got the transients. Get a Domme, get off and get gone, no complications, just orgasms. That was Mistress Sixx.

Which worked perfectly.

But there was something more there for the subs she wasn't even realizing she was offering.

And she liked understanding that she did.

Though she didn't like understanding that Aryas was right during that conversation in the booth.

She had it down in practice.

She'd just that moment come to understand the theory.

"I must say, I'm pleased I've earned this amount of dedication so quickly," she told him.

"And if you don't mind, Mistress, I'll say I am too, even though it sucks 'cause I got that, and you're his. But I'll take what you can give not getting yourself off on some power trip you got with some built dude you think you can fuck over 'cause you think he gets off on letting you. You get it. And no offense to your particular sisterhood, but not many of your kind do."

"It seems we need to find someone more worthy of you, gladiator," she murmured.

"I'm finding I'm good where I am right now, Mistress, but you got a friend, I'm open to new experiences."

She smiled at him.

He grinned back at her.

Right.

That grin.

Those eyes.

That body.

That cock.

Sixx made a decision.

Time to play matchmaker.

"Your balls are still bound, Ami," she noted quietly. "Free them and then pull them down as you stroke up."

His voice was thicker and his grin had vanished, his face going dark in a good way, when he replied, "As you wish, Mistress."

She watched him do that, and for the first time in a long time— in fact maybe ever—she wanted to touch a sub. She wanted that cock in her mouth. She wanted to order him to roll to his knees, get behind him, press close, wrap her fingers around his dick, cup his balls, and do that to him until he was begging her to let him come.

A vision of Stellan on his knees stroking his cock flashed into her mind.

She banished it and focused on Ami.

"Faster and harder," she whispered.

"Yes," he whispered back, giving her that.

She closed her eyes behind her sunglasses, and it filled her brain again. It wasn't Ami there, laid out on the lounge in the sun, touching himself at her command.

Stellan's eyes were hot on her, his cock hard for her, his balls heavy for her.

God, she was going to come.

In an effort not to let that happen, she opened her eyes and saw she wasn't the only one in that state. A bead of pearly wet glistened at the tip of his dick.

"Would you like to come for me?" she asked.

"Very much," he grunted.

"How I like it?" she pushed.

"Any way you like it, my Mistress."

"Then get on your hands and knees," she commanded.

He didn't hesitate a second.

He was magnificent displayed on his back, stroking his cock.

But that powerful body was spectacular on its hands and knees.

"Tip, over here," she called, dredging up iron control not to allow her legs to shift restlessly as wet excitement snaked up her pussy. "Now."

Tip moved from where he was, face still stuffed in Jennifer's crotch, to standing by the side of Sixx's lounge.

"Jennifer, get a towel and some oil. Fast."

"Yes, Mistress," she said and took off.

"Ami, spread your knees farther apart," she ordered.

He did, his thick, turgid cock suspended before him, ready to be used.

Damn, she wanted to grab hold.

"Kneel between his legs, Tip, reach between and massage his balls," she demanded.

Tip did as told.

Ami's head dropped.

His Mistress had commanded a man's hand to work him.

And he totally got off on it like it was her hand that was on him.

Because, in essence, it *was* her hand on him.

Jennifer came with the towel and oil.

"Give the oil to Tip," Sixx told her. "Spread the towel under Ami."

"Yes, Mistress," she murmured, carried out her instructions, and Sixx looked to Tip.

"Oil your hands and then reach around the side and jack him."

Tip nodded and obeyed.

That was all for her.

Now something for Ami.

"Jennifer, to the front, Ami, as you please," she said.

Jennifer got on her knees in front of Ami and then her head fell back almost instantly when he shoved his face between her legs.

Strong body and apparently that included his tongue.

Sixx drank sangria and did what any good Domme would do.

What Ami wanted her to do.

In this instance, she got off on watching.

When things progressed, and Ami's powerful thigh muscles were straining, his sculpted ass clenching, he was no longer eating out pussy because he couldn't, his breaths audibly heavy, she whispered, "Drive two fingers inside him, Tip. Hard and fast."

Tip did as told, and Ami's head shot back, his back arching.

God, *better.*

"Finger fuck him, keep jacking him, and make him come," she ordered, her voice husky.

"Yes, Mistress," Tip murmured.

"Take as much as you can, Ami, then blow for me."

"As you wish . . ." he puffed, "Mistress."

He took a lot.

And he had absolutely not lied.

He *totally* got off on giving her whatever she wanted.

"Mistress," he groaned.

"Blow, Ami," she allowed on a gentle whisper.

He strained back, and with a loud grunt, he shot his cum on the towel under him.

Sixx didn't bother stopping her legs from rubbing against each other or beating back the delicate, unhurried, rippling climax that whispered up her cunt and through her lips as she watched him go.

Ami had earned that from her.

So she gave it to him.

"Milk him, Tip, and keep fucking him, get in there, Jennifer, and squeeze his balls," Sixx ordered.

Jennifer moved in. Tip kept at him. And Ami thrust his cock into Tip's hand, his ass moving through the air, making it hard for both of them to hold on, as his big body shuddered, he groaned and kept erupting.

Oh yes.

She needed to find someone worthy of this warrior.

When the convulsing turned to trembles, immediately she said, "Release him and step away. Back to your lounge. This time, Jennifer, you holding Tip's cockhead in your mouth. Take the towel away before you go."

They murmured their acquiescence, Tip bunching up the towel covered in the flatteringly large offering of Ami's cum and whisking it away before they went.

Ami held position, breathing hard, head lowered, body still slightly quivering.

It was a beautiful sight.

And just like that, Stellan juxtaposed over the glorious spectacle of Ami, and that particular vision was so strong, Sixx had to shake her head to get rid of it.

"You've served me well," she said gently, her hand itching to touch him, soothe him, her body poised to move to him, press into him, coddle him.

She'd never wanted to do that with any sub, and she knew it was him she wanted to do that to because he was hers through Stellan.

So he was part of Stellan.

Like Tip's hand had been a part of her.

"I'm glad, Mistress."

"Look at me, Ami," she urged.

His head turned to her.

"Thank you," she whispered.

A flare burned through his eyes as he understood what she was saying to him, pleased at what he'd given to her.

No.

What they'd shared.

She was highly sought after at the Honey.

But she'd never had a moment like this with a sub in her life.

"My pleasure," he whispered back.

"Sixx," she said. "For now and anytime we're not in a scene, for you, I'm Sixx."

She'd never given that to a sub either.

"Sixx," he murmured, lips twitching.

Totally had to find this guy a good one.

"You can get up and take off your belt and cage, warrior," she said. "Get in the pool, relax, recuperate. When you're ready, you get to do whatever you want to Jennifer, and you can make Tip do whatever you want too. Though be sure I'm around, I want to watch."

"Gratitude, Mistress."

She gave him a small smile that his eyes honed in on, keen and hungry.

"No, gladiator, gratitude to you," she said in a soft voice that didn't even sound like it came from her because she'd never heard it like that. "Now go."

He nodded, got up, unbuckled his belt, and let it fall to the deck. Then he went to the pool. Listing to the side, he fell into a hand at its edge before he swung his legs out from under him to slide into the pool in a way that only someone with immense upper body strength could do.

It was an awesome show.

But after his bald head disappeared under the water, her attention went directly to Stellan.

He was still with Victor.

But his eyes behind those aviators, she knew, were locked on her.

And his lips were turned up in a self-satisfied smile that told her he was pleased he'd given her a toy she enjoyed playing with.

Suddenly, she wanted to rush across the deck and throw herself into his arms to express her gratitude.

She wanted to do the same to beg him to take her back upstairs and finish what he started.

And she wanted to do the same to burrow into him and whisper in his ear that Ami was fantastic, Tip and Jennifer lovely, but all she wanted was him.

These thoughts tripped to a halt when her view of Stellan was blocked.

She looked up to see the sun playing on the profuse, glistening, brunette curls of the petite Evangeline Brooks and the deep, shining, auburn waves of the long and lithe Amélie Strand as the mismatched duo gracefully sank in unison, side by side, hip-to-hip, a two-woman, Dominatrix Busby Berkeley show coming to rest on the lounge right in front of her.

"*Chérie*," Amélie started, "would you kindly share what *on earth* is going on?"

"What Leigh is saying," Evangeline put in the second Amélie stopped speaking, "is first, thank you for that awesome show. And second, what the hell is happening with you and Stellan?"

"I—" Sixx began.

"I'd heard you were with him at the pit," Leigh stated. "And by with him it was reported you were *with him*, but I didn't believe it."

"You know there's a gladiator pit in Phoenix?" Sixx asked, mildly peeved she hadn't shared that intel.

Then again, Sixx hadn't exactly been available for very many girlie chats since she came back, what with brooding about Stellan and putting on shows to get his attention taking all of her time.

"Of course," Leigh answered. "Aryas and I invested with Stellan." She turned her head to Evangeline. "And as I've been telling you, Leenie, you really need to come. It's magnificent."

"Does Olly go with you?" Evangeline asked, openly intrigued by this idea just as it was clear Branch would not be.

Leigh shook her head. "Felicia, Mira or Romy. It's not Olly's thing."

Sixx looked across the pool to where Olly was sitting (now, *he* was in board shorts, all big-boy-next-door with a damn fine kink). He was at the edge of the pool—calves in the water, a bottle of beer in his hand, talking to Penn and Shane, who were in the pool.

"Your stallion not playing today?" Sixx queried.

"He's never been to a private party," Leigh explained, shocking Sixx because the guy wasn't twenty-one, and the way he was with Amélie, she thought he'd had to have been in the life for a while. "He wanted to get the lay of the land. I have a feeling after watching your recent demonstration he'll get into the swing of things the next fête Stellan throws."

Sixx wouldn't doubt that. She didn't watch them anymore, but when she had, she'd noted that Olly was a huge showoff.

Then again, if Sixx had what Leigh and Olly had, she'd consider taking that particular show on the road.

"Uh . . . hello? Sixx?" Leenie called. "Earlier Stellan paraded you around his pool like he was introducing everyone to his new fiancée. Are you and Stellan together? And if so, when did this happen?"

There was something in her expression, something intent, beyond curiosity about a friend's love life (way beyond) that she couldn't put her finger on but made her uneasy.

"I think it's fabulous," Leigh stated. "And it's *so* Stellan to find you such an amazing specimen to occupy your time and meet your needs at the same time he doesn't partake or even look at anything, except you."

Sixx's body went completely solid.

"I knew that gladiator was his, I've seen the man in battle, and I was surprised," Leigh continued. "Not anymore, knowing now Stellan acquired him for you."

"It's incredibly generous," Evangeline muttered, watching Sixx closely.

Like she was moving it through treacle, Sixx shifted her head so she could look between her friends and find Stellan.

Felicia had joined Stellan and Victor, and Stellan was looking down at her, laughing at something she said.

Sixx watched, thinking—as per his wont, which was his wont because he knew it would be hers—she was Mistress Sixx out here, with her toys, not his newly unveiled Simone.

But he had not acquired something for himself to pass the time.

She couldn't touch, but she could play. And he'd given her that.

However, it was his party. The kind of party he didn't give frequently, but he threw regularly, and he'd always enjoyed the opportunity to provide his friends—people who shared his way of life—a different scene, a fantastic one, that they could use to partake in that way of life.

And he partook too.

Always.

But she'd just orchestrated a load being shot from a heavy, hard cock on the big beautiful body of an exceptional alpha-submissive, Stellan allowed it, was the man behind it, and he got nothing but knowing he gave her that.

It was then she moved her head around in a hazy way, taking in a pool she'd been to before, but didn't take in the way she was taking it in right then.

The smart, expensive deck furniture. The well-maintained, attractive landscaping. The theme of bright Mexican pots overflowing with succulents, carried through from the front, dotted everywhere. Pots that someone had to cultivate, and that someone wasn't Stellan.

The pool deck was travertine edged in brick. Expensive, and not dusty or dirty. And the pads on the furniture were pristine white.

In the kitchen, the island had been covered in fabulous displays of food, flanked with lavish beverage dispensers filled with fruit and ice, offering two types of sangria as well as margaritas. There were also buckets filled with bottles of beer, chilled white wine and champagne.

There were a goodly number of people there, but there was so much of all of that, half of it would be thrown out.

Maybe more.

They couldn't consume all that.

And then there was going to be a sit-down dinner.

"This turn of events makes me happy for you." It was Leigh speaking, and the change in her timbre of voice, like she was a soft-spoken general imparting an important message to her troops, had Sixx's vague gaze moving to her. "Stellan and you. You've always been somewhat reserved. This was your way. But since your return, this intensified to the point I must admit to having some concern for you. It seemed something had happened to you while you were gone. Something you weren't sharing. Now I see what you were searching for. Stellan too. He would never, not ever be content with someone who did not share that common bond. You were meant for each other. No less equal than a partner who fits the unique puzzle that is the two of you, forming the perfect picture. But a different kind of equal, not two halves that make a whole. Two like-minded souls who share a vital understanding."

"I've got to go," Sixx stated urgently, jumping off the lounge like it had just caught on fire.

"Sorry?"

"What?"

She put her sangria down on an attractive table that was handy (of course), shoved her feet in her slides and took off moving toward the house. "Catch you guys later."

"Sixx!" Leigh called.

Sixx kept moving, eyes to her feet that were directing her to the house.

She opened the French door, shoving her sunglasses up into her hair immediately. She moved into the kitchen/dining room space and avoided looking at the sprawling banquet Stellan had his housekeeper lay out for his guests.

Her clutch and bag were in his room.

She didn't give a shit about the bag.

But her keyfob was in her purse, and she needed that to get into her car and get the hell out of there.

She darted toward the stairs but didn't hit that first step since she was stopped when a set of strong fingers closed around her elbow.

"Simone," Stellan whispered, drawing her around to face him.

She stared at his chest. "I have to go. Something I forgot I had to do."

"Sweetheart—"

His hand was coming up, like he was going to touch her face.

She flinched, tore her elbow from his grip and started to rear back, but she didn't get far before she was plastered to his body, her head immobilized by his hand clamped on the side of her neck, his thumb at her jaw forcing it up.

She looked to his ear.

"What's happened?" he asked.

"I really need to go," she told his ear.

"Look at me, honey."

"A job I forgot about," she lied and kept doing it. "I'll call you."

"What did Leigh say?"

She shook her head against his grip. "You need to . . ." She cleared her throat. "I mean, I need to go, and I gave Ami permission to do what he wanted with Jennifer. But you, I mean . . . I'm going . . . you should . . . um, if Victor's being generous, you should play with her."

"Right," he gritted, letting her go but only to alter the way he'd been holding her.

He clasped his fingers around her biceps and dragged her up the stairs, down the hall, into his room.

This was good.

Her clutch was there.

It was bad when he slammed the heavy (also ornately carved) door, closing them both in.

He yanked her around to his front and clamped a hand on the side of her head, fingers in her hair, palm under her jaw, face in hers in a way she had no choice but to look up at him.

"What the fuck is happening?" he bit out.

"You know me," she found her lips whispering.

"I'm trying to," he retorted.

"You know my name."

"Yes," he agreed curtly.

"*You know me.*"

Stellan went still.

Oh yes.

He knew her.

"I don't belong here," she told him.

"Simone—"

"Stop calling me that," she hissed. "I'm *Sixx*."

"Darling—"

"Stop calling me that too," she snapped.

"Please . . . take a breath and calm down."

"How much did this house cost?" she asked.

An irritated storm cloud of confusion hit his expression.

It was hot.

Fuck!

"Why does that matter?" he asked back.

"Only someone who could afford this kind of house would ask that," she retorted.

That shut him up.

It also cleared up that cloud.

But he didn't let her go.

"Do you have any idea how much that spread cost to lay out or do you just dump cash in an account for Margarita and tell her to go for it?" she pushed.

"If you'd calm down," he said, now using a warm, even tone, "I could explain to you in a way you'll understand why that doesn't matter."

"I'm not a sub," she stated bitingly.

"No. You're not. You're Sixx. Mistress Sixx with a devoted following. You're not a sub. I know that. Not for anyone. But me."

"Not even for—"

"Not for anyone but the men in your life who you can trust to be your true self. Trust to keep that safe."

She snapped her mouth shut.

Stellan didn't.

"You gave it to Aryas, who you adore. And you give it to me."

Holy God.

Their sessions were closed.

They'd been closed.

Goddamn Aryas!

He'd lost his patience and interfered.

"How do you know this?" she asked, the words coming out breathy.

"Because I had Branch Dillinger investigate you, and he's thorough."

Worse!

Her stomach dropped to her feet, and her voice pitched high and panicked.

"Dillinger knows?"

Stellan slid his hand back to cup her nape, and with his other arm, which was latched around her waist, he pulled her closer into his body.

"He will say nothing."

"No one gets to know me."

"He'll say nothing, sweetheart."

"They *can't* know me."

"Because you don't want them to know you?"

"Because you let people in and they fuck you over, and in terms of the life I lead, that kind of fucking over gets you *dead*."

Those words set his face to stone.

"You don't live that life anymore, Simone."

"I was born to that life, Stellan, and when that's the case, that kind of slime never washes away, and more fool the person who tries to pretend it does."

"That's not true," he returned.

"And how would you know?"

"Because I was born to slime too, darling, the designer kind. And it took a sandblaster, but I washed that fucking shit away, and I will *never* tolerate it coming back and infesting the life I built without that slime in it."

She shut up.

He stared at her.

And it was then he knew.

He knew that she knew about him too.

So he asked after that.

"Do you know as a matter of course, since it plays out in the press, or did you look into me?"

Sixx said nothing.

He still got his answer.

"Was it after what happened Tuesday night or before?" he asked.

She kept her mouth shut.

"Before," he murmured, studying her closely. "How long have you wanted me, honey?"

Her eyes slid away.

This giving him another silent answer.

His fingers gripped her scalp. "Look at me."

Her eyes slid back.

"What did Leigh say?" he demanded.

"That she's happy for us. That we're not two halves that make a whole. We're two souls who share a vital understanding. She said we were meant for each other."

His gaze softened and warmed, and watching the beauty of that set a panic in her that was so extreme, it made Sixx prepare to fight in order to get free.

"What did I say about you pulling away?" he murmured.

She calmed.

Instantly.

God!

With no other direction to go, she fell forward, planting her face in his chest.

His hand slid up to cup the back of her head, his arm around her closed tighter, and she felt his lips hit her hair.

God.

"She was beautiful," he murmured.

"Who?"

"Silie."

Lord.

She closed her eyes.

His sister.

His sister who committed suicide.

Because of his father—among other, more terrible reasons.

Yes, he knew she knew.

And yes, he'd grown up with slime too.

"We have a lot to learn about each other, Simone. All I ask for in the present, until we can start to do that in a meaningful way, is that you please just be you."

She opened her eyes and saw white linen.

But she felt strength.

Power.

Warmth.

And it was then she realized she'd never been held this way.

Not once.

In her life.

Fuck.

Were those tears in her eyes?

"Be me?" she asked, her words muffled by his chest, which she hoped hid the throaty that came from the effort of her trying to get her shit together.

"Strong. A survivor. A winner. Come back downstairs with me. Eat. Drink. Enjoy your friends. Stay close to me this time so I can look after you. And when they're gone, we'll make our deal and take it from there."

"Stellan, really, I don't belo—"

"If you say you don't belong here one more time, I swear to fuck, darling, I'll lash you naked to my bed, gagged and blindfolded, and spank you so long and so hard, you'll be glad I've left you on your belly. But your fine ass will sting so badly, just the air in the room will be torture. And I'll go down, eat, drink, enjoy my friends, and return to play with you for as long as it takes to make you beg for release. Something you won't get until you apologize for being so immensely insulting . . . *to yourself*. Then and only then will I let you come."

Sixx pressed her lips together to stop herself from talking.

Or maybe moaning.

"Are these words heard?" he prompted.

She stared at his linen-covered chest trying to figure out if she should say what he'd told her not to say just to see if he'd do what he promised or if she just wanted to ask him to do it.

"Say, 'Yes, Stellan,'" he ordered.

"Yes, Stellan," she echoed.

Her cheek moved with the huge breath he took in, and it moved again when he let it out.

"Though I'm not sure I'm good with going back down there," she shared. "I took off, acting like a frigging idiot."

He pulled her head out of his chest, tilting it back to look up at him as he looked down at her.

"Do you really give a fuck?" he asked, brows raised.

Thinking about it, she kind of didn't.

It was Leigh. And Leenie. And the rest.

They were cool.

"No," she answered.

He smiled, and the miracle happened again.

He got freakishly more handsome.

"Do you think they care?" he asked.

"Yes. I've never done anything like that. They're probably worried about me."

"About the acting-like-an-idiot part," he amended. "Considering the fact you didn't, they wouldn't think that. They'll just be worried about you."

"What do I say to them?" she asked, because she didn't know.

She always had it together. It was imperative in her line of work, for one. But also to keep her shit tight so it didn't blow apart, for another.

"It's none of their business?" he asked back in answer.

"Uh . . . well, I've never really been just one of the girls, but I've been around them enough to know that doesn't work."

He started chuckling and through it said, "I'm sure you'll think of something."

Her gaze drifted away as she nodded.

"Right, darling, let's head back down so they can stop worrying about you."

He started to make a move, but it was then she realized she had her hands fisted in his shirt at his sides and she didn't let go.

In fact, she pressed those fists in and called, "Hey."

He stopped moving and looked down at her, brows again raised.

He looked hot like that too.

Lord.

She totally belonged to him.

And it felt good.

Damn.

"Are you cool with me and Ami? I mean, I—" she started.

"Did you enjoy watching him perform for you?"

She nodded.

"Then yes, I'm cool."

"You're not . . . you don't have . . ."

"I have you."

"Not down there."

"I still have you."

"But we haven't really—"

"We will."

"But—"

"You're a Domme, Simone," he stated firmly.

She didn't reply.

"A specific kind of Domme, actually," he continued. "You know precisely how gratifying it is to give someone something they need without getting anything in return. It remains to be seen, though I doubt it'll be better than the orgasms you'll be giving me. But it's still a beautiful thing that means a good deal to me, giving you something you need, watching you while you have it, seeing how much you enjoy it. But I'd prefer it if you just had it without worrying about it because that worry pollutes the beauty it gives to me."

"Okay then, hot stuff, I'll play with that meat guilt-free," she muttered.

She was about to look away at the same time break away when her body arrested totally.

This was because his expression changed totally.

She stood in his hold, staring into his eyes, suspended in time, simply taking in his sheer male beauty, which was excruciatingly more beautiful with that look on his face.

Eventually, as ever with Stellan, she could take no more.

"What?" she whispered.

"Hot stuff?" he whispered back.

Was that offensive? Coarse?

Common?

"I—"

"Fuck," he growled.

And then . . .

He kissed her.

At first, Sixx stood still in his hold under the gentle assault of his mouth.

It didn't take long before his taste and touch and smell and feel permeated, making her melt into him, slide her arms along his trim waist, press close, tip her head further back, and open herself for more.

It was like she'd never been kissed.

But she *had* never been kissed like this. With that wonderful, wet, tender attentiveness that was all about giving, making her feel warm, wanted, safe.

Tingly.

He broke the kiss, and she almost whimpered at the loss.

Instead she stayed pressed to him, open to him and the experience as he touched his forehead affectionately to hers for a far-too-brief moment, the fingers of one of his hands stroking her spine, and murmured, "We should return."

She didn't want to return.

She wanted to live in his room in this moment with him until she was no longer breathing.

Warm.

Wanted.

Safe.

"All right," she replied.

He let her body go but took her hand and led her back down the stairs.

As they went, Sixx didn't look at the paintings on the walls or feel the thick carpet runner under her slides or the cool of the air-conditioning that had to be a bitch of a bill for a place that size.

She just followed where Stellan was leading.

And headed back to the pool party.

six

Bullshit and Bravado

STELLAN

Stellan stood in the opened French doors, looking out at his lit pool, beside which Simone was standing with Talia, Mira, Belle and Leigh, chatting.

He was trying to understand how she could make him like what she was wearing now better than her plunge-front, scarlet-red bathing suit with the graphic print sarong tied around her hips and the gold tangled in her cleavage.

Totally unconsciously, she looked like a woman who belonged on a beach on the French Riviera or a yacht off Capri, not poolside in Phoenix.

Both when she was in her swimsuit . . .

And now.

It didn't take long to for him to understand.

She'd collared herself for him.

In her state, she might not have realized what she'd unintentionally done.

But as a Domme, she absolutely fucking knew.

This meant he was fighting going hard, seeing the Evening Simone that had replaced Daytime Sixx, the woman who had graced the foot of his table at dinner and was now standing, holding a martini glass in her hand with the gin martini he'd made her in it, talking to her friends.

After her shower, she'd done up her face in a shimmering palette of peaches and pinks that highlighted and defined and made her natural appeal intensely alluring.

On her body was a strapless sheath made of supple cream leather that was not skintight but instead fit her exceptionally, clinging where it should, giving where it should, emphasizing her figure to perfection.

And on her feet were rose gold, high-heeled sandals with two thin straps across the toes that had tiny buckles, and more thin straps around the ankles.

She had long, rose gold hoops in her ears, a sleek, rose gold bangle at her wrist.

And a wide sheet of shining rose gold collared around her neck.

Her short hair and the elegant length of her neck accentuated it perfectly.

And honest to Christ, Stellan had no idea how he wasn't showing his guests to the door so he could power through their talk and then finally get her in his bed.

"So . . . she okay?"

Stellan turned and looked at Olly, who'd positioned himself in the other opened door, his eyes aimed at the pool, but not at Olly's woman, Amélie.

At Simone.

After the pool party, Olly had showered and changed into jeans and a light salmon linen shirt that was quite like Stellan's.

And the reason why he was standing right there was not a mystery.

"Leigh send you in to get the true story?" Stellan queried.

Olly looked to Stellan, grinning. "You guessed it. Sixx acting all 'it's groovy now' when you guys came back after, uh . . . whatever went down did not cut it with my Leigh-Leigh."

Stellan shook his head, his lips twitching, and looked back to Simone. "She's fine."

She wasn't.

However, her panic attack was good. She got some of what was infecting her out.

So she wasn't fine.

But she was better.

"You pretty much know this is gonna be the talk of the Honey for, oh . . . I don't know, maybe the next decade," Olly noted.

"I do pretty much know that, and I much more than pretty much don't give a fuck," Stellan replied and heard Olly chuckle.

"Well, man, we're gonna take off before you kick our asses out so you can pounce on that, but I'm gonna say what I gotta say before Leigh-Leigh gets up in my shit and makes me have a sit-down with you to say it."

That had Stellan turning his attention away from Simone and giving it again to Olly.

And Olly looked uncomfortable, which did not bode well. The man had a natural confidence that was so deep-seated it came out even when he was subbing during a scene.

"What's that?"

Olly seemed to have to rip his eyes from the pool to give them to Stellan.

"You're gonna hafta give it up, bud."

Stellan felt his brows snap together. "Sorry?"

"For her," he went on, tipping his head toward the pool. "That guy you got her, he rocks it. But he's not you. And she might be okay with that for now, but that's not gonna last. She's gonna need it from you."

Stellan straightened, now feeling his face get hard, and turned to Olly.

"This really has nothing to do with you," he said low.

"I know," Olly replied genially, but still uncomfortably. "But I saw it. Leigh saw it. Everyone else was watching her sub. We were watching Sixx. And she was looking at him. But she was thinking of you."

"You might not understand this, but that's the point."

"I do understand it, Stellan, and I'd say I'm in the position to understand it more than you," he returned quietly.

Stellan made no reply because the friendly, helpful bastard was right.

"She switching for you?" Olly asked.

"If Sixx shares that with Leigh, that's her prerogative. But no offense, Olly, it's not mine to share with you."

"She's switching for you," he muttered.

Now Stellan was getting angry.

"We had a rough start," he reminded Olly. "We smoothed that out. Leigh means a great deal to me, I'd prefer that something didn't happen to change where you and I are at."

"I would too, and not just because Leigh thinks the world of you but because you're a solid guy and I like you. She wants you to be happy, and I'll give you it honestly, I do too. I don't know Sixx very well. She's a pretty closed book. But this is making Leigh happy, and if it does that for her, it does it for me."

When he said nothing more, Stellan asked, "Why do I think you're not finished?"

"Because I know you got it in you, man, to go the distance to give the one you've obviously decided is *the one* everything she needs, and we both know how I know that. Whatever Sixx is working through, I'm standing here as your friend telling you, don't play games. The stakes are too high. I've watched her work. Thin stream of seriously fucking chilly that's not my gig but has most the male subs gagging for it. Today, quick thaw. It was all about heat. But her doin' that guy, playin' it like that, and she doesn't lay a finger on him—my guess, and I'm thinkin' it's a pretty fuckin' accurate one, that no-touch business was at your demand, then clearing out like she did, she's dealing with something deep. You fuck around when you got a woman whose head is jacked up, she'll slip through your fingers."

"I'm not sixteen with my first crush," Stellan returned.

"I nearly lost her."

Stellan drew a sharp breath in through his nose at this blunt sharing, but he said nothing.

"I had shit jacking with my head, and I didn't give it to my Leigh-Leigh. Instead I fucked it all up and nearly lost her."

"I don't have shit jacking with my head," Stellan pointed out.

"I know. You got it goin' on. What I'm saying is be Leigh."

Be Leigh.

"She doesn't play games, Stellan," Olly continued. "It's all out there. No matter who you are in Leigh's life, if she's feeling you, you know it."

"Sixx is not under any impression she doesn't matter to me."

"Yeah. *Today*. But you built a gladiator pit for her, Stellan," Olly said quietly. "And I've been watching your dance. You've barely looked at her in months. And we didn't know why you did it until today, but you built a fuckin' sex show for her that, according to Leigh, is raking in the green. You're trying to tell me you're not playing games?" He shook his head. "You got any clue how much she watches you?"

Stellan looked back to Simone by the pool with Talia, Mira, Belle and Leigh, talking.

She was smiling her cat's smile that, when she was playing Mistress, would make any male sub *or* Dom instantly go hard.

Out by his pool with her friends, it was different—no less appealing, just pretty.

And sweet.

But she still seemed removed.

Protecting herself.

Protecting herself from people who care about her.

Which she would do.

Because instinctually, since she'd never had that kind of bounty, she'd still know it was the worst kind of thing to lose.

"How much does she watch me?" he whispered.

"Any time you aren't lookin', man."

He knew she watched him.

But not that much.

That felt very good.

And could go very badly.

Right there, before his eyes, protecting herself from people who care about her.

Yes, it could go very badly.

"I never said it, and I'll say it now," Olly went on, changing the subject because he was a decent man and good at being a friend, and Stellan looked back to him. "I was outta line in the halls that night, gettin' in your face. Should have shown you respect."

"You're just being Olly now," Stellan said slowly, not losing eye contact. "We both know who was out of line that night, and it wasn't you."

Olly grinned at him.

It didn't take long before that grin faded.

"Winning feels good until you look over at the loser. Makes you feel better when you see him get his win. Don't fuck up your win, Stellan. And just sayin', you got good from Leigh. But if you ever need me, bud, you got the same from me, and you know how to find me."

"Christ, next thing I know, you're going to invite me for beers with you and Dillinger and your friend. The owner of the Bolt."

The grin came back.

"Barclay," he shared. "And we could use a Dom in our party. Get Aryas to pitch up. Start evening out our numbers. You guys could add the class."

Stellan did not return the smile. "You're standing there for me, but you're also standing there for her, and you should know it's not unappreciated. You should also know, it's unlikely I'll take you up on your offer to find you should I need to talk to somebody. But that's not unappreciated either. Last, you should know, I don't drink beer. I don't hang with the guys. I make money. I spend money. I travel. I read. I drink wine, Scotch and vodka martinis. I eat good food. And I fuck. But again, the offer is not unappreciated."

Olly burst out laughing.

Not finished doing it, he said, "I eat good food too."

Stellan shook his head, turned it, and stilled when he saw they had five pairs of feminine eyes on them.

Leigh's looked soft and happy, her man and her friend who'd had a rough start standing together, talking, laughing.

Simone's looked guarded, like she thought what she was experiencing was happy, and she didn't quite understand the feeling.

"How about I round up all these lingering assholes who won't get with the program and leave you alone with your woman so you can get some alone time with your woman?" Olly suggested, and Stellan looked back at him.

"If you do that, I'll buy you a yacht."

Olly again started chuckling. "Spread you put on today, Stellan, least I can do. Good party. Thanks for asking us."

"My pleasure," Stellan murmured.

Olly got close and clapped him on the back.

Stellan didn't share he was a handshake man. He just lifted up his chin.

Olly strolled out.

Stellan watched him go.

"Lange, outta here. Say goodbye to her for me?"

Stellan looked again to his side to see Ami, who Simone had wanted to stay for dinner, so he'd showered and put on clothes and stayed for dinner. He was standing there also in jeans, but he was wearing a lightweight, short-sleeved, pattern-on-white, cotton button-up.

"You're not on, Ami, and she's right there. You're welcome to say goodbye to her yourself."

"That's not gonna happen."

Stellan's attention on the man focused.

Fuck.

"You're out," Stellan noted.

"I'll fight for her in the pit. But unless I'm invited to sit at your table like tonight, gotta ask you not to call me. Can't do another scene with Sixx."

Stellan nodded. "I understand that."

"Not that it wasn't good," he assured. "It's because it was too—"

Today, quick thaw. It was all about heat.

Stellan fought his teeth clenching.

"As I said, Ami, I understand."

"Don't know how you can watch, friend," Ami muttered.

Because she's not allowed to touch anyone but me, he thought.

"Because it makes her happy," he said.

Ami studied him intently.

Then he jerked up his chin in understanding. "Yeah."

"I can also understand you leaving without speaking with her, but she might not."

Ami took a moment to think things over.

Then he said, "If it takes time for you to find someone who can hack it without getting in too deep, I'm on call. I'll keep my shit tight. But can't do it too often, Lange. She's yours. You get to keep that. I'm the one walking away. And I'm not so down with watching."

"I understand that too."

Ami's head swung toward Simone, and he murmured, "Guess I'll say goodnight."

That set Stellan again to fighting his teeth clenching.

"Goodnight, Ami."

"Later, Lange."

Stellan watched Ami move toward the huddle of females that Olly was disbursing, and he kept tight hold on a variety of reactions when he saw the warmth in Simone's face when she noticed Ami approaching.

Fortunately, Olly recruited Leigh in the act of getting everyone to leave, and therefore this process didn't take very long.

Indeed, within twenty minutes, he was standing at his front door saying farewell to Belle, Tiffany, Penn and Shane, the last to leave.

However, during this process, he noted that although Simone said her *goodbyes* and *be safe driving home*s with smiles, she didn't stand at his side where she belonged while he did the same.

The next time he'd be certain to share that instruction.

He also noted that once she returned from standing by the pool, often her gaze would go to the staff Margarita had hired to come in late that afternoon to clear away the food, finish cooking the dinner Margarita had prepared, set the table, serve, clear away and tidy up.

In fact, Stellan saw one of the two who'd arrived go to Simone and say something to which Simone nodded, and her gaze slid to Stellan before she disappeared with the woman only to return not long later to stand removed while Stellan watched the last party-goers away.

When he shut the door, he started right to her.

"You all right?" he asked.

"Yeah. Your . . . uh, catering people or whatever got everything sorted. Did a sweep of the pool area and all. They were ready to go, it's late, I didn't want to disturb you, so I gave them both a fifty dollar tip so they could head home."

This did not make Stellan happy.

Therefore he frowned down at her when he stopped in front of her.

"You should have disturbed me," he said.

"It's all good."

"I'll give you the cash later."

"It's all good, Stellan."

There was no reason discussing it. They had other more important things to discuss—then do.

He would simply give her the cash later.

"Would you like another drink?" he asked.

"Are we negotiating this deal you've been talking about now?" she asked back.

"Yes," he answered.

"Then yes," she replied.

That made him grin.

"Another martini?" he offered.

She nodded.

He went to the kitchen.

He heard the sounds of her stilettos alternately hitting his tile then disappearing as she moved with him and traversed tile and rugs.

She stopped opposite the island to him, so he moved the bottles and shaker to her.

He made her gin martini first.

Then the same for him with vodka.

He said nothing while he did.

She watched his hands the whole time he did.

He wrapped his fingers around his martini glass, and after he'd taken a chill sip of the sharp drink, he murmured, "Ready?"

Her brown eyes lifted to his. They were clear, not nervous, perhaps somewhat fatigued, which wasn't surprising considering it was after eleven at night, but that was all.

And that was good. She had no reason to be nervous with him, and she never would.

Not at times like these.

Other times, under his command . . . she'd relish the nerves, he'd see to it.

Simone nodded.

He took another sip before putting his glass down so that he could take her hand, fit it in the crook of his arm, take up his glass again, and start moving her to the stairs.

"Where are these negotiations happening?" she asked when their direction became clear.

"My bedroom."

"Hmm . . ." she hummed noncommittally.

"In front of the fire," he carried on, starting them moving slowly up the stairs.

"You have a fireplace in your room?" she asked.

"You didn't see it?"

"Sorry. I was too busy noticing your French count desk. I didn't notice you had a fireplace too."

"My French count desk?" he queried.

"You have a desk in your bedroom."

"I know."

"Only French counts have desks in their bedrooms."

"Really?" he murmured, not hiding his amusement.

"French counts, English barons, and you."

Stellan started chuckling.

"And when you say 'in front of the fire,' do you mean an actual fire?" she asked.

"Of course," he answered.

"No one lights a fire in their bedroom in June in Arizona, Stellan."

"I do."

"Yes," she whispered, her voice now sounding amused, but also soft, pensive, and Stellan had never heard it like that before.

It was beautiful.

"Only you," she finished.

He said nothing more as he guided her into his room, straight to the couch in front of the fire, and let her go. He opened the drawer in the end table to get the remote that activated the fire, hit the buttons so it was burning as he wanted it, and returned it. He then sat down in the middle of the couch, separated from where she had seated herself tucked tight into the corner.

All right.

Maybe she was nervous, and she was hiding it.

"Did you come up here and turn on the lights?" she asked, glancing around his room, which was lit softly with a few lamps.

"They're on timers," he answered.

She looked to him. "Are they timed to turn off too?"

"Only if I don't turn them off before they're timed to go off."

"So, essentially, even your bedroom is wired to welcome you."

He raised his brows. "Even my bedroom?"

She shrugged, looked to the fire, took a sip of her drink, and said, "You're rich. It shows. Like in your face, it shows. But that doesn't mean it isn't nice. Gracious." Her gaze came back to him. "When I walked in earlier, I thought it looked like your house was decorated in, 'Relax, I got you.'"

That made Stellan burst out laughing.

He was down to chuckling when he saw her again sipping her martini, watching him laugh from under her lashes, and he replied with feeling, "I'm delighted you think that."

She swallowed her sip, took her glass from her lips, looked him in the eye and declared, "We need to discuss Ami."

Stellan felt a clutch of something unpleasant in his chest, a sour taste at the back of his tongue and a low roar in his head.

Earlier, he actually had been good watching Simone enjoy the toy that he himself had provided her.

This was because he'd had practice.

For months he'd watched her playing with her toys, biding his time, preparing, only going in when he was ready for the win.

After she invited Ami to stay, and he saw them exchange a number of words over dinner, at the time, that had not affected him overly much.

But after Ami's hesitancy even to say goodbye to the Domme who'd worked him in a way that had moved him, which was not Simone's normal technique, Stellan wasn't feeling as at ease about the situation.

"I asked him to stay for dinner because he seems freaking cool, when he's naked and hard, and when he's not," she went on, these words not making Stellan any more at ease.

Especially since she was finally right there. Up in his room in front of a fire, looking exquisitely tempting, wearing what amounted to a collar, with a drink in her hand, him at her side and their negotiation imminent. The negotiation of what could be the most important deal he'd brokered in his life.

But she was talking about another man.

"So I needed to get a sense of him when he's not in a scene," she continued. "In order that we can figure out who to set him up with."

Who to set him up with?

Stellan's head twitched. "Sorry?"

"A Mistress," she explained. "I'm sensing he wants something long term. Someone in the life *and* his life. But I don't want to fix him up with someone who does his head in. So we have to vet them carefully, and I'm totally drawing a blank. I haven't been paying a lot of attention to the new players at the Honey who came in since I was away. So we need to go to the club so you can give me the lowdown on them, and I can look them over. If there's no one that works, we might have to go to the Bolt to get a sense of things. No stone unturned, as it were."

"You want to find a Domme for Ami." The words were expressed as a statement even if they were a request for a confirmation.

"Well . . . yeah. I mean, it'll suck, he gets claimed and won't be battling in the pit for me. So it'd be good we find one who's loaded so she can pay for her throne and keep him down there because I think he gets off on that. Or," her lips turned up slightly, "since you're the big man there, maybe you can pull some strings. But she has to be right. I think some of the Mistresses he's found haven't been good with him. So we have to find that perfect balance. Good for him in the scene, and not crazy-psycho lady outside of it, or vice-versa."

Stellan regarded her.

She held his regard for some time before she prompted, "You in on doing this with me?"

She was not thinking about Ami and what they'd shared while she was sitting beside Stellan in front of a fire on a couch in his bedroom prior to talking about their future together.

She wanted the man to have a decent woman in his life.

She wanted to do something nice for a new friend.

"Please come here," he requested quietly.

His request set her head to twitching, but otherwise she didn't move.

"Please, Simone."

It took her a moment, but finally she slid to him.

He rounded her waist with an arm and pulled her to him in a way she had no choice but to curl close, even so far as shifting a knee so it was resting on his thigh, at the same time he lifted his feet and put them up on the table in front of the couch with his ankles crossed.

This was much better even though Simone did not relax in his hold, rest her head on his shoulder, cuddle into his side. She held distant and stiff.

He allowed that, took a sip of his martini, and murmured, "We'll find someone perfect for Ami."

"Cool," she muttered.

He decided not to share at that juncture what Ami had shared with him earlier.

Instead, he pointed out, "If we do, you'll lose him, darling, in more than just the pit."

"I don't have him anyway, and he wants someone to *have him* have him. And he's a good guy, so he should have what he wants."

"Then we'll help him find that."

"Thanks," she whispered.

"It'll be my pleasure," he replied.

She took a sip of her drink.

Stellan breathed in her perfume. It was all her—complicated, contradictory, full of musk and amber with a hint of pepper. Dark and forbidding at the same time warm.

"Are we finished talking about Ami?" he asked.

"Yes," she answered.

"So we can now discuss us."

There was hesitancy before she said, "Okay."

"Shall I propose my deal?"

Stellan had his eyes on her.

Simone had her glass to her lips, her gaze to the fire, and she murmured, "Knock yourself out."

Therefore, through a grin, he began.

"Tomorrow, I'd like to take you to your home, pick up enough things that you'll be fine being here for the next month . . ."

Her head turned sharply his way so she could stare him in the eyes.

Hers were stunned.

He kept speaking.

"We'll move you in, and this is where you'll stay . . . for a month. You'll work. I'll work. If you like, we can go to the club together, but you will not play, nor will I, with each other or anyone else. We can watch. We can have drinks and visit with our friends. But that's all. In the meantime, we'll share my home together. Eating. Sleeping. Fucking. Living. Except weekends. Weekends will be spent playing."

"I—" she got in.

However, that was all he let her get in.

He tightened his hold on her and spoke over her.

"By playing I mean you'll be *my* Simone. That is, darling, I'll play with you any way I please, and you'll let me."

"You want me to . . . *move in* . . . for . . . *a month?*"

He found it fascinating that she sought confirmation on that point of the deal rather than the last.

"Preliminarily. After that month, we'll assess and see where we are."

"You want me to move in for a month," she stated, not a question this time.

"As you already know, I want to get to know you," he explained.

Her tone pitched higher, and her body got tighter in his hold. "And you want to do that by having me move in?"

"I could ask you out to dinner," he pointed out the boring, but obvious. "I could ask you for a weekend away. I could find ways to waste all sorts of time dancing a tired, tedious dance when I already know I want to know more about you, everything, actually, and I want to fuck you, and I want that very badly, I also want to play with you, and I want that very badly as well."

"I get the getting-to-know-you concept, but Stellan, that's extreme."

"How?" he asked, but didn't give her time to answer. "It isn't like we'll be spending every moment of every day together. It also isn't like we'll be spending every moment together when we're both in this house. We'll sleep together. Wake up together. I'll come home to you when your day is done before mine. You'll come home to me when it's the other way around."

"And we agree to this month, and I immediately get on your nerves, what happens then? I pack up and head home?" she asked.

"You won't immediately get on my nerves, Simone."

"How do you know?"

He gave a slight shrug, took a sip of his martini, looked to the fire and answered, "I just do."

"What if I pick my teeth after a meal?"

He turned his gaze back to her. "Do you?"

"I wouldn't know. I don't know all my annoying habits. Annoying habits aren't annoying to the person doing them, just the person who has to put up with them."

He smiled at her. "I just had dinner with you, darling. You didn't pick your teeth."

"You had guests. Maybe I do that after I eat in front of the TV."

"I don't watch much TV," he told her.

"There you go," she stated, like that was enough to prove they were incompatible.

"Do you watch TV?" he queried.

She looked to the fire. "Not really." She looked back to him. "But when I do, I sometimes eat in front of it."

"To set your mind at ease, I can assure you this doesn't fill me with revulsion."

"Okay, Stellan, but that tired and tedious dance people dance they do it for a reason. You can get a sense if you want to have more time with someone by spending small blocks of it with them . . . *first*. Anyone will get on your nerves if you go in gung ho right away."

He tipped his head to the side. "Do you date often?"

She turned again to the fire.

That meant no.

He'd already guessed that.

"Do you date at all?" he inquired, this with a good deal of curiosity.

She took a sip of her drink.

Another no.

Stellan smiled again and gave her a squeeze. "Simone, honey, look at me."

He felt her take in a large breath before she did as he asked.

"I haven't finished explaining the deal," he told her.

She didn't hide her surprise.

Or her alarm.

"There's more?"

He nodded.

"God," she muttered.

"You can't leave, and I can't ask you to leave, no matter what."

Her eyes got big.

He'd never seen that expression on her face.

And seeing it then, he hoped even more that their discussions didn't drone on so he could get her into bed.

Because Mistress Sixx was cold and removed.

But Simone was incredibly endearing.

"That's insane, Stellan," she said quietly.

"Why?" he asked.

"It's insane you'd even ask why it's insane," she informed him.

"How long have you wanted me, sweetheart?" he whispered and had to lock his arm around her because her body jerked like she was going to bolt from the couch.

Anchored to him, she escaped by turning again to the fire.

"Answer me, Simone," he said to her profile.

She sipped her martini.

"Simone," he said low. "Answer me."

"Why does it matter?" she asked the fire. "You know I do, so why does it matter when that started? It doesn't make what you're asking any less crazy."

"Do you want flowers and chocolates and candlelit dinners where you carry an extra pair of panties in your purse with your toothbrush because you know you'll be sleeping beside me anyway but you go home the next day for unnecessary reasons?"

Her gaze came back to him. "If I said yes, I want flowers and chocolates and candlelit dinners?"

"I'd give them to you, but when we came home after, we'd just be *home*."

"We could end up hating each other," she declared.

"We won't end up hating each other," he refuted.

"If we do, what then? If we don't get along, what, Stellan? I lose you in the way I have you altogether because of this crazy scheme that pushed us too far *way, way, way* too fast."

"And what if that doesn't happen, Simone? What if the exact opposite happens?" he retorted.

That was when it came.

Not nerves.

Not more alarm.

It was like her body petrified in his hold.

It was fear.

"Darling," he whispered, sliding his arm up her back, curling her in, forcing her chest to his, her face closer to his. "You don't think this is insane because you think it will fail. You're saying it's insane because you fear it will succeed."

"I'm not a date type of woman," she whispered back.

"I know," he replied.

"I'm not flowers or candlelight," she shared.

"I know that too."

"I'm not a living-together type of woman either."

"How about we just see?"

"Maybe we should stop this here and go back to being just friends?" she suggested.

"Because I don't want to be your friend, Simone," he told her bluntly and watched her flinch.

But he wasn't done.

"I want to be your lover. I want to be your Master. I want to know all your secrets. I want to unravel the mystery that's you and then help you keep it safe. I want *you*, and the way I want you is beside me, in bed, in play and in life."

"You can't know that," she said softly.

"And this is something you'll be learning about me. I *do* know that. I know myself. I know what I want. And when that's identified, I get it."

"And can I ask how you identified that in me? Especially since pretty much all you know about me you got from Dillinger and not any of it is pretty."

"I can get any kind of pretty I desire, Simone," he said darkly. "I can fuck it in the ass, mouth and pussy. I can bend it to my will with a look. I can whip it. I can bleed it. I can brand it. I can mark it. I can make it do ugly, nasty, repulsive, degrading things. I can get it now and have all that. I can get it when I'm ninety and have all that too. I can open my wallet and get any-fucking-thing I fancy, Simone. Anything." He paused. "Except you."

"So I'm a challenge," she whispered.

"Fuck yes," he answered.

"And then what?" she asked.

"I best it, it's mine. But it's mine in a way I earned it, and that's the only thing worth having. And before you twist any of this, sweetheart, you'll also learn I'm a man who does not waste time on anything that does not deserve my time. So if I go after something I mean to have, it's something worth having."

"So Leigh is taken, and I'm the next up?"

It was his body that was now tight.

"Tell me," he growled, "that you did not just say that."

"You had a thing for her, Stellan."

"Yes. I did," he agreed. "I was completely enamored with her. But, you see, as happens in life often, it presented a variety of challenges to me. Amélie did not realize the challenge I was presenting in return for her own reasons, and in the end, that was lost to me because she found someone else. But prior to that, I had *two* challenging opportunities. It was just that at the time Leigh looked elsewhere, the other challenge was lost to me because she took off to do ridiculously dangerous things in order to . . . I don't know. Feel alive. Feel useful. Prove to herself she can. Or finally get herself dead so she can just stop dealing."

Simone pressed her lips together—not because she was angry but because she knew she'd been appropriately chastised.

Stellan didn't hone in on that.

He'd deal with that later.

He had to finish his point.

"It is often I go to a restaurant and wonder if I want the steak or the lobster. But when you're about the business of finding a woman you want in your life, you can't surf and turf. I lost the lobster, and that was disappointing at the time, but now I don't give that first fuck. Because I get steak."

"I've made you angry," she noted quietly.

"You have," he confirmed.

"I'm sorry, Stellan, but I think this proves—"

"Oh no," he slid his hand up her spine to wrap his fingers around her nape, feeling the cool of her collar against his skin and unfortunately not at a place where he could exult in that. "Don't think you can manipulate me, darling. Also don't think there won't be times in the next month that you'll piss me off, or I'll piss you off. The point of going in full barrel is learning each other, including having each other in the good we'll share and learning how to get through the bad."

"Maybe we should start out by taking in a movie," she suggested.

He stared into her eyes.

Then he whispered with unhidden surprise, "Christ. You're a coward."

Her body jolted again, but still no anger came into her face.

The fear was fixed firm in her eyes.

"I just don't understand—" she started.

Stellan moved suddenly, stretching his arm to put his glass on the end table. He then took hers and put it beside his.

After that, he kept his hand at her nape but placed his other unyielding on her jaw and drew her nearer.

"This is, and you know it, Sixx, the only way I have even the remotest chance to win you," he stated.

Her eyes narrowed in confusion. "What?"

"I have to go all in because if I don't, all is lost before it's even started."

She stared at him.

"You know I'm right," he pushed. "You know if I leave any slack, you'll run. But if I tie you to me, at least I have a chance at proving what you already feel in your heart is true. That you can trust in me, believe in what I'm offering you, and maybe for once in our life allow yourself to experience not just the concept of being happy, but actually being fucking *happy*."

Stellan didn't know what it was that he'd said, but something had forced her to waver.

Therefore, obviously, he took advantage.

"We're getting your things tomorrow," he declared. "You're moving in for a month, committed to a life with me for that time, no excuses, no backing out, no running away, not for any reason. Not any reason, Sixx. Do you understand me?"

"Why are you calling me Sixx?" she whispered.

"Because Sixx is the coward full of bullshit and bravado that hides Simone, who lives down deep. And that's who I have right now. But Simone is the real survivor. She's the one who keeps you living and breathing, who you're fucking terrified to let free, thinking you're protecting her, not having that first idea you're suffocating her. And if you don't stop, and soon, she'll be lost. Gone for eternity. And you'll be stuck in this half-life you're leading, a junkie hooked on adrenaline for the sole purpose of proving to yourself you're still breathing, but any promise of anything even remotely worth having will be forever dead."

Her eyes slid away, so he lifted his hand at her jaw and put pressure on her cheek.

"Look at me," he growled.

Her eyes came back.

"I'm offering you everything," he stated.

"I know," she replied heartbreakingly.

She knew.

And she was still intent on denying herself.

He pulled her closer so that he would be all she could see.

"They do not define you," he bit out.

She swallowed.

"It's arguable about their end, but *you* didn't deserve to die in that room with the vile excuses for parents who were further vile excuses for human beings."

"Stellan—"

"You didn't, Simone."

Her voice was so small, it made his throat get tight when she whispered, "I don't want to talk about this now."

"Then agree to be with me," he pushed.

"Okay," she said.

Fucking brilliant.

"My home. My bed. My life," he kept at her.

Her head nodded in his hold, and she repeated, "Okay."

"Weekends, you submit to me, Simone," he declared.

"Yes, Stellan."

"All weekend, darling."

"All weekend, Stellan."

Yes.

Fucking.

Brilliant.

But he was still pissed.

"I'm not taking you tonight," he announced. "Right now I want to strap you, then I'll want to take you by the hair and force-feed you my cock. Therefore I'm not in the mood for vanilla fucking, and you're not there in your head to be used in the way you've earned."

She nodded, lips pressed together again, but said nothing.

He took in her chastised look and got angrier.

"I can give you beauty," he clipped irritably.

"What I don't understand, baby," she whispered, "is why you think I deserve it."

She was lucky she called him baby.

But not that lucky.

"If you ask me that question in a month, darling," he drawled, "I'll walk away from you, and you'll never see me again. That is my vow to you, Simone. By the end of the month, I'll make you understand. Now I'm done talking. Sit beside me, fucking cuddle into me, and relax in front of the goddamned fire."

"Okay, Stellan."

He let her go.

She moved as told.

He reached to her glass, handing it to her.

He then reached to his and threw back half of what was left.

He scowled at the fire.

He'd gotten everything he wanted, including Simone tucked tight to his side, sipping a martini, but not including the night ending with them naked in his bed with him buried inside her.

So it was no wonder he was bloody fucking furious.

But it wasn't that.

Why you think I deserve it.

It was fucking . . .

That.

seven

She Made It Until Morning

STELLAN

Stellan woke alone in bed.

This meant he was out of it, reaching for his jeans on the floor, and tugging them on even while striding toward the door.

He only stopped when he saw the Valentino clutch sitting on his desk, now with the flap opened.

But it was still sitting on his desk.

He drew in breath while doing up his fly. He glanced around the room, listening to silence while buttoning the button.

No noise.

No sign of Simone.

He moved back to the steps up to his bed.

On the nightstand were her choker, bangle and earrings. And over the chair in the corner Simone's dress was thrown, her heels on the floor, her Bendel bag close to her shoes.

All where he'd put them.

He looked to his side of the bed, and the shirt he'd worn the day before and tossed to the floor the previous night was gone.

He pivoted and strode to and through the door, down the hall and down the stairs.

He didn't have to go to the driveway to ascertain if her car was still there.

He saw her through a set of doors at the back by the pool.

She was sitting in a chair at a patio table outside, wearing his linen shirt, her back to him, a mug on the table in front of her, knees drawn up, heels to the seat.

Stellan moved that way, glancing toward the kitchen as he did to see a mostly full pot of coffee.

Simone was making herself at home—his kitchen, his coffee-pot, his patio furniture, his shirt.

His breath started coming easier.

He only noticed when he got out the door that her head was bent and her arm was moving.

On bare, thus silent feet, he walked to her, got close and stopped dead.

Against her thighs she had a large, top-ringed sketchpad.

On it were blocks of different sizes made of precisely drawn lines and in them in black and white was a series of carefully crafted, intensely interesting, utterly distinctive drawings intermingled with white shapes filled with text.

And white bubbles filled with dialogue.

Fascinated, eyes locked on the pad soaking in all he could see, he took another step toward her.

"Darling—"

He immediately took a step back when she jumped violently in her seat, the pen she was using went flying, hitting the deck, and her head whipped around so fast, she had to have strained something.

She slammed the sketchpad to her chest and puffed out, "Jesus, Stellan, you scared the hell out of me."

"Good morning," he murmured, staring into her makeup-free face, her short hair messier than the purposeful mess she normally styled it in, her pad moving up and down with the rapid rise and fall of her chest, thinking, on his deck, in his shirt, after a night spent in his bed (even if it was a morning after he did not fuck her), she'd never looked as shatteringly pretty.

"Morning," she mumbled, took in a deep breath and shared, "I made coffee."

"I noticed."

She held the pad to her chest and continued to look up at him but said nothing more.

"I saw it, Simone, you don't have to hide it," he told her gently.

She pulled the pad away from her chest, flipped the cover over quickly, hiding away what was inside, and then made a move as if to get out of her seat, saying, "I'll get you some coffee."

"I can get my own coffee."

"Then I'm just going to—"

He put a hand on her shoulder and pressed her back down into the chair.

She resisted a second, then sank to her ass.

He moved to stand at the arm of her chair, looking down at her.

"What is that?" he asked, dipping his head to the pad she again had protectively clutched to her chest.

"Just doodles," she lied.

"It didn't look like doodles to me," he replied.

"Well, they are. It's something I do when my head's a mess to clear it, just not think of . . . I guess . . . anything."

"May I see?" he requested.

She shook her head and reached for her coffee with the pad still tight to her chest. "They're just nonsense."

They were absolutely not nonsense.

"It looked like a graphic novel," he noted.

She turned her attention to the pool, sipped coffee, swallowed, and told the pool, "It's just a load of nothing."

"Do you carry it with you everywhere?" he asked.

Still talking to the pool, she answered, "I keep it in the car for when . . . you know," she cleared her throat and set her mug back down, finishing what she was saying like she'd missed a variety of words, "at the ready."

"You leave it in your car?"

"I take it out when I'm home."

"Ah, and you're home now," he stated meaningfully.

That bought him her eyes, her temper clearly snagging, and she snapped, "Apparently. At least for a month."

"This would be getting to know you, Simone," he pointed out. "You sharing your 'nonsense' with me."

"It's not interesting," she told him.

"Now see," he whispered, "that's a lie."

"It really isn't," she clipped.

"Everything about you is interesting," he told her the truth.

"Everything about *Sixx* is interesting," she shot back.

"No," he drawled. "Everything about Sixx is excruciatingly boring."

Waking up thinking she'd left him only to find she hadn't, but when he approached her, having her shut him down, shut him out of something he sensed was important . . . no, *crucial* to understanding her, had put him in a certain mood—not a good one—and the words came out.

And it was the wrong thing to say.

She was up out of her chair and rounding the seat, moving away from him and doing it rapidly, indeed before he could make a move or even blink.

And she was speaking while she was escaping. "I'm going to get dressed, and then, if you'll—"

Stellan could move fast too, and he did, catching her elbow.

She halted and her eyes shot to his. "As I was saying, if you'll trust me to go home alone and get my stuff, I'll go do that now."

"I'd like to go with you."

"I'd like you to take your hand off me."

"Not until you return to your seat, we talk through what's

somehow become a rocky start to our first morning together, and we decide what's on for the rest of our day."

"Oddly, if I can't go home and get my stuff by myself, I'm feeling like being in your house together . . . but alone."

"Not oddly, darling, I'm not feeling that same need."

Her eyes squinted. "If you think I can't take you to your ass, you're very wrong."

"You cannot."

"Try me."

"Sweetheart, we'll wrestle, but I'd prefer we do it somewhere more comfortable, not on the pool deck."

"Stellan—"

He pulled her closer. She resisted fully that time, but she didn't take it past resistance.

With her career, she had to have moves.

But she was not stronger than him.

So when he got her close enough, he said low, "You don't have to show me if you'd rather not."

"I'd rather not," she hissed.

"And I apologize for that remark about you being boring. It was unnecessary as well as untrue. I woke up to you gone, thought you'd left, broken your promise already, and last night had not ended as I'd hoped."

"I agreed to your month thing."

"You did, and I'd hoped for that. But I'd further hoped that would be celebrated with mutual orgasms, not me brooding into the fire and you passing out on my chest and then stumbling half-asleep through taking off your clothes while I helped you before you fell into my bed for the first time. Regardless, I shouldn't have said what I said. When annoyed or frustrated, I can be biting. I'd hoped you'd learn that, perhaps, the last day of our month together, after, of course, I spent the thirty days prior convincing you to try happiness with me. Not within hours of this exercise we agreed on for getting to know one another."

He heard her take in a deep breath through her nose.

"Shall we try this again?" he suggested.

"What?" she asked.

"Good morning, sweetheart."

She was not ready to let it go and shared that by replying acidly, "Can I get you some coffee now?"

"I can still get it myself," he murmured. "Sit back down. Finish yours. I'll get mine. We'll take a moment to breathe, you in an effort to forgive me, me to reflect on my mistakes so I don't repeat them. Then I'll make us breakfast. We'll get dressed. And we'll go collect your things."

She still wasn't ready to let it go, and she shared it again, this time by saying, "I'm not going to break my promise, and it's insulting your first thought on our first morning was that I did."

"Then I apologize for that too," he returned smoothly.

"I'm so grateful you gave me this opportunity to have beauty, Stellan," she said drily, and sarcastically. "I can already see the path and how bright and cheery being happy is going to be."

"Please, honey, don't say anything more," he whispered. "I surprised you when you were doing something private. I insulted you. And before all that, I doubted you. It's already bad enough. Don't make it worse."

She looked to the French doors for a moment before she heaved a breath.

"Get your coffee," she murmured, pulling lightly on her arm still in his hold.

He let her go but otherwise didn't move a muscle.

She headed directly back to the chair she'd vacated.

Stellan waited until she sat, and only then did he move back into the house.

He could well imagine Susan's response to all of that and decided that the sister of his heart who'd replaced the sister of his blood (who'd also had his heart) might be a woman he told everything.

However he would not be sharing this clusterfuck of first-thing-in-the-morning, first-day-of-what-could-be-the-rest-of-their-lives-together, colossal fuckups.

He made his coffee, took it out to the pool deck, and noted the pad was still closed, sitting on the table. She'd retrieved her pen, and it was resting on the sketchbook. And she was seated as she had been, curled into herself, now likely unconsciously due to self-protection, the fingers of both hands wrapped around her coffee held up to her chest, her eyes glued to the pool.

He sat at the angle beside her, not opposite her, stretched out his legs and crossed his ankles.

He sipped, openly studying her.

And he did this with an emerging feeling of shock.

This shock came from the realization that in the entirety of his life he'd wanted precisely six things that he could not buy, broker, maneuver or simply take.

His father not being a weak, pompous, self-important, self-indulgent, supercilious, useless mound of flesh.

Segueing from that, his father not marrying his second wife. A woman who'd had a brother who'd hidden the monster within from everyone but Stellan, who'd hated him on sight, and Silie, who'd done the same and thus avoided him like the plague that he was, only to be raped by him when left alone in the house together.

Segueing from *that*, his sister, unable to deal with the fact that their father would not allow any form of justice to be served, for if it got out he'd allowed a monster in his own home, a monster who'd torn the innocence and light and beauty from a fourteen-year-old girl who'd never even been kissed, he'd never live it down, so she'd made the momentous and terrible decision to end her own life.

Fortunately independent of that, he'd wanted Amélie.

And independent of that, Simone.

And finally, he wanted very badly to thoroughly peruse what was inside that sketchpad.

Simone broke the silence, mercifully alleviating the pain forming in his chest that felt like someone had parked a building on it.

"In case you didn't notice, I'll share I can be a screaming bitch when my feelings are hurt and hold on to that a lot longer than I should, not to mention, I strike out when I'm feeling cornered."

He fought back his relieved smile and murmured, "That was noticed, darling."

"And I don't want you to go to my place because it's a pit," she declared, talking to the pool, as she had when she broke their silence. "And not a pit because I'm a slob, which I am, but because my place is just simply a pit, so it's not worth being tidy but also because my place is such a pit, I don't spend a lot of time there in order to actually tidy."

"I have a housekeeper," he reminded her.

"This I know," she muttered.

"You can be as much of a slob as you like. Margarita will, of course, ride your ass about it, as she does mine every morning she shows and finds my clothes on the floor or my towels in the sink. I just ignore her, and she's glad I do because if I wished to pick up after myself, she wouldn't have the ass of another member of her brood to ride."

"I doubt very seriously she'll like picking up some random woman's clothes off the floor, Stellan."

"Considering no random women have slept in my bed and she'll know what it means when a very much *not* random woman is sharing my home with me, you'd be wrong, Simone."

That earned him her eyes. "You've never had a woman in your bed?"

"I didn't say that," he replied. "They've never *slept* in my bed."

Her lips twitched.

"They've been fucked there," he elaborated.

"I'm sure," she mumbled to her coffee at her lips before she took a sip.

"I must admit, darling, they've also been tied there," he shared carefully.

"I'm sure about that too," she returned, sounding unfazed at having that information.

"And I'll allow there might have been a catnap or two," he muttered.

Her eyes twinkled.

Christ.

It was now, in his shirt, by his pool, eyes twinkling, that she'd never looked more shatteringly pretty.

"But I'm afraid, as ungentlemanly as it may seem, they're gone before morning," he finished.

"I feel like you should award me a crown with a pink satin sash placed over my chest with the glittery words 'She made it until morning.'"

"My sashes, my darling, are black, they're silk, not even a hint of glitter, and I'm relatively certain I could be creative with your enchanting chest, but their more frequent uses are at wrists and ankles."

She shook her head, now fully smiling, took another drink from her coffee, and looked back at his pool.

"I don't care where you live, Sixx, because you live here for now," he said quietly. "And if my home says I'm wealthy and have exceptional taste in interior designers, your home will say you lead an interesting life and you don't spend it doing things that are not only uninteresting but are a waste of your time."

"Stellan Lange, will of steel, demonstrated even when he's determined to see the best in me," she remarked.

"This is true, with one alteration, that being when I'm determined to introduce that to you."

Her gaze slid to him and that . . .

Now that . . .

The warmth and gratitude and sweetness.

Stunning.

"Shall I make us breakfast, darling?" he asked quietly.

"You're criminally gorgeous, insanely wealthy, excruciatingly generous, irritatingly intelligent, and you can cook?"

"Are you beginning to understand my frustration at you not jumping at my offer in front of the fire last night?"

"I forgot ridiculously arrogant."

He burst out laughing, did it rising from his chair, bending to her and catching her behind the head.

He kissed the top and straightened, letting her go but dipping his chin to look into her eyes.

"Eggs and toast or pancakes?" he asked.

"Surprise me," she answered.

He smiled.

Her gaze fell to it and it came back.

Warmth and gratitude and sweetness.

"I'll be back," he said.

"I'll be here," she replied.

Yes.

Yes, she would.

Stellan moved into his house, for the first time that morning breathing easy.

"I told you it was a dump."

Stellan had closed the door to her dark, cramped studio that was not cramped due to Simone having a good deal of belongings, but cramped because, no matter how many belongings she had, it would be cramped because it was miniscule.

And he stood there marveling at the fact it also smelled dank when it hadn't rained in Phoenix for over four months.

Dillinger had given him her address, of course, and he'd noted it, of course, but the south side of Phoenix was not his stomping grounds.

He had no idea.

He also had no idea if he could wring the miracle he needed to wring in just a month—finding a way to free Simone Marchesa from the overbearing protection Sixx held her under at the same time allowing Sixx to remain at liberty to be all the glorious parts, with none of the damaging ones, she'd formed herself into being.

But even if he failed in besting the greatest risk he'd ever taken . . .

She was never moving back here.

"Can you tell me why you live here?" he asked.

"Relatively central," she stated, throwing open the door to a closet whereupon a foot-high expanse of feminine paraphernalia rolled out onto the floor. "Shit," she muttered, bending to paw through it and finishing, "And cheap."

"It's my understanding you were paid handsomely for the ridiculously foolish things you used to do and still moonlight doing, even if you're also paid handsomely for the legitimate job you have at Joel's firm."

Her back shot straight, and her eyes cut to him.

"Joel?" she asked.

"Your employer is a long-time friend of mine."

She rolled her eyes to the ceiling, muttering, "Naturally."

"Simone," he called.

She again looked to him.

"You live in a twenty-first century hovel in a developed country, and you own McQueen, Valentino, Bendel and were last night wearing a pair of eight-hundred-dollar Giuseppe Zanotti sandals standing by my pool." He looked pointedly side to side and back at her. "What the bloody fuck?"

"Those Zanotti sandals are life," she replied.

"Yes, and we'll be exploring their various functionalities when you're submitting to me next weekend," he returned. "But that isn't an answer to my question."

"I can't have those sandals and a go bag in my secret hiding place that's filled and will get even more filled with cash to get me out of the country and keep me clothed, fed, and safe for an indeterminate amount of time when life turns to shit—as life has a tendency to do if you have the last name Marchesa if I have to pay expensive rent somewhere I'm never going to hang."

Stellan was again not breathing easy.

"Perhaps we should not talk about this right now," he suggested.

"Perhaps," she replied, returning her attention to her closet.

"Pack everything," he ordered, and she swiveled back to him woodenly, her lips parted. "If you don't have enough luggage, we'll go to Scottsdale Fashion Square and pick up some at Louis Vuitton."

"I'm not taking everything to your house, Stellan," she declared.

He looked down at the tangle at her feet, and at a glance saw the lipstick-red sole of a Louboutin, the heel of which was twined with the silken ankle wrap of a Birman trapped around the signature chain of a McCartney Baby Bella tote.

He then looked to the door that had a lock on the knob that turned on a pinch and that was it.

There wasn't even a chain.

His attention went back to Simone.

"Pack everything, Simone."

"Stellan—"

"It won't be here when you get back. It's actually a monumental surprise any of it is here now. And since you risked your ass repeatedly to get it, practically giving it to some meth-addled buffoon is not going to happen. So pack *everything*, Simone."

Her eyes narrowed. "Sundays are supposed to be fun days, hot stuff. Here we are on a Sunday, and we're entering domestic bliss, and you're all cranky."

"Darling, I've not fucked since well before our affecting night at the gladiator pit, unless you count the multiple handjobs I gave myself as I imagined all the ways I was going to fuck you, play with you, and lately, punish you for not calling as I ordered you to do, which I personally don't count. I'm afraid that makes a man like me cranky."

Now her mouth had fallen open.

Adorable.

His patience was draining swiftly.

She shut her mouth only to open it again to ask, "You've not fucked for nearly a week?"

"The last slave I was inside was over three months ago, and the last vanilla fuck I had was before that, this after I made the decision that empty fucking was something I'd allow you to do while I was biding my time to make my move with you, but it wasn't doing a thing for me."

She seemed to have taken a mental trip to another world before she snapped back, and he realized she'd been harking back to any time she'd seen him at the Honey when she breathed, "My God, that's true."

He swung a hand to the mess at her feet.

"So if we can hurry this along," he prompted.

"I wasn't empty fucking either, Stellan," she declared.

And yet *again* he was fucking fighting fucking clenching his *fucking* teeth.

"Sweetheart, you've had nearly every male sub at the Honey who swings your way, always at least in twos, frequently in threes and fours."

"I command them to touch each other or fuck each other. I rarely engaged in the first and never the last."

"But you played."

"You did too, and you touched."

Stellan shut his mouth.

"I was trying to get your attention," she whispered her admission.

"You succeeded," he whispered his reply. "Now you need to pack, darling, everything, before I throw you to that absurdly small bed with sheets that I can see have polyester fibers and bury myself inside you up to your womb."

Her eyes heated in a manner that was not helping him control his urge to throw her on the double bed that was taking the majority of the space in the room before her mouth curled up in her cat's smile.

"You're such a snob, baby," she murmured.

"The first time I have you is not going to be in a hovel on polyester sheets. And just to make things perfectly clear, Simone, I'll *never* be having you in anything remotely resembling a slum or on a bed that's not even as long as me or on sheets that prove all the inadequacies of the world that they've touched your skin."

"I'm beginning to like you," she stated teasingly.

She was completely in love with him.

She was also even more fuckable when she was teasing.

Thus she was beginning to be a problem he was painfully impatient to solve.

"Simone," he replied warningly. "*Pack.*"

She looked down at the mess at her feet, grinning and mumbling, "As you wish."

She could speak no sweeter words.

Rather than fuck her on a pile of designer gear, he looked around for a suitcase to assist her in hauling that gear out of that hellhole.

In the end, they went back to his house, switched out his Tesla with his Maserati Levante, loaded his suitcases inside, hit Fashion Square, purchased a full set of LV luggage for her, and went back.

It took two trips.

All she owned worth moving were clothes, shoes, handbags, accessories, drawing supplies, sketchpads and mysterious keepsakes she tried to hide, shoving them in her new cruiser bag when she thought he was occupied with something else.

The rest they left behind.

Then Simone wasn't moved in with enough for a month.

She was just moved in.

And suddenly Stellan wasn't cranky anymore.

That afternoon, Stellan was stretched out on his mahogany leather chesterfield in the lounge area off the dining room with his book when Simone returned from his room where he'd left her to unpack.

He'd done this with two goals.

One, she'd be unpacked, thus moved in, thus at a place where she could start settling into his home and her life as it would be with him.

Two, because it was not lost on him that she was a woman who'd lived a life taking care of herself by herself and it would do him no favors to be constantly invading her space. He needed to show her that she'd have her times where she would be alone with her thoughts or her sketchpads or however she needed to settle her mind and emotions.

He'd blown it that morning.

That was not going to happen again.

Even so, he was immensely glad when she sauntered in and threw herself with one leg tossed over the arm of the armchair at the end of his couch.

However, he was not glad she'd thrown herself in a chair and not on him.

He took her in. Her tailored, black short shorts. The dark gray knit top that had one arm bare and the other arm partially covered by a fall of material. She'd taken off the pewter gladiator sandals she'd changed into when she'd changed out of her t-shirt dress when they went shopping, so her legs and feet were bare.

Her hair was a sexy mess, and except for a sweep of blush, a thick line of black eyeliner and a couple of coats of mascara, she had on no other adornment, including jewelry.

"I'm done," she announced.

Finally it was time to fuck.

"And just to say," she went on, "that was no easy task. Your closet is heaving. You have more clothes than a girl."

He dropped his book to his chest and spoke truth. "My closet is twice the size of your entire apartment. It might be heaving now with the addition of the evidence of your addiction to leather and designer apparel that emerged as if by magic from that microscopic closet in your hovel. I'm not surprised you opened the door and it rolled out at your feet. What I'm surprised about is that when you opened the door it didn't explode in your face."

She grinned at him.

Definitely time to fuck.

"But my closet was not full when you began," he concluded.

"I counted," she returned. "And you have fifty-two suits."

He raised his brows. "Is this a crime?"

"Who needs fifty-two suits?" she teased.

"Apparently me," he drawled.

She rolled her eyes.

He looked at her long legs and took a moment to gather his control before he had her turned in that chair with her shorts around her ankles and his cock planted inside her.

When his attention moved back to her face, he noted she'd grown distracted, and she'd done this because her eyes were moving the length of his body.

It seemed they shared a common frame of mind.

Excellent.

"Simone," he called.

"Mm?" she hummed.

"Are you all right?" he asked.

"I like that shirt," she mumbled.

He didn't look down at his graphite-colored linen shirt.

He studied her, attempting not to smile at the same time attempting to control his cock, which was getting hard.

"And you look really good in jeans," she continued mumbling.

Stellan felt his lips twitch.

"Simone," he called again.

"Mm?" she repeated her hum.

He reached out and put his book on the coffee table before ordering, "Come here, darling."

Like she was on autopilot, she rose from the chair, moved to him, and when she got close, he lifted up only enough to wrap his fingers around her hand. It took no effort at all to tug her down to him so that she was stretched out on top of him whereupon he rolled, trapping her against the back of the couch.

Yes.

This was much better.

Her vague eyes hit his.

"Would you like something to eat?" he asked quietly.

"I don't think so," she replied.

"Would you like me to make you a cocktail?" he kept at the game.

Her gaze dropped to his mouth.

"Maybe later," she murmured.

Definitely later.

"Simone," he said.

Her eyes drifted up to his.

Stellan dipped in close and whispered, "We're going to fuck now, sweetheart."

Her hand resting on his chest clenched into his shirt, her body coasted toward his, her gaze again dropped to his mouth, and Stellan kissed her.

Although he'd planned to do this last night, starting the proceedings on his couch in his bedroom, that didn't happen.

So he carried out his plan there.

Thus he communicated with his firm, wet kiss that he was not going to mess about, but he also wasn't going in hard and fast.

This was not going to be a quick fuck to take the edge off.

This was going to be their first fuck.

Something to remember.

He realized his mistake while crafting this strategy almost immediately.

He had not taken into account how he would react to her response.

Especially when it was like it had been during their first kiss the day before—sweet, almost innocent, like he was the first man who'd ever had her mouth.

This included Simone melting into him, tipping her head deep, her lips soft, her mouth an open invitation, her taste exemplary, her perfume weaving a spell.

Therefore it was time to take this to his bedroom, or she'd be bare ass to mahogany leather, he'd be out of control, and this would be a quick fuck to take the edge off.

He broke the kiss, drew away from her, but did it pulling her gently out of the couch with him.

On their feet, he held her in his arms and kissed her there. Light, soft, quick touches and tastes as she held onto his shirt in fists to hold her steady in order to fully absorb them through her lips.

Then he disengaged, moved them around the couch, through the room, up the stairs and down the hall to his room.

He stopped her at his side of his bed, turned her back to it, her front to him, and looked down at her gentled face as she peered up at him with the slow burn he'd created openly exposed in her eyes.

Beautiful.

He took her face in his hands, gliding his fingers across the skin, over her ears, in her hair, his gaze roaming, his mouth murmuring, "You probably have no earthly idea how pretty you are."

"I'm hot as fuck," she tried to quip, but her words were breathy.

He gave her a small smile. "You are, my darling, but you're also uncommonly pretty." He rubbed a thumb across her lips, whispering, "I could look at you for hours."

Simone was finished with talking, definitely not in the mood to stand there and let him look at her, and she communicated that by arching into him.

He used his hands at her face to pull her up and again captured her mouth.

It took effort, and control, to build the heat of his kisses slowly, especially when she started making little mews that formed in the back of her throat but filled his mouth.

And most especially when she rubbed her breasts against his chest through the fabric of their shirts.

But when her patience snapped and her hands became urgent, lifting up the untucked tails of his shirt and hitting the skin at the sides of his waist, immediately trailing everywhere she could reach, her touch slipped the knot he had tied on his control, and Stellan returned it.

Under her shirt, he wrapped his fingers around her sides. The pads going up her back, his thumbs dug in at the front.

Her skin was smooth, soft, warm, gorgeous.

Gliding up, his attention snagged as his thumb snagged a ridge of skin that shouldn't be there.

Although he'd seen them the night before when he'd helped her undress, it surprised him enough to break contact with her lips.

But he wouldn't have had to.

Her body abruptly cranked to the side, and if he didn't tighten his hold on her to keep her where she was, he'd have lost her.

Their eyes met, and her breathing was no longer ragged simply due to his kisses.

"I—" she started, panic seeping into her gaze.

"I know about it," he whispered, feeling her tense as he dragged the pad of his thumb back over one of two scars he knew she'd received when she'd sustained gunshot wounds.

"It's—"

"Not for now," he finished for her.

"Stellan—"

He pressed in at the scar but took his other hand from her skin to hold her at the side of her head.

He put his lips to hers and said, "I know what brought you back to Phoenix, darling. And we'll talk about the whys later. For now all you need to know is that I don't give a fuck about it. It doesn't bother me. It's part of you. It comes with you. It's a piece of your history. And in case you've been missing my message, honey, I want all of you. Now settle down so that I can get inside you."

She stared into his eyes, her breath still coming fast with excitement as well as panic, and before he could guess her intention, she pulled back, tore off her shirt, tossed it aside and came at him with hands up.

Fingers fisting in his hair, she dragged his mouth down to hers.

She thrust her tongue between his lips.

He thrust it out, taking hers briefly, then tore his mouth free.

It was high time to move things along.

"Shorts off," he growled.

She moved instantly, shimmying them down, and it was his turn to pull away, not bothering with the buttons but yanking his shirt over his head.

When she stood there in nothing but a black, net lace bra, one that exposed high, small breasts and dark, budded nipples, Stellan shoved a thigh through her legs, drawing it up.

She gasped when it hit her, and he used it to lift her, moving in, taking her onto the bed, going with her, falling on top of her.

And finally she was beneath him.

He possessed her mouth with a scorching kiss that he didn't allow to last long because he refused to wait any longer.

After what amounted to years of watching, years of wondering, it was finally time to discover a different taste of his Simone.

On his way down her body, he only stopped long enough to jerk one cup of her bra down and pull hard with his mouth on her tight nipple, giving himself the sharp sound of her pleasure, before he moved down further.

When he reached his destination, it was Simone who threw one leg over his shoulder, the other she lifted and let fall wide.

The invitation was brazen.

And exquisite.

His hard cock throbbed inside his jeans, and he went in.

Arching her back, rocking into his mouth, he'd barely slid his tongue along her clit before he felt and heard her coming.

He took that, he pushed it, he clamped his hands on her hips and held her to him, fucking her with his tongue, feeding on her delicious wet, sucking on her clit as she gasped, moaned, whimpered and squirmed against him.

Christ, she was magnificent.

So magnificent, eating her as he ground his hard cock into the mattress, Stellan took more.

And more.

Suddenly, she wrenched free and he felt her hands on his jaw, pulling him up to his knees, to her, putting her face to his, and she panted against his moist lips, her foggy, burning, molten brown eyes somehow managing also to be intensely focused as she pushed out, "You. Now."

"I wasn't finished," he growled.

She came in, eyes locked to his, sinking her teeth sharply in his bottom lip. He felt pain and instantly tasted blood, but she yanked back, pulling his flesh with her, and *Christ*...

Christ.

He felt his cast-iron cock start to weep.

She let his lip go and forced out hoarsely, "You. *Now.*"

Not thinking, suddenly and for the first time in his life at someone's command, his hands went to his jeans.

He handled the fly. Simone was at the ready right when he got the zip down, and she dragged them over his ass.

His cock sprung blissfully free, and Stellan had to shove her hand away to take hold of his own damned self and wrest back the control that she'd seized.

With his other arm, he rounded her hips, pulling her up to him.

He positioned.

She again caught hold of his jaw with both her hands.

He drove in.

"Beautiful Christ," he groaned when her sleek tight closed around him.

On a gust of breath, her head falling back, her hands slid into his hair, up, so her forearms were holding him at the back of his head.

He dropped her to her back on his bed and started moving.

She rounded his shoulders with her arms, righted her head, caught his eyes, and rocked with his thrusts.

"Faster, Stellan," she ordered, locking on to him with her heels in his ass.

"Patience, darling," he gritted, going slow, enjoying learning every silken inch of her, *intimately*.

Her head came up swiftly.

His reared back at the same time he lifted his hand to her face, forcing his thumb into her mouth, holding her tongue down with the pad.

The edges of her teeth sank into his flesh, causing a sting, making his balls draw up, and he felt the smile on his lips when he drove in slow, deep, putting his face to hers.

"Settle down, Sixx," he whispered. Her eyes narrowed, he swiveled his hips on an inward glide, and his smile grew as he watched her eyelids flutter at the same time he felt the walls of her pussy do the same. "You had your moment. We fuck my way, honey."

He moved, unhurried and deliberate, completely enjoying every wet thrust.

She changed tactics and licked his thumb.

He carried on moving just as he liked.

"Yes?" he prompted.

She glared a moment.

He swiveled again.

Her eyes rolled back into her head.

"Yes?" he pushed.

Vaguely, she nodded.

He ground in as her reward.

Her chin tipped back, and she automatically sucked his thumb in deep.

It was then he went faster.

"Round my waist with your legs," he commanded.

She did as told.

And Stellan went even faster, this time doing it harder.

Hazily, she caught his eyes and sucked frantically at his thumb.

He drew it out and exchanged it with his tongue.

She took his cock, and he gave her the thumb she'd wetted at her clit.

When he did, one of her hands clenched in his hair as she flung the other arm over her head and fisted it in his comforter, moaning into his mouth.

And when she needed it, could take no more, he released her lips.

"Don't come," he ordered gruffly.

"Stellan," she breathed, her hips meeting his thrusts wildly.

Fuck, she was amazing.

"Don't you come, Simone," he warned thickly, pounding inside her now, pushing it for himself, desperate to explode, needing more to watch what he was building in her, watch her struggle to obey his command, unintentionally doing anything in her power to snap his control so she'd be freed to let her own go.

"Baby," she whispered her plea, arching up into him, rubbing against him, rocking with him, pulling out all the stops.

He kept at her with cock and thumb until it was Stellan who could take no more.

"Now, darling," he whispered.

She shoved her face in his neck and flew apart.

And he sank his teeth deep into the flesh of hers, and his world turned white.

Everything obliterating, drawing down to nothing but the taste of Simone in his mouth, his cock pounding into her sleek, soaked beauty, his balls draining, skin rubbing and slapping against skin, sex mingled with her perfume, his cologne permeating the air, and his whole body fucking, *fucking* finally covering hers, buried in hers as Stellan climaxed inside his Simone.

When the world turned to color again, and he had it in him to unlatch the hold of his teeth and automatically begin to lave the mark he'd left there, it hit him that Simone was not stroking him. Not petting him. Not quivering under him in her own aftermath.

Legs about his waist, one arm below his shoulder blades, one hand on the back of his neck, she was holding on fast. Hard. *Tight.*

He moved his thumb from her clit to put his weight into his forearm in the bed.

But even as he took that from her, she didn't let go.

So he slid his lips to her ear.

"Are you all right, honey?" he whispered.

She didn't answer verbally.

Just nodded.

He lifted his head to look down at her.

And grew completely still.

He didn't move until the tear slid out the side of her eye, along her temple, to disappear in her hair.

He bent to touch his lips to the trail and then laid his hand there, positioning his face right in hers.

"Simone, darling, I asked if you're all right," he repeated gently.

"Thank you," she whispered.

"For what?" he asked.

"For thinking I deserve you."

Her words caused his entire chest to cave in, and he growled.

Then he kissed her hard and deep.

And when he was done, he decided that was for another time.

Now, they were celebrating.

And they were doing that by engaging in a mind-boggling amount of fucking.

But when he broke from her mouth, he queried, "Now would you like a cocktail?"

She stared in his eyes. Eventually her lips quirked.

And finally they moved.

"Absolutely."

*   *   *

Much later, Stellan lay naked on his back on his couch in his bedroom in front of the fire.

Simone lay naked partly on him, partly draped down his side, her forehead in his neck, her cheek on his collarbone, her top leg thrown over his thighs, his arm around her, the warm, round cheek of her ass in his hand.

She was out.

Asleep.

Done in.

As she would be.

Driven by something that had nothing to do with the lapse of time between his acquisitions of pussy, and everything to do with the woman right there at his side, he'd used her liberally to explore some of the surfeit of possibilities of drawing her to climax.

On the table before them was the detritus of the remains of raids on the fridge as well as a bottle of gin, a bottle of vodka, a bottle of vermouth, an almost-empty jar of olives, two martini shakers, a silver bucket of mostly melted ice, two empty martini glasses and the sludge left behind of a half-eaten gallon of ice cream that should have gone back into the freezer three hours ago.

His room had lit itself when the time came, lamps here and there, offering a welcoming light.

Stellan's eyes were on the fire.

His breaths were coming deep, relaxed. Easy.

His last deposit of cum was seeping out of Simone, all over his thigh.

"Now this is fucking more like it," he muttered.

And then slowly . . .

He smiled.

eight

A Man Who Has Everything

STELLAN

"Hold it."

"Baby."

"What did I say?"

"But, I—"

Both of them sitting up, Stellan's hands were gripping the cheeks of her behind as she rode his cock. He adjusted one, gathering her wet then sliding his middle finger up her ass.

He watched her head drop back as she moaned, *"God.* That is *not* helping."

He shoved his face in her throat, and as she fucked him, he fucked her ass.

"Faster, Simone," he ordered.

"If I do that, I'll come," she whimpered.

He drove his finger deep, and with his other hand caught her hair in a tight grip, maneuvering her face to his own.

"Faster," he growled.

She bounced on him faster, staring in his eyes, gasping against his lips, her gaze fuzzy, scattered, glorious.

He started fucking her ass again as he brought her mouth to his, tilting her head to the side, capturing her lips, and he assumed the same rhythm she was using on his cock with his finger and his tongue.

She took it for an admirably long time before she made a desperate noise down his throat.

He broke the kiss and whispered, "Now you can come, darling."

She flew back in a total body arc, still bounding on his cock, head back, chest thrust forward, pure sex, pure beauty, all Simone, all his.

He slid his finger out, pulled her off his cock, but kept her on her knees.

Shifting out from between her legs and moving around her, he walked on his knees into her, pushing her closer to the headboard, grunting, "Tip."

She lifted her ass.

He guided his cock and drove it home.

Jesus, yes.

Home.

Her head slammed into his shoulder.

Stellan again shoved his face in her neck as he fucked her fast, deep, and so rough, she had to reach out and latch onto the headboard to lock her arm or he'd drive her right into it.

"*God*, I love your cock," she breathed.

This verbal confirmation was unnecessary.

But he was still delighted to get it.

He lifted his head and clipped, "Mouth."

She turned her head and offered it.

He took her mouth, pounding inside her so hard, noises came from her throat, driving down his with each thrust until he broke the kiss, groaned, "*Fuck*, sweetheart," his world cleared, went blank of everything but Simone, and he exploded inside her.

He came down with his cock buried to the root, his ass to his calves with Simone straddling his thighs, resting into him, essentially sitting on his shaft. His forehead was in her neck, one arm tight along her belly, the other arm slanted up, fingers wrapped around her throat.

"Just to say, baby, I'm not sure it's necessary for you to make up for all the fucking you missed these last months in the expanse of twenty-four hours with me," Simone joked breathily.

Smiling, he started stroking her throat but didn't otherwise move his hand.

He did move his head to glide his lips up a cord at the side of her neck to her ear.

"Are you not enjoying yourself?" he asked there.

He felt her fingers curl around his forearm at her chest, and he lifted his head to catch her turning hers to look into his eyes.

"I didn't say that," she whispered, and her warm brown eyes got warmer. "Nice wakeup call, hot stuff."

He felt his face get soft, then he moved in and kissed her even softer.

Unfortunately, he had to end it and say, "I need to shower and get to work."

"And I need to test my walking and see if I've been struck bow-legged."

He found himself laughing, then caught himself while doing it.

He'd never laughed while inside a woman, not in his life.

Thirty-nine years, innumerable partners, the same amount of playthings.

Not once.

"Stellan?" she called, the odd note of open concern in her voice, something he'd never heard her give so nakedly, taking him back to her.

"I've never laughed when I've been inside a woman," he shared with her, just as openly.

He saw the surprise flicker in her eyes only a moment before they shut down.

Oh no she did not.

Not then, in that moment.

Not ever.

His fingers that were light at her throat, tightened.

"Simone," he warned.

She was looking at his cheek.

She was also murmuring, "You need to get to work, and so do I."

"Can you explain to me why I'm still hard inside you, we were sharing something beautiful after sharing something beautifully pleasurable, and now you're miles away from me?"

She moved her gaze to focus on his eyebrows and replied, "Because we both should probably get a move on."

He pulled out, and she cried out when he lifted her, turned her, and planted her astride his lap, sitting on his ass in his bed, caging her with his arms and pinning her in with his thighs.

"So, we got through the first day, and it was not painless," he began. "But for you, it was relatively easy considering there's a good deal of difficult issues to go over, and we haven't even started. I own my company, so I can go in whenever I like. And I know Joel allows you to make your own schedule considering most of your work is out in the field, so even if he forced you to a schedule, he'd never know if you kept it. Since we can do as we wish, how about we start tackling those issues now? Hmm?"

"How about we not," she retorted, her body and voice stiff.

He felt his eyes narrow. "That wasn't actually me giving you a choice."

"Stellan," she snapped.

He moved one arm so he could use his thumb to press in at the scar on her lower right abdomen that he'd snagged the night before, then he moved it to the one that was an inch up and in and pressed there.

"Shall we start with these?" he suggested.

So abruptly he braced, she stared him direct in the eyes.

And spoke.

"I haven't had a man inside me for over a year. And the last man was a sub I took in Aryas's club in Vegas. And I took him because he reminded me of you."

Stellan ran his hand up her side, over her ribs, breast, chest, to her neck, murmuring, "Simone."

"I hadn't had an orgasm in months, until you gave me one at the pit," she declared. "Not even a handjob or likewise."

"Darling," he whispered.

"You want to go over issues? You want me to be real? You asked how long I've wanted you, Stellan. Here's your answer, baby. Since the first second I laid eyes on you."

"Simo—"

"Back when you were in love with Amélie."

"We went over that, sweetheart," he reminded her quietly, realizing he'd made another mistake, poked the lioness, and now he needed to soothe her back to a purr.

She tipped her head sharply to the side. "I've been hung up on you for years. Still feel like I'm a challenge?" she asked.

"Yes," he answered simply.

He could tell she processed that by the stunned flare in her eyes, but he couldn't tell how she'd done it when she immediately pushed past it.

"I've never been on a date. Not one. Not in my life."

"All right, honey, perhaps you should slow down."

She did not take his suggestion.

"I've picked up men and fucked them, though not often. Before I met you, however, not rare. And they got the ride of their lives when that horny girl they thought was going to give them a sloppy, slutty good time tied their asses to their beds and used their cocks for her own purposes. Though they got off on that shit. Every." She got closer to his face. "Last." She got *in* his face. "One."

Stellan decided to stay silent and let her get it out.

She moved away but only as far as his hold would let her go.

"It wasn't until Aryas read it in me and explained it to me that I knew what it was. I always thought I was a freak."

He couldn't let that pass without comment.

"You're not a freak."

"Did Aryas tell you about me?" she asked.

He felt his brows draw together. "Tell me what about you?"

"That when I subbed for him in training, I *subbed* for him. Was it him who told Dillinger who told you?"

"No, darling,' he said calmingly. "Dillinger shared Aryas trained you. I guessed that part."

She seemed to deflate, like thinking Aryas had betrayed her had blown her up to the point her skin was a fragile membrane that couldn't hold the pain and was about to explode.

"He didn't betray your confidence," Stellan further assured. "I see how you are with him, and I know you trained under him. There's a slight deference you give to him that you don't give anyone else. It's independent of the feelings you have for him. It's indicative of you having history of submitting to him, and not just because you did that in training. Even so, it was still a guess."

She turned her head to look away.

"I know you're damaged, Simone," he said gently, carefully. "And if you think that's a turnoff, I can assure you it isn't."

She looked back to him and announced, "I'm not damaged, Stellan. I'm a mess."

"I believe those are not mutually exclusive," he murmured.

"You're wrong. Because damage can be fixed. A mess is just a mess."

"A mess can be sorted out."

"Not my kind of mess."

"You're very wrong."

"*God, Stellan!*" she shouted suddenly, shocking him with her out-burst to the point his body went solid all around her and his hold on her increased. "Don't you see I'm trying to *protect you?*"

"From what?" he asked, his voice lowering, his patience bleed-ing, and he was trying, but failing, to stem the flow.

"*Me*, you big idiot," she snapped.

"And shall I return the favor?" he asked.

The frustration ebbed out quickly as her expression grew con-fused. "What?"

"Shall I protect you from me?"

"What is there to protect me from?"

"Well, I don't know, darling. Perhaps the fact I live in terror that some hint of my father will slither from somewhere deep inside me, and I'll find out that the vast effort I've expended since I could form a coherent thought *not* to be *one thing like him* would all be for naught? Or perhaps I should share the delightful memory of walking into the garage to find my sister in my running car, looking asleep but being very *dead*."

Her hands lifted to hold either side of his face, she dropped her forehead to his and she whispered urgently, "Stop, baby. Just stop."

He didn't.

"Or should I share how I felt about the fact the wife before the last one that my father married was of an age to be my bride? Or how the last one was too young even for me? The woman was four years out of high school, for fuck's sake."

"I think I know how you felt. I saw you in D.C. Meeting with them. Giving him the direct cut," she admitted, still whispering. "And since I did, I have a good feeling how you felt."

His head jerked while she spoke, and he felt his brow snap low and heavy.

"Sorry?"

She slid her hands to his neck and lifted her forehead away. "I was in D.C., for a . . . um, job. I was at that restaurant. I saw you. That's when I, well . . . after that happened, I looked into you."

"You were there?"

She nodded.

Stellan could not believe this.

"Why the fuck didn't you say anything?" he demanded.

"We weren't exactly super-close when I got back, and it's not something you slide across a booth at the Honey to say to some-body. I mean how would that go? 'Hey. How's it going? Just, you know, wanted you to know that I saw you tell your father to go fuck himself in D.C. Well done with that.' "

She was being amusing.

He did not laugh.

"Not now. *Then*. In D.C. Why didn't you come to me?"

"I was going to get your attention, but you looked pretty ticked."

"After repeated communications to him never to get in touch with me for any reason, as usual, when he heard I was in D.C. for business, and he was there for the same, my father ignored that and called me to meet him for lunch so that he could introduce me to his fiancée and ask me to be his best man, *again*. Something I'd refused *two times before*. Of course I was ticked."

"Obviously, I figured that out when I looked into you," she muttered.

"Jesus Christ, Simone. You knew how to get in touch with me. All you needed to do was call Aryas or Leigh, and they would have given you my number. We could have met in D.C. Fucked. And now been together for over a year."

She stared at him, for the most part, if you could stare at someone and do it repeatedly blinking.

"You find something in what I said surprising?" he asked drily.

"Been together for over a year?" she asked back incredulously.

"Darling, the first time I was inside you, when we were done, you wept. We were meant to connect. We're just meant *to be*."

She poised to take flight.

He took her to her back and covered her with his body.

"Oh no, honey," he whispered menacingly. "There's no escape from that, and you know it. You're in the mood to be real? You're ready to ride through our issues?"

"Not so much anymore," she answered.

But he wasn't asking a question.

So he spoke over her.

"You're thirty-three years old, never had a date, never had a man who means something take your mouth, never had a man make love to you, and that's what we did the first time, sweetheart, in the way people like us do it, and it drove you to tears. You're big, bad Sixx who could put a man on his ass and survive multiple gunshot wounds, but you submit to me in *everything*. You've moved in with me. You won't come unless I allow it. You endured a life filled with shit and you forged your way through it for the express purpose to be right where you are right now. I can have any woman I want. But the only one I want is the one that was *made for me*."

"I honest to God don't want you to get angry, baby, but I need you to *see* how that's difficult for me to believe," she stated earnestly.

"You're missing the fact I already see it, Simone. Why do you think your ass is right here and your clothes are in my closet? I'm not missing even a second at having the chance of shoving the answer to that right in your face. I vowed to you I would make that clear. And I'm going to do it. I've had you thirty-two hours, and you're already splitting wide open for me. Can you still doubt where this is going? Can you still doubt *me*?"

She pressed her lips together, and her eyes explored her own eyebrows.

Bloody hell, only she could be that fucking adorable when things were this extreme between them.

"Simone," he growled.

Her gaze snapped to him.

"Okay, jeez," she mumbled, then spoke clearly. "The sex is spectacular and you're awesome and I'm hot and you think I'm pretty and we're both royally fucked up so we belong together because apparently, if there's an all-powerful being, he or she means for me to sit like a fat cat in a Phoenician mansion and be spoiled by a hot guy. I give up. You think I'm worth it, it won't be me anymore trying to talk you out of it."

"Stop being amusing," he ordered.

"I can't. That's me. I'm a badass, a hardass and a smartass. It is what it is and you picked me so get over it."

Stellan did not waste time marveling over how she could annoy him, frustrate him, amuse him, delight him, electrify him, rouse him and warm him, all at the same time.

He just decided to rejoice in it.

As well as her giving in.

So he rolled off of her only to roll her to her belly and then roll right back on.

While he did this, she cried, "Stellan!"

"Open your legs," he commanded.

"Stellan," she whispered breathlessly.

"Do it, Simone."

She did.

His hips fell through.

"Reach up and grasp the edge of the bed," he ordered.

"Are you seriously going to fuck me again?" she asked.

"No. I'm *seriously* going to fuck you again," he answered, sliding a hand over her ass, and in.

Her body stilled.

Then melted.

His lovely, irritating, endearing, infuriating, enchanting Simone.

He put his lips to her ear as he glided a light caress over her clit, and she started trembling.

"We're going to celebrate your capitulation, darling."

"I'm down with that," she murmured huskily.

"Excellent," he replied, then nipped her earlobe. Her body jolted before her hips pushed up into his. "Hold onto the edge of the bed and don't let go," he repeated.

She did as told, asking, "Are we done talking?"

"If you'd like to share more of your mysteries while I fuck you, be my guest. But as for me, yes. I'm done talking."

He slid his hand back over her ass, her hip, and went in at the front just as he slid his cock in from behind.

And apparently, except for emitting a delicious sigh when she accepted his cock that heralded other such noises as she took her fucking, Simone was done talking too.

"Pardon?" Simone asked in his ear through the phone as Stellan walked down the hall to his office an hour and a half later.

"Dinner," he started to repeat what he'd inquired about ten seconds earlier. "What are we doing?"

"Uh . . ."

"Would you like to go out?" he asked.

"Can we talk about this later?'

"Is there something claiming your attention now?"

"Yes, I'm doing my hair."

He stopped dead outside Susan's office.

"I beg your pardon?" he queried.

"You called while I was doing my hair," she reiterated then asked, "Couldn't we have talked about this before you left?"

"You were in the shower when I left when you should have been in the shower with me, but I allowed you not to be since you passed out for a power nap after I gave you your third orgasm of the morning."

A member of his staff walked by him, a man who now had wide eyes, eyes that were trained on him but moved away immediately when he caught the look Stellan leveled at him.

"So no," he kept talking and again walking, "we couldn't, so now we are, and I'm curious to know why you doing your hair precludes us from making dinner plans."

"You put product in your hair," she stated.

"Yes," he agreed, smiling and tipping up his chin to Susan as he walked by her desk, heading to his office.

"You put it in your hands, whisk it through your hair, and the miracle that is the gloriousness of Stellan Lange takes over and it looks perfect. I was awake for *that*, so I watched. It was admittedly difficult because you did it standing in the bathroom wearing nothing but a towel, and your chest is hefty competition in the attention stakes, and normally, it would win out to you running your fingers through your hair, but not by much. I'm not so lucky. My situation requires product, roller brushes, hair dryers, more product, a lot of fiddling, a skilled hand at wielding hairspray, and *concentration* to make it look windswept and blow away and adorably fuckable."

Standing by his chair, he turned to face his desk, changing hands on his phone as he shrugged off his jacket, and he did all this smiling and replying, "We'll go out. I'll ask Susan to make a booking."

"Susan?"

"My assistant."

She sounded suspicious when she queried, "Does she look like a Victoria's Secret model?"

"She's lovely, married, one child down who I'm godfather to, one child on the way, and her father's a prick, so I danced the father-daughter dance with her at her wedding."

Simone said nothing.

"Darling?" he called.

Her voice was soft when she demanded, "Tell me when and where and what to wear and I'll be there."

"You'll be at home. We're going together."

"Tell me when and what to wear and I'll be home to get ready to go together," she amended.

He laughed quietly.

"Are you done distracting me from killer hair?" she asked.

After throwing his jacket around the back of his chair, Stellan sat in it but did it with his eyes on Susan, who had planted herself standing across from him at his desk with her arms crossed on her chest.

"Yes."

"Catch ya later, hot stuff."

"See you tonight, sweetheart."

He rang off and put his phone on his desk.

"So?" Susan demanded.

He grinned at her.

"You grinning like a lion lounging on the remains of his kill does not answer my question, Stellan," she pointed out.

"I'm thinking it actually does," he retorted.

"Stellan," she said warningly.

"Would you care to use more words to form your question?" he requested.

"You had your new girl who sends flowers and wears leather at your house for a big party with your sex friends, and I'd like to know how that went."

He often reconsidered the amount of sharing he did with his assistant.

And then he always shared with his assistant.

"She moved in over the weekend."

Her face grew pale.

Then she nearly screamed, "*Say what?*"

"It's fine," he noted calmly.

She slowly adjusted her body to stand in front of then aim her ass at the chair before his desk, landing with a plop on it.

Then she asked, "Have you lost your mind?"

"No," he answered.

"Stellan..." She drew in a breath. "Okay. No offense. You know. Okay? So, *you know.* You're the most intelligent man *I* know. By far. And don't ever tell Harry I said that. If you do, I'll deny it all the way to my grave. But you know. You know that about yourself, and you know I think that about you. So you also know you're a whale. A mark. Every female con artist's dream come true."

He sat back in his chair, rested his elbows on the arms, and linked his fingers together at his chest as he replied, "She's not that person, Susie, and I understand why you'd be concerned, but that's not Simone."

"You had one date, and she's moved in."

"Yes," he confirmed.

"Just saying, honey, no woman in her right mind would do that unless she's messed up, she wants something or she's up to something."

"It was my idea, and I had to talk her into it."

"I bet you did," she muttered, her concerned-thus-distracted focus falling to the top of his desk.

"Sue," he called.

She lifted her gaze to his.

"I know what I'm doing," he told her.

"But—"

"I want you to meet her. You and Harry and eventually Crosby."

She closed her mouth.

"She needs time. A week. Two. Then we'll set something up," he continued.

"This isn't you," she whispered.

She was right.

Then again, he'd never had Simone.

"Yesterday, she woke before me," he shared. "Went to her car and got a sketchpad. I startled her in the middle of drawing. I only saw seconds of it, but what I saw, she was drawing a graphic novel that seemed to feature a female superhero by the name of Sixx, the name she's given herself that everyone but me knows her as, who wears leather and looks like her, except scarred, facially, and to extremes."

"Oh God," she said softly.

"She became incredibly agitated and secretive, hiding it from me the minute she noticed I was there, and she used anger to conceal fear when I asked to see it and unwisely did not back off when she refused."

"Yes, Stellan, that wasn't too bright," she mumbled.

He smiled softly at her. "I eventually let it go, smoothed things over. But Susie, honey, she's not using me. She's terrified of me. And she's going to try everything she can to drive me away before life how she understands it takes me away or the life she leads takes her away from me."

"What if the life she leads takes her away from you?" she asked.

"It won't."

"What if it does?" she pushed.

"I won't allow it."

"You're pretty powerful, Stell, but you're not omnipotent. You can't control everything."

"I'm aware of that."

"So . . . if you lose her?"

He felt his face get hard, and it came out in his voice. "I won't."

She studied him closely and for some time until, hesitantly, she suggested, "Maybe there's a reason she protects people from her."

"She thinks there is. But I know there's definitely a reason she needs to stop doing that."

"We're all not broken and set on a course of self-destruction like Silie, honey," she pointed out gently, and cautiously. "But even if some of us are, if we're set on that course, no one could save us."

"I'm not saving my sister, Susie. I'm falling in love with the only woman I've ever met who fits me."

Her face turned melancholy. "I hope so."

"I know so. Meet her and you'll know too."

"You know I'll meet her. I'll be there with bells on, and I'll be hilarious and protective, and if she's falling in love with you too, she won't be able to stop herself from falling in love with me."

"She already loves me, Susan. She fell in love with me the minute she met me, probably then thinking I actually am omnipotent and the only person who could withstand the destruction she's convinced herself she's had some hand in that's followed in her wake." He grinned. "Now she's doing it because she's headstrong, smart as hell, and I'm the only person she can't bulldoze or freeze out with her personality. Not to mention we're exceptionally sexually compatible."

She lifted a hand, palm out his way. "TMI, boss man."

Sensing the course of their conversation had shifted, he took advantage.

"I believe I shocked Frank in the hall when he overheard me speaking to Simone and mentioning the three orgasms I gave her this morning."

"Please say it isn't so," she begged, clasping her hands to her chest to dramatize the words. "I won't be able to leave my office for a week. They'll all want the skinny."

He smiled.

And shrugged.

Eyes on him, suddenly she straightened in her chair.

Then she brightened.

"What?" he asked.

Finally, her expression calmed.

"You're happy," she declared.

"I am," he confirmed.

"Right. Good. Now I'm all set to meet her."

"We'll do that, but I need a booking tonight for her and me. Try Buck and Rider first."

As his cell on his desk rang, she stood, saying, "I'm on it, boss man."

He took up his phone, shot her a smile, and looked down at the display as Susan turned and moved to leave.

He sighed at what he saw on his phone, took the call, and lifted his eyes, watching Susan go while answering.

"Aryas."

"Got home yesterday, drove by your house to have a face-to-face, saw Sixx's Cayenne there, decided against it. So this has to be on the phone," he stated as the door closed behind Susan. "I hope you know what the fuck you're doing."

The news had made the rounds.

Not a surprise.

"Aryas—"

"She'd have my balls, she knew I was givin' this to you, but this isn't play, brother. Not for her. I want this, for both of you. I rode her ass to do somethin' about takin' it there with you. But you gotta know, it's not play. Not for Sixx. Are you feelin' me?"

"If you'll give me a second to speak, I can assure you I know that."

"Does Sixx know that?"

"Simone knows everything."

He heard Aryas pull in a sharp breath, and he knew why considering no one knew who "Simone" was.

Except Dillinger because he'd investigated her.

And, he now knew, Aryas.

Though he wondered if Simone knew that.

He wasn't going to ask.

"She moved in this weekend," Stellan shared.

"Oh fuck," Aryas muttered.

"She won't be moving out."

"That went fast," Aryas noted.

It didn't seem very fast to Stellan.

"Too fast," Aryas went on.

"It's as it needs to be," Stellan replied.

"She's sub, man," Aryas said quietly, like he was breaking a confidence.

Which he was.

"Just leave it at that," Stellan returned. "You go deeper in this conversation, she finds out, it would cause harm, and I'm trying to avoid that."

"She's also straight-up Domme."

"I'm aware of both."

"Yeah. Took her to the pit. Gave her a warrior. Got her a toy for your party." There was a pause when Stellan imagined Aryas was shaking his head before he said, "Fuck. I hope you know what you're doing."

Deciding it was best to change the subject, Stellan did that.

"I need a Mistress."

"Say again?" Aryas demanded.

"For the warrior I gave Simone. She wants to find someone for him that will work well with him, in a playroom and out. As she describes, someone who's not psycho-crazy in one zone or the other. My take is it would be something like Leenie gives to Dillinger, perhaps more hardcore, though I can't know how Dillinger likes it played. Do you have any suggestions?"

"You two are finding another Domme to be with the sub you got for Sixx to work?"

"Yes."

"You don't know what you're doing," he muttered.

"It's what she wants for him."

"And who's she gonna work, brother?" Aryas asked.

Stellan said nothing.

Aryas didn't let it go. "Those times she needs to work someone over, what's she gonna do?"

"We'll sort something out."

"You do know that we're talkin' about her and you. Her and *you*. How long's it gonna take before you can't take it anymore, Stellan, watchin' her do her thing with another guy?"

"*Our* thing is not even a week old, Aryas. So I'm a little focused on a number of other variables that take precedence. We'll deal with that when it happens."

"You're sure?"

He was finished with this conversation and thus moved to draw a line under it.

"I'll do anything to make her happy, so yes, Aryas, fuck yes. I am absolutely sure."

Aryas fell silent.

He also broke that silence.

"There's that story, the thorn in the paw," he began. "It may play that way for you, and I hope it does. But other side of that coin is the beast rips his healer's throat out. Have a care, my man, and I like you, I respect you, you're good people. But I love her. If you fuck this up, and she tears into your throat, it'll hurt like fuck, but you'll heal and move on. She'll never forgive herself. She'll never let anyone close again. And we'll all lose her forever."

Yes, Aryas knew far more than Simone thought he knew.

Before Stellan could form a reply, Aryas had dropped the line.

"Sage bastard," Stellan growled at his phone.

When he did, a beep came with a text that showed a tiny picture on his screen.

At the name, and the picture, he pulled it up.

There he stared at a selfie of Simone winking at the camera cheekily from behind a tempting, windswept hank of hair under which it said, **Adorably fuckable.**

And the conversations with Susan and Aryas were lost when Stellan burst out laughing.

He was still doing it as his finger moved over his phone.

He texted her back with *X*.

And then he saved the picture to Simone's contact and changed the name to "Adorably Fuckable."

That night, walking into Buck &Rider with Sixx wearing a white leather, body-skimming slip dress with a scooped neck, thin straps and a hemline to her knees paired with gray snakeskin pumps, he knew every man whose eyes followed her did not think she was adorably fuckable.

They thought she was just fuckable.

And he had never walked into anywhere with any woman on his arm feeling the way he was feeling escorting Simone to their table.

Like a lion roaming the savanna taking in his domain.

His father didn't understand this feeling.

He wanted it, even so far as convinced himself he had it, but deep down he knew he wasn't strong enough to earn it.

"Hey," she called after he seated her and took the chair at the angle to hers.

Stellan looked at her, saw his mark at her neck, and felt his cock stirring lazily at the memory of how it happened and the knowledge that every man whose eyes followed her to that table, every man who was surreptitiously watching them now, knew how she'd earned his mark.

As much as he liked that, he also saw her throat bare and decided to have collars custom-made just like the one she'd worn Saturday night, but in real rose gold. And yellow gold. And platinum.

"You okay?" she asked.

He took his napkin, shook it out, and put it on his lap.

Then he turned again to her.

"I'm never going to be my father," he announced.

Her chin jerked back into her neck, and her brows drew straight down like she'd personally been insulted.

"Of course you're not," she snapped.

His father didn't understand that kind of reaction either.

"Damn, I'm sorry, Stellan," she said quietly, reaching out and wrapping her fingers around the side of his hand. "The stuff that came up this morning is messing with—"

He turned his hand and gripped her fingers hard.

"It's not."

Her fingers gripped hard back.

And his father would never have that either.

"Then why are you talking about it?" she asked.

A server approached.

Stellan stared him down.

The server retreated.

Stellan looked back at Simone.

"My assistant means the world to me, and I'd like for us to have dinner with her and her husband, perhaps next week."

"Okay," she said hesitantly.

Whether her hesitancy came from the change of subject or his statement, it didn't matter.

She was meeting Susan, and they were done discussing his father.

"I order for you," he instructed. "Before the server returns, tell me what you want to drink, and before he comes back, tell me what you want to eat. You sit there owned by me tonight, darling."

Her fingers tensed in his, she wriggled a little on her seat, heat flared in her eyes, and she repeated, quieter this time, "Okay, baby."

He liked her response.

And he was very much looking forward to that weekend when he'd be breaking her into that part of their lives.

But they had other things to get straight.

"I asked Aryas to help us find Ami a Mistress. He's good for another session or two with you, but that's all, Simone. For his sake, you'll need to cut him loose. We'll find a way to meet that need for you, but you'll be losing Ami. You decide the when, you can have him in a playroom at the Honey with the blinds down or my playroom at home. Either way, I'll be with you. Watching."

"You have a playroom at your house?"

"I should have given you the full tour. I'll do that tonight when we return home."

She gave him her cat's smile, and again he didn't know if she was giving it because she wanted him to play with her there, or if she wanted to play there.

That didn't matter either.

"I'll be dismantling it, Simone. When I work you, the way I'll work you, it'll be in our home and in our bed. We've got the resources to assuage your alternate needs, and when we want a change of scenery, we have the resources to find that too."

She nodded and held fast to his hand, her expression turning searching.

"Stellan, are you sure you're okay?"

"Of course. There's no reason not to be. I'm a man who has everything," he replied.

"Seemingly," she returned. "But no one can have everything."

He stared her straight in the eye, squeezed her fingers tight, and repeated, "I'm a man who has everything."

She understood him, he knew, because her gaze grew warm, her face soft.

But her lips murmured, "God, you're impossible."

"How's that?"

"You know that happy you're so determined for me to have?" she asked.

"Yes."

"Well," she started like she was grousing, "I'm actually beginning to see the path, it *is* bright and cheery, which means you were right, within less than forty-eight hours, and that's annoying."

As he was finding he often did with Simone . . .

Stellan burst out laughing.

nine

A Force onto Him

SIXX

Sixx sat in her car, her digital camera with the long telephoto lens attached to it up and aimed.

Thus she took a variety of pictures of the man who was doing yardwork two houses down—mowing the lawn, blowing debris, bending, bagging and hefting the bags into the back of his truck.

When she had a number of snaps, she lowered the camera and muttered, "People are so stupid."

Particularly that man, who had taken yardwork-for-cash jobs when he was alternately suing his employer for supposed injuries on a manual labor job that left him physically unable to work, at the same time collecting disability checks from the government.

What was on her camera meant at least the lawsuit was over.

Now she needed to send the photos to the attorney on the case, check her email, and tie things up for the weekend.

And considering she didn't have a workspace at the firm, mostly since her work happened in the field, if she had to hook in she usually opened her laptop in a coffeehouse or bar somewhere. This was because she didn't have Wi-Fi at her "hovel."

But since she was done for the day, she decided she'd just go back to Stellan's and deal with everything (he *did* have Wi-Fi, and about a gazillion Wi-Fi extenders, so it was fast as a shot throughout the house). He'd be home soon anyway, and then they could have dinner, hang, fuck, sleep, and then . . .

She stilled her mind, set her camera on the passenger seat, and shifted the Cayenne into drive, putting her foot on the gas to head to Stellan's.

It was Friday.

The end of the best week of her life.

Bar none.

So much the best, it blasted everything out of the water.

Not that there was much competition.

It was just that living with Stellan was . . .

Sublime.

It was not a surprise the man was phenomenally talented in bed. She'd only seen him at play, but what she'd seen, the veneration in which his subs held him, that two and two definitely equaled four million, and the reality proved that.

But it wasn't that.

It was that he thought she was funny.

God, every time she made him laugh, she felt like a god, like she'd wrought some miracle.

He was happy. Happy to be with her.

She'd never made anyone happy in her entire life.

She was a definite smartass, so she'd had occasion to make people laugh.

But it was different with Stellan.

It moved her completely that she could give that to him.

It was . . . she couldn't describe it even in her head.

It just meant everything that she could make Stellan happy.

The rest, regardless of how much of it there was, and there was a lot, was frosting.

Not the sex. Sex with Stellan was definitely moist, rich, delicious cake.

But the rest felt like she was on a game show, and she'd jumped through all the hoops to win the million-dollar prize, and then the confetti dropped and the band played and she'd been told she'd also won the fabulous all-expenses-paid vacation to Italy, the new car *and* the yacht.

Seriously, he looked like he looked, dressed like he dressed, fucked like he fucked . . . and the man could cook *and* he liked to cook, but mostly, he liked to cook for her.

He also adored his assistant, spoke about her like she was a beloved member of his family, with humor and devotion in his voice and a look on his handsome face that Sixx felt pierce right through her heart (in a good way) and warm her down deep in her belly.

He further spoke with respect and amused affection about "M," (though Sixx had not seen Margarita since she arrived at the pool party, she'd seen the effects of her taking care of Stellan . . . and now Sixx).

There was also how attentive he was to Sixx. And how he didn't hide he found her fascinating. How he listened actively to anything she said, like he wasn't just interested but absorbing it, breathing it in like it was as essential as oxygen.

Not to mention she simply just loved watching him. He was comfortable and confident in any surroundings—his home, the restaurants he took her to, everywhere (she'd now had three "dates," if you included when they went to the pit, though two of them were dates where she went home with her date—Stellan liked to cook but he also liked to eat out).

And last, he could make a mean cocktail.

They hadn't gotten into anything heavy after their Monday morning together. He asked about her day and listened. She asked about his and definitely listened. He read, so she bought some ebooks for her laptop, and she read on opposite ends of the couch to him, their legs tangled. They cooked (or she sipped the cocktails he made her while he cooked, Sixx didn't cook if she could avoid it, and so far in her life, she'd been able to do that). They took night swims in his pool. They had lots and lots (and lots) of sex (including sex in the pool).

It was awesome.

It made her . . .

Happy.

But last night, while eating Stellan's astounding hamburgers (he even made hamburgers extraordinarily, the insides having homemade bacon bits, sautéed mushrooms and onions, and cheese, they were *incredible*), he'd told her that, "Your weekend of submitting to me, darling, will start Saturday morning, the minute you wake."

Tomorrow.

It was not lost on her that he'd been guiding her toward what would be happening over the weekend all through the week. He had a commanding personality naturally, but the things he said and expected of her were not entirely about that being simply a part of who he was. Not to mention, he'd tell her straight when he wanted her in her role, when he was slipping them into a modified scene, like he did at Buck &Rider when he took control of ordering for her.

She was not only a Domme who had worked subs; she'd been to a variety of sex clubs seeing other Doms work their subs.

And she'd seen Stellan work his.

But that was in a playroom at the Honey.

He'd told her he'd be dismantling the fully kitted, seriously-the-bomb playroom in his house because the way he'd work her would be "in our home and in our bed."

Sixx had no idea what that meant.

But it was making her nervous.

For a variety of reasons.

She forced herself not to think about it as she made the trek to Stellan's house, and then she had to force herself to buck up when she saw the Toyota Camry in the drive as she headed toward the four-car garage where she now parked her baby.

She suspected that Camry belonged to Margarita, and she suspected it had not been lost on Margarita that someone was sleeping with Stellan in his bed considering the fact the half of his closet that hadn't been filled was now full of leather and designer fabulousness and his clothes hamper had women's panties in it (as well as other things).

She parked in the garage next to Stellan's Maserati (when did something like that become part of her life?), took a breath, grabbed her workbag, her camera, and pulled herself out.

She was wearing a pair of loose-fitting, black leather short shorts and an oversized dark gray tank that dipped so low in the front it nearly showed cleavage, these with a pair of simple black T-strap sandals.

And for the first time in her life, she wondered what someone would think of her outfit (this did not count Stellan, she always wondered what he thought of what she wore, at the club, in a playroom, and especially recently—then again, recently, she was in no doubt. He could express a good deal of appreciation just using his eyes).

She hit the button to close up the garage and entered the house through the door that led to a laundry room that would bring many women to tears. The area offered so much counter space, cabinetry and mounted drying racks that even Sixx got excited when she saw it, and laundry was never exciting.

She came into the back hall that led to Stellan's home office, which was nicer than her boss's office-office, and bigger than her entire apartment (then again, nearly every room in Stellan's house was bigger than her apartment; there was a powder room on the lower level that wasn't, but that was it), a library, a game room and the door to what was very unusual for any home to have in Phoenix—a basement.

Along with a home theater (yup, he had a four-seat home-freaking-theater), a walk-in wine cellar and a lot of storage, Stellan's vast playroom was down there.

She hit the kitchen with some trepidation because she knew Margarita made the bed every day, dealt with the laundry, and tidied up breakfast dishes as well as kept the entire place spotless, so there was a possibility she could be anywhere, including the kitchen.

And Stellan respected and adored her, and thus Sixx felt the bizarre need for Margarita at least to respect and like Sixx.

She wasn't even letting herself think about meeting Stellan's assistant, Susan, and her husband, Harry.

The only good first impression she'd ever cared she'd make was getting the man behind the money who was hiring her for a job to do just that.

She'd never had to make people like her.

She didn't know how to do it.

And Margarita was a Mexican-American grandmother who had the opportunity to see Sixx's entire collection of leather, knew she'd moved in and was sleeping out of wedlock with Margarita's employer (though, Stellan shared, he kept the playroom under lock and key, and Margarita did not have that particular key).

She didn't think that was a good first impression already.

"Sixx!" Margarita exclaimed when she saw her.

"Hey there, Margarita," Sixx replied with a nervous, forced smile, seeing Stellan's kitchen counters were littered with burlap grocery bags in various stages of unpacking.

"I just got back from the grocery," Margarita declared unnecessarily.

Sixx dropped her camera and workbag on the counter. "Yes, I see."

Margarita grabbed a package of strawberries and a bag of Bing cherries and headed to the fridge. "Stellan said you're in all weekend, so I got you covered."

"That's cool," Sixx replied, trying to read anything on her that might be negative, but all she seemed was to be happily buzzing along in her duties. "Can I help?" she asked.

"Nope. I mean, if you want," Margarita came out of the fridge and shot her a smile, "but you don't have to." Her eyes fell on Sixx's expensive camera and came back to Sixx. "Are you a photographer?"

She shook her head. "Investigator."

Margarita's eyes got so big that they made Sixx give her a genuine smile.

"Like, a detective?"

"Sort of. I'm the in-house investigator for a law firm. If they have a case that needs someone to do some digging, I do that digging."

"*Interesting*," Margarita said, like she found it just that and then some.

Sixx's lips quirked. "It actually is."

Margarita's face suddenly fell as her gaze went back to the camera. "Do you," she turned her eyes again to Sixx, "have to take pictures of unsavory things?"

She nodded. "It's a bummer but yes. Sometimes. I can't share what I got snaps of today, it's all confidential. But at least today's work wasn't icky."

Margarita started chuckling, loading her arms with tortilla chips, boxes of crackers and a bottle of fat olives before heading to the pantry, muttering, "Icky."

"If you're down with putting all this away, I need to send these snaps into the office, but seriously, if you need help, I'm in, and the snaps can wait," Sixx called after her when Margarita disappeared into the large walk-in pantry lined with shelves and cabinets with countertops that she kept stocked with pretty much everything.

"I'm down with doing this," Margarita called back. "I won't be long, and then I'll be out of your hair."

"You're not in my hair," Sixx started with a loud voice but ended it normal when Margarita came back. "And, uh . . ." How did one do something like this? "If you, well . . ."

Margarita stopped moving and looked to Sixx after pulling two bottles of Hendrick's out of a burlap bag.

Two bottles.

Guess she didn't want them running out.

Or Sixx was enjoying too many of Stellan's excellent mixology skills.

"If I what?" Margarita prompted.

"Need me to . . . you know, do anything. To make things easier on you. What with me being here with Stellan now and—"

She interrupted. "It's my job to make things easier on *you*."

"It's that for Stellan but—"

"No, Sixx. I take care of Stellan, and this household. In other words, I take care of anything important to Stellan that revolves around this household. And since you're here, and you would not be if you weren't important to Stellan, I take care of you too."

That was sweet.

But . . .

"I can make the bed in the morning," Sixx offered. "And he told me you, well . . . get on him about it, so I can make sure Stellan hits the laundry hamper, which I noticed he's not wont to do."

Or even get close.

The man dropped his clothes where they hit and that was that, even if it was rooms away.

She didn't get all she said out before Margarita shouted with laughter.

Sixx didn't know what made her laugh so hard, so she just stood there, smiling that confused smile people who weren't in on the joke smiled, waiting to be let in on the joke.

"*Querida*," Margarita began after she quit yukking it up, "the only thing I beg you to do is *not* take care of the things I do for Stellan . . . and you. What excuse would I have to keep an eye on him if you made the bed and got him to hit the laundry hamper, which could grow to you doing his laundry and then the shopping and then where would he be? Considering the state of the individual who calls herself his mother, someone has to . . ."

She trailed off when she took in the look that hit Sixx's face.

The state of the individual who calls herself his mother?

When Sixx had done her deep dive, she'd seen pictures of Brigette Lange. Older ones where she was startlingly beautiful and hanging on the arm of the then-handsome Andreas Lange—the heir to a hotel empire and the beauty who'd caught his eye.

She'd also seen pictures that were not recent but were more recent than those. Pictures of a woman still retaining her beauty even if it looked like a veil that did not conceal the haggard wasteland of the grief of a woman who'd lost her young daughter to suicide.

She hadn't dug deeper than that into Brigette. It was enough to learn what befell Silie Lange and the public disintegration of any kind of relationship Andreas had with his son after they lost Silie and it came to light precisely *why*.

"He hasn't spoken of her," Margarita noted in a horrified whisper.

"We're still getting to know each other," Sixx replied, saw the expression on Margarita's face and quickly assured, "There's much that's difficult for both of us to share. We're . . . it's too much, Margarita. We're parceling it out. But he will tell me. He's honest about everything. So you shouldn't worry you broke a confidence. It's just that we've known each other for years, but what we have is relatively new, and we haven't gotten around to certain . . . details."

Margarita was nodding repeatedly, but Sixx could still see she was shaken.

"I'm glad he has you," Sixx said quietly, and Margarita's troubled gaze came to her. "I won't make the bed, and I'll let him drop his clothes to the floor, so he'll be sure to keep you. But honestly, I hope you know he'd do that anyway, even if he had to unmake a bed I made so he'd have the excuse."

Margarita's head tipped to the side.

"Did you ever expect to have a woman thanking you for not making your bed?" she asked unsteadily, trying to inject humor into what had become heavy.

"No. Then again, I never expected to live in a house where someone comes in every day to make the bed, so lately, my life has been full of surprises."

Margarita gave her a tremulous smile.

Sixx's return smile was steady.

"If there's anything you'd like . . . I know what Stellan likes, and he has Susan call with any additions. But if there are things you want to have around or things you like to cook . . ." Margarita offered.

"I hate to give you a poor impression of me, but I never learned to cook because I never had the desire to learn, and thankfully, God offered frozen dinners and microwaves and fast food, so I don't go hungry."

Margarita looked alarmed until Sixx finished what she was saying.

"But the only thing I want around is Stellan, and since he lives here, does the cooking and likes doing that, I'm good."

"Can I admit something to you?" Margarita asked abruptly.

"I'm feeling like breaking open the gin, getting us both sloshed, but before that texting Stellan to warn him he's going to have to drive you home. So since we're here, we might as well go for it."

"If I were to have guessed who he'd pick, it would not be a woman like you."

Damn.

Sixx fought stepping away or even turning away to hide how deep that stung.

"But after I saw you, I thought about it, and now that I know more about you, I think you're perfect," Margarita went on. "He is nowhere near your average man, so why on earth would he choose an average woman?"

Why on earth would he choose an average woman?

"Margarita," Sixx whispered, not knowing what to say, not even knowing how she was feeling.

Just that it was good.

The woman nodded smartly. "She'd need to be unique. Individual. A force onto herself *and* him. Exciting and daring and beyond the pale. Someone who has an interesting job and wears leather shorts in Phoenix in the summertime, looking like a Hollywood starlet." She kept firm hold on Sixx's gaze. "And someone who would also offer to make the bed to make things easier on me."

"When I saw your car, I was worried coming in here," Sixx

admitted. "When Stellan talks about you, I can tell how much he cares about you, and I really wanted you to like me."

"Well then, mission accomplished, Sixx," Margarita replied, back to her bright smile.

"Simone," Sixx blurted.

Margarita appeared confused. "I'm sorry?"

"People I . . . I mean, I'm known by everyone as Sixx. Except Stellan. He . . . I'm Simone to him. That is, I'm Simone. That's my name. But . . ."

Saving her, Margarita said firmly, "Simone."

Sixx cleared her throat, then asked, "Do you drink gin?"

"I drink wine and I drink tequila, and I have a husband who will come and get me if I drink too much of either. So you send your pictures, and I'll finish up here, and we'll share a drink. And if that becomes two, I'll call Ernesto, and all will be well."

Sixx grinned at her. "Cool. Be back in a bit."

"See you in a bit."

Sixx grabbed her workbag and camera and headed for Stellan's office, pulling her phone out as she went.

She sat at his desk and texted, I invited Margarita to stay for a drink when she's done doing her thing. Cool?

She'd powered up and was loading the pictures on her laptop when his reply came back.

Cool. X

Stellan was not a verbose texter. He got the job done and that was it.

But that was his thing.

X.

Sometimes that would be his only reply.

X.

Sending her a kiss.

So Sixx thought he really didn't need to say much else.

That was all she needed.

✻   ✻   ✻

"I'm not sure how Ernesto feels about my girlfriend liquoring up his wife."

Sixx was sitting at Stellan's island, watching him cut up cucumbers that he was apparently going to throw into a salad made of corn he'd grilled on his restaurant-quality stove, chickpeas, mint, oil, lime juice and, obviously, cucumbers.

"I'll admit, things got out of hand," she mumbled into her muddled gin. She took a sip, swallowed, and finished, "But only because she's a lightweight."

Stellan shot a megawatt smile at her.

He had amazing teeth.

And he'd called her his girlfriend.

Did men like Stellan Lange have girlfriends?

It was he who called it.

So she guessed they did.

And that was her.

Seriously.

How was this happening?

When he tossed the cucumber in, mixed it all up, put it in the fridge, and went back to the tuna steaks, she tried to sound casual as she noted, "You've mentioned your dad, but you never speak of your mom."

He didn't look up from whatever he was doing to the tuna as he murmured, "Ah, so M has a big mouth when she sips tequila."

He didn't appear tense or pissed or hesitant, so Sixx kept at it.

But she did it covering for Margarita.

"She let something slip, freaked, I moved her past it, but she didn't really say anything."

He stopped with the tuna, put the heels of his palms to the counter, and looked to her.

"What did she say?"

"She just mentioned her."

"How?"

Sixx lowered her voice and replied, "If you don't want to talk about this, Stellan, that's totally all right."

"She's a bitter alcoholic who's managed to burn through the enormous settlement she obtained from my father, the healthy additions I've given her in the interim and, regularly, prior to the end of the month, the monthly alimony she still receives. Thus prompting my healthy additions. She's the reason his prenups are extreme. He's still supporting her and her excruciatingly slow commission of suicide, but this isn't why he chafes against it. He simply wishes she'd fade from memory. He's not a fan of being confronted with his failures since he vastly prefers kidding himself that he doesn't have any."

"Baby," Sixx whispered.

"I understand her bitterness," he carried on, seemingly effortlessly. "I even understand her addiction. She adored my father. In early years, I remember us all being very happy. However, I think she got a wrinkle, and his love for her died. She was completely unprepared. She thought she'd live the fairy tale forever. And she couldn't ever imagine how that nightmare would turn into something darker than anyone could believe."

"I shouldn't have brought it up," Sixx stated quickly when he paused in speaking.

"Why not?" Stellan asked. "We're getting to know each other. This is part of my life. A part of my life that you'll discover, and with something like that you should be prepared."

"So maybe—" she tried.

But he kept going.

"She lives in a beautiful home outside Sedona. She meditates and wears clothes that appear to be crafted solely out of scarves. She has Tibetan prayer bells installed in her garden, and she drinks three bottles of wine a night and can lapse into rages about a marriage that ended thirty years ago like she just discovered her husband was unfaithful the moment before. She comes down too often and stays with me. When she does, she sits cross-legged by the pool on a Buddhist rug to balance her chi. Later I'll have to assist her to bed because if I don't, I'm not certain she'll make it to her room without injury. She's delighted I have not married, or even become serious with a woman, because she's convinced I'll destroy their life, like my father did before me. And if you told her she thought that, she would be stunned and affronted. However, halfway into bottle of wine number two, she would not be able to stop running her mouth about that very thing."

When he stopped speaking, without anything else to say, Sixx said, "I'm so sorry."

"I am too," he agreed. "I remember her as beautiful and full of life, in love with her husband, and she adored her children. Besotted with us. It was unfortunate the bitterness settled in with permanency quickly, so even Silie lived it. Obviously, I cannot know what was happening in my sister's head when she made the decision she made. And obviously, I've thought of it often since she made it. But I think it was not simply due to the fact she'd been raped by what amounted to a member of our family. It was that after she was, with her mother that bitter, already twisted, completely self-involved and so far down the path to alcoholism there was no turning back, Silie had no one to turn to."

"Except you," Sixx whispered.

He nodded once. "Except me, and your sixteen-year-old brother is not the confidant needed to deal with something that hideously ugly. I did my best, but it was never going to be good enough."

In that moment Sixx was unfairly and irrationally angry at Silie Lange.

Because she *hated* that Stellan *ever* thought he wouldn't be good enough at *anything*.

"Really, I'm so, *so* sorry I made you speak of these things, baby," she said gently.

And when she did, he pinned her with his blue stare and returned, "I speak openly of them, Simone. I do not bury it. I do not hide it. I do not ever attempt to convince myself that it did not affect me, alter me, and those for the worse. I miss my sister. I mourn the life she could have had. I miss the mother and father I knew when I was young because they've both died as sure as Silie is gone. It is a fact of my life. It is part of what's made me. I don't turn away from it. I face it. I do that even if there's no lesson to learn from it. No desperate silver lining to try to wrench from it. Every human being on this earth experiences heinous things. Some less extreme. Some so extreme, they're unimaginable. If there's a meaning to this life, that's it. You find a way to deal or you die, whether by making yourself stop breathing or living a life not worth living."

Sixx looked to her glass before she took a healthy sip.

"That's not an indictment, darling," he said softly.

She turned her gaze to the pool.

"Some of us do the best we can do," he continued.

She cut her eyes to him and looked him up and down, from lean waist to fabulous head of thick, beautiful hair in his stunning kitchen in his Phoenician mansion.

"And some of us do better," she returned.

"I found my sister dead in a garage. That marked me. I have a weak father and an equally weak mother, and that marked me too. I did not watch my parents get murdered and do it miraculously surviving a bloodbath. After what you've endured, the fact that you're not a junkie, or a prostitute, or a drug dealer, or anything but the magnificent creature you've formed yourself into being is frankly no less than a miracle."

Okay, she hated she put him through that.

But now she *really* wished she hadn't brought it up.

"Are you going to cook that tuna or—?" she began.

"You couldn't have saved them," he stated.

"I know that," she snapped.

"I'm not talking about your parents."

Sixx actually *felt* her face pale.

Oh God.

Oh no.

God.

He knew *everything*.

She threw back the rest of her drink.

"They made their choices," Stellan kept after her.

She glared at him.

"You are not responsible for those choices," he declared.

"They were my friends," she clipped.

He raised his brows. "Did you inject them with your uncle's heroin?"

"Now we need to stop talking about this," she bit out.

"No we don't," he returned smoothly.

"I'm sorry I mentioned your mother. I'm sorry it brought up your father and your sister. But in this getting-to-know-you thing we have going on, I'm not ready for this."

"Will you ever be?" he asked.

"Absolutely not," she stated clearly.

"Then now's as good a time as any," he fired back.

"Right then, did Dillinger tell you their parents didn't let me go to their funerals?" she queried.

"No. But I'm not surprised. They needed someone to blame. So they blamed a seventeen-year-old girl who had nothing to do with it."

"He was *my* uncle, Stellan."

Abruptly his face got hard, and he leaned toward her, grinding out, "Simone, you weren't even fucking *there*. He was known as a charmer. He was good-looking. He'd had two counts of statutory rape dropped on him, according to conjecture by the police, because he'd bought off the parents. He was known to party with young girls, give them drugs, get them hooked as clients and available bodies. Your two friends had been there repeatedly without you being there before he fed them tainted heroin. *Repeatedly.* Other kids at your school said they were your friends for the sole purpose of spending time with him to get access to his drugs and his attentions. Did you know that when it happened?"

She shook her head. "Of course not."

"You just had friends over from school like any girl does, not having any clue they were using you."

"I should have known."

"How?"

"Because that was my life, Stellan, and it might have been all I knew, but I still knew it was wrong. I just had to pretend. I had to pretend I could be normal and do normal things."

"And that's wrong?" he pushed.

"I should have protected them!" she snapped loudly.

"You were no more than a child. It wasn't your job."

"I was their friend, so yes, maybe they were using me, but I didn't know that, and it doesn't matter. *I* thought *I* was *their* friend, so you are one hundred percent *wrong*. It *was* my job."

"I understand you think that, Simone, but how could you do that when you weren't even *there*?"

She looked away.

"Look at me," he ordered.

"Fuck you," she spat.

"Darling, look at me," he called gently.

She looked at him and yelled, *"Fuck you!"*

"Come here," he murmured.

She put her glass down and slid off her stool, sneering at him. "No. You can't be sweet Stellan now. Hold up the mirror and show me how it really is, then pull it away and try to weave your spell to make me think it looks different. It's never different, Stellan. Never. And this shit . . ." She twirled her hand in the air. "It's done. I'm going to take a ride. I'll come back and get my stuff sometime over the weekend."

She started to walk away, but of course she didn't get very far.

Stellan barred her path.

She stopped and looked up at him, her voice vibrating its warning. "I will seriously land you on your ass if you don't get out of my way."

"You promised not to leave no matter the reason," he replied.

Tricky bastard.

With that talk about his family, she'd fallen right into his hands.

She'd even brought it up.

"Apparently I lied," she retorted.

She went to sidestep him, and he moved in front of her.

Her eyes caught his, she smiled without humor and noted, "Last warning, baby."

"If you leave me, all will be lost," he declared.

"No shit?" she asked.

"There isn't another for me."

"Oh there is, handsome," she stated snidely. "Just open up your wallet or waltz into the Honey and they'll be lining up."

He lifted his brows again. "Is that what you want for me?"

No.

The thought of Stellan having someone who wasn't unique. Individual. Exciting. Daring. A force onto *him*.

No.

She didn't want that.

It killed her to even think about that.

But she was done with this.

"Get out of my way," she hissed.

"No."

"Stellan," she growled.

"If you're correct, and you can land me on my ass, that would sting my pride. If you walked out on me, I survived my parents, my sister killing herself, but honest to Christ, Simone, in just one week of having you by my side, I have real fear that would destroy me."

Sixx went solid.

And Stellan went in for the kill.

"You make me laugh, honey. Even Susan, who was dead set to think you were taking me for a ride, or at the very least would put me through the emotional wringer, got over it when she saw I'd found someone who made me happy. It had not occurred to me in my life of plenty that I was missing anything, but I've learned I was. I started this in an attempt to make *you* happy. What I'm discovering is that it's happening the other way around."

His beloved assistant saw it.

She saw that Sixx was making him happy.

She was making him *happy*.

Sixx looked at his throat.

She looked at the buttons of the shirt on his broad chest.

She looked over his shoulder.

She made a decision.

Then she looked to him.

"I can't talk about that anymore," she whispered.

"We'll leave it for now," he whispered back.

Still whispering, she said, "I want this. I want us."

"I know you do."

"You're going to have to be patient with me. I'm not used to anyone giving a shit."

"It breaks me, but I know that too."

"I also don't have anyone . . ." She swallowed. "I don't have anyone who's glad I found someone that makes me happy."

"You do."

"Just you."

"That's not true. There are many of them, Simone. You just haven't noticed, and you also haven't let them in."

She couldn't do that now either.

"I watched my mother—"

His normally silken voice sounded hoarse in beautiful and terrible ways when he cut her off. "I know."

"It was my father who got in front of me."

"Stop it for now and please come here."

Sixx went there.

Stellan folded her in his arms.

She wrapped hers around him and pressed deep.

He held her tight.

"You're going to have to give me time," she said.

"All right, darling."

"After dinner, I'm going to need—"

"Take your sketchpads wherever you wish. I'll be somewhere else, and you can come to me when you're ready."

She closed her eyes tight.

And he thought she deserved him?

How could that be?

"I'm sorry," she murmured.

"Don't be," he said into the top of her hair.

"So yes," she cleared her throat, "there we go. We're both royally fucked up."

"Royally," he agreed.

"You might be gorgeous and rich and able to cook and have a way with hiring household staff that are awesome because Margarita is just awesome, but when she's tipsy, she's hilarious-awesome, but in the royally-fucked-up stakes, I totally beat you."

His body moved with silent laughter.

It was the best feeling in the world.

She tipped her head back, and when she did, she found him looking down at her.

Just amazing.

"Are you going to feed me?" she prompted.

"Whatever you need."

That was Stellan.

Whatever she needed.

Sixx got up on her toes and pressed her lips to his.

He bent into her, taking her back to the soles of her feet, and took the kiss deep.

When he'd used his mouth to fill her up with all things Stellan Lange, he led her back to the kitchen, made her another drink, and finished cooking their meal.

After they ate, she took her sketchpads to the library and saved the day on paper in ways she could never have done in real life.

When she was ready, she found Stellan.

And he was right where she needed him to be.

ten

Pondering

SIXX

Sixx woke up the next morning to find she was alone in bed.

She sat up, looked around the room, and saw she was just plain alone.

This was a surprise. She and Stellan had had a heavy night the night before, but they'd ended it together, that day heralded them adding a new level to their relationship, and she thought Stellan would want to start that right off the bat.

And she had to admit, she wanted him to start it right off the bat.

She was nervous (her—*Sixx*—frigging *nervous*).

But she was also curious . . . in that sexually-stirred-up-in-a-good-way kind of way.

She threw the covers off, pulled herself out of bed, and padded through one of the archways to Stellan's luxurious master bath (he had chandeliers and columns in there too, not to mention a flat-screen mounted on the wall).

She stopped when, on the vanity by the sink she used, she saw the glossy cream box with the frosty-blue satin bow. This was sitting on top of what looked like the white linen shirt Stellan had worn at the pool party last weekend. And both of these were beside a full mug of coffee that was resting on one of those individual coffee warmers.

She moved toward it and saw there was a thick-stock notecard sitting on it embossed at the top with Stellan Petter Lange.

Of course the man didn't just dash something off on a scratch pad.

Always class with Stellan.

She smiled before she even picked the thing up.

Written on it, it said,

S-
Come down wearing this, darling.
I want you adorably fuckable.
-S

Well, that explained him not being in the bedroom.

Sixx felt butterflies hit her stomach.

Actual butterflies.

And they got worse when she opened the box to find an extraordinary set of pale yellow lace underwear. The lace was divine. The demi-cup bra exquisite. The panties a wide strip of lace across the hips with just a narrow gusset between the legs. And they were the perfect size.

She figured "adorably fuckable" meant he wanted her prettied up (in the way Sixx could get prettied up) and good to go for the day. Therefore she took a shower, gave herself a close shave, lotioned up, did a light makeup thing and a full hair thing, all of this while sipping coffee.

She donned the underwear that even felt like sheer decadence, shrugged on the shirt, and took her empty coffee mug down with her.

She saw Stellan was out on the patio, back to the doors, eyes to the pool, cell to his ear.

The heat had finally hit, and Phoenix was experiencing upper

90s/low 100s days, but that wasn't the reason Stellan was out there with his broad shoulders bare.

She saw his legs covered in a pair of the loose-fitting, knit, masculine lounge pants he wore when he was working a sub (that was, he wore them when he was wearing anything, it was either those pants, or when play had reached a certain point, nude).

She knew what those pants meant considering he slept naked.

A tremor shivering up her inner thighs, she set down her mug in the kitchen and moved out the door to the patio.

The instant he heard her approach, he turned and looked over his shoulder at her.

And the instant he did that, it took everything she had not to stop dead in order to put everything she had into memorizing that moment right there.

Mostly Stellan wearing her favorite look: at his home, relaxed, in his element, surrounded by all he'd wrought, his hair not styled to project the man he was out in the world, his suits in his closet.

No, right there with his dark hair falling on his forehead, messy from sleep and making love before he did that, face relaxed, dark blue eyes soft and content and admiring and pointed toward her. He could give her diamonds and pearls and entire islands, but the best gift she'd ever receive was him sitting there, looking at her just . . . like . . . *that*.

He tipped up his chin indicating he wanted her to come to him.

But she was already going to him. She would have gone to him if getting there meant going to the ends of the earth and she had to do it slaying dragons and battling trolls.

And when she arrived at his side, he kept his head back, his eyes falling to her mouth, telling her what else he wanted.

But Sixx would have dropped to touch her lips to his even if she knew, prior to doing it, it would be the last thing she'd do in her life.

This is love, she thought, feeling his soft lips light against hers and adoring the feel. *I'm in love.*

When she moved an inch away, thrown by her realization, she stopped only because he'd caught her at the back of the neck.

Up close, Sixx looked in his eyes and realized that was the last thing she wanted to see before she took her final breath.

Stellan looking at her, completely content because he woke up in a home where she would wake up and find him.

"One moment," he said into his cell, then immediately to her, not covering up his phone, not giving that first shit whoever was on the other line heard him, he said, "Good morning, darling."

"Morning, baby," she whispered, her voice throaty with the realization that had just dawned, but as thick as her throat was, for once in her life, her mind was crystal clear.

He pulled her to him to brush her lips against his again before he let her go and indicated with a tip of his head the chair he wanted her to sit in.

Sixx moved there, lowering herself in the patio chair Stellan had angled facing his.

After she sat, he bent forward and did it deep, sweeping her feet up into his lap by hooking his forearm around her ankles. He then sat back, resumed his conversation, and did it one-handed massaging her foot.

"I'd wanted it taken care of yesterday, it wasn't," he said into the phone. "And we'll discuss how I feel about that on Monday. For now, you've taken enough of my weekend. My woman is awake. We're done talking." He paused, listened briefly, then said, "Monday."

And that was obviously that because he pressed his thumb on the screen, tossed the phone on the table, and looked at Sixx.

"Sleep well?" he asked.

She nodded.

He engaged his other hand to massage her foot.

Heaven.

My woman is awake. We're done talking.

Lord, she'd fallen in love with him. Not from-afar love that was mostly deep, abiding fascination but in the end really just a crush.

No, it was real-life, sitting opposite him with your feet in his lap wearing beautiful underwear he bought you after a night where you had an ugly emotional row while discussing viciously painful parts of your past but you ended it cuddling, then making love, then sleeping in each other's arms, only to wake up to a foot rub . . . *love*.

"You all right?" he asked.

Was she?

Was she all right?

Was she like he'd looked when he'd peered over his shoulder at her? Content. Relaxed. Quietly . . . *happy*.

Or was that crystal clear of her mind a tactic to hold at bay other thoughts that wanted to crowd in? Terrifying thoughts. Thoughts about how perfect this moment was, how it and the last week and even how Stellan had ended their discussion last night had been everything any girl could ever want—but she was not that girl who got what she wanted.

She was that girl who'd been born to nothing and worked her way to having a bunch of leather and designer gear, one (and a half, as she counted Carlo) true friends, and a lot more of nothing.

"Simone?" he prompted.

"I'm good," she replied, swallowing instead of clearing her throat when it came out husky.

He gave her a gorgeous, understanding smile, and she wondered what he understood (and was worried about it) as he moved his hands to her other foot.

"Not after last night," he declared.

"Pardon?" she asked, for her part, totally not understanding.

"We're not playing," he explained. "Not after last night. We need some time to just be. Be with each other. Clear our heads. Let that go. If you like, we can have a session tomorrow. But now . . . no."

Yes.

God yes.

She was in love with him.

She needed to clear her head.

She'd never really done it, but it sounded heavenly to just . . . be.

That said, what was with the underwear?

"So the yellow lace is a non-starter?" she asked.

He shook his head. "I did buy it for you to wear while I played with you, but now it's just a gift. Though I put it out as I did to see how you'd respond. And considering it was a sort of test, I'm pleased to note that you passed."

Deciding for now just to live in the moment, this glorious moment, Sixx kicked playfully at his hands, doing it so he wouldn't stop because she never wanted him to stop as she shot him a fake-annoyed look that totally didn't work since she was also grinning.

He grinned back, dug his fingers in at the arch of her foot, she bit back a moan, and he asked, "Do you want more coffee?"

She focused her gaze on him, and she was no longer grinning.

"If you want to play, baby, I want to play," she said quietly.

That was awarded with a sexy flash in his eyes, but he shook his head again.

"I love that, sweetheart," he replied in her same tone. "And if you're there, I'm thrilled. We'll have our session tomorrow. But this morning, I'll get you some coffee and bring out some breakfast. We can then go to a movie or go downstairs and spend all day watching them here. I have an extensive library, or it's set up to get anything online we might want to see. Or we can go to the Botanical Gardens or instead, to Papago and walk the loop. We can also just put on our suits, get our books and have a lazy day by the pool. Your choice."

Her choice.

Even when she was wearing underwear he'd told her to put on or he was ordering for her at a restaurant, it was her choice.

She had a feeling if she lived the dream of a life where he was in it for decades, in one way or another everything would be her choice.

Which would be his choice.

Okay, yes.

Her mind was no longer crystal clear.

She was terrified.

She was also Sixx.

And Simone might fall apart (she wouldn't know, she'd never allowed Simone to handle anything too intense . . . or anything at all).

But Sixx . . .

Now Sixx could handle anything.

At least until it was time to bail—however that bailing needed to be to protect herself, protect Simone.

Or in this case, to protect Stellan.

In the meantime, he had to know.

And before she chickened out, she had to tell him.

"You make me happy too," she blurted.

His fingers dug in at the ball of her foot.

"You should know that," she said when he said nothing. "And the biggest part of that is knowing that I give it to you."

His dark look and the dark words that came after did beautiful things to her.

"Get up, bend over the table, lift my shirt to your waist and pull your panties down to your thighs."

She was frozen in the beauty.

"I thought we weren't playing," she whispered.

"We're not," he replied smoothly. "We're fucking. Or I'm fucking you. Now do as you're told, Simone."

She did as she was told, wet and ready for him before he moved in behind her, placed a hand firm on the small of her back, the other curled around her hip, and drove his cock inside.

Instantly, she was lost in him, happily lost being filled with him, connected to him, *one* with him, and that didn't change when he started thrusting and ordered, "You don't come. You're bent over and on offer for me, darling. If you earn it, I'll let you come tomorrow."

God, *beauty.*

"This isn't playing?" she asked, her voice wispy.

"You'll understand the difference," he answered, pounded in, stayed in, ground in, waited for her moan, and finished, "tomorrow."

Sixx said no more.

She let him use her. She got off on letting him use her. She thrilled at beating back her own response while listening to him build his. Holding steady, pulsing tight around him to give him more, listening to his soft sigh but feeling his thrusts intensify as he came inside her, and glorying in the invasive caress that was him slipping in and out as he came down.

He slid all the way in and bent over her to say softly, "Breakfast then movies here. You get one pick. I get one pick. And we'll agree on a pick. Then we'll have a nice dinner out here by the pool."

That sounded like the perfect day.

She started counting.

Now she was at seven perfect days. Seven. The first seven of her imperfect life.

"Works for me," she murmured, eyes closed, feeling his breath at her neck, his chest warm against her back, his cock still buried deep, not caring even a little that her clit was buzzing, her nipples tingling, her thighs quivering with the aftermath of holding back an orgasm.

Because she'd given him his.

And honest to God, that was all she needed.

Sixx moved down the hallway toward Stellan's office.

It was later. After their movie spree in his at-home theater. After they'd gorged on snack food and she'd made him watch *Man on Fire*, he'd made her watch *No Country for Old Men*, and thus feeling in a Coen Brothers mood, they'd ended it watching *Fargo*. After that, they'd trudged back up for Stellan to start dinner only to get interrupted by a phone call, "I really can't ignore it, sweetheart. Back in a bit."

He'd then taken off, leaving things happening in the kitchen, and since Sixx knew nothing about what happened in a kitchen, she went off to find him to ask about what she should do with the stuff he left happening in the kitchen.

She didn't think he'd mind if she interrupted him.

She was getting the feeling he wouldn't mind anything when it came to her.

But she didn't make it to his office.

Because he was in the library.

Sixx was still in the yellow underwear and his shirt. He was still only wearing his lounge pants. That day was a day of togetherness and decadence, and she was wearing makeup, but other than that, for both of them, the day had been all about the chill.

Until she saw him standing in the library, his tan, muscled back to her, the span of those broad shoulders, his amazing ass encased in those beautifully fitting lounge pants, one arm up and cocked, hand holding the phone to his ear, head turned, looking down, one arm out, finger touching the cover of her sketchpad.

Sixx stopped moving.

She also stopped breathing.

That sketchpad was one of twelve. The other eleven were filled from cover to cover with all the foul shit she'd seen, she'd done, she'd heard bragged about, she'd heard whispered about. From when she was a little girl and her first living memory was watching her mother stitch up a gunshot graze on her father's thigh in their tiny kitchen, a wound he got for reasons she was too young to ever know, to various incarnations of her saving that little girl, doing all the things she had to do to keep her safe and protected and innocent and loved.

Sixx was the one who'd seen all those things, not Simone.

Sixx was the one who'd done all those things so Simone wouldn't have to.

Heard the things.

Lived the things.

Every adventure left a scar on Sixx that would never heal. All over fictional Sixx's body—her back, chest, legs, arms, face—there were scars.

Fictional Sixx in her sketchpads was a walking healed wound, a miracle of a still-existing, still-ready-for-the-fight hero, even after what she'd endured, determined to keep going because if she didn't, Simone would have to face those realities.

And standing in the hall, having padded there unnoticed on bare feet, she saw in his profile precisely how badly Stellan wanted to open that sketchbook. Open the cover that opened the window to her psyche, exposing everything, exposing the entirety of the mess he'd taken on, exposing the wounds that were inflicted deep down inside that could never heal.

She almost cried out, screamed, stomped in and demanded to know what the fuck he was doing.

She didn't because Stellan skated his fingers across the cover of the pad then turned away, moving to the window, speaking in low tones on his phone, stopping to look out at his fabulous landscaping.

It was then she knew.

It was then she knew that of course he wouldn't.

Of course Stellan wouldn't break her trust like that, trespass in places he knew she didn't want him to be, betray her in a manner he knew she couldn't forgive.

Of course not.

He'd wait.

Wait for her to offer it to him.

Wait for it like it was a gift he lived to receive.

Sixx sucked in breath and forced herself to walk on unsteady legs to the kitchen. She turned everything off. If it was ruined, it was ruined. Stellan would start again without getting upset, or he'd go out and get them something. With her, he was that even-keeled.

A ruined dinner he'd spent time preparing was nothing.

Sixx thinking she had anything to do with her friends dying at her uncle's hand, now that was worth getting pissed and in her face about.

She walked out to the patio, went to the remote that controlled practically everything, including the pool light and the water feature.

She turned both on then went to a lounge, curled in it, legs tucked tight to her chest, arms wrapped around them, and watched the halogen pool light lazily navigate a variety of different colors. Purple. Blue. Green. Red. Purple. Blue. Green. Red.

"Simone."

She didn't jump, even if she hadn't noticed him joining her.

She just tipped her head back and looked up at him.

"I didn't know what to do, and I didn't want to disturb you on your call, so I just turned everything off," she told him.

"It's pasta. It's fine. If it's ruined, I'll cook more," he replied impatiently, then got to what he wanted to talk about, she knew with the intense look he had focused on her face. "Are you all right?"

She was not.

She wanted to show him. She wanted to be brave enough to take him to her sketchpads and hand them over and give herself to him fully. Show him the unrelenting ugly. Show him how he was the first real beauty she'd had in her life. Show him how Carlo was a prankster, a pain in her ass, a part of her life who could disappear, but even so, he'd always be there when she needed him. Show him that Aryas was the first person she'd ever truly trusted.

Show him that he had already hit her sketchpads, and he was going to be the second.

Show him everything.

He'd be able to handle it.

She was not a mighty Goliath, capable of facing everything, not once sustaining a scar.

He was.

And in superhero land there were two ways that could go.

He was either the hero's source of strength, the calm in the storm, the safe haven that was always there to return to.

Or he was her mortal weakness. The being the cyclone of evil out there was always threatening to destroy. The being she loved the most, and no matter how strong he was, he would be lost to it, and when he was, it would break her.

And that would be a wound that would never heal.

So she'd have to keep him safe.

And to do that, she had to stay away from him, lose him, sacrifice their love so he could go on without her to live the life he deserved.

"Simone," he called, his voice sharp with worry, his body angling down to sit on the lounge at her feet. He wrapped a strong hand with his long, elegant fingers around her ankle and ordered, "Talk to me."

Tell him, tell him, tell him! her mind screamed.

She turned her gaze to the pool.

"I'm just trying to get used to it," she said.

"Used to what?" he asked.

"Just . . . everything."

Coward, her mind sneered.

"Give me an example of 'everything,'" Stellan demanded.

"We watched movies all day, me in my underwear, you in what amounts to pajamas," she explained.

"And?" he pressed.

"I've never done that." She looked from the pool to him. "I've never had that brand of awesome."

"So you're sitting out here, looking lost and alone, reflecting about a day you thoroughly enjoyed?" he asked, like he wanted confirmation that she was as insane as she sounded.

"Baby," she said quietly, "you signed on for the mess. You're not allowed to question it."

"Sorry, darling, I absolutely signed on, but that was not a caveat."

He was right. It was not.

Wishful thinking never worked for her either.

"This has been a great day," she declared.

"And so you're by my pool brooding."

Her back went straight. "Men brood. Women ponder."

His lips twitched and he amended, "And so you're by my pool pondering."

"Yes, pondering how a day can be this perfect and you can be this annoying because you've given me a perfect day."

He burst out laughing.

She loved the look, the sound, everything.

But she glared at him.

Still chuckling, he stated, "So you're not out here pondering. You're out here thinking about how dead set you were against this deal we have, and it hasn't been a full week, but you like it here, you like being with me, you're happy, so now you know how very wrong you were, and this means you're pouting."

"Don't gloat, handsome. It's unbecoming," Sixx retorted.

He continued chuckling as his hand slid up the inside of her calf and he leaned toward her, this taking all her attention.

"Would you like to sit out here continuing to ponder about how I was very right regarding how spectacular we are together," he asked in a silken drawl. "Thus how you were very wrong. And how much more spectacular we're going to be after I play with you tomorrow, something you know because you can't even take my hand on your calf without giving everything away. Doing all this while I go in and cook more pasta so we can eat?"

"It's your self-appointed role to give me everything I might desire, and you've done a bang-up job so far so no sense stopping. Therefore, yes. As it's been two full hours since we ate up all Margarita's fabulous homemade salsa with those chips, food would be good," she returned, making him continue to laugh softly, which was her intention entirely.

Stellan slid his hand down the inside of her thigh and she shivered.

Which didn't make him stop laughing, but the sound of it turned to something far more affecting.

"Ponder all you want, darling. I'll be inside boiling pasta and waiting," he purred.

"Stop turning me on when you're not going to let me come when we start *getting* it on," she shot back.

"Oh," he murmured, his fingers gliding in a there-and-gone touch across the gusset of her panties that she knew he didn't miss were soaked with her wet, and probably didn't miss his nearly imperceptible touch made them wetter, "I advise you get used to that, Simone. But I have a feeling you'll not learn to like it, you'll learn to love it because you like it very much already."

"Tease," she snapped somewhat breathlessly.

"Temptress," he whispered in return.

Before it could go on any longer, he bent in and kissed her knee before he squeezed the inside of her thigh affectionately and straightened from the lounge.

"Come in when you're ready," he murmured, giving her a tender, loving smile before he sauntered away with his confident swagger in those lounge pants that at just a glance made her wet(ter).

He gives you everything, and you give nothing, her mind pointed out. *How are you going to keep him if you take and don't give?*

"That's the point precisely," she muttered to the door Stellan entered, watching through the windows as he moved to the kitchen.

So it's better to have loved and lost than not to have loved at all? It was a scoff.

"No," she looked back to the pool. "It's better to give the little I can give before he gets too deep and then get the fuck out of his life so he can find someone who deserves to have him."

You're a fool.

"I'm a hero," she told the mellow rotation of tranquil colors of the pool. "We'll do anything, sacrifice it all, to protect the ones we love."

Her inner tormenter had nothing to say to that.

Then again, she knew all too well that was just plain true.

Sixx liked taking Stellan like this best of all.

On her belly, her legs spread wide, his cock driving deep, his body covering hers, his face in her neck, his arms around her, fingers touching her, teasing her, driving her crazy.

Second best was missionary or riding him with him sitting up. It was vanilla, but she didn't care. She liked face-to-face, getting to watch him, seeing how much he got off on watching her.

She liked how she was taking him now more, though. She could feel his power better like this, his chest pressed to her back, his hips pounding into her ass, his cock thrusting deep, his breath rough on her skin, his warmth everywhere.

She was his like this. Hers only to offer, but his to take, to use, to give only what he wished and have anything he wanted.

She was not allowed to come. He'd told her that when they started, and he was pushing her, testing her, training her in a way she knew that when they got down to serious playing, her endurance had to be at a point she could take whatever he wished to give.

So that night she'd already held it through him eating her, spending so much time on her nipples, it was beautiful torture, and now this . . .

Having him, his cock, his power, knowing she'd also get his cum, having to hold on to control that felt constantly like it was slipping, heavily greased with the need he'd built, made it straight-up painful not to be able to let go. Not only from all he'd done, but mostly because he was going to go over the edge and she'd feel it, hear it, have his seed deep inside her, and she couldn't go with him.

It was astounding.

And it wasn't even play. Not Stellan's kind of play.

It was preparation.

So tomorrow was going to be *insane*.

Sixx couldn't wait.

With every lover she'd had it had been about taking.

Except with Aryas. With Aryas it had been about trust.

With Stellan it was about giving.

Giving the only thing she had.

So she had to bite her inner lip when she felt and heard him taking himself there, holding her in his arms as he did it, and she had to close her eyes and brace her whole body when she heard him slip over, clutching her close, burying himself as deep as he could get.

She had to steel herself even as she listened to him coming down, his breaths steadying, his face stuffed in her neck, his fingers leisurely keeping at their torment.

Finally, he pulled out and rolled to his back, but immediately he hauled her on top of him and trapped her in his arms.

Sixx rested her forehead against his throat.

She was going to draw this moment in her book, graphically, vividly, her legs straddling his thigh, his arms tight around her, his cum gliding out of her and onto his skin.

Eventually, he drifted a hand down to trail his fingers at her upper ass.

"How are you, darling?" he murmured.

"How are you?" she asked.

"I'm excellent."

"Then I'm that too."

His fingers stopped trailing and moved to grip her at her waist.

They usually fell asleep like this. Unless they'd made love in the morning and were getting up to get ready to face their days, after Stellan had come inside her, she kept him there. Unless she had to, she never wanted to wash him away.

So when his grip eased and he was simply holding her, his chest moving with his steady breaths moving her, she was lulling to sleep, thinking he was doing the same, when he spoke.

"I fear you're not believing in this."

Her eyes, which had drifted closed with oncoming sleep, opened with ready alertness, like in the next instant she'd need to take flight.

"How do I get my Simone to believe?" he asked in a tone where it was clear he did not expect her to answer.

So she didn't.

She lay naked in his arms against his long, lean, warm, strong, naked body, held by him, feeling him seep out of her, wondering if she'd ever find a way to believe.

"You know life isn't perfect, Simone," he whispered. "It burns in me that you know that all too well. But days like this happen, sweetheart. They're what get us through the days that aren't like this. It's just that you haven't ever experienced that, so you don't understand it isn't about surviving, it's about living for days just like today."

"Can we go to sleep?" she asked.

He held her in a way she knew he was, for once, not going to give her what she wanted.

But then he gave her what she wanted.

"Of course, honey," he murmured.

She snuggled in, cuddling closer.

His arms tightened and stayed that way.

And Sixx drifted to sleep held tight in Stellan's arms knowing two things.

She'd kept her promise to Aryas. She'd found some happy.

So that was all good.

She also knew that this would be the memory she'd keep with her, the flashback in the novel of her life that would keep her strong and ready to face anything until she faced the end—movies and togetherness and pasta and falling asleep in her lover's arms.

It would be bittersweet when she went on not having it.

But it would serve her to keep on keeping on.

Because she'd know in her heart that for one shining moment in her life, she'd been the woman who deserved it.

eleven

Forever

SIXX

Sixx opened her eyes when Stellan slid a finger down her cheek.

She lifted her gaze up to him and saw he didn't look sleepy in the slightest.

"Prepare for me, darling," he said softly, and she felt the heat hit her chest, between her legs, in her face . . . everywhere.

It was time.

Time to play.

"Coffee in the bathroom," he went on. "I'll meet you by the pool."

He straightened, and her eyes tracked him as he did, but he didn't walk away.

He said, "Hurry."

That was when he started moving away.

She watched him in a new pair of lounge pants, and again no shirt, take five steps (she counted).

Then she threw the covers back and dashed into the bathroom.

No glossy cream box that day.

No.

Spread across the vanity counter was a one-piece black lace number that was panties attached to a V of material just above the pubis that swept up over her breasts and narrowed over the shoulders. Thin straps ran down the back to a bra-like fastening under the shoulder blades that came from a strap just under the breasts at the front.

The panties were hipsters, so the beautifully placed ribbons that started where the V came up above the pubis were designed to curve over hips at the waist, highlighting those swells, drawing the eye. At the back, straps started to form on the panties at the sides of the hips and met the straps curving along the waist, to attach in a complicated crisscross to a diamond-size panel of lace that did very little to cover an ass.

It was the most feminine, most beautiful wireless teddy cage she'd ever seen.

And she could not fucking wait to put it on.

On the counter above the sexy teddy was her rose gold choker.

Her legs trembled, and with all due haste her hand darted to her toothbrush.

She wasted no time preparing for Stellan, even if she went all out with heavy makeup around her eyes and full-force, adorably fuckable hair.

She put no jewelry on other than what Stellan had laid out for her.

The choker.

And after she finished placing it around her neck and looked in the mirror, she whispered, "Oh hell."

Sixx her own damned self bought Stellan something he could collar her with.

God, she'd collared herself *for* him.

Harking back—and she could likely remember every single one she'd seen him with—she'd never seen him collar a slave.

Not one.

But their first time playing, he wanted her collared.

On this thought, honest to God, she nearly orgasmed right there staring at herself in the mirror, smoky eyes, racy-but-classy teddy, collar, ready for him.

Instead, she took a deep breath to steady herself because she had a feeling she had a variety of challenges waiting for her, and she was not going to let him down.

She was going to give to him exactly what he wanted exactly how he wanted it even if it killed her.

She took her empty mug down with her, and as she hit the bottom of the stairs, she saw him in the same seat by the pool in the same position as he had been the day before, except he didn't have a phone to his ear. But he did have his elbow on the arm of his chair, a cup of coffee held up at his side.

She noted there were dishes on the table beside him, a folded napkin, some kind of cutlery, like he'd had breakfast.

There was also a folded bath towel.

My, my, my.

Her legs stated trembling again.

Her determination to have it together took another huge hit just seeing him there, gazing at the rippling waters of his pool (the water feature was on), drinking coffee . . . waiting for her.

Waiting to play with her.

So the time it took her to walk her mug to the sink and then move to the doors, she spent psyching herself up.

This was going to be awesome because it was going to be with Stellan.

This was going to be hot because it was going to come from Stellan.

And this was going to mean everything because she got to take it from Stellan.

And give it to him.

When she made it through the door and he peered over his shoulder that morning, he did not look content and relaxed.

His eyes moved the length of her body in a way that made her feel like each step she took, she'd get shorter and shorter as she melted into a puddle of Sixx goo slithering her way toward him.

She stopped at his side and looked down at him as he looked up at her.

She wanted to kiss him.

She actually felt that need drive right up her pussy, she wanted it so much.

"The cushion, darling," he murmured, "on that chair. Put it on the deck between my feet and sit there."

She watched as he spread his thick thighs and her mouth watered so intensely, she had to swallow.

She started to move but stopped when his fingers closed around hers.

She looked down at him again.

"Forget something?" he asked.

Did she?

Was there something else on the bathroom counter he wanted her to wear that she missed?

No. There was nothing. She never missed anything, but she for certain wouldn't miss anything that morning.

So was she supposed to ask him if he wanted more coffee?

Her two submissive scenes with Aryas had occurred in the red room at the Honey. They'd been private, controlled and contained. There wasn't coffee to get for her Dominant. The only kind of service expected was sexual.

"Did you want more coffee?" she asked, but it even sounded like a guess.

"No, Simone," Stellan answered. "What I want and what you know I want, when I give you a command, is for you to answer appropriately."

Top to toe, her body stiffened.

He expected her to call him Master.

Already she saw the differences between him being a dominant sexual partner and actual Dom/sub play.

She wanted to give him everything.

She wanted to make this everything he wanted.

But she'd forgotten about that.

And Sixx couldn't do that.

She was a Mistress. She gave the commands.

And she'd been a slave to her early life. She took no commands from any Master.

Stellan as her everyday Stellan, yes.

Stellan dominating her, yes.

Stellan as her Master.

She couldn't do it.

Christ, she was falling at the first hurdle.

"Can I just call you Stellan?" she whispered.

"Can you just call me Stellan . . . what?" he pressed.

"I can't do that, baby," she said softly.

His fingers around hers tightened before he let her go and said, "Get the cushion and position as I asked, Simone."

He'd given in, which was somewhat of a relief.

But she'd disappointed him.

Already.

Which was oh-so-*not* a relief.

It's a word. Just a word. In play. This isn't real life. It's fantasy. It's sex. It's trust. It's love, her mind reminded her.

Trust.

Love.

Shut up, she returned.

You want him to rule you, your body, your heart. You couldn't wait to get down here, her mind kept at her.

Shut up! she snapped.

Stilling her thoughts, Sixx got the cushion, dropped it to the deck between his spread legs and then dropped to her hip on it.

She looked up at him.

"Can I please expla—?" she began.

She didn't finish because his fingers spanned her jaw, but his thumb pressed on her lips, pushing in, the pad of it digging into the edge of the ridge of her lower teeth.

"Speak when spoken to, Simone," he said.

Well at least she could do that, especially with his hand holding her jaw and mouth prisoner.

"Lean against my leg," he ordered.

She could do that too, so she did.

He ran the pad of his thumb along the edge of her teeth.

"It's important to me you call me Master," he stated, removing his thumb but using it to stroke hard across her cheek, pressing the inner flesh into the side of her teeth. "You may speak."

"Can we start into that slowly?" she asked.

He removed his hand and reached to the table.

He came back with a cube of watermelon.

He touched it to her lips, and when she opened them, he murmured, "No."

She didn't know if that was a "no" to opening her mouth or a "no" they couldn't start slowly.

But she closed her lips.

He slid the cube along them and watched himself doing it, his expression schooled, appearing like he was lost in thought.

She let him and tried not to squirm.

"Tongue," he ordered quietly.

Sixx slid out her tongue.

He placed the watermelon on it and said, "Eat."

She took it in, chewed and swallowed, all while he watched.

As he did, something inside her melted, and Sixx slipped into a sub daze, realizing even more now than with her experience with Aryas how glorious it was to perform, to do as told and let her Dom watch. They were barely five minutes in, he was simply viewing her while she swallowed some fruit, and she was so focused on him, focused on giving him what he asked for, she didn't hear the long sheets of water falling from the stone feature into his pool. She didn't feel the heat already on the morning or the cushion under her hip.

She felt his calf, knee and thigh at her back. She saw his face. She even could convince herself she heard his breathing.

He reached and brought back another piece of fruit, half a juicy strawberry this time, and rubbed it along her lips.

She waited for permission.

He watched the fruit trace her flesh like he could do it for days.

And it felt like days. It felt like an eternity.

"Did you call Aryas Master?"

In her state, his question surprised her, and her gaze that was resting in a sub daze sharpened to focus on him.

"No," she answered.

His head cocked to the side. "No?"

She shook her head.

"Did he punish you for that?" he queried.

She fought a squirm and nodded.

Stellan appeared to take that in.

And he did so not liking it.

"Tongue," he commanded.

She gave him her tongue and took the fruit when he laid it there.

She brought it into her mouth, started chewing, and he slightly shook his head.

"Did I tell you to eat?"

Sixx stopped chewing.

"You'll have to finish now," he said.

She finished chewing and swallowed.

"Sorry," she muttered.

He reached for another piece of fruit and came back with a cube of cantaloupe.

Rubbing it on her lip, he asked, "Do you know what bothers me?"

Oh God.

Something bothered him.

Now they were not even six minutes into their first scene, and something was bothering him.

But of course it would. Practically the first thing he'd asked, she hadn't given.

She almost spoke, but he did it before her.

"That you gave what was mine to Aryas."

It came out before she could stop it. "Stellan."

He pressed the melon between her lips, placing it on her tongue.

She held it in her mouth and stared up at him, seeing now there was a tightness around his mouth, a hardness in his eyes.

Lord, it *did* bother him.

"It's irrational, I know," he went on. "I also don't care. The very thought of Aryas commanding you, if I don't stop myself thinking on it, it could grow to rage." He cupped her jaw with his hand and ordered, "Eat."

She chewed and swallowed.

"But you knew," he continued.

She sat between his legs and looked up in his eyes and as commanded, said nothing.

"You knew," he stated. "From the moment I laid eyes on you, you knew you were mine. And you gave yourself to him."

She opened her mouth to say something, leaning into him, but his thumb came again, this time pressing against the front of her teeth.

"Don't speak, Simone," he growled.

All right.

She had Stellan the tyrant. The Dom who expected his subs to obey. He called them slaves for a reason. When he was with them, he *owned* them.

And he was with her now, and he owned her.

But then again, he'd always owned her.

Always.

He was right.

It started the first second she laid eyes on him.

It took effort, but she managed not to bite the lip he was pressing against, shift her legs because what was happening between them screamed for her to move, writhe, rub her thighs together or plunge her hand between them and rub . . . *hard*.

"The first time I touched you as your Master, you climaxed for me," he declared.

She did.

God.

"So I met you while you were in training, before you subbed, and even then, you were mine. You've been mine for years, but you gave yourself to him, and now I finally have you, and you won't give me what's mine."

She stared up into his eyes, holding herself perfectly still.

Abruptly, his thumb went away, his whole hand did, and he reached back to the fruit. He returned with a blackberry dipped in yogurt.

He spread the yogurt across her lower lip and murmured, "At least you didn't give that to him."

She couldn't stop her teeth from coming out and scoring her lip anxiously.

He watched and when she was done, he pressed the fruit into her mouth.

"Eat that and when you've swallowed, lick your lips clean," he commanded.

Holding his gaze, she did as told.

He watched.

It was agony and it was *awesome.*

"Up on your knees, Simone," he said.

She got up on her knees between his legs.

"Put your hands on my knees."

She did that too.

"I'm going to feed you. As I'm doing that, you may speak freely, but you take what I put in your mouth, chew it and swallow it while you make your explanations to me."

Thank God.

She was going to get to explain.

He dipped a strawberry half into the yogurt, pressed it between her lips, she chewed and was about to swallow, then speak, when he asked, "Now, explain how you're going to apologize to me for what you did at the pit."

She blinked.

What she did at the pit?

"At the time, I warned you that you'd need to offer your apology," he carried on, reaching for another blackberry, dipping it in yogurt and feeding it to her. "When you looked at that gladiator with invitation even while sitting by your Master."

Oh man.

Another piece of fruit, melon this time, slathered in yogurt went into her mouth.

"Your apology?" he prompted when she was chewing.

Honestly, she hadn't even thought about it. It seemed years ago, and so much had happened since, it entirely slipped her mind.

"I see," he murmured.

And he knew it had.

Damn!

She swallowed and started, "Stellan—"

Suddenly, he gripped her at the back of her neck, pulled her up to him even as he dipped his face to hers.

"*Master,*" he hissed.

She said nothing.

"Say it," he insisted.

"I can't," she whispered.

"You will," he warned, then let her go and reached back to the table.

Not for fruit this time.

Toward the bath towel.

He flipped it open and Sixx nearly groaned.

There was a Lelo INA Wave there, a large, bulbous G-spot massager with a clit stimulator.

Just that. No lube.

Thank God she was as wet as she was because the internal part was not small.

Stellan took it up, but when he stopped, her gaze went from the vibrator to him.

"You'll be having your breakfast, Simone," he said. "And you won't be coming for some time. I have a number of plans for you today, and it would be a shame if you didn't enjoy them to their fullest."

Sixx had a feeling "enjoy" was a relative term in this context. But she said nothing. Only nodded.

"Yes?" he pushed.

"Yes," she whispered.

Something flashed in his eyes. It looked like annoyance, or maybe it was excitement.

"Be still," he said.

She nodded again.

He wrapped one hand around the side of her neck, leaning deeply into her.

She felt the toy nudge the lace between her legs aside, and she held his gaze, peering deeply into his heated eyes. Hers, she suspected, were far more heated, as he slowly slid the vibrator inside her. He positioned it perfectly, internally as well as against her clit, and she couldn't bite back the little mew that she emitted when he turned it on.

God, that was nice.

In her state, *too* nice.

Damn.

She couldn't bite that mew back, but she was proud it was just that with the electric shock the toy sent surging through her body. Her fingers tightened on his knees, and sweet, hot satisfaction saturated his eyes.

Right, she liked him content and peaceful, watching her walk to him sitting by his pool.

But that look just hit second best to the look right there that was all she could see.

He was getting off on this.

Not a surprise, that was part of the point, but him not hiding it from her was.

He was remote with his slaves, almost removed in some scenes, just like her, but his was stern, assertive. The tenderness and affection only came when he needed to use it to get what he was after.

But he was giving it to her right there, nothing hidden.

He loved her on her knees before him.

And that just made it worse because it made it *oh so much better.*

"Stay still for me, Simone," he said, sitting back, and she almost went with him, she so didn't want to lose that look. She didn't want it distant from her either. "You can chew and swallow what I give you. But remain motionless except for your mouth."

She did as told, already feeling the fronts of her thighs start quivering, her fingers digging into the muscle around his knees as a response to his command, what was happening between her legs.

"Say, 'Yes, Master,' " he urged gently.

"Yes . . ."

He waited.

She couldn't finish.

He smiled a sweet, hot, wicked, magnetic smile that sent another pulse through her as if he'd turned up the vibrator working inside her when he had not.

Then he reached to the table to dip a blackberry in yogurt and feed it to her.

He fed her and himself as she knelt between his legs, gazing at his face, gripping his knees, chewing and swallowing and fighting the ripples of pleasure swelling from cunt to nipples to scalp to knees all the way down her shins straight to her toes.

She was trembling and finding it difficult to concentrate on chewing and swallowing when she thought he was going to take pity on her as he murmured, "Enough breakfast, darling."

She drew in a breath and released it but sucked in another one when he kept speaking.

"Now for your punishment for what you did at the pit."

Damn.

She thought that had been her punishment.

Okay, she wanted to give him everything, she wanted to be everything for him, and she'd fallen at the first hurdle.

And now she might fail at this.

But she couldn't. She just couldn't.

That said, she had a feeling it was going to take all she had.

"My waistband, Simone," he said. "Bring it down. Expose me. All of me."

Oh yes.

It was going to take all she had.

The moan surged up and out before she could catch it, and things didn't get better when she looked down at his lap, seeing him hard and straining against the knit fabric of his lounge pants.

Yes, hell yes.

He was getting off on this.

The pants were dark gray. The waistband black and elastic.

If pulled down to expose his cock and cup his balls, it would undo her.

He had a beautiful dick. Unsurprisingly, it was just like the rest of him, thick, long, and exquisitely formed. Giving him head was a religious experience.

Doing it close to climax with a g-spot vibrator and clit stimulator working inside her might kill her.

"You'll learn," he said softly, "that I don't like repeating myself. Now, my waistband, Simone."

She lifted her eyes to his, then forced her hands to move.

Curling her fingers into the waistband of his pants at the sides, she pulled them a couple of inches down before she ran her fingers along the front, tugging the elastic over his cock.

It bounded free, and at the sight of it she had to suck the insides of her mouth between her molars and bite hard to beat back everything that exposing his beauty made her feel.

It didn't get better when she worked the waistband under his balls, the elastic cradling them against the root of his shaft.

She could sketch that. She'd give it an entire page. Then she'd do something she never did—rip it out and frame it so she could look at it whenever she pleased.

He was that gorgeous.

"Glistening, Simone," he whispered, "every inch. Once you have me as I wish, hold my cock in your mouth and do not move."

It was close to the order she'd given Jennifer at his pool party, and having her own command turned on her turned her *on*.

Or considering her current state, turned her on a whole lot *more*.

Willing herself to withstand this for him, Sixx rested her hands on his thighs and bent in, tongue out, and did as she was commanded. She licked him to wet every inch. The taste of him, the musk of him, the feel of his steel under the soft skin of his cock, the vulnerability of his sac, just the fact he was formed perfectly, it was torture, and the pads of her fingers were convulsively contracting and releasing in his flesh as the world narrowed to his dick and balls and her cunt and clit.

His voice had grown thick when he ordered, "Now slide me inside, take me as deep as you can, and hold."

Okay, yes.

This might kill her.

She slid him inside and held.

Having that beautiful cock held deep in her mouth was a fabulous agony.

God, she was going to come.

Just holding him in her mouth, she was going to come.

She felt her entire body tremble.

Fuck, she was going to come.

She gripped his thighs so hard she fancied she could feel each sinew of his muscles under her fingertips, and that didn't help a thing.

She was going to explode.

She was going to let him down.

She was going to *come apart*.

She felt him trail a finger from the layered hair at the nape of her neck down that helpless line to the knot at the top of her spine.

And at his touch, she entered the zone.

Her mind cleared.

She was his.

She was owned.

She was slave to Stellan.

She was serving and she'd done wrong, so she was being punished.

She felt the ache and pulse between her legs, the throb at her clit, and they were elegant in the pain they caused of her need to release. Every inch, every *centimeter* of his cock she held in her mouth was a gift. Serving him was her purpose.

It was what she was born to do.

And she was not allowed to come.

So she would not.

Until he told her to.

Her fingers stopped convulsing and just gripped him tight as she held strong and did as Stellan bid her to do.

"That's it, darling," he murmured tenderly, having felt it, felt her give over, felt her settle into service, that good of a Dom, that attuned to Sixx, he didn't miss it for a moment. Drifting his finger back up and caressing the nape of her neck, he continued, "Now suck."

She sucked, madly, wildly, like working his cock was her only reason for being.

His finger left her nape so all of them could sift into her hair. They tightened and pulled, and she knew to bob.

"Yes," he growled, and she felt his body tauten all around her.

She blew him, sucking hard, slipping him in and out fast, digging her nails into the flesh of his thighs.

He pulled her off of him using her hair, and in a rough voice commanded, "Up."

She surged to her feet.

He instantly slid the vibrator out from inside her, tossed it on the towel, then grasped behind her thighs, hauling her toward him.

She moved into the seat, her knees at his sides, her head tipped down, looking him in his eyes as his body slid lower in the chair. He used his hands to position her. She felt the thick, slick head of his cock shifting the lace aside, he jerked her down on him, filling her, and her head shot back.

Glory.

Hallelujah.

"Watch your Master as you serve him," he growled.

She immediately bent her head forward, and his open palm landed on her ass.

Fucking *fabulous*.

"Move," he demanded.

She moved.

"Fast, Simone, grip me, milk your Master," he ordered throatily.

She went faster, constricting around him, watching his dark face get darker, satisfaction and domination filling his features, making them so handsome she could have wept at the honor of witnessing the sight as he wrapped his fingers around her buttocks. Digging in. Using her flesh to pull her down, up, down, crashing her into him.

She started panting.

"Open the lace, expose your breasts to me," he grunted.

She moved her hands instantly to do as told.

"Hold them on offer to me."

She did that too, rounding them at the bottoms, holding her breasts in her hands, still driving down on his dick.

A magnificent sneer hit his face that pounded between her legs as sure as his cock was doing. "Who are you?"

She didn't even think.

Sixx was gone. Sixx had never even existed.

It was all her now.

Simone.

Simone Marchesa.

The woman who belonged to Stellan Lange.

"I'm Simone," she breathed.

"Who owns you?"

"You do," she gasped.

"Rub your thumbs over your nipples."

She did and moaned, having to fight tipping her head back at the same time holding on to her orgasm, determined not to let go.

Saving herself . . .

For him.

Serving herself . . .

To him.

"Who's your Master?" he asked.

She stared into his eyes. "You are, baby."

"Say it," he whispered.

God.

His fingers dug into her ass.

"Say it, Simone," he pushed.

She moved faster on him, arcing her back but keeping her head tilted so she held his eyes.

But she didn't say it.

"You'll give that to me," he told her.

She kept riding him.

His hands left her ass, moved up her back, clenched in her hair, and he dragged her head to his. Their foreheads colliding, she watched from close as his eyes flashed, then closed as a heavy breath escaped his lips, fanning over hers, and she felt his body tense and strain under her.

"Hold," he grunted.

She stopped, full of him, as he climaxed under her.

She did it.

She made it.

She gave him what he wanted.

She felt like shouting her triumph, and the need to orgasm had never been so huge.

But she held on, squeezed his cock with the walls of her pussy, and took in his soft sigh as she did.

Slowly, his grip on her hair loosened, his eyes opened and looked into hers.

They were languid . . . beautiful.

His breath was evening.

She was still panting.

"You've done well, darling," he murmured.

Thank God.

"I'm glad, baby," she whispered.

"Clean you up, eat you out, then when you're ready, set about giving you your reward."

Oh hell.

He was talented at giving head, and she knew being "ready" was not getting a reward after getting an orgasm.

"Go upstairs, wash me from you," he ordered. "When I join you, I want you on our bed on your knees with them spread wide, facing the headboard. I want you riding my face."

Shit.

Just the visual that brought to mind took her right back to quivering.

"Okay, Stellan," she muttered.

His hands slid down to her neck, and one over the other, squeezed.

"You'll give it to me," he told her quietly.

She knew what he meant.

Declaring him her Master.

And she wanted to.

But she wasn't sure she could do it.

"When you believe," he whispered.

That was just it.

She'd never believe.

She swallowed.

He didn't push it further.

"Slide me out, darling. And go do as I say."

She nodded. She slid him out, moved off of him, and on unsteady legs, the ache between hers, the heaviness in her breasts, the intense sensation at her nipples, the sensitivity of her skin had been downshifted significantly, but they were nowhere near gone.

She started to move around his chair but stopped when he hooked her with an arm along her belly.

She looked down at him.

"I took you there. I took you there with just a touch, and you know what that means," he said gently.

Sixx stared at him, beginning to tremble for a different reason.

"Untested subs, Simone, they do not find it easy to go there," he continued.

He was right.

Submissives new to the scene required a lot more time and work to guide them into the headspace where they could give over control, slip into the zone, find themselves languishing in the agony and ecstasy of being at the mercy of someone else's will, not content but wholly rapturous they were used to serve their Dominant.

Their first full scene, and she'd found herself right there.

Except calling him Master, something he was. He knew it, she knew it. It was just something she could not say—he'd guided her right there.

Because that was her as it was him.

From the moment they met there was no other way it could be.

"Stellan—" she whispered.

"How much more proof do you need that you're mine, Simone?" he asked.

She didn't have an answer to that.

"Undeniably mine," he stated the answer she refused to say. Then he went in for the kill. "Forever, sweetheart."

Forever.

She knew she was.

She was his.

Forever.

The thing was . . . that was true, absolutely, without a single doubt true.

But it didn't mean what he thought it meant.

And she was going to give him what she could.

Then she was going to have to do something about it.

twelve

Sealed

SIXX

Sixx lay on her belly between Stellan's cocked legs, holding his balls in her mouth, resting the side of her head in the juncture of hip and thigh, recovering.

He'd eaten her . . .

And eaten her . . .

And eaten her . . .

Not unrelenting, he slowed to give her time to pull herself together, but he kept her riding his face for what had felt like hours. She was surprised the sun was still shining through the windows, for she had withstood the work of his mouth so long she felt the sun surely had gone down and the moon should be filling the sky.

Stellan's fingers were stroking gently along the line of her hair at her neck, as she stared up close at his distended cock, memorizing every line, ridge, vein and swell, thinking in her current state what she thought not in her current state.

Seriously.

His cock could have been sculpted by an artist.

"Lift your eyes to me, Simone."

She knew he meant her to keep him in her mouth as previously instructed, so she did that and tilted only enough to look up the textured sections of his abs, over the bulging crests of his pecs, past the corded column of his throat, to his adoring, languorous, dark blue eyes.

It was then, in the zone, his to do with as he willed, she shot right back into herself.

Mira looked at Trey like that when she worked him.

And Leigh looked at Olly like that.

Now she had that.

She *had* that.

From Stellan.

God.

"Do you understand now the difference between when you're simply mine and when you're mine in play?" he asked.

Man, did she ever.

She blinked once.

His lips curved up in a way she felt buzz in her clit.

"You've earned your reward now, darling," he murmured. "Release me, cover me and come up to straddle me."

Her body a mass of electrified nerve endings that she'd grown accustomed to, but were nevertheless an enduring, splendid misery, she slid his balls out of her mouth, shifted up, adjusted the waistband of his pants so it covered his privates, then she moved up to straddle him even as he kept his legs cocked, not making it easy.

When she got in position, she discovered a new beautiful misery, feeling him hard against her wet, needy core and knowing she could do nothing about it.

Stellan slid his hands across her waist to the small of her back and up the sides of her spine, her skin so sensitized, if she let go, even an inch of his touch could drive her to climax.

But she held strong.

She had no clue how she did.

But she did.

For him.

He pulled her down to him as his hands moved until she was resting chest to chest on him, her fingers curled over his shoulders.

"Our first time as Master and his pretty, stubborn slave, I've something special planned," he told her.

She was in little doubt that something special would not be something special.

It would be something spectacular.

The question was . . . would she survive it?

"Are you ready?" he asked.

"Yes," she whispered.

That one word came out shaky because she said it, she wanted to mean it, she just wasn't sure she actually did.

One of his hands slid back down, between her legs, under the lace, through the wet to rest at her clit.

Her body jolted, and she had to seize her lower lip between her teeth and bite down, the pain helping her hold her control.

Stellan's wicked smile came back.

"I thought I cleaned all that wet away," he remarked.

"Mm," she hummed, incapable of further considering her entire focus was on her clit and what he might do with it, considering he'd told her that her reward was imminent.

"So I can assume you enjoy spending time with my balls in your mouth?" he queried.

"Yes," she pushed out.

More like, *God, yes.*

Holding him like that. Serving him like that. His cock that close for her to see.

Bliss.

Aching bliss but bliss all the same.

His eyebrows arched. "Yes . . . ?"

It was a prompt.

"Yes," she whispered miserably, not giving him what he wanted.

She had to give it to him.

She *had* to give it to him . . . before she set about losing him.

But damn it . . .

She couldn't give it to him.

He bent to her and touched his mouth to hers, and Sixx breathed that touch in like oxygen because he hadn't kissed her at all, light or hard, not the entire day.

And then he shattered her world, demonstrating how deeply he understood her and giving her something more she wanted badly but really could not have.

"You wouldn't be you if there wasn't a little Sixx somewhere in there, being stubborn, holding back," he said gently. "The Mistress coming out, *my* Mistress, submitting to me at the same time making *me* work and slave to earn something."

Her body stiffened from all he'd said.

However . . .

His Mistress?

"It would be boring if it was no challenge at all, darling," he went on, flicked her clit with his fingers, making her moan, her body jolt again, and he finished, "But I'll best it, Sixx. You'll submit to me too, as Simone does. I guarantee that."

"Stellan—"

"Come," he said, removing his hands, curling up, taking her with him as he exited the bed, putting her on her feet. He wrapped his fingers around hers. "Time for your reward."

He tugged at her hand, and she walked with him out of his bedroom into the hall, down the hall, the stairs and along the back passage toward the laundry room, only to stop at the door to the basement.

It was then her heart started pounding as he led her down the stairs.

He'd said their play would be in their bed, their home.

But she had a feeling he wasn't taking her to the home theater or the wine cellar (though both would be interesting).

No.

He was taking her to the playroom.

His fully-kitted playroom.

Benches. Vaults. Tables. Suspension apparatus. Crosses.

He also had equipment—chains, flogs, whips, paddles, crops, switches, candles, ropes, cuffs, shackles.

Further, he had cabinets filled with toys—vibrators, clamps, phalluses, plugs, gags, masks, corsets.

Sixx had not once seen him go hardcore on any of his subs, but that didn't mean she hadn't seen him get creative with a cross, a set of clamps, toys, restraints, anything with a handle and more.

She had not, however, seen him do any of that with a slave new to his playroom.

He could be a tyrant, but he was a break-'em-in-easy kind of guy. It was the surprise they received when he took it deeper that got him off.

She was licking her lips and hovering somewhere between pulling her hand from his and running away and tightening her fingers around his and dragging him to the playroom herself when they made it to the door.

He opened it, drew her inside, and she honest-to-God nearly melted to his feet.

This was because there were three gladiators in there—Ami, as well as the one who had won in the pit and then gone to his partner and force-fed him his cock, and that partner who'd been forced to suck cock.

The two partners were wearing locked leather shorts that had a zipped-up-the-sides panel at the front covering their packages that could be opened to free their cocks, this locked to the belt at the waistband. The shorts also had a zip between the legs that was locked closed at the back waistband that could be opened for access to other parts.

Currently, they were all closed in tight.

But it was Ami she couldn't take her eyes from as Stellan led her into the room.

He was fully naked.

And with a complicated strapping of black rope around his waist and over his shoulders, he was somewhat suspended from the ceiling with his wrists tied behind his neck, the ropes going down his back, along his waist, and fed through the eye of the anal hook that was inserted up his ass.

His feet were on the floor.

But barely.

His back was to the room so they had the full view.

And she didn't take her eyes off that superlative view even as she felt Stellan arrange her in his lap as he sat them both.

"I take it you're enjoying your reward," he murmured amusedly.

Slowly, she turned her eyes from the spectacle before her and looked to Stellan.

They were cocooned in the wide seat in what could only be described as a modern throne. It was upholstered in blue velvet almost the exact color of his eyes. A broad, curved hood rose gracefully out at the sides and up high over their heads.

The king was in attendance, and she was his slave queen, settled in to watch their servants perform on command.

Unable to hold it back, she shivered full body in his hold.

"You're enjoying it," he whispered, his lips forming a sexy, satisfied smile.

She raised her hand to the side of his neck, curled her fingers in and lifted up so her lips were at his ear.

"Ami," was all she said quietly.

"Is all in, but ungagged and has a safe word," he replied in her tone.

She pulled away, looked him in the eyes, and nodded.

He curled her into a closer hold in his arms, inclined his head toward the room, and when she turned hers at his unspoken command, he ordered, "Position him to face us and one of you drop to your knees and take his cock."

The partners moved; one turned Ami on his hook so he was no longer back to them, the other one fell to his knees, and the minute he had Ami's engorged cock within range, he grabbed onto it with his hand and took it deep in his mouth.

Ami let out a low groan.

Lord, a man blowing a man was almost as fabulous as a man fucking a man.

But a man blowing a restrained warrior that was suspended on an anal hook was *sublime*.

Sixx squirmed in Stellan's lap, eyes riveted to the bobbing head of the man on his knees.

"Not enough, darling?" Stellan asked.

This wasn't a reward.

It was more torture.

She lifted her gaze to Ami's face.

His eyes were locked to her, his face flushed, the muscles in his neck straining, his gaze a scorch of heat.

Totally in the zone.

Performing for her.

His Mistress had entered the room as a slave, and he still gave it up for her.

She felt her face soften.

Then she heard Stellan bark, "Take his face."

Ami immediately started thrusting so hard, the guy on his knees had to lift his hands to Ami's hips to hold on and not fall back.

"Release the panel and the zip. Rosebud," Stellan ordered.

The free man moved immediately. Crouching beside his partner, he unlocked the locks, unzipped the back down through his legs as well as the panels at the front. Sixx couldn't see the latter, but she did hear his thankful grunt, so she suspected his cock was hard and releasing it from its confines was a relief.

The free sub then moved to one of Stellan's cabinets, opened it, selected a rosebud plug, lubed it, and moved back to the players.

Situating himself to the side so he didn't obstruct the view, Sixx watched and listened as another, deeper grunt muffled by thrusting cock sounded in the room as he plugged his partner's ass.

A wave of wet hit between her legs.

"My queen can't see," Stellan called.

The man on his knees tipped his ass so she had a better view.

Okay, plugged ass getting fucked in his face by a restrained warrior . . .

Now *that* was sublime.

So enthralled, she had no idea she let out a purring mew.

And then it happened.

What she should have known would happen simply because Stellan was Stellan.

But she definitely should have known it would happen after he mentioned her giving herself to Aryas.

And now, here was Ami performing how he was performing.

Stellan had a number of messages to send.

And he was sending them.

Thus they were up, Sixx in Stellan's arms.

Then he turned around, sitting her back in the chair but suspended over it, her legs splayed wide to the sides, his eyes locked on her, his mouth issuing commands.

"Unhook him. Fuck his ass. Come inside. Ami, shoot your cum down his throat. My queen can listen."

But he actually had no intention of her listening.

Because Stellan drew his waistband back down over his big, thick, hard cock.

Curving it under his balls, he moved into her, whispered, "At your pleasure," and slammed inside her.

Taking him brutally, ready for it, gagging for it, so loving every inch that invaded her, Sixx's heels dug into the sides of the chair. Her back arching, her pussy rocked into his hips, she came immediately, staggeringly, all her molecules scattering. Her head pressed back into blue velvet as her body lurched violently in the chair from her orgasm and from taking her Master's cock.

For leverage, Stellan had his hands planted in the arms of the chair close to the back, the drives of his body keeping hers from exploding off her perch, but the world had fallen out from underneath her.

She had to find purchase, and she did that on him, throwing her arms around his shoulders, digging her nails into his flesh, crying out again and again and again, rolling her hips out to meet his thrusts also again and again and again, her first staggering orgasm shifting into another one, this one *dazzling*.

"Stellan." His name came as a plea, a brand, a claim, a demand, an appeal, a wish ... the realization of a dream.

This was her dream.

Spread for him.

Offered to him.

Serving him.

Taking her fucking from him.

Nothing but *his*.

He owned her.

But he could only do that because *she owned him*.

"Fuck," Stellan groaned.

She shifted her hands so she could curl her nails into the back of his neck, and her eyes focused on his.

"Fuck me. Keep fucking me," she commanded breathily, still climaxing, lost to it, destroyed by it.

Ruined.

He pounded into her, their eyes locked, a snarl curling up his throat and lacerating the air.

Yes.

He kissed her.

His tongue was a lifeline. The noises he drove down her throat sustenance. She clutched him with her pussy, her fingers raking up, gripping his hair. She took her branding, her claiming, the demands of her Master, but there was no plea, no appeal ...

He was staking his claim of her.

For the gladiators.

For Ami.

For Stellan.

For Sixx.

He ended the kiss but left his mouth at hers, their breaths clashing.

She vaguely heard the strident chorus of manly grunts in the room, pierced by her feminine gasps and cries; nothing existed for

her but taking her fucking from her Master, her marking, her claiming, and giving him *everything*.

She succeeded and climaxed again when she watched Stellan's
head jerk back, the veins in his neck pop out and felt his thrusts turn
savage as he came inside her, and she found a new struggle, orgasming at the same time, forcing herself to watch him do the same.

Sixx joined him as he shuddered through aftershocks, her body
absorbing his, and his hers, and she shifted her hands to his hair,
stroking it as he dropped his forehead to hers, and their panting
breaths mingled.

A deep, guttural masculine cry rent the air as someone else in
the room came.

But as lush as that sound was, her entire focus was on the eyes
in front of her.

It was only then she realized that he'd given it all to her but
even doing it in a room with three other people, he'd given them
nothing.

She was entirely hidden and he hadn't even pulled his pants over
his ass.

He'd fucked her, and (except for the one on his knees) they'd
probably watched him fuck her, but really they'd seen nothing.

He'd given it to her, he'd claimed her before them, he'd taken
her for himself . . . and the only ones who got anything from what
they shared was them.

Man, he was a genius.

Just the thought of it made her tremble again.

"Nice reward," she muttered breathlessly.

"Cheek," he returned gruffly.

"Stellan?" she called like he wasn't right there, his cock still embedded inside her, his eyes staring into hers from less than an inch
away.

"Right here, darling," he responded gallantly, even if he knew
he didn't have to.

"I might not be able to say it, but you know it, what you are to me."

Those eyes, so close, flashed with triumph that was so resplendent, it made her heels dig into the sides of the chair, her pussy clamp on him so tight he gave a slight grunt, and her fingers fist in his hair.

"I still want it from your lips, Simone," he said.

She gave him a small smile, and he drew back so he could drop his eyes to it and watch.

Whatever he saw, he liked, because he flexed his hips into hers.

She bit her lip.

He gave her his wicked grin.

Another deep, masculine groan filled the air.

God, he was awesome.

"Can I watch now?" she requested.

"Anything, darling," he murmured.

Yes, anything.

And yes, she'd take anything.

Because it meant giving Stellan as much of everything as she could give.

For their month.

Just their month.

They had three more weeks.

And then more than ever before, not for her, for Stellan . . .

She had to be history.

The instant Stellan slid a hand around her hip and in, flicking at her clit and growling, "Now, Simone," she came.

Hard. Stars exploding behind her eyes, body locking, pussy rippling, clit convulsing, lips parted and pants escaping . . . *hard*.

She kept at it as, on her knees, she took his deep, vicious thrusts that, with her arms restrained in satin sleeves laced tight together from upper biceps to wrists behind her back, fingers curled in, nails biting into her palms at the small, she had no choice but to accept, to allow to drive her cheek deeper into the bed. She shuddered again, not with aftershocks.

Another climax.

His finger still at her clit, his other hand holding her ankle almost tenderly where it rested against his calf through her second orgasm, he kept at her and forced a sharp gasp from her throat followed by an incomprehensible, *"Please."* If she was of a mind to think clearly, she wouldn't know what she was begging for because Stellan was giving her everything she needed.

She would know what she wanted when he reached deep with both hands. Gripping her at the insides of her thighs right below the juncture to her sex, sending waves of pain and pleasure shooting up her cunt, she quivered in front of him in multiple mini-climaxes as he let out a grunt that turned into a groan when he exploded inside her.

Stellan kept her filled and stroked the insides of her thighs as the aftershocks scoured through her. Sixx struggled to catch her breath, and then his hands moved over her hips, her bottom, the backs of her thighs, down her calves to curl around each ankle and hold her there while he caressed her pussy with his cock, slow and sweet.

She stayed positioned for him in their bed, trying to will her mind and body back into her command.

The gladiators had been released. She'd been fed a light lunch at the feet of her Master. And now they were back in Stellan's room. Stellan had removed her teddy, then Sixx had found that her reward was long-lasting and included a myriad of creatively culminated, mind-boggling orgasms.

Eventually, Stellan pulled out, released her ankles, and fell to his back beside her, not hesitating a second to draw her over him, still restrained.

But he positioned her like he normally did after they'd had sex, her thighs cradling one of his, his cum seeping out of her, her forehead in his throat.

She'd find the kink factor was a spectacular addition when his soft, loving, postcoital touch traced down her bound arms, slid under her immobile wrists, and back out for his fingers to lace into hers, which could do nothing but allow them and curl into his.

"What am I going to do with you?" he murmured.

The question was a surprise for a variety of reasons, considering he'd demonstrated plainly he knew a lot of things to do with her.

But Sixx had a feeling he wasn't talking about play.

"You're here, right here, all here, all mine, at the same time miles away from me," he said, and she blinked at his neck. "How do you manage that?"

She was bound for him, her pussy still throbbed from taking him, his cum was gliding out of her, but this was not a Master-and-his-slave conversation.

"Stellan—" she began as a warning.

Suddenly, his other hand laced between the fingers of her free one. Using her straightened, trussed arms as leverage, he pulled her up as he crunched up, forcing her to go with him in a way she was straddling his hair-roughened thigh, her soft, sensitive, wet flesh against his hard, dry, bristly heat.

When she was face-to-face with him, his fingers around hers curled in cruelly.

And she had the impatient, frustrated tyrant.

"I could keep you suspended astride my cross and beat you for hours and that wouldn't break you. I could keep you hovering close to climax without release for weeks and that wouldn't break you. So how, Simone? How do I force it out of you?" he asked.

"It's just a word, baby," she whispered pacifyingly.

"I'm not talking about the word, Simone."

She shut her mouth.

"I could give you everything, in my case literally, and it still would be nothing," he stated, and her insides frosted over that he'd think such a thing.

"That isn't true," she whispered.

"You're pulling away even when I'm inside you," he stated flatly.

She looked away, terrified but at the same time moved he'd sensed that from her, read it in her, knew her so deeply.

"Don't look away from me, and that is not a command as your Master, that's your man demanding that of you, especially when we're talking about this," he said, and he furthered the words by letting her fingers go and starting to unlace the restraints.

Slowly, she forced her gaze to his.

"We're having a good day," she said softly. "Let's just have this beautiful day."

"And then what?" he asked as she felt the laces loosening.

"And then tomorrow we'll have a different beautiful day."

"And then?" he asked, the laces loosened, he slipped the sleeves off and tossed them on the floor beside the bed.

She had a feeling M wasn't going to be picking those up and that was because Sixx would, and she'd put them away.

"Simone," he clipped.

She focused on him.

"We have three more weeks."

It was then her world collapsed. Like in the movies when the massive earthquake hits, the mighty crack opening in the earth, swallowing everything inside as it crumbles and disappears, letting out a mighty poof of dust that annihilates everything.

This was because his face assumed an expression like she'd struck him.

Stunned.

Hurt.

Wounded.

Arms released, she lifted both hands to his face.

"Baby."

"It's just time spent," he declared, "Or rather, time served for you."

"No, it's not," she rushed to say. "It's brilliant, beautiful, perfect. You're making me happy."

"And you're still going to leave me," he stated. "Fulfill your promise and then leave."

God, how did they get *here*?

"I need you to understand," she said.

"I'll never understand," he returned. "After this week, Simone, honestly? You can ask that of me?"

Her hands gripped him harder. "You don't get it."

His hands came up and gripped her just the same, positioning her so they were nose-to-nose and his eyes were drilling into hers.

"Then explain it to me," he bit out.

She automatically retreated, trying to physically, which he disallowed, so she did it verbally.

"You push too hard," she snapped.

"Learn this about me, darling," he drawled ominously. "When there's something I want, and I have it in my sights, I will do anything, absolutely *fucking anything*, to secure it. You think this is pushing hard, you know nothing about me."

"You're not making this better," she warned.

"Why won't you allow yourself to be happy?" he asked, irate.

That question, one Aryas had posed to her using different words what was now years ago, made her move so violently, she tore out of his arms and was across the bed before he could snatch her back.

Naked, on three limbs, the last held up, palm out toward him, when he made to lunge at her, she hissed, "Don't get near me."

His face turned gentle.

As it always did when he took it too far and she snapped.

Then fear spiraled up her spine when that wiped clean and his expression set to determined.

Switching tactics.

Doing absolutely *anything*.

"Get over here," he ordered.

"No," she denied.

"Get over here, Sixx," he bit.

He called her Sixx.

He knew precisely who he was dealing with.

God, he knew *her* down to her soul.

And that terrified her most of all.

"No!" she yelled and moved to throw herself off the bed.

He caught her around the waist and dragged her back, and this was good.

This was great.

With this, she could show him precisely who he was dealing with.

He said if she took him to his ass, it would sting his pride. But the man Stellan was, she knew if she did that, it wouldn't just sting his pride. It would alter who they were to each other forever.

And when she went at him with no holds barred, it tore her apart at the same time it gave her hope that she'd finally found the means to save him.

She discovered the faults in this hastily-formed plan immediately.

The facts were that Stellan might be well-bred, well-dressed and wealthy.

But a predator was a predator no matter how polished he appeared to the world.

And when an urbane predator was pushed to claim something that was his, he was an animal.

In the ensuing battle, she had a few openings, and he bested her at each one. He was strong, he was sly, and he was a fucking cheat.

He—her Stellan, the man she was in love with, the man who looked at her adoringly when she held his balls in her mouth or *anytime*—knew he was bigger than her, stronger than her, and as she'd expected him to do, something he did *not* do, he gave her no quarter.

It could be Ami he was grappling with.

So when he had her facedown on the bed, her arm torqued up her back so tight, the pain in her shoulder was acute and almost blinding, but definitely immobilizing, and he commanded, "Spread your goddamn legs," she did it.

He kept his hold on her even as she sensed him reaching, heard a nightstand open, knew he was doing something just out of sight, so she didn't know what it was until she had a scant second to feel it and tense the muscles she needed to tense to refuse it.

But the latter had no effect.

He rammed the plug up her ass, which set her groaning and sliding slightly up to her knees.

Then he spanked her, and if she thought the sharp blows he'd given her the day of the pool party had a good sting, this was a damned *thrashing*.

"Stellan," she breathed.

"*Master*," he bit.

"Baby," she tried.

His hand hitting her flesh was his only reply.

He gave it to her and he gave her more, holding her wrist twisted up her back, until she felt the pain in her shoulder rocket down her ass, gathering with the pain he was inflicting there, and scattering between her legs, down the backs of her thighs, and without any warning and thus with no control whatsoever, she started coming.

"That's it, darling," he growled, she knew, taking her flesh from pink to red and welted.

"God," she whispered hoarsely.

"No, sweetheart," he returned, the spanking ending, the torture beginning. He held her down and dove his hand between her legs. "*Master*," he finished.

She quivered, she shook, she shuddered, she came again and again and again from deft, talented, relentless clit stimulation and deep, hard, penetrating finger fucking until her body was not her own . . . at all, even a little of it, all the way to her marrow.

It was his.

Only his.

"I can't . . . no more," she begged feebly, but her muscles clenched and another orgasm burned through her.

He took hold of the plug and started fucking her ass, and she shoved her face in the bed and moaned.

"Sorry?" he called.

"Please." The word was muffled in the bed.

He filled her, and his hand went back between her legs.

Abruptly, of its own volition, she shuddered in surrender.

Her body going lax, her legs spreading wider, she turned her face again so her cheek was to the sheets and whispered, "Please, I can't take more, Master."

In a blink, the plug was out, she was up, in his arms, her body wrapped around his, his arm tight at her waist, his other hand cupped to the back of her head, and he was kissing her deeply.

Shifting his hips, he slid inside, and using his arm around her waist to lift and lower her, he was fucking her gently.

He pulled her mouth from his, shoved her face in his neck, and moved her on his cock. Each time he filled her, she sighed against his skin, too spent to do anything but hold on and grip him as hard as she could with her pussy.

"You won't be able to leave me," he declared thickly.

She closed her eyes and centered on the pull and release, the push and seal.

Seal.

Seal.

Sealed.

His orgasm was lazy and so beautifully orchestrated, having Sixx in the state he put her in, she could do nothing but hear it, feel it, absorb it in every way that could come to being, accepting it as the precious gift he had every intention of giving.

When he was finished, he impaled her on his cock and held her in his arms.

"I thought I knew what I was doing," he murmured. "But you're full of surprises. And in matters of meaning, in other words, battles worth winning, I adore surprises, sweetheart."

Great.

"You need a firmer hand," he decided.

She didn't think she could have it in her, but apparently she did because she shivered.

He chuckled.

She loved the sound.

God!

"I think every weekend we play, I'll command a day where I get Simone and a day where I get to break Sixx," he said.

And he could also find a way to get off on the messed-up insanity of her split personalities.

Fabulous.

"Yes?" he asked.

"I think you're more nuts than me," she muttered against his skin.

"I said something once that, at the time, I didn't even realize how true was its meaning," he shared.

Sixx had a feeling she didn't want to know.

She also had a feeling he knew she didn't.

But Stellan didn't give a damn.

"Sweet pussy is worth any hassle. But to earn the attention of a queen . . ." He curled his hand around her jaw and used it to force her to look at him. The touch was dominant, but gentle, and achingly sweet, and when he caught her eyes, he concluded, speaking every word in a way each was laced with steel, "I. Will. Do. *Anything.*"

"You have my attention," she whispered.

"I have your utter devotion," he retorted, and she felt her body freeze. "But your devotion is twisted, Simone. In the way Sixx protects you, she's trying to protect me. Shut me out, force me down. I can break your body. I can earn a 'Master' from your lips. But that is what I'm going to break to make you mine. And you can fight it, my sweet darling. Fuck, I want you to. It'll make the process all the more interesting. But in the end, you'll bow to your king and then take your place at his side. Trust me."

"I could disappear tomorrow," she told him the truth.

"And I would find you," he told her his.

His was probably more true.

She dropped her head so her forehead rested against his and lifted a hand to stroke his cheek.

"I wish I could give you what you want," she said quietly.

"You already do," he replied. "I just have to prove that to you." He pushed her face away slightly and said, "You're finished serving, darling. I'll make us some dinner, and we'll have a quiet night in front of the fire."

When he let her jaw go, beginning to move like he was going to pull them from the bed, she caught his jaw tight and he stilled.

"It was him. It wasn't her," she whispered huskily. "It was always him."

Stellan said absolutely nothing. He just stayed perfectly still and stared into her eyes, his having gone so hyper-alert, they felt like a laser burning through her.

"There wasn't much but he . . ."

She trailed off.

He stayed silent.

"He loved me," she pushed out.

When it was Sixx who went silent, he urged gently, "More, honey."

"The bullets. He took those bullets for me."

"Okay," he whispered.

It was nearly guttural when she shared the awful truth.

"It's not safe to love me."

Understanding flared in his eyes so bright, it was like a beacon that lit up the room, and a growl so low, so predatory, it scraped against her skin as it rumbled from his chest, and he spoke like he'd spoken earlier, but there was a fiery flint to the steel of the words he gave her.

"By God, Simone, I. Will. Prove. That. Is. *Not true.*"

"You need to stay safe for me," she said urgently.

"I will."

"Always," she begged.

His arms around her went from strong and firm to gentle and sweet.

"Always, honey."

"Even if it's me that has to make you safe."

He hesitated on that, and she about opened her mouth.

But he spoke first.

"We shall see."

thirteen

Happily Ever After

STELLAN

The next morning, leaving Simone standing at the bathroom mirror in her underwear making her hair adorably fuckable, with his suit jacket in his hand, Stellan walked down the stairs.

With Simone as she was in their bathroom, he did not want to leave her.

With what he knew was downstairs, he had to leave.

He found what he expected to find after he'd sent the text he'd sent last night, hiding in the bathroom to do it.

He was not annoyed he was reduced to hiding in his own bathroom to do what he had to do.

Any tactic, any ploy, *anything* . . . he would do, without embarrassment, without remorse.

M was in his kitchen.

M was usually in his kitchen at this time of day to make him breakfast, but also to keep him company considering she worried about him living in this big house by himself.

He'd asked her to give Sixx and him a couple of weeks to get used to each other before they resumed regularly scheduled activities.

After what Stellan had discovered last night, he wasn't moving cautiously forward with his Simone.

She thought he was pushing too hard?

She'd learn what that meant.

"*Mijo!*" M cried in that welcoming way of hers, like it hadn't been mere days since they'd seen each other last, but years. She was turning from whatever she was doing in the kitchen to him, giving him one of her big, bright smiles. "Good morning."

"Good morning, M," he murmured, throwing his jacket over the back of one of the stools at the island.

She frowned at his jacket.

She gathered his clothing from the floor, laundered it, and put it away or took it then picked it up from the dry cleaner's.

She was always riding his ass to take better care of his things.

And thus would have preferred him draping his jacket around the chair, not tossing it over the back.

Her gaze went from his jacket to his twitching lips to his eyes.

"How is Simone?" she asked.

And there it was.

He'd discovered on Friday that Simone had invited M to call her by her real name.

It had been a surprise at the time, a good one, but nonetheless a surprise. Stellan wasn't certain anyone but Aryas and Dillinger knew her true name, and neither man used it.

At the time, whatever accord they'd reached that led them to drinking tequila he was delighted with and thought it was progress.

And he felt more progress had been made over the weekend.

But it was time to stop going slowly.

It was time to end Simone's self-enforced loneliness and show her that being loved and being around the ones who did it was the safest place she could be.

Not the other way around.

Stellan didn't answer M's question.

He moved right to her, in her space, toe to toe, and watched her eyebrows arch up as he tipped his head down.

Since it was time to speed things up, there was no time to waste.

"I'm losing her," he whispered.

Shock and upset hit her gaze.

"What?" she whispered back.

"Her parents were drug dealers."

M's eyes became huge.

Stellan continued, "When she was twelve, they were killed when they were meeting their supplier and a rival supplier made a play to claim new territory. She was there when it happened."

"I-I-I . . ." She shook her head disconcertedly. "I can't even comprehend this," she said softly, her voice filled with horror.

"Her father stepped in front of her to protect her."

Now her voice was pitched high. "Why was she even *there*?"

Stellan shook his head as well, doing it with two meanings. One that he didn't know why such a thing occurred, and the other that it didn't matter.

"As shocking as this is, sweetheart, that's a moot point now. She was. And it's clear she did not have a close relationship with her mother. But there was something between her and her father. What made matters worse in a situation that didn't seem like it could get worse, when they died, she did not go to a relative who would show her love and care and give her what she needed to deal with what she'd witnessed. She went to her uncle, who is arguably worse than those two."

"How could he be worse?" she asked incredulously.

"That doesn't matter," Stellan answered gently. "What matters is that he clearly did not counsel her or get her the help she'd need to understand what happened in that room when she lost her parents. She's twisted it, not surprisingly. She thinks it's not safe to love her."

"That's ridiculous," she snapped, not upset with Simone, upset about the story Stellan was sharing.

"It is to you, to me, to anyone," Stellan agreed. "To her, perhaps the only person in her life who showed her affection, kindness and his version of love was shot dead stepping in front of her. At twelve, it was all she knew. She was too young to understand what they did to make a living was wrong, that taking a twelve-year-old to a meeting with their supplier was wrong. All she knows is the only person who loved her died saving her."

"This is . . . it is . . ." Tears filling her eyes, M looked away and didn't finish.

Stellan put a crooked forefinger under her chin and brought her back.

"She's in love with me, M, and utterly terrified that will in some way harm me."

"You need to get her into counseling," she advised shakily.

"I need to be certain she doesn't disappear off the face of the earth first."

"How do we . . ." She cleared her throat. "How do we keep her with us?"

Us.

Stellan almost smiled.

Instead he answered, "We do not let go."

He kept his finger under her chin, moving his thumb to hold her there when that chin started trembling.

Suddenly, fire flashed in her eyes. One emotion fled and another took its place, and his thumb was unnecessary.

She nodded her head resolutely once.

"We will not let go."

He grinned at her, removed his hand and said, "Thank you, M."

Her head tipped to the side, and her gaze grew shrewd. "You're very much in love with her."

"In the story of her life, I'm her happily ever after," Stellan replied simply.

Brightness immediately hit her eyes again as they got wet in a way she could not fight.

"Shh," he shushed, rounding her with his arms and pulling her against his body. "We've a fight on our hands, but that part is the good part. Not something to cry about."

Her voice hitched through her, "I know. And it makes me very happy because the world never seemed right to me, the handsome prince going so long without meeting his fair maiden."

It never occurred to Stellan that the story went both ways.

But it fucking did.

He'd lived a long time just living. Not searching for a woman to share his life with, more than likely, he realized in that moment, because he held fear that in the end, he would be like his father, and he'd lay a path of devastation in his wake.

But he'd never do that to Simone.

Never.

Apparently, the "handsome prince" had some healing to do as well . . . and Simone was his healer.

For her part, Simone would probably laugh herself sick at being thought of as a fair maiden. She was the scarred heroine who sacrificed everything to keep the people she loved safe.

But her story was about to change.

And so was his.

Stellan gave M a squeeze and another smile, and it was M who pulled out of his arms.

And then M did what M did when it came to Stellan or anyone she held close to her heart.

She bossed him.

Going right to a little dish filled with a number of pills in a variety of colors and shapes, she tapped it on the counter once before she nudged a tall, slim glass of cranberry juice toward it . . . and him.

"Vitamins, *mijo*," she murmured and moved away.

Stellan went to his vitamins and began to take them with the juice.

As M got busy doing something, she asked, "Is Simone coming down for breakfast?"

"She was doing her hair when I left her, but yes. Though I'll warn you, M, I did not tell her that you were resuming your normal schedule. She has no idea you come in the mornings to cook breakfast for me."

"Good," she muttered, "the element of surprise. Keep her on her toes."

He knew he'd just recruited an excellent ally.

He simply had to hope like fuck they could pull this off.

Stellan took all his vitamins and drank his juice before M got on his ass about doing either.

He'd made himself a cup of coffee, refreshed M's, taken his cup to his office to load his attaché, and was returning when he saw Simone wandering to the kitchen, her gaze locked on M.

When she saw him out of the corner of her eyes, she glanced at him only briefly before M, who from his position in the hall Stellan could not see, called, "Good morning, Simone! Did you have a nice weekend?"

"Yes, M, hey," Simone replied as Stellan moved out of the hall and into the kitchen. "Did you?"

"Excellent," M replied, headed toward Simone, and Stellan almost barked with laughter as he saw she had a little dish in one hand, a tall, thin glass of cranberry juice in the other.

She placed the dish in front of Simone with a sharp crack.

"Vitamins," she declared firmly and another crack, less sharp, but still a crack, sounded and the glass was down. "Cranberry juice." She immediately started poking the pills. "That's Stellan's multi. I'll get one for women for you. But you'll take that today. Vitamin C, no explanation. B-12, energy. Fish oil for your joints—"

"I—" Simone tried to get in.

M spoke over her, and Stellan had to swallow a chuckle with his sip of coffee.

"Green tea, there are two of those. You should take two more during the day, at least. Unless you drink some of the actual tea. Those are antioxidants. And L-lysine. In case you don't know, it's an enzyme your body naturally has to strengthen the immune system. But as you age, it depletes. You need to keep that strong. You take those, and you'll have my breakfast burrito with fruit this morning. Vitamins are good, but always the best source of getting them is in healthy, fresh, plant-based food. So be certain to have some fruit and vegetables for lunch, and I know that Stellan makes sure you have your veggies in the evening. If you do all this, it will make me happy."

Simone stared at M, moved her stare to Stellan, who gave her a slight smile and a one-armed shrug, but somewhere deeper he was feeling a good deal more, witnessing Simone processing a woman showing she gave a damn for the first time in her life, before she moved her gaze back to M.

"Listen, M, I—" she tried.

Another crack of the dish on the marble countertop. "Take these, Simone. Now, *querida*. I'll finish with breakfast." When Simone didn't move, M prompted, "I can't make you breakfast if you don't take them, and if I don't make you breakfast, both of you will be late for work."

Simone slowly reached out to the dish.

M didn't move until Simone had taken half the pills.

She then went back to the stove.

Stellan made his way to Simone, bent, and kissed her cheek as she finished with the vitamins.

Her eyes turned to his, and there was query in them.

He did not have to ask after that query.

"Did I not tell you?" he asked.

She shook her head.

"I'm so sorry, my darling," he murmured. "I texted M to tell her to resume her regular schedule. When you first moved in, I asked her not to come in the mornings while we got settled in together. Now that we are, she's back."

Her eyes said a thousand words that with M there her mouth could not say.

He just wasn't listening.

"Coffee?" he asked.

"Yes," she pushed out.

He moved to the coffeemaker, trying not to smirk smugly.

"All the juice, Simone," M ordered.

"I—" Simone started again, and Stellan didn't turn to watch as M cut her off.

To that, he listened.

"If you don't like cranberry, I'll get you something you like. As you know, we have orange and grapefruit right now. But if you prefer apple or grape or pineapple, I'll get it at the grocery today. Or pomegranate. That's very good for you."

"Cranberry's fine, M," Simone mumbled.

"I'll get some pomegranate anyway."

Stellan walked Simone's coffee to her, seeing her gulp down cranberry juice.

At the sight, he couldn't stop his smile.

She gave him big, annoyed eyes.

He ignored that too.

And set about enjoying breakfast with two of his favorite girls in the world.

Forty-five minutes later, having left Simone being coaxed into taking cooking lessons from M, Stellan was halfway to work when his phone rang.

He took the call and spoke into the car.

"Yes, darling?"

"Do you want to tell me what that was?" Simone demanded.

"What what was?"

"This morning."

"Breakfast," he explained easily.

"Stellan—"

It was Stellan who interrupted her this time.

"You don't have to learn to cook, honey. I like cooking for us."

"I—"

"And speaking of that, we'll have dinner at home tonight, but tomorrow, we'll go out. After dinner, we'll enjoy drinks at the club."

"The club?"

"The Honey," he clarified.

"I'm not sure—"

"I'll call Leigh. Ask her and Olly to meet us there."

She made no response.

"Have a good day, darling. I'll see you tonight."

Her whisper filled his car.

"It's not going to work."

His steady voice vibrated through the car.

"Oh yes it is."

"I shouldn't have started this with you," she stated, like she wasn't talking to him.

"You're very wrong, Simone. Deciding to do that was the best decision you've made in your life. Now say, 'Goodbye, Stellan. I'll see you tonight.' "

"Kiss off, Stellan, I'm going to kick your ass tonight."

He burst out laughing.

He also made sure she heard it.

She loved it when he laughed and failed every time trying to hide that she did.

Then he hung up on her.

When Stellan walked through the door to Susan's office, he did not offer her a greeting, pass by, and go to his office

He offered her a greeting, walked to the opposite side of her desk, and stopped.

She studied him, did not return his *Good morning*, and instead said, "I don't like the look on your face."

Stellan again didn't delay.

"I know it's difficult to find a babysitter for Crosby, so how about we take that out of the equation and you, Harry, and Crosby join Simone and I for dinner at my house, perhaps Wednesday? Or if that doesn't work, Thursday."

Her brows headed toward her hairline. "You want Crosby there?"

"Yes."

"No offense, boss man, you picked her, I'm sure she's something else. But the woman is a fixer and I've never met one but even so, I'm not sure they'd be hip on dinner parties including eighteen-month-olds. I can't say I remember every second of every episode, but I'm pretty sure Olivia Pope never has been near a baby, but I could guess, considering the shenanigans that go on, she wouldn't have a lot of time for one."

"It'll be fine," Stellan assured.

"Does she like kids?" Susan asked.

"I've no idea," Stellan answered. "Though if I had to guess, I'd say they terrify her."

It was clear she caught herself before she rolled her eyes.

But she didn't let this effort stop her from saying, "Well then, take this woman's advice about your woman who I don't know but we both share at least that in common. Do not have her meet members of your family in a way that's more uncomfortable than it's already going to be."

"I have a variety of reasons for asking you to bring Crosby."

"You always have a variety of reasons for anything you do," she muttered. "First and foremost, you don't do it unless you can get everything you can out of it."

Very true.

"She needs to meet you," he went on. "She needs to get to know you. She needs to get to know me better. You're Crosby's mother. I'm Crosby's godfather. Harry is a very good friend of mine. You're all an important part of my life. I see no point in drawing out the inevitable."

"And?" she pushed.

"And I'm going to find it very interesting how she responds to a toddler considering I have every intention of impregnating her eventually, and also repeatedly, so I would say that's important to know."

Her mouth actually dropped open.

"You might wish to close that," he advised, tipping his head toward her, eyes to her lips. "You never know what you'll catch."

She snapped her mouth shut but opened it immediately to state, "You've decided, one date, one week with this woman, to have *children* with her?"

Stellan nodded. "For the most part, yes. We still have things to discover about each other, obviously. But I know she has good taste in films. She likes my cooking, can't boil water herself, and I don't care. She's stubborn but hilarious, and made M fall in love with her somehow through a single conversation, and now she's been adopted."

Susan assumed a stunned expression.

"Holy Moses, M adopted her?" she breathed.

"Yes, you belong to three sisterhoods with her now, by my count. The obvious one that involves you both sharing the same body parts. The one that involves me. And now the one that involves M deciding you'll need a mother until you die, even though you have one and even if you leave this earth at ninety-eight. If she outlives you, she'll mother you. Same with Simone. She forced a dish of vitamins on her this morning. I'm relatively certain I've pulled something with the effort it took for me not to laugh. But she took them."

Susan had an amusing look that was hilarity warring with incredulity when she said, "So with all that, you've decided to make babies with a fixer."

Stellan felt his good mood shifting.

"You need to let go of this idea of her as a fixer," he shared.

She didn't back down. "But isn't that what she does?"

"Not for very long."

Her expression changed again.

This time she looked worried.

"Stellan, I don't have to tell you that for a century or so women have been pretty intent on finding ways to make certain decisions for themselves. Like, um ... what they do to spend their time, how they make their money, being able to go out and *make* money, stuff like that."

Stellan lifted his attaché and rested it on her desk before explaining, "Simone doesn't do what she does because she enjoys doing it. She does what she does because it's the persona she needs to inhabit. It has a variety of uses including making people feel the need to keep distant from her as well as tricking herself into feeling alive. And last, giving life the excuse to do what it will with her, the sooner the better. If she did what she did because it was a genuine part of who she is, I wouldn't say a word. That's not why she does it."

"So you have her all figured out," she noted.

"Not close. She doles information out only under duress. But I have every intention of getting it figured out, so this I will do."

Susan knew that to be all kinds of true.

"You should have been a psychologist," she remarked.

"My innate abilities in that arena allow me to be very good at what I actually decided to do."

She grinned up at him. "Does she have any idea what she's gotten herself into?"

"She thinks she does, but she has no clue."

Her grin turned into a smile. "Right then, this I've gotta see firsthand. That's to say, Harry and I don't have anything on ever. The minute I popped Crosby out, our social life stormed out and slammed the door behind it, like a teenage girl who was denied tickets to the boyband concert she wanted so badly to see but she didn't keep her room clean. Though to give your girl a fighting chance before we enter the mix, we'll say Thursday. I'll call Harry to make sure it's good with him. Do you want us to bring anything?"

"If I say no, are you still going to bring a bottle of my favorite Scotch, flowers for Simone and some dessert you made anyway?" he asked.

"Yes," she answered.

"Then . . . no."

She dissolved into laughter.

Stellan smiled.

And watched indulgently.

Sitting at his desk, turned to the side, eyes to the non-view, Stellan listened to his phone ring in his ear.

The ass made him wait five rings.

He almost hung up.

But considering he'd do anything, he was doing anything.

"Lange," the man answered.

"Fred," Stellan replied. "Do you have a few minutes?"

"If you're calling about that council vote, I thought we had an agreement about that."

"We do. I'm not calling about that, unless what I'm calling about makes its way to being about that."

Fred didn't speak.

Stellan didn't need him to.

He needed the buffoon who was a buffoon in a variety of ways—however not in terms of the work he did, in that he was lethally successful . . . literally—to listen.

And agree.

"It's my understanding you farm out certain jobs to Sixx Marchesa," Stellan stated.

He visualized Fred straightening in his chair as he said alertly, "Where's this go—?"

"You're going to stop," Stellan finished.

"I am?" Fred asked.

"Yes you are."

"You wanna explain how you're makin' this decision for me?"

"Not really, but I will. She means something to me."

"Right . . . you're both a member of that club."

"No," Stellan negated. "She's living with me."

He heard a whistle in his ear as he crossed his legs and stared at the sprawling desert city.

"She's not who I woulda called for you," Fred remarked.

Stellan had no interest in what kind of woman a man like Fred would call for him.

A man like Fred, the kind who had zero legitimate concerns and thus made his money, raised his family, and went to sleep beside his wife as a criminal, but wanted to move into legitimate concerns way too late to even begin to wash the black marks from his soul—mattered not a thing to Stellan.

Except for the fact he ranged the edge of Sixx's life.

And that had to stop.

"So, if you should have another job, you'll find another resource," Stellan declared.

"Don't know, my man," Fred drawled, proving one way he could be a buffoon. "After Dillinger left it, the field got empty. Tucker refuses to work for me because that mouthy wife of his hates my guts. I need something done, what'm I supposed to do?"

"You have a creative way of dealing with human resources, Fred. I'm sure you'll come up with something."

And this was true. For instance, when someone did something Fred didn't like, if that someone was a man, Fred had his balls cut off, put in Formaldehyde, and they sat on a shelf behind his desk.

Again, not someone he wanted around Sixx.

And whatever jobs a man like that would throw her way?

Absolutely not.

"You're leaving me at a disadvantage here, Lange, without offering me anything to even that shit out," Fred noted.

"If I remember correctly, I'm having words with a couple of council members about that parcel of land out past Queen's Creek you want so badly."

"That's a deal, we agreed," Fred said roughly.

"Sadly, before they play out, some deals need to be renegotiated."

Fred didn't like to hear that, and as a man known to have a short fuse—which kept him in his position of lowly-criminal-with-a-moderate-empire, one he put great effort into keeping rather than elevating past, even in the world he inhabited—he didn't wait to share his displeasure.

Complete buffoon.

"You sittin' like a fat cat in your skyscraper—" Fred began.

Stellan uncrossed his legs, swiveled to his desk and cut him off.

"Listen to me," he growled. "It amused me to do something for you, and it suited me to hold a marker from you. It turns out I'm calling that before I expected to. And you'll allow me to do that. You'll not contact Sixx for any jobs before that land deal goes through, and you'll not do it after. If you do, we'll have issues."

"*We'll have issues,*" Fred mimicked. "Think you're a big man, throwin' your weight and connections around, think your money and all that protects you, but you're a pussy in a suit."

"Sylvie Creed has no issues working with me," Stellan said quietly. "You're correct. She does dislike you. Quite intensely. She'd enjoy fucking with you and your business. I wouldn't have to pay her, even though I would. And if you even thought of touching Sylvie, Tucker Creed would find you and rip your throat out with his bare hands. But listen to me, Fred, I might start out letting Sylvie have her fun with you, but I wouldn't let it end that way. I look like I look because I have taste and a good barber. I would not underestimate me if I were you."

"Excuse me for not quaking in my boots," Fred returned snidely. "What's a pussy like you gonna do to me?"

"If you engage Sixx again, I'll eliminate you."

The fury was tangible when Fred replied, "Are you seriously threatening to kill me?"

"Of course not," Stellan returned unperturbedly. "There are a variety of ways to eliminate someone, Fred. And I'd get creative."

"Yeah," the snide was back, "pussy."

"If you put Sixx in harm's way, which I define as her being any-where near you or your business ventures, I will make you hurt. And I'll enjoy doing it."

"We'll see how that goes," Fred retorted.

"The land deal is off the table."

"Fuck that, I don't need that shit."

He did.

And he'd never get it without Stellan.

The fool.

"And any further attempts to increase your legitimate dealings will be cut off at every pass, something you very much want to hap-pen because your wife wants you to reach retirement age, and she sees her future foursomes of golf not including you."

"We'll see," Fred muttered, letting slip a nuance of discomfort at how much and how personal Stellan's information ran.

"And you can forget the nail parlor and smoothie shop. Neither can launder your money anymore considering I purchased the prop-erties both inhabit last week, and I'm revoking their leases."

Fred had nothing to say to that.

Stellan turned back to the view and crossed his legs, asking, "Have I lost you?"

"Set up that play," Fred whispered. "You set up that goddamn play before you even promised me those votes."

"I never enter negotiations without complete understanding I have the upper hand."

"That was a smart play, but this one isn't," Fred warned.

"No, what isn't a smart play is dealing with someone who has a variety of things you want and not giving him the only thing he asks for, something that means nothing to you. Doing that simply in an attempt to communicate you have the bigger balls, when doing it means you do not. Now, if I read your response right, you're threat-ening me. And I can assure you that if you test me, I'll retaliate."

"And if I test your woman?"

Stellan's neck got tight.

But his voice was smooth when he returned, "Then Sixx will retaliate, and you'll feel humiliated when she lands you on your ass. But I'd wager that's the last thing you'd feel before she carved a blade across your throat."

"So you know the reputation of this bitch you're so fuckin' hot to keep outta the game," Fred noted.

"I know there's one worse enemy you can have in Phoenix outside Sixx Marchesa, and it isn't me. It's Branch Dillinger. And if you hurt her or me, before either of us could make a play, you'd be dealing with him."

Not surprisingly, the specter of Dillinger worked.

Then again, even Stellan might think twice before he crossed Branch Dillinger. Unless he liked you, and there were few in that club, the man was cold as stone. And vengeance served up from a man with an elite set of skills who looked at the vast majority of humanity as globs of matter that shared space with him was not something anyone would wish to elicit.

"Fine. You want it, my man, you got it," Fred spat. "Figure you callin' me means you're doin' this without her knowin', so it's gonna be you who's gonna be on your ass."

The truth was, Stellan was very curious what Simone's response was going to be.

And after their match in bed the day before, he was hoping she'd give that avenue a repeat try.

"Don't call this number again, asshole," Fred finished.

"Delightedly."

"Pussy," Fred muttered.

"Buffoon," Stellan returned clearly.

"Fuck you."

"Aren't we done?" Stellan asked.

"Yeah we—"

Stellan made them done.

He hung up.

He didn't have time for that.

He had other calls to make.

"Stellan, my brother," Aryas answered.

"Aryas," Stellan replied.

"Good news for you," Aryas told him before Stellan could begin talking about why he'd called. "Got a Domme in training. She could use an experienced sub, and from my take on her, the boy you talked to me about would be good for her. If he's up for a session or two, I'd waive the guest pass he'd have to normally pay. Can't waive the background check though, so he'd have to make an appointment to come in, fill out the paperwork, and talk with Dillinger."

"That's good news, I'll speak with Ami," Stellan said and added another phone call to Sixx on his list of things to do that day.

"Let me know what he says, and I'll chat with the Domme."

"Right. I'll do that," Stellan agreed. "Do you have a few minutes to talk?"

"Shoot," Aryas invited.

"When's the last time you spoke with Sixx?" Stellan asked.

"Spoke with her as in, got deep into a conversation about life and love and the meaning of it all? Never. Got into a conversation that lasted longer than it took for us to share a drink in one of my booths at the Honey? Never. Shared a drink with her at the club and didn't get into anything that means anything, even though I'd try but she'd cut me off at every pass? A couple of weeks. Got into a conversation over the phone with her to ream her ass about stupid shit she does to make money? It's been a while, since she stopped doing stupid shit."

"She hasn't."

There was silence.

"She works ad hoc jobs for Fred Carvelo, among others."

"Fuck," Aryas bit.

"I've been making a few calls," Stellan shared. "This work will dry up, starting today."

Another wave of silence, but Aryas broke it. "Have you lost your mind?"

"No," Stellan answered calmly.

"I take it you're makin' these calls, she doesn't know this work is gonna stop coming her way."

"You take it correctly."

"Okay," Aryas began. "Goes without sayin' I do not want our girl doin' stupid shit for dirty assholes who infest the underbelly of Phoenix. But I'm thinkin' that's not the way to go with makin' that stop."

"And how has reaming her ass worked so far, Aryas?" Stellan asked.

There was a pause before he muttered, "You got a point." He spoke clearly when he continued, "I'm still not thinking good thoughts on this, Stellan."

"I need you to help me pull her in," Stellan told him.

"Say again?" Aryas demanded.

"I need you to help me pull her in. You and Leigh and Olly and Leenie. I need her grounded. I need her centered. I need her supported. I need to build a foundation for her that she believes in. That she knows in her heart will never crack."

Aryas sounded perplexed when he replied, "She's already got that."

"No, she doesn't. She has no idea that she has that, which means she does not have that. She understands the concept that she has good people in her life. She absolutely does not understand the concept that they form the foundation of a life that will see her through the best of times, the worst of times, and all the minutiae in between."

"You're digging under," Aryas whispered, no concern in his voice, just respect.

"I am."

"You're getting in there."

"That I'm not doing," Stellan admitted. "So I'm calling for reinforcements."

"I'm in. So in. All in," Aryas declared. "I'll talk to Leigh. Leenie. Get her ass to the club. She'll have so much foundation she'll think she got herself a pair of cement boots."

Stellan took in a deep breath and let it out, saying, "Thank you."

"No need to thank me. Thanks goes to you, my man. And we'll be with you all the ways we can."

"We'll be at the club tomorrow night," Stellan shared.

"And so will I. See you then . . . and Stellan?"

"Yes?"

"Good luck, brother. Good fuckin' luck," Aryas said low.

After that, he hung up.

Stellan put his phone on his desk and turned back to the view thinking he could use all the luck he could get.

And hoping he didn't need a miracle.

"I'll want to meet her," Simone said that night from where they sat, both of them ostensibly reading, but mostly talking, on the couch in front of the fire in their bedroom.

Stellan made a note to make yet another call, this time again to Aryas so he could arrange for the Mistress that he wanted to work Ami to meet Simone.

"I'll see if Aryas will ask her to meet us at the club," Stellan replied.

"Ami should also be able to look her over," Simone said.

Stellan fought back a sigh at yet another call he'd need to make.

"Once you approve her, I'll discuss it with him."

"Good," she murmured, eyes to her tablet where she was reading a downloaded book.

Not her sketchpads. Those usually disappeared after she worked at them. He'd only ever seen her leave one out—last Friday, after their intense conversation—and it was likely left out because of their intense conversation. An oversight.

He needed to get into those sketchpads.

But he had a feeling if he did that without her permission, it would be an invasion she'd never forgive and a betrayal she'd use to end things with him in a way even he could not resuscitate.

As he studied her across the couch from him, doing it considering pulling her feet into his lap, she lifted her gaze to him.

"I'm not sure about the club tomorrow night, baby," she said softly.

She used "baby" to get her way quite often.

He liked it when she called him that so much he should allow her to get her way so she wouldn't discontinue its use.

However, with the stakes this high, that would be counterproductive.

"Why not?" he asked.

"We're not going to play, right?"

He nodded. "We're not going to play."

"So what's the point?"

"The point is to have a drink in a place where we can fully be who we are around people who are comfortable being fully who they are. One of the few places, outside our home, that allows that. *Our* place."

At his last two words, she turned to the fire.

Stellan examined her profile.

In doing so, he noted she was trying to hide it.

But she was scared.

And there were likely a myriad of reasons why.

She was scared of being his in a place where she had a carefully constructed façade she did not wish to be dismantled due to what it would expose. Scared of going there with him for no reason but to be with him, with her friends, and how much she'd like that, which would mean it would demonstrate how much she'd miss it when it was gone—or better, how much she wouldn't want to let it go. Scared of what it might convey, her with him, as they were both Doms, and as erroneous as it was to make that assumption, it was the way of the world, not simply the way of Simone's nature, that it would be assumed if one of them would switch, it would be her.

"I've never known you to go there just for a drink," she said softly.

"You haven't been there every time I've been there," he replied quietly. "That said, it is rare that I would go just for that purpose." She turned again to look at him. "But I've also never had a woman in my life who shared my way of life."

"I think it's too soon."

If she thought going to the Honey was too soon, she was not going to appreciate the news she'd be meeting Susan, Harry and Crosby on Thursday night.

"You're thinking wrong," he replied.

"Stellan—"

"We're going," he said decisively.

Her back got straight. "I'm not your submissive Simone right now," she snapped.

He looked down to his book, stating smoothly, "You always are, darling. You'll come to realize that and take comfort and contentment in it."

"Not when there's something you want to do that I *don't* want to do in terms of just living life."

He looked back at her. "Give me one reason, only one, but it has to be a good one, why we would not go to the club tomorrow night,"

Giving him one good reason would expose too much, therefore she shot back, "I don't feel like it."

"That's not a good reason."

"It should be," she retorted.

Stellan decided to stop playing nice.

"My pretty little coward," he whispered.

Her eyes flashed.

His lips curved.

She looked down at her tablet, shutting him out at the same time giving in.

He fully smiled.

Then he ordered, "Put your feet in my lap, sweetheart."

"Go to hell, asshole," she muttered.

He set his book aside, captured her feet, and brought them to his lap. She struggled, but only for moments, deciding not to give him the pleasure of subduing her.

Wise.

He started in on massaging the soles.

"You're insufferable," she told her tablet.

"You're adorable," he told her.

Eyes still aimed at her screen, Stellan caught a brand-new look on her face. It was pinched with frustration.

Definitely adorable.

With one hand, Stellan continued to massage her foot while with the other, he grabbed his book to give the impression he'd resumed reading.

He did not.

He fought the urge to crow.

She'd given in.

She could have fought it. She could have refused to do it.

But some part of her wanted to be on his arm as he walked them into the Honey. To be with her friends there. To be in their space.

She could be unconsciously taking everything she could get before she took herself away.

Or she could be learning to enjoy everything she was going to have.

Stellan decided it was the latter.

He also decided to read two more chapters.

After that, he was making love to his Simone, and they were going to sleep.

Tomorrow, they'd battle again.

And he was looking forward to it.

fourteen

Multivitamin

SIXX

Sixx came down the next morning prepared for what she'd face.

She did not have to wait for it.

"*Buenos días*, Simone!" M greeted in that way Simone was becoming accustomed to, like she hadn't seen her just yesterday but like Simone had reentered their world from her decade-long sojourn in a parallel universe, and M wasn't used to having her back.

"Hey, M," Sixx replied, scanning the area, looking for Stellan.

"He's in his study," M told her. "Your vitamins are in that dish on the island. I bought you a woman's multi and I got pomegranate juice."

Sixx had never had pomegranate juice and wasn't sure she wanted pomegranate juice.

She'd also never taken a vitamin in her life before yesterday.

She went right to the island and took her vitamins with pomegranate juice.

She further decided, next time M served that up, she'd find some way to cut it without M knowing. The stuff was bitter . . . and strong.

Perhaps with the way things were going with Stellan, she'd pick gin.

"Hello, darling."

She turned her head.

And there he was. The man of her dreams who was currently the orchestrator of her nightmare.

A nightmare that came when you lived a dream you knew was going to die.

She narrowed her eyes at him.

His mouth twitched as he moved her way, *right* her way, into her space, doing it seemingly to kiss her cheek, but after he did that, he slid his lips to her ear.

"For a woman who came three times last night, begging for that third, you seem in a vile mood," he murmured there and moved only far enough away to look into her eyes.

She was not going to reply.

She was not going to do anything.

But ride this out.

Two weeks and six days.

Then, even if it killed her (and she already knew it was going to kill her), she was gone.

"*Huevos rancheros* today," M stated into their staring contest. "Take seats, *mijos*, I'm serving."

"I'll get your coffee," Stellan murmured to Sixx, moving away.

She watched him.

Then she sat at the island, and M put a plate of food that looked better than any breakfast she'd had in her life (that was, any of them she'd had before yesterday) in front of her as Stellan slid a mug of coffee just like she liked it by her plate and then sat next to her to be served his own.

They'd eaten like this the day before. Side by side at the island with M chitter-chattering at them, Stellan murmuring fond "mms," "hmms," and "ahs" and Sixx struggling with all of it.

The delicious taste of homemade breakfast. The feel of the room, warm and pleasant. The act of starting the day sitting beside the man she slept beside, sharing time with a woman with a kind heart and a way with a spoon.

In all that had happened with Stellan, for some reason that was the toughest to handle.

They felt like . . .

She didn't have much experience with it, but it felt like . . .

A family.

Except for memories of her mother grudgingly pouring sugary cereal in a bowl with some milk or the times when her father would wake up in a good mood and make "my famous French toast for my baby girl!" she'd never sat anywhere for any family meal.

As pathetic as it totally was, that included not a single birthday, Thanksgiving, Christmas.

Ever.

If her father remembered, while her mother was out doing business, making buys, soliciting sales, he'd take her out for pizza on her birthday, and if she was lucky, that was followed with an ice cream cone.

She did not consider that a family meal. Since they had pizza delivered for dinner two or three times a week, it was just what it was . . . except somewhere else.

As it had yesterday, and right then, Stellan's huge home closed in on her in a way that, having spent the time in it she'd spent, it never had.

She had the urge to look around to see if the walls were moving, but she didn't.

Even so, it couldn't be escaped that now that the seal had been torn off, even when they were sharing dinner and sitting by the fire last night, his luxurious, intimidating mansion had ceased being that and instead had become something else.

It was where people slept. And showered. And read books. And made love. And ate side by side.

It was a home.

It was where she slept, showered, read books, made love, ate side by side with the man in her life.

It was *her* home.

"Not to your liking, *querida*?" M asked with concern, and Sixx's head shot up.

She dug in to the food, her voice uncontrollably husky when she replied, "No, M. It's delicious. Just have a job today that's on my mind."

Sixx felt both M's and Stellan's eyes on her, but she avoided them, cutting through the egg, gathering it up with the homemade salsa, some Spanish rice and fresh avocado, and putting it between her lips.

It was heaven.

This was heaven.

All of it.

And because it was, Sixx was in hell.

It got worse when Stellan's hand landed on her back, gliding down light but warm to rest at its small, and she turned her head his way to catch the penetrating, worried look on his handsome face.

"All right?" he murmured low.

"Peachy," she lied.

Her lie didn't shift his focus or expression, it just intensified both.

Sixx couldn't deal.

She turned back to her food.

She'd taken a multivitamin purchased specifically for her.

She was eating breakfast.

Why did that make her want to dissolve into tears?

Some unspoken accord was reached, and M resumed her cheerful chitter-chatter, and after a few loving circles, Stellan removed his hand from her back and returned to his breakfast.

Sixx ate while she pulled her shit together.

Two weeks.

Six days.

She could do it.

She could take it.

She could give the little she had to give.

Then she'd be a memory.

That night, Sixx stood at the sinks in the Dom Lounge at the Honey, her lipstick in her raised hand arrested on its way to her face, staring at herself in the mirror.

As they'd walked in, Sixx knowing all eyes in the bar were coming to them—Mistress Sixx and Master Stellan arriving together, a couple, an item, living together—Stellan had murmured in her ear, "I forgot to mention, Susan and Harry will be over for dinner on Thursday. They're bringing Crosby."

She honest-to-God almost threw up, right there on the spot.

Instead, before Stellan could seat her in the booth he choose— *not* one in a corner, *not* one in a shadow, one right smack at the center of the side wall so everyone in the room could see it . . . *them*—she'd said she had to freshen up.

Then she'd escaped.

God, in two days she'd have to meet his precious Susan.

And Crosby!

What the hell was she going to do around a kid?

"Sixx?"

She jumped a mile and turned, feeling her eyes grow big with surprise, her heart beating wild in her chest as she saw Amélie standing there, studying her with some alarm.

"Are you all right?" she asked.

Sixx shook herself, cerebrally and literally.

"Yes. Fine. Sorry, you caught me off guard."

"You . . . I . . . you," Leigh unusually stammered. "I didn't know you could be caught off guard."

Sixx didn't either.

Damn.

"And you can see the door open in the mirror from where you're standing," she continued.

Damn again!

"I have things on my mind," Sixx murmured.

"Would you like to share?" Leigh offered.

She did.

God.

She did want to share. With somebody, anybody. She'd talk to a vagrant on the street.

But definitely Amélie, who knew Stellan, liked Stellan, knew Sixx (of a sort) and liked her.

And there was utterly no way she was going to talk to Leigh.

"I'm good," she replied, turning and finally lifting her lipstick to her lips, leaning into the mirror to freshen it up.

"Sixx?" Leigh called.

"Hmm?" Sixx responded, not taking her eyes from her lips.

"You know I'm here, anytime, right?"

Shit, damn, *fuck*.

She was going to cry again.

Sixx finished her lips and turned to Leigh with what she hoped was a neutral expression on her face.

"Yeah. Sure," she answered.

"And Leenie too," she pushed it. "Mira. Felicia. Romy. Anybody. The start of a new relationship can be wonderful. But even if it is, it can also be confusing. So if you want to talk anything through, any of us would be there for you. Not just to talk through something like that. To talk through anything that might be troubling you."

"As I said, Leigh," Sixx started nonchalantly, "I'm good. But just to say, I'm not starting a new relationship."

Leigh's perfectly arched brows hiked up. "Sorry?"

"I think you have the wrong impression," she shared.

"About . . . you and Stellan," Leigh stated hesitantly, finishing, "*living together?*"

That did sound stupid.

But she had to go with it.

"We aren't really. It's a temporary thing. We have a spark. We're working through it. It's not going anywhere."

Like someone swiped an eraser across it, Leigh's face went blank.

But her voice held a distinct timbre when she asked, "Does Stellan know this?"

Sixx nodded. "Absolutely."

She should have known she couldn't pull shit with Leigh.

And Leigh didn't hesitate to remind her she couldn't.

She did this declaring, "He's falling in love with you."

Lord, she wished she could have sustained that with no reaction. She, however, could not.

She flinched and cast her eyes away.

"If you're playing with him, Sixx, you need to have a conversation with him so emotions can be held in check."

Sixx again met Leigh's gaze. "He's aware. He just doesn't want to listen. You know Stellan. He wants what he wants, and that's all there is."

"Is there a reason you don't want him?"

"We don't suit. Not for the long run."

"And how's that?"

Sixx swung a hand low, her meaning clear but she underlined it saying, "Uh . . . pretty much in *everything*."

"Stop it," Leigh whispered, and Sixx went perfectly still.

Leigh's expression was no longer a blank slate. Her tone was not cool and unconcerned.

God, she almost looked in pain.

She definitely sounded it.

"Leigh—"

"You're perfect for each other and you know it. And something is very wrong, and you know that too. If you don't wish to speak about it, *chérie*, I will not press, even though everything in me is screaming to do just that. I will only reiterate that I care for you. I want the best for you. I care for Stellan. I want the best for him. Now that the idea of the two of you has been brought to light, I feel deep in my heart that the best for both of you is each other. That said, the last time we spoke of this, you rushed away, which is wholly unlike you. Only for you to return wearing a mask, which, I mean no offense, is not. Now, I've taken you by surprise when you're always entirely aware of your surroundings, and you're saying the man you've moved in with who is obviously enamored with you and that is only intensifying with time is someone you're just playing with." Her head tipped sharply to the side. "Are you switching for him? Is that what's bothering you?"

"I thought you said you weren't going to press," Sixx, feeling like a bitch, pointed out.

Leigh shut her mouth.

Sixx shook her head, lifted her hand, dropped it.

"That was bitchy." She straightened her shoulders. "And yes. He's an excellent Dom. We're exploring some things. But that isn't it. I'm just a temporary kind of girl, and Stellan knows the score so don't worry. He's aware of where I'm at, and he'll be fine when it's over. You know he will."

"I know nothing of the sort," Leigh returned.

Back to the bitch, Sixx pointed out, "He was in love with you maybe a year ago."

"You were not here maybe a year ago."

God, why did all her friends have to be so damned smart?

"Amélie—"

"I would say, don't hurt him, because normally, I would suspect Stellan could survive absolutely anything. With you, the way he looks at you, the change in his manner when he's around you, I cannot say that's still correct. But I won't say that. I'll say don't self-harm and do that by denying yourself something that's good for you for whatever reason that might be. If you're concerned about switching, I know a switch. He's perfectly at ease with both sides of that coin, and although a man, I still believe speaking with him would be useful for you. If it's something else, I can only say what I've already said more than once. I'm here to listen, and it would be my honor, my privilege, Sixx, for you to share with me whatever is on your mind."

To end this awkward conversation, Sixx replied, "Thanks. If I need to talk, I'll reach out."

"Promise me."

Sixx looked her right in the eye.

And lied.

"I promise."

The disappointment and distress Leigh didn't hide shared she knew she'd just been lied to, right to her face, by a friend.

Well, there you go, she thought. *Perfect. So when you're gone, now Leigh will realize she's not missing much of anything. Not that she probably didn't know that already.*

Leigh said nothing of it.

Instead, she shared, "I just need to use the loo. Olly is out with Stellan. If you want to wait, we can walk out together. If not, I'll see you out there."

Leigh also didn't hide that Sixx's response was disappointing when she said, "See you out there."

She just nodded and moved toward the toilets.

Sixx shoved her lipstick in her clutch and headed to the door.

She wanted to sit in a booth with Stellan, Olly and Leigh now a whole lot less than she wanted to do it before, and she wasn't fired up about it in the first place.

This was on her mind as she made her way through the halls back toward the bar.

So she hit Surprise: Part Two of the night when Aryas boomed, "Yo!" Her head shot up, and she saw a smiling, huge Aryas in front of her.

Right in front of her.

They were less than a foot away.

"Lost in thought, trajectory *me,*" he teased. "Not sure I could be bowled over, but Mistress Sixx on another planet threw me, so you were about to do it."

"Aryas," she said in greeting, taking a step back.

The jovial light in his eyes extinguished, and one she was getting too damned used to took its place.

"Christ, what the fuck is up with you?" he asked.

"Nothing," she lied . . . *again.* "I just have an annoying job on the go and it's on my mind."

Aryas was not nearly as mannered as Amélie.

Not even close.

He demonstrated this with his reply of, "Bullshit."

She was at the end of her rope with this crap, and she didn't feel the need to be mannered about it either.

"Listen, I've got something going down at work that's messing with me, and I don't need anyone else to mess with me. I just need a drink and time to relax, and tomorrow I'll be back in the grind, getting it sorted."

"You are scared freakin' shitless that Stellan's doing it for you, and it's not about a cush mansion and taking elegant cock among the strains of Mozart or however that dude keeps it tight when he does vanilla. It's that you finally got what you want, you have no idea how that feels, it's blowin' your badass mind, and instead of womaning up and getting your head straight, you're gearing up to run as fast as your stiletto boots will get you gone."

Her eyes narrowed. "Did you not hear me just say I don't need anyone else to mess with me?"

"You've had what you wanted, or more to the point, what you didn't want at all, and really did not need, for a long time, Sixx. Now it's time to pull that pretty head right out of that sweet ass and focus on the right goals for a change."

"If I want a conversation with you about my goals, Aryas, don't you worry. I'll seek you out."

"You wouldn't do that even if I paid you a million goddamn bucks to do it, and I'll prove that right now. One million. In cash. By the end of the week. You come to my office right now and open up to me."

She stood stock-still and stared in his confrontational but warm and uneasy eyes.

She also said nothing.

"I knew it," he whispered.

"Stop it," she whispered back.

"Open up, Sixx. To me. To Leigh. To Leenie. Or best of all, to Stellan," he urged. "But bottom line, just do it with *somebody*."

"I need you to stop."

He was Aryas.

Physically, he was huge.

But he'd have to be to have a body to hold that big of a heart.

"Always here," he murmured, letting it go.

"Thanks," she mumbled, moving to pass him.

She had a lot to do in the short time it would take to get from that place in the hall to the booth where Stellan was, considering she was not going to break down and throw a scene, taking off or demanding to leave once she got there.

In other words, that "lot to do" was getting her head together.

So she said nothing else to Aryas as she made her way.

But he called her name.

And again, he was Aryas.

So she stopped and turned back.

"I have no idea what broke you," he called along the distance between them and managed to do it gently. "So I cannot begin to try to fix you. I just wish like fuck you'd give me or anybody a shot."

"I'm fine, Ary, promise," she lied.

"You know, the people who think a great deal about you not knowing shit about you says it all, baby. What they feel from you, when you're not giving a thing. Can you imagine, if you split open just a crack, what that might bring?"

She could.

And she liked them all enough to save them from it.

I love you, she thought.

"Can I go get a drink now?" she asked.

"From me, Sixx, if I can give it, you can have anything."

Goddamn *shit*.

She was going to cry again.

She sucked in breath and did not.

She simply nodded, turned, and walked away.

Two weeks and now five days.

Two weeks.

And five days.

She hit the door to the bar area, and as she walked down the line of booths, she saw Stellan had positioned himself on the side where he'd see her coming.

Therefore, as the gentleman he was, he slid out of the booth prior to her even arriving at it in order that she could slide in immediately, protected from absolutely nothing as he took the seat at the open end, but if they lived in medieval times or some shit like that, he'd have her covered.

Olly was across from her, smiling, and she just could not wait (not) for Amélie to join their happy party.

"Hey," Olly greeted, still smiling.

"Hey," she mumbled.

"I didn't know what you'd want to drink, darling," Stellan put in. "So I waited to order for both of us."

Of course he did.

"Gordon's cup," she said and watched his head turn immediately, his chin jerking up to call over a server.

"How's things?" Olly asked as the server came up to the table.

"I woke up breathing," she replied.

Olly laughed, but he did it with his kind gaze speculative on her.

Stellan ordered, and Olly, obviously waiting with Stellan for her to arrive, ordered for him and Leigh.

Sixx sat there, miserable and wanting to flee.

She needed her sketchbooks.

She needed to sketch her way out of this, only there having control over the entire situation, making it so she could take herself away and do it leaving them happy and whole just . . . without her.

Fortunately, or unfortunately, depending on how you looked at it, Leigh arrived at their table on this thought, and Olly slid out of the booth just as Stellan had so that Leigh could be protected from the nonthreatening bar-at-large by a cocoon of his solid strength.

Leigh had that, finally she had that, a man to have and to hold, to love and to play with, who thought he'd struck the jackpot getting that back from her.

Sixx was thrilled Amélie had that.

But she was terrified that it appeared she had that same thing too.

And a-fucking-*gain*, Sixx wanted to dissolve into tears.

It only got worse.

It did this when Stellan's hand found hers resting on her thigh, curled around it in a warm, reassuring grip, and his lips also found her ear.

"We'll have our drink and go home," he whispered.

He pulled away and looked into her eyes.

He knew how she was feeling, he knew how deeply it ran, and last, he knew how badly she needed to escape.

And like the gallant knight in the fairy tales, he was going to save her from the burdens that threatened her.

"I'm fine," she whispered back.

Another lie.

"We'll see how you feel after your drink," he returned.

"I'll feel fine," she lied again.

He said nothing more, too cultured to continue a discussion that would only turn into an argument about nothing.

"You really must consider not missing the next book club, Sixx," Leigh said, and Sixx hesitantly turned her attention to her friend, a friend she just had an awkward conversation with in the bathroom. "We're reading Tiffany Reisz. *The Mistress*, obviously. It's excellent. Have you read it?"

Sixx studied Leigh for a moment, seeing she'd completely shut out what had happened in the bathroom. Now, it was just casual conversation among friends in a booth in a sex club.

"Not yet," Sixx replied, jumping right into that game.

"Best nights are the nights my Leigh-Leigh does some reading for that book club," Olly muttered.

"One must always keep one's skills sharp and one's imagination turning," Leigh murmured back.

"Like you need books to do that," Olly returned.

Leigh gave him a slow smile.

Stellan started to stroke the side of Sixx's palm with his thumb.

It felt wonderful.

Leigh turned her attention to Stellan and declared baldly as well as apropos of nothing, "It's been some time since we discussed you getting a pet."

Sixx's hand convulsed in Stellan's hold at the very thought of Stellan lounging on his couch reading with a canine's head on his knee, Stellan's long fingers buried in fur, or a feline curled up in his lap, purring.

God.

Olly's eyes went directly to the ceiling. "Here we go again."

"What?" Amélie asked her man, like she didn't know.

The woman volunteered at a veterinary clinic that also operated a small, no-kill shelter. She was always on people to adopt pets.

Though not Sixx.

She knew better than to ask Sixx.

"I think I have my hands full with my current new pet," Stellan replied drolly.

Olly shot them both a big grin.

Leigh kept her mouth shut.

Sixx wondered what was taking so damned long with her drink.

Leigh's eyes wandered, but they didn't wander far before they narrowed.

It was like Olly had a sixth sense when it came to his woman. The instant she reacted to whatever she saw, he looked at her and then turned his attention to where she was looking.

He also frowned.

Stellan shifted to peer over his shoulder.

It didn't take long before he shifted back—this, blessedly, because the drinks had finally arrived but also because he was too classy to be caught staring over his shoulder at anything.

Sixx tried very hard not to snatch her drink out of the server's hand and down it in one gulp, and she managed to succeed at this endeavor, taking it up only when it was placed in front of her and swallowing back only a healthy sip.

"I'm not sure you should get involved in that, baby," Olly said low.

"What?" Sixx asked after she swallowed.

"Talia and Bryan," Leigh stated immediately. "She's selected him again. And I fear, with the look on his face, that he might get on bended knee before, or after, she strips him red, takes his ass and drains him dry."

Damn.

Sixx looked to the side as Talia walked by their booth, sending them a toothy, carefree grin. She was followed closely by Bryan, who was not looking at the ground but at her ass.

He'd pay for that.

Which was the point when Talia noticed him doing it, something he'd make sure she did.

After they disappeared behind the door to the playrooms, and after Sixx took another hefty sip of her drink, she said to Leigh, "I'd been meaning to discuss that with you."

"And I've been meaning to discuss it with Talia . . . and Aryas," Leigh replied.

"Don't go there," Olly said at the same time Stellan put in, "I would leave that alone, Leigh."

"She's in love with Aryas, and Aryas her," Leigh retorted.

"It's none of your business, sweetheart," Olly told her.

"Talia is a new Domme," Leigh declared. "She might not know what she's doing."

"Talia *was* a new Domme," Stellan amended smoothly. "She's also headstrong, and at this point in her experience, she would not welcome your input."

"Bryan's heart is involved," Leigh returned. "Hers is not."

"I beg to differ," Stellan stated, and Sixx turned her head to look at him as he continued to speak to Amélie. "You are correct. At first, she was selecting him in order to punish Aryas for his inattention. But Aryas has continued his course of inaction, and now she's moving on. I can't say I pay close attention to their play, but the last time I saw them together, it was not about selecting a sub that appeals to her to get them both off as she's biding her time for Aryas to take notice. The tone had changed. Significantly."

"I hadn't noticed that," Leigh murmured.

"Me either," Sixx said under her breath, finishing with, "Poor Ary."

"Indeed," Leigh said, and Sixx looked at her. "Poor Ary." Suddenly, a sly smile spread on her face. "We should go watch."

Yes, the bathroom situation was entirely shut down.

Amélie was letting it go.

She was a good woman, a good friend, and in another life, Sixx would have liked to have gotten to know her better.

She would miss her.

But now she had her.

So she smiled back. "Let's."

Without her having to ask, Stellan slid out, as did Olly, but it was only Stellan who said, "Enjoy. The men will keep the booth warm for when you return."

Sixx exited her seat and saw Leigh already out, reaching a hand toward her.

She took it and refused to look back at the man who slid out of the booth to let her free without her even asking, the man she loved, the man she had sat beside for the first time in *their place*, and would return to when she and Amélie were done, as Leigh tucked Sixx's hand in the crook of her arm and headed them toward the playrooms.

As they walked, Leigh leaned her head Sixx's way and said conspiratorially, "It's good Olly's not coming. If Talia does something inspired, later he won't know I'm copying her."

"Thank you," Sixx said in reply.

Amélie stopped with her hand on the door to the playrooms and looked at Sixx, not hiding her confusion. "For what?"

"For being you," Sixx explained.

The confusion fled, and Leigh gave her a small smile that was both concerned and sad. But she didn't get into either.

She replied, "I can hardly say 'you're welcome' for that."

"Then don't," Sixx said, put her hand on the door too and pushed through, taking Leigh with her.

They moved through the hallways, connected, two Mistresses, two friends, enjoying a night at their club together.

A memory Sixx would take with her.

A memory Sixx knew she'd be glad she had for the time when she wouldn't be making memories like this at all.

The ride home was silent.

Stellan was who he was.

Therefore he knew she needed that.

And he gave her that.

After they walked into the laundry room and he guided her down the hall, Stellan, being who he was, gave her more.

Stopping her outside his study, he looked down at her, lifted a hand to cup her jaw, and she watched his face in the darkened corridor coming close to hers.

When he was a breath away, he said gently, "Go to your sketchbooks, honey. I'll be waiting for you in bed."

With nothing more, he touched his mouth to hers, let her go, and she watched his tall, shadowy figure move gracefully away, wondering if she knew him as well as he knew her.

And she realized she did.

For instance, she knew he did not let whatever happened during his days get to him. He talked about it, but even if it frustrated or annoyed him, he shared only that it did. Other than that, he left it at the office when he came home to her. And then he was just home with her, giving her all of him, taking everything she'd give in return.

She further knew he understood his past and how bleak it was, and he'd found a way to live with it, not against it.

And last, she knew, for reasons she did not understand, he was falling in love with her.

On this thought, Sixx moved directly to the library where she'd hidden her current sketchpad and pencils in a place Stellan wouldn't find (though she'd already learned he wouldn't look, even if she left them out, but M might).

But when she retrieved them, she didn't go to a chair or his desk in his study or out by the pool.

She went to a corner of the room, turned, sank to her ass on the floor, held the sketchpad tight against her chest with her thighs, and she stared in the dark.

That day she'd taken a woman's multivitamin bought specifically for her.

And she'd fall asleep beside Stellan that night.

Alone, solitary, safe, unable to hold them back any longer, the tears came slow at first, one chased leisurely by another.

And then they came faster.

In the end she had to shove her face in her knees and endure the pain it caused as she held back the noises just in case Stellan came looking for her, her shoulders and back and chest and ribs heaving with the effort.

"I wanna be normal," she whispered brokenly to her knees.

You've always wanted to be normal, her mind reminded her. *You'll never be normal. And he doesn't want normal. He wants you. He's not normal, not nearly normal, and you want him.*

She wanted him.

She wanted *him.*

And she wanted *them.*

We'll have our drink and go home.

Behind her squeezed-shut eyes she saw him there, sitting close to her in a booth at the Honey, her safe place, their place, holding her hand, knowing from the time they walked in to the time she fixed her lipstick and returned to him that something had happened, she needed to leave, and he was going to make that so.

This morning it's my famous French toast for my baby girl!

Her head shot up, and she pushed herself off the floor. She hurried to her hiding place, stashed the sketchbook and pens, and dashed her hands on her face to clear away the tears as she moved out the door.

She noted Stellan's timers had lit her way with a lamp at the base of the stairs, which she turned off, and one in the hall, which she also turned off.

She hit the bedroom and saw Stellan in bed, sitting up against the headboard, covers to his waist, chest exposed, book in his hand.

He looked up the minute she entered the room.

She twisted her arms behind her to pull the zipper down on the little red leather mini-dress she was wearing.

He put his book aside on the nightstand and watched her make her way toward him.

She drew the dress off her shoulders at the front, let it drop, and stepped out of it, all with only a moment's hesitation in stepping over it when it hit the floor as she continued toward him, up the steps, to his side of the bed, wearing nothing but a barely there red bralette made of see-through lace and a pair of black pumps with thin ankle straps.

"Darling," he said quietly, gaze on her face, not her body.

She didn't stop moving, even at the side of the bed.

She threw the covers off him and saw he was ready for bed, and also ready for her.

He was naked and hard.

Lord God.

So beautiful.

She put a knee to the bed and swung the other leg around, straddling him.

His hands went to the backs of her thighs.

Her hands went to his wrists, pulling them away, lifting them over his head, pinning them to the headboard, her eyes looking directly into his.

She saw them flash.

"Simone," he whispered.

She lowered herself on him, rubbing her wetness against the underside of his rigid shaft.

His jaw tightened, his eyes darkened, and his voice roughened when he repeated, "Simone."

Yes, Sixx knew him.

She also knew his body.

So she bent to it, putting her mouth to him, going to places that she'd learned were responsive.

The skin under his ear, the expanse where his head met his neck. And down.

His nipples were sensitive. If he was ever at her command, she'd manipulate them for hours, torturing him with it.

She moved to them, pulling his hands down slightly so she could hold them away but pressing her weight into them as she did so he'd get her message.

She felt his fingers ball into fists, but he allowed her to hold him as she worked his nipples, licking, sucking, scraping the edge of her teeth down them, feeling his body respond, hearing the low masculine purrs drift up his throat, his hands tensing and flexing in her hold.

She moved further down, over the ridges of his abs, to where he liked her best, where any man was most sensitive.

"Simone," he groaned.

She kept going, having to release his hands to do it.

He spread his legs, her body slipped through, his fingers slid into her hair and he whispered, "Darling."

She took up his shaft then swallowed it deep, thrilling when his resulting grunt drove up her pussy.

Sixx again grasped his hands, pulling his fingers out of her hair and pushing them into the bed by his hips as she sucked him off relentlessly, dragging hard, moving fast, seeing his legs cock up reflexively at her sides, taking his thrusts as his fingers wrapped around her wrists and her work forced him to move.

She let him fuck her face because that was what he wanted, what he *needed*, and while he had her, she would give him anything, everything, all she had to give.

Sixx did this until it was time to give more.

She drew deep as she pulled him out, then surged up over his body, taking his wrists with her, pinning them again to the headboard.

Catching his heated, frustrated, beautiful blue gaze, she transferred his wrists to one hand, reached between them, wrapped her fingers around his cock, positioned him, and then plunged down on him, fast and hard.

His eyes narrowed dangerously, and he hissed through his teeth.

She started riding him, staring into blue.

Holding her gaze, his wrists moved in her fingers, but Sixx replaced her other hand there, pushing both of his into the headboard with as much of her weight as she could use and all of her strength as she rode him fast, squeezing him with her pussy as she went, her breaths escalating, his going uneven.

"I want to touch you," he growled.

She said nothing, just kept moving on him, milking him, fucking him, quick and hard.

She felt his hands flex then form into fists again, but he didn't break her hold as he demanded, "At least kiss me."

Sixx didn't.

She held contact with his gaze, riding him rough, merciless.

"Simone," he warned low.

Her breath was coming with difficulty, her focus shifting from what she was giving him to what she was giving herself. She kept at him but had to drop her forehead to his, their connection there rolling as she drove herself down on him again and again, taking him, refocusing where she needed to be.

Only giving to him.

"Sixx," he bit off, pressing his forehead into hers, and she saw it beginning.

"For you," she whispered. "Just you."

"Goddammit, *Sixx*," he groaned.

His head snapping back with nowhere to go, it slammed against the headboard, and Sixx kept moving on him, working him, taking him through his orgasm.

When he was done, she settled, full of him, and his head slid down the side of hers so his forehead rested on her shoulder.

She closed her eyes and memorized that moment to commit to her sketchpad later.

When she had, Sixx let his wrists go. His hands immediately moved to grab her, but she was quicker.

She swung off, disconnecting them, exiting the bed.

She walked to the bathroom and cleaned up.

She walked into the closet and took off her bralette and shoes, pulling on a shapeless T-shirt nightie.

She walked out of the closet, back into the bathroom. She cleaned her face, brushed her teeth, turned out the light, and surprisingly, found the bedroom dark when she entered it.

But then again, it wasn't surprising.

Stellan would guess that was what she would need.

So he made it so.

Sixx pulled back the covers and got into bed, settling on her side only to be drawn directly into Stellan's body.

She closed her eyes and braced.

"I get it," he said into the back of her hair, tightening his hold on her, pulling her closer, molding her back to his front. "I understand now."

He'd never understand.

He was too strong.

Too right.

Too good.

Too beautiful.

He could lose his parents, and go on.

He could lose his sister, and go on.

He would lose her, and go on.

"In your scenes, why it's always about them, your subs," he continued. "Why you barely touch them. Why you let yourself have nothing. It seems you're detached, removed, indifferent, but you aren't, my darling, are you? What it is for any good Dom goes doubly for you. Doesn't it, Simone? You're giving them exactly what they want, entirely focused on giving them precisely what they need. Sacrificing your own needs to hone in with utter absorption to give to them what they want the most. It isn't a disconnect. The reason they're begging for it is that they've never had it so good."

"I need to sleep now, Stellan," she replied.

"If you ever need that again, Sixx, you ask me to the couch, another room, lead me to the playroom, but not in our bed. In our bed, you climax, even if it's eventually. Sixx and Simone sleep at my side, but only Simone fucks me in this bed, including when I have to break through Sixx to get to her. Is that understood?"

It was very much understood in a number of ways.

Including that he would give that to her again if she needed it.

He'd do anything for her.

Even take an orgasm it was she who would not allow him to return instead of the other way around.

He gave her a squeeze. "Simone, is that understood?"

"It's understood," she mumbled.

His arm loosened . . . somewhat.

She lay in his hold and stared at the dark.

"What made you cry?" he whispered.

Of course he didn't miss that.

Then again, she hadn't hidden it.

I'm in love with you.

"Simone, sweetheart, what made you cry?" he repeated when she did not answer out loud.

I never want to leave you. I want to stay forever and knock myself out to make you happy.

Stellan burrowed his face in her hair and murmured, "That's all right, honey. You don't have to answer."

Of course she didn't.

"I'll get you there," he promised quietly.

No you won't.

"And when you're there, I'll make you happy."

That isn't the goal. If that was to happen, it would need to be the other way around.

"He'd want you to be happy, Simone," he said gently.

That had her shutting her eyes tight.

This morning it's my famous French toast for my baby girl!

"Please, stop talking," she begged.

"All right, darling," he murmured.

Stellan held her.

Sixx let him.

He did not fall asleep before her.

And she did not fall asleep before she prepared herself mentally and knew when the next day dawned, she could endure.

Two weeks.

And five days.

Then the torture would be over.

For Stellan.

fifteen

Rare Slices of Perfection

SIXX

"I get that you have a life. I'm glad that you have a life. It's fantastic
to learn a friend of mine is part of that life. Stellan is a good man,
and I see good things for the two of you. Now that you're seeing
each other, I realize I should have thought to set you up with the
guy. You're perfect for him. And honestly, I knew the good stuff had
to end eventually. A woman like you wouldn't be able to give us
twenty-four-seven forever. But you need to let us know if we need
another investigator, Sixx. Even if part-time or on contract. I'll make
it clear your position is not in jeopardy. You're allowed to have a life.
We've enjoyed having you available to us, like, we've been able to uti-
lize you for longer than we should have, frankly. But the work still
has to get done, and we're up against a wall with this one, and we've
got nothing to go on."

Sixx sat opposite her boss in his office, and even though he was
telling her she was falling down on the job, what she heard repeated
in her head was *I actually should have thought to set you up with the guy, you're
perfect for him.*

"How did you know about me and Stellan?" she asked, and Joel
Trebek's eyebrows went up.

"Sorry, was it a secret?" he asked back.

"No, I just haven't shared about us in the office."

In fact, Sixx didn't share anything at the office, and not just
because she rarely came to the office. So she definitely had not shared
that.

He nodded. "Yes, but you were at Steak 44 with him last week.

A mutual acquaintance saw you, spoke briefly with Stellan, he introduced you. His wife told my wife who told me."

Of course.

Sixx got them back on track. "The trial with this guy starts Wednesday?"

Joel nodded again. "And we have nothing, but there can't be nothing to find. You did the computer work, it's not there. That tells me if there's something to be had, it's going to take fieldwork."

"I'm on it," she told him. "If there's something to get, you'll have it by Monday."

At that, Joel shook his head. "Sixx, we've contracted with outside investigators before. We can pull one in on this. You knew this wasn't a nine-to-five job when you took it, but you've gone above and beyond since you started with us. If you need some time—"

"I don't need time." She drew in a breath and did something she'd never done in her life with any "employer" (not that she had many legitimate ones before Joel): She invoked her personal life into her professional one. "I'll speak with Stellan. He'll understand."

She said it, but she wasn't sure that was true.

Stellan would give her anything, and she wouldn't renege on the dinner the next evening with his Susan. But she was going to have to put in the work—nights and weekends—and she had a feeling with the full-court press he was doing to get her to believe, he wasn't going to like it.

Especially weekends.

Joel gave her a close look. "You're sure?"

"Stellan gets it, and he gets me. He'll get this," she replied.

Joel smiled. "Great. But if you need an assist, give me a heads-up. We'll get it for you."

That was not going to happen. She partnered up only rarely, and when she did there were only three people she'd do that with—Carlo, Sylvie or Tucker. Joel might be cool with contracting with Sylvie or Tucker. Carlo would scare the holy hell out of him.

"Best get on this," she muttered, rising from her chair.

"Tell Stellan I said hello and we should get together for a drink or a meal. I'll talk to Tammy. We'll set something up."

Dinner or drinks with her boss, his wife, and Sixx's man.

How very normal.

Yikes.

Sixx nodded, lifted a hand in a wave and walked out of the office, not wondering how she'd let work slide considering she always went balls to the wall, day or night, for whatever job she was on. She didn't have the "or night" part of that being with Stellan.

What she wondered was how she let an assignment slide so badly her boss had to chat with her about it. He was being cool, and that had to do with the fact that she was good at what she did and he knew it. However, it also could have to do with the fact she was with Stellan and they were buds.

But she'd been so focused on Stellan, nights with him, dinner with him, going to bed with him, having their weekend together, she'd blown off work. That wasn't like her, and she needed this job.

At least until she took off.

But if she decided to go totally legit, she'd need the reference.

This is good, she told herself as she walked through the offices, making eye contact, dipping her chin or lifting it to secretaries and paralegals (or whoever they were) that she passed. Staff whose names she didn't know and didn't make any effort to know or remember if she learned them, unless she was working a job for the attorney they worked for.

And she thought this was good because she could fight Stellan's all-out offensive with this, an excuse he couldn't really counter for her to have time away from him . . . them.

And if he *did* counter it, she had ammunition to fight another way because for real, normal people in the real, normal world, it was absolutely not cool for some guy to ask his woman to put her job in jeopardy to spend time with him.

In fact, she decided as she tagged the button for the elevator, Stellan's office was on the next block, so she'd go there now, killing two birds with one stone since she'd have to be on the job that night and thus away from him, they should have this out sooner rather than later.

But also, Susan worked for him. She'd be there. And Sixx could meet her before tomorrow night, take the edge off, show the woman what she'd be dealing with, and then tomorrow night, she'd just have to deal with the husband . . . and the kid.

Perfect (ish, she still had to deal with the husband . . . and the kid).

She rode the elevator down, left the building, and was sure to take her sunglasses out of her metallic silver envelope clutch and slide them on even though she only had to walk half a block and cross a street to get to the terrazzo-covered forecourt of the skyscraper that Stellan not only owned but also conducted his business. That business taking up two floors. The Phoenix sun was blinding on its own, but bouncing off buildings and pavements, it was killer.

When she arrived in Stellan's building and again took off her sunglasses and tucked them away, she noted there was a security guy you had to pass unless you had a card to get through the secure, automated half-gates that led to the elevator bay.

Sixx tucked her clutch under her arm, walked right up to him, told him her name and who she wanted to see.

He'd done a top-to-toe as she walked up and did two top-to-tits over the high partition of his desk as he asked, "You got an appointment?"

"He'll see me," she replied.

The guard gave her a look that said he didn't doubt it and picked up the phone.

Not two minutes later, he was reaching for a drawer, nodding, muttering, "Uh-huh, uh-huh. Right." He hung up, slid the card he got from his drawer across the high shelf at the top of his desk toward her and said, "Use that. It's a temporary pass. They say they'll set you up with a permanent one up at Mr. Lange's office."

She wanted to snatch up the card and hold it to her chest like the boy she'd had a crush on in high school out of the blue gave her a rose after class.

Sixx did not do this.

She just took the card, lifted it up, murmured, "Thanks," and walked to the security stanchions, slipping in the card and moving through the gates when they opened.

She thanked God for long-wearing lipstick when she hit Stellan's floor and saw the wide, sweeping reception desk made of a gleaming wave of undulating wood that was adorned with two enormous bouquets of fresh flowers in the wide, sweeping, elegant reception area. A desk that was not being manned only by a receptionist. Instead, it was populated by a receptionist, four loitering women, and an equally loitering guy.

News had gotten out the boss's woman was on her way up.

All eyes came to her as she walked across the marble flooring toward the desk in simple, but kickass, high-heeled, black patent Louboutin So Kate pumps. She was wearing a silvery-gray-leather pencil skirt that fit her like a glove and hit her at her knees. She was also wearing a skintight, silk knit, sleeveless, mock turtleneck tee.

Her only adornment was her square-faced Michele watch and a pair of small diamond studs in her ears.

Really, the skirt and shoes were all she needed.

And the bugged-out eyes fastened to her proved that to be true.

"I'm here to see Stellan," she shared with the receptionist when she arrived at her desk. "Sorry," she went on, belatedly realizing who she was speaking to. "Mr. Lange."

"I, uh . . . yeah, uh . . . right, um . . . obviously," she stammered, clearly unable to cope with Stellan Lange's girlfriend showing up in her sphere. "Uh, let me—"

Sixx heard from the side, "Allow me to put Maureen out of her misery and take you back."

She looked that way to see a very pretty, petite, blonde, well-dressed woman who had a knowing smile on her face and a measuring look in her eye.

The glorious Susan.

God, she even looked like the perfect baby sister you lived to adore.

Sixx inwardly drew her shit tight, gave a small smile to the receptionist and her other onlookers and moved toward the blonde.

"You're Susan, yes?" she asked, lifting her hand when she got close.

"I am. And you're Simone."

That threw Sixx for a second, so much she let it show.

"Sixx," Susan said quickly. "Sixx. Sorry."

"No apology needed, Simone is fine," Sixx told her as Susan took her hand, gave it a firm squeeze, and they both let go. "I was in the neighborhood, and I had something I needed to share with Stellan, so I figured I'd just pop by. Am I being a nuisance?"

"No. Absolutely not," Susan assured. "Though he's on a call and told me he didn't want to be disturbed." Susan was speaking as she indicated a hall to Sixx with a swing of her arm, and they both began to walk down it. "I haven't shared you were here yet as he should be wrapping it up soon. And I suspect he'll do that even if he wasn't wrapping it up when we poke our heads through to show him you're here."

"I don't want to bother him, or you. What I have to share shouldn't take long." That was a partial lie. It might, she had no idea how Stellan would react or how long that would take. "I can call him and leave a message on his cell. I was just a block away, though, so I thought—"

Susan cut her off. "No worries. All good. In fact, you here will make his day."

Sixx examined the well-appointed hall off of which were large rooms filled with well-appointed cubbies. Sprinkled around were fabulous art and more fresh flower arrangements.

She was taking this all in despite the fact she was not quite able not to think about making Stellan's day, but for her sanity, she wanted to.

"I'm glad we have a chance to meet anyway," Susan went on, and Sixx looked to her. "Take the pressure off tomorrow night."

Sixx had never met anyone that mattered to a beau. She'd never even had a beau. And most the people she dealt with, nothing mattered to them but power and money.

It hadn't occurred to her Susan might be on edge too.

"Right. So I'll give you the honesty and share that was also behind me walking a block in one-hundred-and-seven-degree heat in a leather skirt to have a word with Stellan," Sixx admitted as Susan led them into a well-appointed office that was large, had comfortable seating around, and a huge desk filled with what appeared to be lots of work scattered on top as well as one of the bigger fresh flower arrangements at the corner of it.

"That skirt is something else, to be sure," Susan replied, stopped in front of her desk, and looked up at Sixx. "How do you wear leather in the summer in Phoenix?"

"Like every other Phoenician, I limit my time outside in the summer to racing from the air-conditioning of a building to the air-conditioning in my car and vice versa. So it really doesn't matter what I wear since most of the time I'm enjoying a soothing seventy-something degrees. And if I spend any time outside, it's in a bathing suit by a pool, no leather to be found."

Susan gave her a big smile. "Too true."

Sixx hesitantly returned the smile.

"So, I'm just going to say, since we're being honest," Susan began. "I figured you'd be daunting, the woman who caught Stellan's eye. But, you know, meeting you, you're not daunting. You're *terrifying*."

Oh no.

"I'm not, really, it's the leather. It's a power material," Sixx tried to joke.

"It is that, but it's also the fact you walked a block . . . or *anywhere* . . . in those shoes. I'd break an ankle or fall flat on my face."

"You can best anything with practice. That's how I did it."

"I sucked at ballet, so I'm thinking you're wrong."

Sixx gave her a less hesitant smile and lowered her voice to share, "I'm just a person, Susan. I'm no different from you or anyone else."

"You look like the famous ex-wife of a rock god who dumped his butt the minute she found out he cheated on her, proving he's the most idiotic man on the planet and unworthy of her time. Then she went on to get more famous just for being awesome but also building a designer handbag dynasty. At the same time she tamed an until-then-untamable, unspeakably handsome and glamorous playboy, earning his utter devotion and a one-hundred-and-fifty-thousand-dollar, custom-designed wedding gown to top the five-carat diamond engagement ring he slid on her finger aboard his yacht."

Sixx blinked at her.

"I don't know about the rock god part," Susan went on. "But I know the second part is true, and so is the last part since Stellan's already told me I can pick your engagement ring, and I'm seeing from taking in all that is you that five carats is the way to go."

At hearing these words, unable to stop herself, Sixx reached out with her fingers to Susan's desk and leaned into them, staring at the woman and trying with everything she had not to hyperventilate.

"Oh God, I've freaked you," Susan whispered in horror.

"I'm a mess," Sixx whispered back, so off-kilter from what Susan had just said, not to mention being the recipient of such open honesty, unable to stop that too.

"You're the most put-together woman I've ever seen," Susan kept up the whispering.

"Camouflage."

"I don't believe that."

"It's true."

"I still don't believe it."

"He's going to give up on me," Sixx shared, yes, also still whispering. "I'm such a mess, I'm going to make that so."

"He never gives up on anything that matters to him," Susan was still whispering in return. "And you really matter to him."

"Then I'm going to have to leave him before I hurt him."

Susan suddenly looked panicked. "Leaving him *would* hurt him."

"You don't understand—"

"He'd slay dragons for you," Susan declared desperately.

Sixx shut her mouth.

"He would. He would," she said like she was chanting, leaned in, and continued fiercely, "*Let him.*"

Sixx took a step back, looked side to side, realized what the fuck she was doing, and opened her mouth to find a way out of the mess she'd somehow created.

Seriously.

This was Stellan's Susan.

She couldn't talk to Leigh, but she could know Susan for all of five minutes and let this vomit out of her mouth?

"My dad's a dick, excuse my language," Susan declared suddenly. "And my mom let him be that to me. So outside of Harry and Crosby, Stellan's all I've got that's *mine*, and there isn't a single woman on the planet I'd think was worthy of him, not one. That was, I thought that until I just met you."

Sixx shook her head. "You don't know me."

"I know why he's falling in love with you."

Sixx clamped her mouth shut again.

"Do you want to know why?" Susan asked.

"Because he likes a challenge?" Sixx asked in return.

"Because you're the only woman on this planet who wants him for nothing but him, even the part of him that wants nothing but to love you."

Sixx looked to Susan's desk, mumbling, "Damn, I'm going to cry."

"Oh God! Don't do that," Susan exclaimed, lifting a hand and curling her fingers around Sixx's upper arm. "He'll think I made you cry, and he'll get ticked at me."

Sixx looked at her, shaking her head. "He'll know it's not you. I've been on edge lately."

Susan nodded knowingly, taking her hand. "Weirdly, impending happiness does that to you. I honestly would not allow myself to think Harry was real. I mean, this sweet, cute guy thought I was funny and adorable and got this big smile on his face any time he saw me? What was wrong with him? Didn't he see what my dad saw in me? This big, fat loser who got B's on her report card and lost the race to win class secretary? That right there was a double fail. I should have run for president. And won. Hands down."

"A B isn't bad," Sixx pointed out.

"Not for my dad. For my dad it was the end of the world and proof positive he'd produced a huge dunce," Susan replied.

"You do know that's more than a little bit crazy," Sixx shared.

Susan gave her a close look that communicated a lot of things and said, "I didn't, until Harry . . . and Stellan."

God.

Stellan believed in her too.

And look at her now.

Sixx couldn't handle that.

Instead, she went on, "And that class officer stuff is just a popularity contest. He could be equally pissed you didn't win prom queen."

"He was ticked at that too."

"What a douche," Sixx decreed.

"Word," Susan agreed.

They looked at each other.

Then as one they burst out laughing so hard, both of them had to lean against the desk to hold themselves up.

Still laughing, Susan eyed the door to her office, and Sixx looked that way to see someone scurrying down the hall.

"I freaking love this," Susan stated, and Sixx turned back to her to see her daintily wiping away tears of hilarity from under her eyes so as not to disturb her mascara.

"What?" Sixx asked, pulling herself together, thinking she'd never noticed it, but laughing did a lot toward taking the heavy and making it light again.

"You, being absolutely fabulous. Of course, this means my life will be hell because everyone will want the gossip. But seriously, what more can I say? All questions are answered with just you showing here. You're edgy, awesome, amazing, and Stellan is Stellan. It was meant to be."

Sixx tried to ignore that so she didn't lose it again.

Sixx found it impossible to ignore that.

"I really am a mess," Sixx told her quietly.

"Join the club, babe," Susan replied airily, then flicked a wrist toward her doorway. "They'll never know that because I will never share, on threat of death." She crossed her heart then held up two fingers. "But for me, I can now avoid the inferiority complex I've been gearing up to nurture until my dying day."

"You do know, he adores you with every fiber of his being, and when he said we were having dinner tomorrow night, I nearly vomited on the spot," Sixx shared.

Susan burst out laughing, and Sixx couldn't help it. It was laugh, cry or scream, and laughing seemed to work great, so she took the path of least resistance and laughed with her.

It was then she heard a door open, one of the double ones at the side of Susan's office.

Susan twisted her neck to look over her shoulder, and Sixx just looked over Susan's shoulder.

Thus they both saw Stellan standing there, no jacket, blue tie, light gray vest, fabulous striped shirt, tailored light gray trousers, fantastic brown shoes, brows raised, lips quirked . . . *gorgeous*.

"Hey, boss man," Susan called. "Surprise visit from your cool chick."

"As she's standing chatting with you in your office," Stellan replied, moving from the door into the room, "it would appear the surprise is no longer a surprise to you."

"Nope," Susan agreed.

"And will you be sharing why you didn't tell me she was here?" Stellan asked, arriving at Sixx's side and claiming her instantly by putting a hand to her hip and then sliding it around her back all the way to the other side, doing this pulling her to him.

"You said not to disturb your call," Susan answered.

"Make a note, Susie, that in future, if Sixx is here, you disturb me. I don't give a fuck if the President of the United States is sitting in my office."

"Note made," Susan replied.

Stellan finally looked down at her. "Hello, darling."

"Oh my God!" Susan cried before Sixx could even open her mouth. "You call her 'darling!' I am literally standing here *melting.*"

Stellan turned back to Susan. "You do know what the word 'literally' means, do you not?"

"You don't feel me, Stell. My feet are actually just puddles right now," she shot back. "I don't know how I'm remaining standing."

"Perhaps we should put you out of your misery," Stellan suggested.

"The misery hasn't yet begun," she returned. "It'll start the instant you disappear, and then there'll be a stampede to get the lowdown on Sixx."

"Then perhaps you should share with them that I'm considering revising the Employee Handbook to state that anyone caught gossiping faces immediate termination," Stellan replied.

"Roger that," Susan said, beginning to move around her desk.

Stellan began to move them both toward his office.

"Great to meet you, Susan," Sixx called as they went.

"Right back at you, cool chick," Susan returned.

Stellan led her into the most kickass office she'd ever seen, all contemporary wood paneling, built-in cabinetry and floors that went forever, plus recessed lighting and leather with hints of black, cream and chrome.

After closing the door behind him, he also led her right to his desk and around it. He pressed her slightly back so she was leaning against the desk before he took a seat in his chair turned her way.

She dropped her clutch to his desk, crossed her ankles and looked down at him, thinking only Stellan could be seated while she was mostly standing and still seem to dominate the situation.

"Everything okay?" he asked, and she wanted to laugh because outside of "Hello, darling," that was the first thing he said to her, and he'd had an exchange with his beloved assistant, walked Sixx through his huge-ass office, and settled her against his desk in the time in between.

"You're adorable with her," Sixx proclaimed.

"She's adorable, so it's impossible not to fall into that," he returned.

"She loves you more than breath," Sixx told him.

His brows quirked. "It's good to know she returns that sentiment."

"I like her."

"I knew you would."

"I had a meeting with Joel this morning," she shared abruptly.

Not missing a beat, he murmured, "I was wondering why the world was being treated to that charming skirt today."

She felt her lips curl up. "They have a case, trial starts Wednesday. Two business partners who started things the best of friends but it didn't carry on that way."

"Mm?" he prompted.

"One of the partners is our client, and I've been tasked with digging something useful up that would prove he was correct about flushing his friendship and business venture down the toilet, then suing his ex-buddy."

"Yes?"

"I've failed at digging something up, mostly because I haven't tried very hard due to the fact that I've been wrapped up in what's happening with us."

"Ah," Stellan said on a sigh, sitting back in his chair, putting his elbows on the arms and steepling his fingers like an evil mastermind, except a wildly attractive one whose bones she wanted to jump and do that immediately.

"I'm going to have to start up again with working nights, Stellan, and weekends."

"Of course."

She stared.

He spoke.

"I'm delighted you gave us the time you did, Simone, but you have a job, you have responsibilities to your employer. You also have my house key, and your Cayenne is programmed to open your garage bay. If I'm asleep when you get home, all I ask is that you wake me so I know you're home safely. And if you need to work evenings, nights and weekends, just share your schedule with me with as much notice as you can, so I don't plan anything when you need to be working."

Easy as that?

"I work a lot, Stellan," she warned.

"I do too, Simone. I also enjoy my work. If you became clingy and nagging and demanded I stop, this would make me unhappy. Why would I do something like that to you?"

"Men think about these things differently than women do."

"Not all of us."

She narrowed her eyes at him. "You know, you could at least try to be a pain in the ass sometimes."

He grinned. "Why on earth would I do that?"

She crossed her arms on her chest and looked down at her beautifully shod toes, muttering, "No reason."

Stellan gave it a moment before he noted softly, "You were laughing with her."

"We shared a few moments," she told her toes.

"How long were you in her office with her?"

She slid her eyes to him. "Maybe five minutes."

He gave her a warm smile. "She has that effect on people."

She straightened her head and looked at him directly. "I didn't pop in to be a pain. I was in the office, I'm not often in the office, and since it's close to your office, and I had something to share, I decided to walk down and share it. But you should know I also came to meet her so it wouldn't seem so heavy tomorrow night."

"That's perfectly understandable, and she obviously didn't mind, nor would I expect her to. I don't mind either. Ever. Anytime you wish to see me, I'll make myself available to you. To that end, we'll get you a passcard before you leave."

"I think Susan already has that going," she told him.

"I'll bet she does," he replied.

"You're leaving last night alone," she noted, again changing the subject abruptly, because he was leaving it alone but she, seemingly, could not.

"There are things about you, Simone, that are yours, and they will never be mine to have unless you choose to give them to me. Your sketchbooks, for one. Whatever occurred last night, another. I'm thrilled you're in my life. I'm delighted beyond measure to share my home with you, M with you, Susan with you. If there's anything you want from me, need from me, and I can give it to you, it's yours. Materially, emotionally, my attention, my time. I'm fully aware that I've chosen a woman to spend my life with that is not at this point ready to offer me the same. I can wait. And honestly, Simone, if you never are, but you give me the beauty we have now, then that will make me far from unhappy."

God.

She loved him.

"Really, it'd be a big help if you could be a pain in the ass even infrequently."

He dropped his hands to his lap and smiled.

"I should probably get out of your hair," she muttered.

"Actually, I'd prefer you pull your skirt up to your hips, your panties down, and spread your legs."

Her heart thumped in her chest, her clit pulsed, her nipples instantly budded hard, her lips parted, and her eyes stayed riveted on him.

"Susan," she whispered.

"Knows better than to disturb us, or allow anyone else to, but regardless, I locked the door."

"Stellan—"

"I told you what I wish you to do, Simone. Please do it," he said low.

Holding his eyes, she hesitated for a long moment, two, before she uncrossed her ankles, came up from the desk, shimmied her skirt up her hips and then pushed her thong down them until it fell to her ankles.

She kicked it aside and leaned back against the desk, bare-assed, and spread her legs.

Stellan didn't watch her face while she did it.

He watched her do it.

She was so wet she was surprised she wasn't dripping down the inside of her thigh not only doing it, but watching his face darken while she did.

Like he had all day, he took his time getting up from his chair and moving to stand between her spread legs.

Sixx stared up at him, positioned for him, exposed to him, and decided the beauty of Stellan surrounded by all that defined him out in the world was hot *as fuck*.

She was certain he'd fuck her on his desk, and she was ready for it. In fact, the longer he stood over her, looking down at her, not touching her, she was tempted to beg for it.

But then she couldn't hold back her gasp when he dropped to his knees in front of her, shoved his mouth between her legs, and immediately commenced eating her.

Hard.

Her head rolled back.

Stellan threw one of her thighs over his shoulder and went deeper.

Amazing.

She moaned and rolled into him.

He began to tongue fuck her.

"God," she whispered, lifting her head, looking down her body, seeing Stellan Lange on his knees before her. His dark hair and his broad shoulders and the shiny material at the back of his vest, all that between her legs, her white thigh thrown over one of his shoulders. "Baby," she breathed, lifting a hand to drift her fingers into that thick, soft hair.

He adjusted, sucking in her clit, but she saw his gaze catching hers along the length of her body.

She locked her calf along his back so the trembling in her legs didn't take her off his desk.

Eyes to hers, he drew hard at her clit—and primed by him just being him, giving her that command, doing this right there how they were doing it—that was all she needed. Her body convulsed, her head fell back again, and she came in his mouth.

She lost him and her purchase on the desk when he lifted her up and planted her ass firmly to the edge of it. She heard a zip go, tried to focus, but in the grips of the climax he gave her, she couldn't, even when both her legs were yanked high and wide. With Stellan's hands behind her knees, he bent over her and drove inside.

"Stellan," she panted, her back arching, her chest pressing into his.

"Look at me while I fuck you, darling," he ordered.

She righted her head and found his eyes right before his mouth took hers.

She tasted him and herself and it was the best taste *in the world*.

He fucked her to another orgasm and then let go of her knees, allowing her to round his hips with her legs as he curled his arms around her. One hand at the back of her neck, one arm holding her steady at the waist to take his thrusts. And he kept fucking her, staring in her eyes until he orgasmed quietly. But the veins popping in his neck, by his temple, the hardness of his jaw, the depth of his claiming drives as he fucked her through it told her it was a good one.

Sixx knew he hadn't fully come down before he was kissing her again, tasting her with his tongue, giving her his own, his cock planted to the root and staying there.

When he broke the kiss, he again caught her gaze.

"I've been wanting to do that since you walked down to breakfast this morning in that skirt."

"I'm glad I gave you an early opportunity."

He grinned, touched his nose to hers, and when he did that, a simple gesture, but so goddamn sweet, Sixx got lost.

Lost in the idea that this could be their life. Her in the neighborhood, as it were, using her passcard to pop up and have a banter with Susan, a chat and a quick fuck on his desk with him. That she'd work, and he'd work, and she'd come to him asleep, wake him up to let him know she was home safe. Come down to breakfast wearing something he wanted to take off her, down her vitamins every morning and listen to M chatter.

But scars were forever, and hers were crippling.

They didn't heal.

Did they?

"I might be late tonight," she said quietly.

"Can you meet me at The Gladly for a quick dinner?" he asked.

She nodded. "I'll try. I'll let you know."

"If you can't, darling, that's all right."

She nodded again.

"Do you want me to clean you up, or do you want to do it?" he queried.

"Do you have your own bathroom?"

"Of course."

Of course.

"Show me the way, and I'll take care of it," she said.

He slid out.

She missed him the second he was gone.

He helped her to her feet and pulled up his trousers, but didn't do them up before he bent and nabbed her panties from the floor.

He handed them to her, fastened his slacks as she yanked down her skirt, and then he took her hand and led her to what looked like just another wood panel on his wall but when he reached to it, she saw the cleverly hidden latch. He opened the door and exposed a fabulous bathroom with beautifully tiled walls in mellow browns and grays, contemporary fixtures and wood-framed cabinets covered in sliding doors of milky glass.

"Your interior designer really is amazing," she mumbled.

"I'm very good at finding the very best of people, and when I do, holding on," he drawled in reply.

But she stopped dead in the doorway, turned her head his way and looked up at him.

His handsome face was soft, sated and serious.

"Get cleaned up, sweetheart," he murmured, using a hand in the small of her back to push her into his bathroom.

She went.

He closed the door behind her.

She found a pile of plush, thick, perfectly white washcloths in a cabinet. She cleaned up, put her panties back on, rinsed the cloth well and hung it over the side of the sink.

She then walked out to find Stellan standing behind his desk, looking down at a laptop open on it.

He didn't have a PC. Just that laptop.

He also had a view of the Valley spread out along the entire side of his office where she could see Camelback Mountain in the distance.

She moved to him, looking at the view, and only turned her attention to him when she had to skirt his desk.

When she got close, he pulled her into his arms.

"I'll walk you to the elevators," he declared.

"I'm not sure your staff could handle that," she quipped.

"I don't give a fuck," he returned.

Before she could say anything, he bent to touch his lips to hers and then he picked up her clutch, handed it to her, and moved them toward the door, not holding her hand, not curling her fingers around his elbow, but with his arm around her, their hips and legs brushing as they moved, his hold making it impossible for her not to curve her arm around him as well.

His hair was slightly messy from her fingers being in it, and he hadn't fixed it (not that he should—as with everything Stellan, it was hot). It was too late to mention it when he unlocked and opened the office door and guided her through, not letting her go.

"Sixx is heading out," he informed Susan. "Did you get a pass-card for her?"

"Right here," Susan replied, lifting up a card and shaking it in the air.

Stellan moved to the desk, took it from Susan, handed it to Sixx, and let her go long enough for her to tuck it in her clutch.

When she was done, Stellan claimed her back immediately, but Sixx looked to Susan, who spoke.

"See you tomorrow, babe. Totally cool to meet you."

"Right back at you," Sixx replied, earning a huge smile from Susan.

She returned one not as huge, but definitely genuine as Stellan moved them into the hall.

"You know, this is actually kind of cruel to do to your hungry-for-your boss's-business staff," she noted under her breath as they moved along.

"I find I have absolutely no response to that," he replied, pull-ing her closer so she looked up at him to find him gazing down at her as they walked. "I don't get into their lives. They really have no place getting into mine."

"You're rich, gorgeous and wear a suit way too well. When you're that, it happens."

He smiled down at her.

"No. Seriously. Have you ever seen David Gandy in a suit?" she asked.

"I don't even know who David Gandy is."

"Google him."

"I don't Google."

She stared up at him.

"Who doesn't Google?" she asked.

"I have so far found no need to Google, but if I did, I have staff to do it," he answered, then suggested, "I could ask Susan to Google him."

"I wouldn't do that unless you wanted to lose her for the rest of the day."

His brows went up. "That attractive?"

"She mentioned Harry, didn't say much, I could still tell she was devoted, but regardless, she'd drop him like a rock if Gandy crooked his finger at her."

"And you?"

Stellan Lange just ate her out on his knees at the side of his desk then fucked her on it.

David Gandy was . . . well, *David Gandy.*

But Stellan was *Stellan.*

"I think I'm good."

He threw his beautiful head back and shouted with laughter.

She watched him do it, not having any idea how gentle her face was and how openly blissful she looked doing it.

She did notice they were in the reception area but only because he stopped her by the elevators and tagged a button.

"Call me about dinner," he murmured, pulling her around to his front and trapping her in both his arms.

She lifted her hands and placed them on his pecs. "Will do."

He bent and touched his mouth to hers then twisted his neck to touch his mouth to her jaw before he went even further and brushed his lips at the skin behind her ear.

She pressed closer as she shivered in his arms.

He lifted his head and looked into her eyes.

"Can I share how elated I am that you decided to drop by?"

"I've been noticing you seem to like me," she muttered.

"I'm glad you're noticing," he murmured in return.

Suddenly, it all came back, all of it, hitting her like she'd been hurled bodily at a wall.

"Stellan—"

His face came right into hers and he whispered, "Don't fuck it up. Please, God, Simone, this has been one of those rare slices of perfection in life. Let us both have it, honey, without fucking it up."

She closed her mouth and nodded.

He took in her nod, got closer, touched his lips to hers again, and when he lifted his head, the elevator binged.

He moved her to it, scooted her in, and stood outside as she stood inside, looking up into his dark blue eyes.

"Later at dinner, darling," he bid.

"Right, baby," she murmured.

The door closed him off from sight, but the entire time they slid shut, he did not move.

She stared at them, thinking she was supposed to remember something . . .

But she couldn't quite . . .

Wait.

I've chosen a woman to spend my life with . . .

He'd said that.

He'd said, *Spend my life with . . .*

"Oh God," she whispered to the doors.

He was lost too.

Stellan was in love with her.

And that was all Sixx could think about as she made her way out of his building, down the street and into the parking area of the building that housed her own office.

Which meant she didn't think, not once that day, that she was down to two weeks and four days.

And hours later . . .

After she tiptoed into their room, quietly got ready for bed, and slid in beside him only for him immediately to pull her into his arms, then roll to his back with her mostly draped on his front while she whispered, "I'm home safe, baby," to which he replied, drowsily but with a squeeze of his arms, "Good," and then they promptly both fell asleep . . .

She still would not consider the fact that she didn't think it at all.

sixteen

Right to the Sun

STELLAN

The next evening, Stellan was in the kitchen, his light rock Pandora channel coming through the speakers built in around the house, his hands engaged in preparing the salad they'd have with dinner that night, when he heard the garage door go up.

This was followed surprisingly shortly after by a cacophony of sound that could only be a hurrying woman entering a home.

He didn't look to his watch to know that Susan, Harry and Crosby were due to arrive in fifteen minutes.

What Simone didn't know was that, when it didn't have to do with work, after Crosby was born, Susan was routinely at least ten minutes late, usually more to the tune of twenty, so he was prepared for them not to be on time.

He probably should have shared that.

"Oh God! Shit! Fuck!" Simone exclaimed the minute she rounded into the kitchen, dashing straight to him on gold, no-heel sandals, wearing dark gray harem pants and a butter-yellow suede top that fell off one of her shoulders, making that street chic look *haute couture*. "I'm late. So late! I'd hoped to be home in time to help. But you . . . would not . . . *believe*," she declared directly prior to practically accosting him in order to press a hard kiss on his jaw.

She did not tell him what he would not believe. She also didn't give him a chance to say anything, for instance, ask what she thought she could do to help considering she had no interest in the goings-on of a kitchen, including when drinks were being mixed, except the end result of all of that.

"I need to freshen up real quick. Gah!" she cried, moving swiftly away from him, finishing, "Be back as fast as I can!"

With that, she threw her purse and laptop bag to the table at the foot of the stairs and raced up them.

Stellan stood still in his kitchen and stared at his stairs long after she disappeared.

Something had happened the day before.

Something had broken.

In Sixx.

He knew this because Simone was shining through.

Everywhere.

They'd had dinner the night before on a break from whatever it was she did to do what she did for Joel, and they'd had breakfast that morning with M.

In other words, they had not shared a lot of time together since she'd come to his office the day before.

And still, he knew.

It was that blatant.

It was that beautiful.

The woman who just arrived in his home had just come *home*.

She'd come *home* to *him*.

He smiled down at the baby spinach leaves in the bowl just as his cell rang.

He looked to where it was sitting on the counter, suspecting it would be Susan unnecessarily sharing they would be late.

It was not.

He frowned.

It was his mother.

He did not ever want to take a call from his mother, particularly not then.

But it was of an hour in the evening that if he did not pick up, she would simply call again. And again. And again. One right after the other.

He had little hope of making it quick, even if he had an excuse to do so. But if he turned off his ringer, he might miss a call from Susan, and dealing with his mother's petulance that he didn't pick up was worse than dealing with her rambling when she was nearing the end of bottle number one of the night.

He sighed, wiped his hands on a dish towel, and picked up the phone, taking the call.

"Mother."

"My son," she replied, and it was not slurred.

A good sign.

"I have——" He started to share his excuse that he could not talk long, moving away from the island toward the windows to stop and stand, looking out at his pool with its light flowing through different colors, the waters rippling from the water feature.

"I'm coming down, spending the weekend, starting tomorrow," she cut him off to announce.

Stellan stood still and stared at the pool, feeling a surge of fury rush through him, the kind he had not felt in years.

She did not ask how he was.

She did not ask after his health.

She did not ask if maybe he'd met someone he enjoyed spending time with.

She did not ask if he might have plans this weekend and perhaps could not entertain his mother.

She called about her, not to talk to him.

"I have some shopping to do, and the symphony is doing Stravinsky," she carried on. "I thought I'd make it a long weekend, visit some friends, go home on Tuesday. Can you see to Susan getting tickets for us and have Margarita put fresh sheets on the bed in my room?"

He kept his voice carefully modulated when he replied, "You can't come down this weekend."

"I'm sorry?" she asked.

"You can't come down this weekend," he repeated.

This was met with silence.

"Actually," he continued. "You can't come down at all, Mother, not for the foreseeable future."

"I . . . for goodness sakes, why?" she asked, not hiding her shock.

"Because this isn't your home to call and announce you're coming down and you want my housekeeper to make your bed," he answered.

"You're my son. I'm your mother," she returned. "And I haven't seen you in weeks."

"I no longer live alone," he shared abruptly. "A woman who means a great deal to me has moved in. At an appropriate time, we'll come up to Sedona, take you out to dinner so you can meet her and start to get to know her. However, until she's comfortable with you, you cannot come down and stay with us."

"You've moved a woman into your home?" she queried, quiet, wary and sidling toward wounded.

"Yes."

"One I haven't met?"

"Yes."

"Have you been . . . *hiding* her from me?"

"Of course not," he sighed.

"Then why have I not met her yet?"

He didn't answer that and not simply because it was none of her business.

He said, "I can't get into this now. We're having company for dinner and they're arriving soon. I'll call you when I have time, and we'll talk about when Simone and I can come up and have dinner with you."

"This is . . . Stellan, this is *outrageous*," she declared.

"I'm not certain how it's outrageous, Mother," he replied.

"You're not certain?" she demanded. "You're living with a woman who hasn't met your mother!"

"I'm hardly at an age where I need my mother's approval of the women I see," he returned.

"You're always at an age where you should respect your mother," she fired back.

And it was then, Stellan was done.

Done with the kind of people in the world who thought they could produce children and then leave them entirely to their own devices as they attempt to learn to become functional human beings. Done with dealing with family members you had to endure rather than enjoy.

His mother had once been a good mother, loving and nurturing.

Life had then surprised her simply by sharing the knowledge she'd chosen the wrong man to love, to make a family with. And for decades, she'd been entirely unable to cope, and there was no nurture, no support, no tuition. Instead, she had railed and scorned and exhibited every selfish, self-involved behavior you should *not* teach a child.

She had not lived a life devoid of love or access to anyone in it that could give that to her.

She had not witnessed her only anchor in the world being gunned down right before her eyes directly after he'd moved to protect her.

She had been relatively wealthy and privileged before she met his father. And after him, she had not been forced to learn a trade or fend for herself.

And it occurred to Stellan right then that she was one of those women who simply could not function without a man to take care of her, and she had decided precisely how she should be taken care of.

Therefore, when Brigette Lange lost her husband, and she was saddled with two children after being spurned by a powerful, rich, well-known man and of an age where it was easy to convince herself that her prospects were few and certainly none of them had the promise of an Andreas Lange, she'd given up.

She had been in her late thirties, had decided she was washed up, and had set a course for her life to make that so.

And simply because Stellan was bored of her nonsense and entirely unmotivated to deal with the fallout should he make the effort to exit her life, he'd unwittingly enabled her dysfunction by negligently supporting it.

He was done with that as well.

He also didn't hesitate to share he was.

"And can you explain how it's respect to call your son the day prior to your arrival to share you'll be coming to spend time in his home, not to mention tell him to bother his assistant and housekeeper to see to your wishes, also without any notice?" he queried.

"I—"

"It's not," he answered for her. "It's not only disrespect, Mother, it's rude. It always has been. I had no reason to share this with you before because your selfishness would only affect me, and I'd had decades to become used to it. Now, should I allow it to continue, it would affect Simone, and I'm afraid that's unacceptable, so I'm telling you it will no longer continue."

His mother spoke in his ear.

But he didn't hear her.

Because he felt an arm slide around his waist and a warm body press against his side.

Simone was there, looking up at him, her pretty face beautiful with gentle concern.

That wasn't Simone breaking, cracking open, letting him in.

That was just Simone.

He wound his arm around her and shook his head to share he was all right and she had no need for concern.

The expression did not shift, nor did the position of her body.

"Are you listening to me, Stellan?" his mother's shrill voice sounded in his ear.

He pulled Simone closer and looked back out the windows. "Simone just joined me, so no, actually, I wasn't."

"I was saying I have plans with friends. Lunch set with Jenna. I—"

"Then stay with Jenna."

"I can't stay with Jenna!" she snapped. "At this late date, it would be rude to ask."

Did she even listen to herself?

"I know precisely what you mean," he stated.

"Stellan—"

"You're not coming here this weekend, Mother. If M is here should you arrive, I'll instruct her not to let you in."

"So this is why you never gave me a key, so you could shut me out when you needed to," she bit.

"No. I never gave you a key because this isn't your home, it's mine. I don't need a family member with access to take care of pets or handle mail when I'm away. I also am of an age I don't need my mother sauntering in when I'm having dinner guests or I'm entertaining a woman. It would seem perfectly obvious to me considering your penchant to do whatever the hell you want whenever the hell you want to do it that my not giving you a key was tacit communication that I desire my privacy. However, since that was not made implicit, I'll make it explicit. You are not welcome here unless you're invited here. Is that clear?"

There was a long, heavy moment of quiet before Brigette Lange, not getting her way, unsurprisingly lifted her foot and stepped well over the line.

"I cannot believe you, my only child after I lost Silie, that you'd treat me—"

Automatically, Stellan turned into Simone, took his arm from around her, lifted his hand and curled it tight around the side of her neck while he bent so he saw nothing but her liquid, warm brown eyes.

"Do not even *consider* bringing Silie into this conversation," he growled.

He felt Simone's hands curl deep into the sides of his waist as she rolled up on her toes and pressed her forehead to his.

"I only have you left, Stellan," his mother returned sharply.

"You're right. You do. But I'll point out something I should have shared some time ago. The simple fact that you just said that *you* lost Silie when we *both* lost Silie tells me precisely how little you're aware of the fact that your son has feelings, emotions, and now a life that you know nothing of because you never made the effort to know of it. And because I reached this age with a mother who is more interested in making certain she doesn't run out of wine than understanding her son has made decisions in his life that mean he no longer will be living it alone, I myself feel no need to make the effort to share. Case in point, you haven't told me you're happy for me, Mother."

"This is because I'm wondering how long she'll last," she sniped.

"Because I'm unworthy of earning a good woman's love?" he asked, and Simone's fingers dug into his flesh.

There was a moment's hesitation before, "I'm not going to be a party to this conversation anymore."

"Answer the question," Stellan clipped.

"I'm hanging up now," she declared. "Don't bother phoning to set up dinner with that woman who lives with you. I'm suddenly feeling the need to get away. Perhaps Coronado. Or Napa. I don't know when I'll return."

Stellan held Simone's gaze and her neck even as he lifted his head slightly away. "I'm sure you'll choose Napa."

"Perhaps, it's beautiful there."

"And offers an endless supply of your only reason for breathing," he pointed out.

Simone's eyes got big, and she held on to his waist as she pressed her front to his.

"That's unspeakably insulting," his mother snapped.

"It's also what has so far been unspeakably true, though now I'm speaking of it."

"Why am I not surprised?" she asked acidly. "This cruelty. I knew you had your father in you, and here it is, finally coming out. Just like him, hidden under the dutiful son until you have something else you want, and then you throw away what you already have. I hope this woman in your life knows how temporary she undoubtedly is."

"And there it is, coming out even when you're mostly sober. Now you can't deny it, Mother. And I won't either. I've found someone I want to risk it all with, and instead of being happy, if concerned, for me, as a mother should be, it's somehow about you. Simone has nothing to do with you. But the truly unfortunate part is, through your own actions making it so, I have nothing to do with you either. And just to make it clear, the unfortunate part about that is that's been the case for decades. You just didn't realize it until now. But I always did."

"I have endured—"

"You have endured what thousands of women have endured, and you did it with your health and your beauty intact and a wildly generous settlement. Most of the rest don't have that. They still carry on and make no excuses because they don't have a choice. With what you have and what you squandered, you especially have none."

"I think we're done here," she bit out.

"Since the last time I saw you when you were well into bottle number three, you have not been this honest with me. In other words, agreed. We are very much done here."

He knew she didn't disconnect, waiting for him to think on his words, and back out of them.

So he disconnected.

"Baby," Simone whispered immediately, pressing close.

"I'm fine," Stellan said curtly.

"No way you're fine," she replied gently. "That sounded ugly and intense."

"Then it sounded what it was."

"What happened?" she asked.

"She decided to come down for the weekend. I decided that I'd rather she not."

"And you told her about me."

"And I told her about you."

"And she wasn't a big fan of that."

"You didn't factor. That isn't how Brigette Lange works. The fact she could not come down for the weekend factored, and it degenerated from there. She just used you as an excuse."

"You got into the drinking," she said hesitantly.

"Yes, I did."

"And she lashed back with—"

"This whole thing proving that I'm like my father."

It was in that precise moment, Stellan's world changed.

Like it did when he climaxed with her, it wiped clean, and there was nothing.

Nothing but her.

But when his climaxes would fade, the world would come back as it was and always had been.

This time, it did not.

This time, there was a different kind of climax.

And when it was done, he knew nothing would be the same.

It started with Simone stating, "You . . . have got . . . to be *kidding me.*"

"Simone, I told you that she would say things like—"

She pulled free from him by taking a huge step away, but leaning immediately back toward him and screaming, *"You have got to be kidding me!"*

Stellan went still in the face of her fury.

It was a mistake.

She moved like a flash, tearing his phone out of his hand.

Unfortunately, it was still engaged so she did not have to enter his password.

Therefore, she was open to going to his recent calls, which was something she did.

"Darling," he murmured, moving toward her.

But she shifted away and did it quickly.

Not to escape him.

To begin pacing.

"No," she snapped into the phone she'd put to her ear. "It isn't Stellan calling to apologize. This is Simone. And I just witnessed that happy mother-and-son convo, Ms. Lange, and it turned my god-damned *stomach*."

"Hey! What's—?" came from the side, and Stellan's gaze went there to see Susan had let herself in as usual (she most definitely had a key), and there she was, Crosby in her arms, Harry coming up the rear dragging the copious equipment they deemed they needed for whenever they came with son in tow.

Susan and Harry got the vibe and immediately stopped, Susan getting pale, Harry's eyes going big.

Crosby did not get the vibe, reached his arms toward Stellan and shouted, "Steyan!"

Torn with which way to go, Stellan went with the only real choice he had, shaking his head at Susan as he walked to her and then catching her son, who launched himself at Stellan when he got close.

"No," Simone bit off, "I'm not listening to your wine-addled nonsense. We're going to get a few things clear, woman-in-Stellan's-life to woman-in-Stellan's-life. We'll start with the fact that you do not *ever* mention his sister to him again, and we'll move on to you not *ever* even *coming close* to accusing him of being like his father."

"Holy Moses," Susan breathed, her eyes now also big.

Then they narrowed.

"Uh-oh," Harry, having caught his wife's narrowed eyes, muttered.

"Steyan!" Crosby screamed again and latched onto Stellan's ear.

Susan burst forward, slapping a bouquet of flowers she'd brought down on the dining room table as she made a beeline toward Simone.

Harry moved to Stellan and asked, "Is it too soon to pull out the Scotch?"

"You know where it is," Stellan answered, turning his attention to Crosby, who was still tugging on his ear. He then stole his nose, and Crosby dissolved into giggles as he made a grab to get it back.

"No worries," Simone snapped. "Rest assured, it will be *quite some time* before Stellan and I meet you in Sedona. Enjoy Napa. I'm sure the local economy will appreciate your visit."

To that, she took the phone from her ear, stabbed it with her finger, and turned enraged eyes to Stellan.

"Mark these words, handsome. I do not *ever* want to meet that woman *in my life*. And more, she doesn't want to meet me, or I'll scratch her goddamn eyes out," she clipped, blinked, looked at Crosby, shot straight then muttered, "Sorry, that would be gol-darned."

"*What happened?*" Susan near-on screeched.

Crosby heard his mother's tone and started fretting.

Stellan put his nose back then took it again and regained Crosby's attention.

Simone tore her eyes off Stellan holding Crosby and looked at Susan like she was unaware of her arrival.

"Stellan and his mother had words," she explained.

"I got that part," Susan returned.

"And she said some unpleasant things," Simone went on.

Susan pivoted to Stellan.

"I *never* liked that woman," she snapped.

Stellan looked to Susan's husband. "Harry, you were getting Scotch?"

"On it, brother," Harry muttered, on the move.

"And get Sixx some wine while you're at it," Susan ordered.

"Simone drinks gin as a pre-dinner cocktail," Stellan shared.

"I may never drink wine again," Simone declared dramatically, making Stellan beat back laughter.

"Maybe I'll have gin too," Susan decreed.

"Shit," Harry, now at Stellan's wet bar in the family room area, muttered.

"How about you?" Stellan asked Crosby. "What are you feeling like having to drink tonight?"

"Jooz!" Crosby shouted.

"Water," Susan said.

Crosby turned his attention to his mother. "Jooz!"

"Water, baby," she said softly.

Crosby glared at her for a moment before he turned and stole Stellan's nose.

Stellan smiled at him.

And he did it hiding the fact that he no longer needed anything more from Simone Marchesa.

Not her deepest mysteries. Not access to her sketchpads.

Not anything.

He had all he needed.

Because Simone and Sixx had become one with his phone to her ear and his mother on the line.

The sensitive soul and the superhero both had stepped out of the shadows.

And he was in love with her.

He was going to make a family with her.

And he was not ever going to let her go.

"So, that's your boy and your man, yes?" Simone said to Susan.

"Harry, Sixx, Sixx, Harry," Susan introduced perfunctorily, coming toward Stellan.

"Hey, Sixx, cool to meet you," Harry called across the room with a bottle of Scotch in his hand.

"You too," Simone replied with a smile aimed his way.

"And this . . ." Susan stated, pulling Crosby out of Stellan's hold, causing a mad screech she completely ignored. She then walked right to Simone and plopped him in arms Simone had to quickly move to catch him with, "This is Crosby. Center of the universe."

Crosby stared at Simone.

Holding herself and the child awkwardly, she stared back.

After a while, she slowly looked to Susan. "I'm not, well . . . I don't have a lot of experience with kids."

"I didn't either," Susan returned. "Then I popped him out and *boom*, instant expert in all things Crosby."

Simone looked startled. "It happened as easy as that?"

"No, that's a total lie. I was a mess. I read about five thousand baby books before he showed. I still didn't know anything. But you know, in the beginning, they cry, you feed them, change them or try to get them to sleep. You figure out which cry means which. He figures out which buttons to push to get what he wants. It's a give and take. I give. He takes. And we both love every bit of it."

Simone looked back to Crosby.

Crosby studied her, then twisted, reached out to Stellan, and cried, "Steyan!"

"He likes his god-daddy," Susan muttered.

Stellan came forward and relieved Simone of the child.

Crosby instantly went for his nose.

Stellan avoided him but bent in for a blow on the neck from his lips.

When he pulled away, Crosby yelled, "Mo!"

Stellan gave it to him.

"And this is why he loves his god-daddy," Harry stated, handing Stellan a glass of Scotch. "One 'mo,' and Uncle Stellan doesn't hesitate."

Stellan took it, noting, "You're early."

"We were on time," Susan returned.

"Yes. You're early."

Susan rolled her eyes.

"What can I get you to drink, Sixx?" Harry asked, making himself at home back at the drinks cabinet.

"I'll make hers," Stellan said.

"Sooz?" Harry called.

"My choices are nothing alcoholic, nothing alcoholic and nothing alcoholic, so who cares, honey. Just give me something wet," Susan answered, coming to stand close to Stellan and her son.

"She's pregnant," Harry explained to Simone.

"Wow. Congrats," Simone said to Susan with another smile.

"I cried three times before getting in the car to come over here just thinking about hearing Stellan call you 'darling' again. In other words, like the last one, it's gonna be a rough ride."

"Crying?" Simone asked.

"Crying all the time, and my nipples were hard and hurt like heck for seven months straight, and I actually broke a window when I threw a jar of jelly through it that I couldn't open, and that was in month five. It went downhill from there."

"Good Lord," Simone muttered, no longer smiling even a little bit.

Susan shrugged and shoved her face in Crosby's.

Crosby patted her cheek.

"Worth every minute," Susan whispered.

Simone looked to Stellan, caught his eyes on her, and looked away.

He grinned into his Scotch before he took a sip, handed Crosby to his mother, and headed back to the abandoned salad.

"Honey, will you get out Stellan's Scotch and Sixx's chocolates?" Susan asked her husband. "And when you do, hide those chocolates. You remember month three with Crosby."

Harry smiled to himself as he pulled a bottle of Scotch out of a diaper bag, "Yeah, I'm remembering month three pretty clearly."

Stellan was about to open a can of mandarin oranges when he caught Simone standing still but with her head tipped well back.

He took her in and realized she was looking at the speaker in the ceiling.

Then she dropped her chin and looked right into his eyes.

And the open longing exposed in hers again shifted his entire world.

That was when he heard Loggins and Messina's version of "Danny's Song."

Stellan felt his gut drop, his throat get tight and that perfect moment grew exquisitely more perfect when Susan started singing with the song while swaying and dancing around with Crosby in her arms with the addition that he saw Simone felt exactly the same about the moment.

His mother disappeared.

His father disappeared.

His sister disappeared.

Her mother disappeared.

Her father disappeared.

Her uncle disappeared.

Stellan was going to give Simone Marchesa his name.

He was going to make a family with her.

But right then, already, they had a family where there once was none.

And they both knew it.

He called softly, "I forgot your drink, darling."

She moved slowly to him and replied in the same tone, "I'll live. Where are the vases? I'll put those flowers in water."

"I've no earthly clue," he admitted.

She smiled a smile at him that was the first he'd ever gotten from a Sixx who was openly Simone.

It was the brightest, most beautiful thing he'd seen in his life.

Like flying right to the sun.

"Holy Moses, what are you going to do?" Susan asked.

It was after dinner. They were still sitting at the dining room table. Susan had a drooping Crosby in her arms, giving him his bottle.

And Stellan had just learned what Simone had told him earlier he would not believe, but never shared what that was.

Simone shrugged. "Nothing much I can do. It isn't like a lot of our clients aren't schmucks," she answered Susan's question.

"That's gotta suck," Harry noted.

Simone gave her attention to Harry. "Usually, the other guy is a schmuck too so it doesn't. But this time, all I'm getting from the guy we're suing is that he's a decent person. It was our guy who syphoned off the top, regularly blew everything they made, from what was in petty cash to expensing his fantasy football draw party in Vegas and made deals with his buds the business couldn't support," Simone explained.

"And you broke into the good guy's house and saw all his notes on this?" Harry asked.

Simone grinned at him "Not officially. Officially, we have no idea that our opponent has kept profuse notes throughout their deteriorating personal and professional relationship. Notes that are of significant detriment to the case. But unofficially, his lawyer is pouring over every word I took pictures of in hopes of coming up with good answers for all this stuff when it's introduced in court."

"Is he gonna come up with good answers?" Harry queried, and Simone's grin turned into a smile.

"Nope. But all the time he's spending on it is billable hours, so it's a win for the firm either way. But it'll eventually be a loss for the client in two ways, and it's appearing he deserves that double-whammy."

Harry chuckled.

"If this guy is such a jerk and did such jerky things, why would he sue his ex-business partner?" Susan asked.

Simone lifted her drink from the table, answering before taking a sip, "The sun rises, and a variety of jerks rise with it. Who knows why they do what they do? In this case, the only thing that's important is prompt payment of bills."

Susan looked shocked. "Your attorney won't advise him to drop the suit?"

Simone put her drink down. "Our attorney spent two hours

this afternoon trying to convince him his case is weak at best, and he should reconsider this course of action. He refused and accused the firm of not preparing appropriately to efficiently put forth his suit. I think at this point no one will be too cut up to mark one in the loss column."

"People," Susan muttered, "I don't get them."

"You and me both, sister," Simone muttered back.

They shared a small smile.

Stellan looked from them to Harry, and then the men shared a small smile.

"Should I break out those chocolates you brought?" Simone offered.

Susan groaned.

"Totally," Harry answered.

Simone shot Harry a huge smile. "Where did you hide them?"

"Pantry, behind the olives. And just to say, you guys got a lot of olives."

"We both drink martinis," Stellan muttered.

"That explains it," Harry muttered in return.

Simone got up, and Stellan, lounged back in his chair that was across the table from Harry and Susan—not at the head, so no one was odd man out in seating—turned his head to watch her move to the pantry.

He felt something and looked to Susan.

His gut didn't drop at witnessing her look.

It warmed.

"Just in case, you know . . ." Harry started quietly, gaining Stellan's attention, "you didn't get it from the drama we walked in on and the night being a good one, we approve."

Stellan inclined his head.

"We better be seriously in the black this year, boss man, because I'm totally going five carats for that girl," Susan shared.

"You have an unlimited budget," Stellan told her.

She beamed.

The beam died and she asked, "You okay about your mother?"

"Absolutely," he answered, turning his head as he sensed Simone coming back. He caught her eyes, gave her a soft look, and then he again gave Susan his attention. "The only thing troubling me is the fact that I realized I should have done it a long time ago."

"Preach that, my man, so maybe my woman will officially break ties with that ahsweepay she calls a father," Harry put in.

Stellan's attention riveted on Susan.

"Oh boy," Simone muttered at his side, flipping open the box of chocolates on the table.

"You're speaking to him again?" Stellan asked.

"I had to tell him he was going to be a grandfather . . . again," Susan answered.

"Considering all the love and devotion he's given Crosby, and obviously you, but of course," Stellan drawled sarcastically.

"That's it, bro. Tell it like it is," Harry said.

"Shut up, Harry," Susan hissed.

"No way, baby," Harry returned.

"He's my father," Susan reminded her husband.

"I'm a father," Harry retorted. "So I know what a father is, babe. And that man is no father."

"Damn right," Stellan agreed.

Susan's narrowed eyes came to him. "You can pipe down too."

Stellan opened his mouth.

But got nothing out.

"Leave her be."

He looked to his side and watched Simone pop a chocolate in her mouth.

"Darling, you don't know the story," he pointed out.

"Nope, I don't," she agreed after swallowing. "What I do know is her telling her dad about the baby is not for her dad. It's for her. She's a good person doing the right thing. The right thing sometimes is not easy but it's still right, and the goal is for her to be able to rest her head on her pillow and sleep at night because she did right even to a man who has done her wrong. So stand down, big brother. She's got the real kind of love, so she can deal with him and be all right."

Before Stellan could kiss her terribly inappropriately in front of Susan and Harry, Susan spoke.

"I am *soooooooo* seeing how having another being with female parts in our little family is going to work for me. Which means I *soooooo* hope this new one is a girl so she can totally even out the numbers." Susan smiled at Simone. "And check it, baby-girl shopping and then toddler-girl shopping and then little-girl shopping followed by teenage-girl shopping. I mean, *decades* of that goodness. I'm going to be drowning in princess dresses until she gets married."

"If it's a girl, I'm throwing it back," Harry declared.

That was when Stellan chuckled, he heard Simone's soft laughter, and Susan looked in pain because with a now sleeping Crosby in her arms, she couldn't punch her husband.

Stellan stretched an arm along Simone's shoulders and pulled her to his side.

She didn't resist. She rested into him and reached for another chocolate.

"Shove those closer to me, Sixx," Susan ordered, Simone complied, and Susan reached for one, telling Harry, "I'm totally ballooning up with this one and doing it with forethought."

"Baby, I don't care if I have to cut a new door for you to get through, just deliver me a healthy kid with you the same and it's all good."

Simone melted closer to Stellan's side as Susan's pique vanished.

They enjoyed more easy conversation, but with a sleeping baby who needed his bed, it didn't last long.

However, this time, when Stellan stood on his front walk after saying his goodbyes, and while watching Susan and Harry load up and drive away, Simone stood in the curve of his arm at his side.

After the brake lights dimmed when Harry pulled out onto the road, Stellan guided Simone into the house. He closed the door. He locked it.

Then he pulled her in front of him and pushed her back into it, moving in close to her front, his hands coming to her jaw, bending his neck so his face was close to hers.

"Well, hello there," she murmured, her brown eyes warm and dancing.

"Susan hates my father and has little time for my mother, most likely that will be even less now. Margarita hates my mother and doesn't even mention my father. But neither of them has confronted her. Perhaps they feel it isn't their place. Perhaps there's been no opportunity to do so. You could have felt both those things, but you didn't. You just did it. And thus there has been no one in my entire life, even Silie when she was alive, who stood up for me against either of my parents when they were treating me like shit . . . except you."

She stared up at him, looking shocked, then panicked, then angry.

"No one?" she asked.

"You can't imagine, and I cannot describe, how beautiful it was to watch you get that angry and protective on my behalf, sweetheart."

The panic was edging back. "I—"

He touched his mouth to hers to stop her from talking, moved away, and whispered, "Don't. Don't pollute that either, Simone. If you fight me on everything we have until you finally bow fully to your feelings for me, I don't care. But don't pollute that. It was too beautiful, and I need it to be exactly that for the rest of my days."

She held her body tense and held his gaze, so he watched as thoughts and feelings chased themselves through her eyes.

He could not read all of them and didn't try. He stayed silent and gave her time.

Finally, she came to where she needed to be and gave him what that was.

"I need you to fuck me now, Stellan, and do it hard."

"That will not be difficult to oblige," he replied.

"Then oblige," she ordered.

He quirked his brows. "Here at the door, or on the floor, or can you make it to our bed?"

"Your choice."

He smiled.

Her eyes dropped to his mouth to watch.

And that decided it.

He fucked her against the door.

seventeen

Two Halves Made Whole

SIXX

Saturday night, Sixx sat in her Cayenne with her Nikon binoculars to her eyes, watching through a window the not-so-riveting show of a broken man sitting alone in his living room watching the Investigation Discovery Channel.

She'd searched his house. She'd searched his car. She'd again run his finances, his credit, his cell records, criminal records, civil records. She'd even done a social security trace, run a driver's history, and hacked into the electronic employee records of two past employers. And she'd followed him now for days.

But the plaintiff in the case her firm was working had a job in the garden department at Lowe's and was barely scraping by due to the loss of pretty much everything considering his best friend fucked him over so badly. He'd had to sell his house and move into a one-bedroom condo. His girlfriend had even dumped him.

He certainly wasn't sitting on a mountain of money he'd scavenged from the company. In fact, the equipment they both owned that needed selling now that the company was dissolved but was in limbo due to the lawsuit would go a long way for the guy.

Most specifically, paying his legal bills, which were eating him alive.

Yeah, some of their clients were schmucks.

And that was being nice.

She set aside her binoculars, started up her car, drove two blocks, hooked a right, and drove two more blocks before she pulled over, grabbed her phone, and texted Topher, the attorney on the case.

I'm closing this down. There's nothing else to get on this guy. If you have any ideas, I'm game to check them out. But I'm clearing out for tonight. Good luck with this one.

She hit "send," eased her baby back on the road, and picked up her phone to read the return text sitting at a stoplight.

Gotcha. At least I'm not going to be blindsided in the courtroom. Thanks again.

She tossed her phone back to the seat, and when the light turned green, headed home to Stellan.

The good news was, though she had some investigative work to do for another case, that wasn't pressing and would be mostly computer work, so she could start it on Monday.

This meant she and Stellan would have all day Sunday to do whatever it was Stellan wanted to do.

And Sixx was looking forward to it.

She was just there, in the zone.

Not in the zone in their sex lives (though she was there too, totally).

But their lives.

And for now she told herself to do what Stellan asked her to do.

Not question it.

Not pollute it.

Not fuck it up.

Just let it be.

Strangely, getting back to her life as it had been, with her work being a large part of it, the only change being going back to Stellan's house with Stellan in it at night, it became just what she did, who she was, a way of life.

It made being with Stellan easier.

No, that wasn't it.

It made being with Stellan just . . .

Life.

More important, it made Stellan happy.

She had two more weeks of making him happy.

And then . . .

A call coming in stopped her thoughts and set her to glancing at her dash.

It told her Jokerman was calling.

Carlo.

She hit the button on her steering wheel to take the call.

"Yo, asshole," she answered.

"In the immortal words of David Cassidy, I think I love you, and I'm always reminded of that especially when you call me 'asshole.'"

She grinned at the windshield.

"To what do I owe the honor of you remembering I exist?" she asked.

"You know a place called the Bolt?"

Her attention to the conversation increased.

The Bolt was another sex club in Phoenix. Not nearly as nice as the Honey, but it didn't suck. She'd heard it used to be a lot worse, got new management, was cleaned up and slightly classed up.

She'd trolled the Bolt only after that had occurred, and since she started at the Honey, it was definitely a step down, and that was a steep step. But it wasn't a pit.

"Yes," she answered. "Why?"

"Well, got a friend who's a friend of a friend of a friend who part-owns the joint, and my friend knows what I do for shits and giggles. This guy who part-owns the place has got two other partners. One is solid. Real solid. Good guy, and from what I can tell from what I've been told, it's him that keeps the place running. The friend of a friend of a friend of my friend is a flake. But not so flakey he isn't worried the last partner isn't up to some fucked-up shit and using the club to facilitate it."

When he said no more, Sixx prompted, "And?"

"And, the good guy partner isn't a big fan of the bad guy partner and the man in the middle wants to keep things as copacetic as he can, so he doesn't want to go to the good guy partner unless he's got something concrete to show him. I'm not a stranger to Phoenix, so my friend contacted me to see if I'd poke around. But I'm nowhere near there right now without any plans to get there so . . ."

"Enter me," she said.

"Yeah, if you can take it on. He doesn't have your usual deposit because, from what I can tell, he spends all his extra cash on weed, X, various hallucinogens and sex toys. But my friend says he might be a flake, he's also a decent guy, and he'd be good for your normal fee on a payment-plan basis. And if you find something, the good guy partner is gonna have to be brought in, and he'll undoubtedly cover you through the club."

If this was coming from anyone but Carlo, she'd hang up on him.

But it was coming from Carlo, and she was facing a slowdown from firm work. On top of that, firm work was never very exciting, so having something juicy to sink her teeth into worked in a big way.

"What's the fucked-up shit the bad guy partner is using the club to facilitate?" Sixx asked.

"Prostitution."

Oh shit.

"On club premises?" she inquired.

"Yeah," Carlo told her. "Books their private rooms in the club, his girls work them, mostly giving, not getting."

"So they're subs," Sixx surmised.

"Nope, they're paid whores who this guy keeps jacked up on meth or smack and pimps out. This doesn't appear to be entirely voluntary, or, say, voluntary at all if you factor out them being slaves to their addiction. An addiction it's considered this guy enables so he can get them to work for him."

Oh man.

Now she was getting pissed.

"Does the paid play get extreme?" she queried.

"No clue about that life but the words 'blood play,' 'burn play,' and 'branding' were said during my brief. I'm taking a wild stab, but I think that would mean a yes."

"It would mean a yes," she muttered.

"You up for a meet with this guy?"

"Can't do anything until Monday, but yes."

"Great. I'll set it up. His name is Josh. Last name Coates, if you want to dig into him in the meantime."

Oh, she'd be digging into him all right.

The problem was, she was in the scene, knew the scene, and was known in the scene. She couldn't go undercover to set herself up to maybe be taken in by this BDSM pimp.

But Sylvie could.

She grinned at the windshield again.

"Keep in touch," she said to Carlo.

"Will do. In other news, things good?"

They were fantastic.

"I haven't handed anyone their ass in months, so I'm getting jittery," she told him. "Other than that, they're what they are."

Which would be fantastic.

"Love a girl who loves to bust asses," Carlo replied.

"That bus with all the squares on it is rolling out, David. Time to grab your microphone, puka shells, feather your hair, and head out."

"You think your smart ass is a turnoff, but I'm totally hard right now."

"I'm pretty sure masturbation is not allowed on the bus."

He burst out laughing.

She grinned at her windshield again.

When he stopped laughing, she said, "Before you go take care of business, how about you? All good?"

He didn't answer.

"Carlo?" she called. "You there?"

There was another moment of silence before, in a low voice, he stated, "You've never asked me that."

Sixx didn't grin at that.

"I just finished a job and have a long drive home," she lied. She was now five minutes away from Stellan's. "Just killing time."

"No you aren't. You've got the hots for me."

That set her to grinning again.

"I've known you four years, I don't know your last name, and you have a way with a switchblade that scares even me, and I'm totally badass. You're not my type."

"What's your type?" he asked, part teasing, part curiosity.

Tall, dark, rich men who are as beautiful inside as they are on the outside, she thought.

"I haven't met him yet," she said, lying to a friend yet again.

"Right," Carlo muttered.

"I'm bored now." And there was another lie.

"Right." That was said on a chuckle.

"I'm also hanging up on you now," she warned him.

"So what's new?" he asked.

It was then he heard her chuckle.

But with her thumb hovering over the button on her steering wheel that would disconnect their call, quietly she said, "I never thanked you, and I should have thanked you. So now I'm going to say it, mean it, and it'll be done until you call the marker that you earned for doing it. Thank you for saving my life, Carlo. I owe you one."

With that, she disconnected.

She wasn't breathing easily, but she managed to get herself together as she completed the drive home to Stellan's.

She parked next to his Maserati, and as she walked in the back door, she could practically taste the martini he'd no doubt make her since she was home at a relatively decent hour and she was now unsure she could live without his excellent martinis (they were that good).

It was on the tip of her tongue to shout, "Honey, I'm home," as she tossed her cell phone, binoculars and purse on the island.

Fortunately, Stellan wandered into the great room from the direction of the stairs before she said it.

"Hey," she greeted.

"Hey," he returned on a smile, coming her way.

She watched, and seriously, threat of death, she wouldn't have been able to pick a favorite between his workwear, his casualwear or his loungewear.

Though naked was the best, him right there in low-slung, burgundy, drawstring knit pants and a short-sleeved, gray Henley that clung to his chest was definitely her current fave.

"You're done early," he noted.

"There's nothing else to get, and watching him watch TV was definitely not a thrill a minute," she replied.

As he came to a stop in front of her, his smile changed in a way Sixx liked very much with certain parts of her body liking it especially.

"I wonder if we can find something that will keep you amused."

She could drop to her knees in front of him, pull that drawstring waistband under his balls and suck him off.

It wouldn't be amusing. But it would be a definite thrill a minute.

"Hmm . . ." she hummed as he bent in and touched his mouth

to hers in a sweet greeting. "I was thinking of starting with a martini," she remarked when he pulled back.

"If there's nothing else you can get on this man, does that mean
you're done with work for the weekend?" he asked.

She nodded.

"Then it's the weekend, Simone, so I might make you a drink
later, but now I'd like you to walk upstairs, get undressed, and sit
naked at the end of our bed with your legs crossed, leaned back into
your hands at your sides. In that position, you'll wait for me to come
to you."

She stared up at him.

He allowed her to do that for a few seconds before he prompted,
"Is there something about those instructions you don't understand?"

"So we're playing?" she queried.

"Is it the weekend?" he returned.

"Yes," she answered.

"Then yes, that's the deal, and obviously play can wait while work
needs to get done, but if there is no work to be done, you're mine."

You're mine.

God, that had an amazing ring to it.

He moved so his face was closer to hers.

"Darling, you're not walking to our room."

"Right," she whispered.

He straightened.

She skirted around him.

Her legs were a little wobbly as she made her way to their bedroom.

They were more wobbly, and her breasts felt heavier—her nipples definitely were hard—as she took her clothes off in the walk-in
and threw them in the hamper.

She took a minute to check her makeup and hair in the bathroom mirror and add a subtle spray of perfume, then she walked out
to the bedroom and sat at the end of the bed like Stellan had instructed.

As she stared at the door, waiting for him to arrive, she could feel the beat of her heart in her neck pulsing right down to her nipples.

And her mind was flashing from thought to thought, imagining what he might do to her.

She'd watched him at play a lot, but this was not a playroom in the Honey or a playroom at all.

And regardless, last weekend, his work with her had been far more intimate than any she'd seen him do with another sub, even when there were three other men in the room with him while he did it.

In other words, what he intended to do to her could be anything.

This meant her stomach felt odd in a fluttery way, and her pussy was drenched, her clit throbbing and her nipples so hard they hurt.

And the longer he made her wait—and the minutes stretched into more and then more—the worse it got.

She knew this game. She'd played this game a good deal with her subs. The longer you sat in a vulnerable position and waited for attention, the longer you had to think on what that attention might be, or what you wanted it to be, or what your Dom was feeling, knowing you were in that state and it was just getting worse, the more worked up you became.

She'd once made a sub wait so long for her to touch him, when she did, he'd come instantly and without permission.

So of course he'd come again, with permission, a much, much longer and far more arduous time later.

In other words, she had to pull herself together and keep it together. She couldn't lose it like that with Stellan.

Not Stellan.

Not her Master.

She uncrossed her legs and recrossed them, staring at the door, trying not to lick her lips, rub her thighs together or call out just to see if he was close.

Stellan made her wait longer.

And even longer.

When she was ready to scream, aware of every inch of her skin, all of it sensitive even simply exposed to the air, brilliantly uncomfortable in a position that was not designed to give discomfort, but with the length of time she had to wait to be in her Dom's presence, to have his attention, it was becoming excruciating, he sauntered in.

Her pussy pulsed when she saw what he had in his hands.

Left, a tube of lube.

The right, a relatively substantial, wide, squat, steel anal plug.

Her mouth started watering.

He walked up the steps and to her, coming to a stop at her feet.

He tossed the lube and plug to the bed beside her then his hands moved to the hem of his tee.

He tugged it off and dropped it to the floor.

Staring at his chest, Sixx bit her lip.

"Take up the plug, darling, and prepare it," he murmured warmly.

More than ready for the games to begin, Sixx turned her head to the bed to grab the toy, but it was forced back with a crooked finger under her chin so he could catch her gaze.

"I gave you an order, Simone, how do you reply?" he asked.

She stared into his eyes, pulling it up, ready to give it to him, *needing* to give it to him.

So she gave it to him.

"Yes, Master," she whispered.

The flare in his heated blue gaze that left it blazing raged up her pussy, straight to her womb.

"Excellent," he whispered back, the adoration in his tone mingled with the intensity in his eyes and settling warmly throughout her body.

He stroked her chin with a finger, lifting it to sweep it across her lips before he straightened away.

Sixx swallowed and turned back to the toy.

With practiced hands she lubed it, and with the width of it, she did this generously.

Stellan took the lube from her, dropped it to the bed, and she sat at its edge, head tipped back, waiting again for her next instruction.

Her entire body started trembling when he undid the drawstring on his pants, let them drop to just below his ass but planted his feet wide so they stayed right there, stretched across his upper thighs with his now-exposed cock standing out thick, long and proud, his balls heavy but drawn up tight.

Damn, it was actually painful not to bend forward and take him deep in her mouth.

But when he said what he said next, it set the trembles she was experiencing to rolling quakes.

"Now, slide that toy inside me, darling, and fuck me while you do it."

Her eyes locked to his, she sat motionless except for the involuntary quivering.

He tipped his head to the side. "Do I have to ask again?"

"You want me to . . . you want to be . . . ?" She couldn't finish.

Master Stellan wanted to be . . .

Fucked?

And *plugged*?

He finished for her.

"Fucked and then full when I play with you?"

"Yes," she forced out.

"That is what I told you to do," he reminded her.

"Do you . . ." Her voice came out pitched high, and his lips quirked. She pulled it together and asked, "Have you done this before?"

"When I display a slave at the Club, it's her I want displayed, it's her I want to have the attention, not me. So when I work plugged, I wear pants. And when I fuck plugged, it's with my front to the windows."

"Oh my God," she breathed.

She'd had no idea.

How hot was this?

Too hot!

"Darling, don't delay. I have something planned I'm looking forward to, and I'd like to get on with it."

Sixx wanted to get on with it too, in a big way.

And she wasn't going to miss this opportunity. So she leaned toward him, reaching around, her neck straining with the deep bend she had to use to keep contact with his gaze because she absolutely wanted to watch his face as she filled him.

"You can use your other hand to open me," he murmured.

Okay.

Man.

God, she was going to come doing this.

She was going to come, sliding inside Stellan.

Suddenly, his hand flashed out, and he pinched her nipple pitilessly.

She jumped and moaned as that pinch exploded in her clit.

"Plug me," he bit.

Sixx wrapped her hand around his cheek, opening him, and with the plug in the other one, she slid it along his crease until the end caught at his hole.

She pressed it to him.

His hand came to rest on the side of her neck but not for long. It went up, and back, fisting in her hair at the back crown and straining her neck even further as he pulled her back and bent to put his face into hers.

She pressed the plug deeper.

He growled.

Oh yes, this was hot.

The lips of her pussy shivered, and her breath started to come out raspy.

She pushed in deeper and then started stroking.

"After you're done filling me, darling," he murmured roughly, "I'm going to turn you onto your knees and fuck your ass. With fingers splayed, face in the bed, you're going to hold yourself open for me and beg me to fuck you deep. Take you hard. Not to stop. Then I'm going to come in you and on you, all over you. And you're going to thank your Master for his cum and ask him for more."

"Yes," she breathed, pressing the toy in deeper, gliding it out, in, out, opening him, pushing it further and further with each stroke.

"I should have thought to find a switch Mistress to fill me," he purred. "They know how to take ass better than anyone." He came closer so his lips were nearly on hers. "But I'm glad I waited for you."

"I am too," she whispered.

She went deeper, and his hand in her hair fisted tighter.

"This will be it, Simone," he told her, his gaze totally turned on and tuned into her, but something had gone serious in it. Dead serious. "I'll have your ass, you'll have had mine, we'll have claimed everything, which means you'll be fully mine, as I will be yours."

I will be yours.

She started shaking.

"Stellan—"

His other hand captured her nipple, pinching and twisting, and she cried out and drove the plug deeper than intended, earning a pleased grunt.

"Who am I to you?" he reminded her gruffly.

"Master," she said.

"That's my Simone," he returned, pressed into the plug, and she got the hint, drove it home, and he commanded, "Hold on to my ass."

She did, with both hands.

Using her hair, he pushed her down. His other hand now wrapped around his cock, he forced it into her mouth.

She accepted it gladly.

Sucking him while he fucked her face and held her head stationary to take his thrusts, she tried to beat back the moans, the writhing of her hips against the bed, the pressing of her thighs against each other, and Stellan didn't miss it.

"If you come, you will be punished."

She honestly didn't care.

Both his hands spanned her skull, and he drove into her mouth relentlessly as she held tight to his ass and let him.

It went on what seemed like tortuous hours but was only tortuous minutes before he pulled out, kept one hand on her head, the other hand he wrapped around his dick and teased her by brushing the glossy silk of the tip against her lips.

"Are you ready to get fucked, Simone?"

"Yes, Master," she breathed.

She just got that out before she was up, turned, positioned with her knees tight together, her ass back and on offer, her face shoved into the bed.

"Splayed fingers, open yourself for me," he growled.

She did.

She vaguely heard something plop on the bed and knew he was lubing himself for extra slickening to ease the way.

But that was the only way he eased his penetration.

One of his hands landed on the small of her back as he drove into her to the root with a glorious grunt at the same time she let out a sharp cry.

And then he took her ass like it was what it was.

His and his alone, for his use however he wanted to use it.

It.

Was.

Glorious.

He thrust deep and stayed planted.

"Beg me, Simone," he bit out.

"Fuck me, Master," she begged into the bed. "Please, fuck my ass." He again took her deep, hard, forcing her body into the bed with each stroke.

"Open wider for me," he ordered.

She pulled herself wider, and he kept at her.

"Don't stop, Master, please. Please keep fucking my ass," she pleaded.

"You're hot up there, darling," he growled. "Christ. Hot and tight."

"Take it," she breathed.

"Is it mine?"

"Yes. Yours," she pushed out. "Only yours." She closed her eyes, her body shaking, it and nothing of it under her control, so the words she said next slipped right out. "Stellan, baby, I need to come."

"Not yet, Simone."

"I . . . can't . . . hold . . ."

"You will hold."

"Baby—"

He made a low, reverberating noise so exquisite, her body locked to give what it could to her Master, her attention shifting from her need to release entirely to him.

He grunted, "Hold," right before he shouted out his orgasm, pulsing his cum in her ass before he pulled out and jetted more on her cheeks, in her opened crease, everywhere.

She felt the head of his cock prodding her flesh and knew he was milking himself and jacking into her, using her as resistance to keep coming, and it was so sublime, she tasted blood as she bit the inside of her lip to hold back her own climax.

She heard him take in a deep, broken breath then felt his thumb slide up her ass, two fingers drive into her pussy, and he commanded brusquely, "You can come for me now, Simone."

She exploded instantly, holding position, shuddering in the ball of body offered up to her Master, face in the bed, ass and pussy his for the taking.

When she started coasting down, her breathing still erratic, his voice came at her again.

"Thank me," he ordered huskily, his fingers and thumb still inside her but now stroking gently.

"Thank you, Master."

"Ask me for more."

"Please, Master, I need more of your cum."

"Lovely, darling," he murmured. "Tonight, you're going to sleep with my cum in you everywhere you can take it. Sleep with it coating your ass and cunt and belly and breasts. Sleep with a plug inside to keep me inside you. Sleep with your Master a part of you, inside and out."

"Yes," she whispered to the bed.

"Crawl to my nightstand, get your plug, bring it back to your Master."

His fingers were still planted inside her, but to allow her to carry out his instruction, he slid himself free, and she crawled to his nightstand to retrieve the smaller plug he kept there.

As she crawled back, he drawled, "When you get here, darling, up on your knees, facing me, hand me your plug, then prepare to take it by opening for me."

She arrived back to him seeing he'd righted his pants and wishing he hadn't.

But that was not her choice.

And God but she liked it like that.

Because she'd get it back, but only when he was ready to give it to her.

She lifted up on her knees slightly spread, gave him the plug, put her hands where he wanted them and did what he'd told her to do.

Only then did she look right into his eyes and say clearly, "Yes, Master."

His face shifted to a pure beauty of vicious possession as another sound came from him, low again, deep, and this time feral as he took her mouth in a hard, wet kiss at the same time he reached around and drove her plug up her ass.

And there was no way around it no matter how she might want to look at it or how hard her subconscious was trying to make her escape from it.

In that moment she knew it.

She.

Was.

Claimed.

His lips slid from hers to her ear.

"It's time to see how my Simone reacts to being restrained," he whispered there.

She shivered, top to toe.

And she could swear she felt his smile against her ear.

Stellan was fucking her face again, and eating her, while she was tied on her back to his bed with black silk sashes, wrists and ankles, both spread wide.

Sixx was watching his plugged ass move as he thrust into her mouth and ate her out, in the throes of agony since he'd played with her pussy to orgasm, and again, and again, then fucked it to his orgasm (and another of hers), so it was excruciatingly sensitive.

And that was after he'd fucked her tits and come all over them.

With a soft grunt sounding intimately against that exact sensitivity, he came down her throat, and she scrambled to swallow as he ordered, "Now," before he sucked hard on her clit, then licked over it, drove his tongue inside, and she came in his mouth.

She shuddered lazily through her climax, focusing more on milking his cum from his cock, so gone, lost in the scene, lost to him, it was almost like it was happening to an alternate Sixx, and she was out of body, watching it.

He'd done what he'd promised, and she was covered in his seed—ass, cunt, breasts, belly—and now it was down her throat.

He took her with him over the edge each time, and then some, so now she was spent, lax under him, her pussy quivering against his laving tongue, her mouth nursing his cock.

Eventually he gently slid out, and she lay there unmoving for him as he slipped the knot on each wrist, each ankle, then positioned between her legs, lowered his body to hers and murmured his command.

"Arms and legs around me, darling."

Like she was in a dream, her limbs drifted to do as she was told.

"Are you even conscious?" he asked, and at the teasing lilt to his voice, she focused on him (mildly).

"I think so," she answered.

"We're done playing, Simone, though you keep the plug until morning, and you won't be washing me away."

"Okay by me, hot stuff," she muttered and felt her most favorite feeling in the world.

Yes, after multiple orgasms and mind-shattering sexual play, what she felt right then was still her favorite.

His body was shaking against hers with his quiet laughter.

That made her focus on him a lot less mild.

His fingers came to her jaw, his thumb moving over her cheek to the corner of her lip, along the lower one, and back as he studied her face.

"You okay?" she asked softly, seeing his face was sated, relaxed, content, but feeling something . . . off.

"You slipped right into role this time."

She grinned at him, giving him her own tease, "Miss Sixx?"

His thumb halted and his eyes grew intense on hers.

His did not hide he was startled.

"I'm sorry?" he asked.

In the peace of the aftermath of a beautiful scene, suddenly, her insides grew cold.

"I don't . . . well, it's . . ." she stammered, drew in a breath and said, "Of course you don't miss her. I shouldn't have mentioned it."

"She's not gone."

Sixx stared up at him.

He continued, "She's right here, where she's always been. Where she'll always be. She's not going anywhere. She's you."

"I thought you wanted—"

"I want you. *You*. And you're Sixx."

"But Simone—"

"There is no distinction, honey. I call you one name. Others call you another. But in the end, they're one in the same."

His words were freaking her out so much her hands went from resting on his back to pushing in between them, not to force him away but to find warmth.

"Sweetheart?" he called questioningly.

She couldn't be both.

It was one.

And it was never supposed to be the other.

But she was out.

She was his.

Simone was his.

As was Sixx.

They just weren't one in the same.

They couldn't be. How could she protect Simone . . . protect *him* . . . if they were?

But there was no denying it, not anymore.

They were both out.

They were both his.

They were both who she was.

Two halves made whole.

His fingers moved back to cup her behind her ear, the pads carefully digging in and even the tone of his voice communicated his concern when he said, "Simone."

"I think I really kind of need to just . . . pass out," she told him lamely.

"That was too intense," he declared.

"I'm . . ." Her head twitched. "Sorry?"

"That scene, it was too intense."

"It was fine, Stellan."

"It asked a lot of you."

"No more than I've seen you ask of any of your subs."

"You aren't any of my subs, Simone. You're you, the woman in my bed, my home, my life. This is just a part of what we have, and we're getting to know each other in that way, and that scene was asking too much."

She was confused. "I can't imagine how."

"It required the strength of Sixx with the openness and acceptance of Simone. They are one in the same. But you clearly don't know that yet, so introducing you to yourself through fucking you was not the way to go."

She was still confused.

"But . . . didn't you do that last Sunday?"

"No, I broke Sixx last Sunday. Sixx submitted to me last Sunday. I didn't have Simone last Sunday. I didn't have her tonight. Tonight, I had it all."

He did.

She'd given him it all.

He moved suddenly, rolling off of her but hooking her with an arm like he was going to drag her out of bed.

All of a sudden panicked, she clamped on and cried, "Wait!"

Stellan lifted a hand and cupped her jaw. "We're showering and then we're—"

"No!" she exclaimed desperately, pushing into him with her body, wrapping her arms back around him, holding on tight.

She couldn't lose what he'd given her that night.

She couldn't lose what she had of him.

She couldn't lose what she'd given of herself.

"Darling—"

She shook her head where it was resting on the pillow. "I don't want to lose you. I don't want to wash you away."

His voice went supremely tender. "Simone, we need to exit this scene completely. We'll talk about it tomorrow."

"No." Sixx kept shaking her head. "We can't. I want to keep it. Don't make me lose it."

He studied her face so acutely she couldn't handle it, shoved it in his throat and held him even tighter.

"Let's just go to sleep, baby," she whispered there. "Can we just go to sleep?"

He hesitated before he replied quietly, "We can, darling. But before we do, I need you to take the plug from me."

She nodded, moving her hand toward his ass.

She didn't get there before he murmured, "Will you kiss me while you do it?"

At the request, being an actual request, from Stellan, so quiet, so beautiful, her hand stopped, her eyes closed, and her heart wrung out like someone was squeezing the blood from it.

It did this only for it to be let go so new, clean, uncontaminated blood could pump through it, through her veins, through her entire body.

She tipped her head back and caught his gaze before she moved in to take his mouth and slid her hand to his backside.

She took the plug from him slowly, gently, absorbing his corresponding purrs in her mouth as he took her tongue and sucked sweetly at it when he'd been released.

He ended the kiss, kissed her chin, her nose, then pulled carefully away, taking the plug from her before he left their bed.

She curled her legs into her belly and watched him walk to the bathroom.

He was not gone long, and he made short work of turning the lights out around the room when he returned.

He then rejoined her in bed, immediately pulling her into his arms, over his body, so she was straddling his thigh, her forehead in his neck, his hand at her ass, his other arm holding her close to him around her back.

"Sleep, Simone," he urged softly.

She nodded against his skin, staring at the shadows of his chest and shoulder, but she knew sleep would not come.

In the dark, held by Stellan, covered with him, filled by him, she looked back at their time together and realized it had happened long before that night.

And because of that, she had no choice but to make a decision.

So she did.

This decision did not make sleep any easier.

In fact, it was just the opposite.

She also knew Stellan did not sleep, probably feeling her awake, sensing her disquiet, but oh-so-Stellan, not prodding at it.

He was like that and would not rest knowing she could not.

This should have made her decision easier to take.

It did not.

But no matter how difficult it was, for the both of them, she had to carry it out without delay.

They had tonight.

And tomorrow . . .

Tomorrow would be whatever it would be.

Though she knew what it would be, and she hoped the night never ended.

But Sixx had learned a long time ago not to hope for impossible things.

That night would end. They always did.

And then it would be tomorrow.

On that thought, Sixx fell into an uneasy sleep.

Only then did Stellan join her there.

eighteen

Dynamic Duo

SIXX

Sixx woke the next morning to an empty bed.

She didn't panic. Stellan was good at giving her space. Especially after things got intense.

Although she didn't panic about that, her belly felt like it was filled with lead, her body like it was encased in concrete, and it was without a doubt the hardest thing she'd ever done in her life, rolling out of that bed.

When she made it to the bathroom, she saw a cup of coffee on the warmer, but other than that, nothing. No lingerie. No note.

Pure Stellan.

He was worried about her, so he was not going to take them there.

That morning it would be Simone and Stellan, maybe a day of movies, or going shopping, or perhaps driving up to Prescott to spend the day out of the heat.

Whatever she wanted.

Whatever she needed.

Yes, God yes, what she had to do was the worst thing she'd ever had to do in her life.

But it had to be done.

She slid out his plug, washed it, and set it on the towel laid out on the counter next to the one he'd cleaned last night.

His and hers plugs.

It was the woman she was, it was the couple they were, that made the sight of their shared intimacy set her nearly to collapsing in uncontrollable tears.

Instead, she did something else she didn't want to do.

She got in the shower and washed him away.

When she got out, she lotioned up (it *was* Phoenix—in that dry climate, no matter what was happening, you couldn't miss that step). But she didn't do makeup or perfume or fashion her hair into adorably fuckable.

She would go to him as she was. Simone "Sixx" Marchesa.

Bared.

Real.

She moved out to the bedroom, right to the end of the bed.

Sixx stood by the tee Stellan had left on the floor and deliberated far too long on whether to nab it or put her own clothes on.

In the end, she was selfish.

She needed it, needed some part of him near, so she bent and grabbed it, pulled it on, went to the walk-in and got a pair of panties.

She slid them up. Stood there. Took a deep breath. Then another. And a third.

Only then did she set about doing what she had to do.

She went to the drawer where she'd hidden them under some clothes.

And she retrieved them.

All of them.

She then walked into the bathroom, got her coffee, walked into the bedroom, through it, and left the room.

On the way down the stairs, she saw him out on the patio, in his chair, with his coffee cup, staring at his pool. Shoulders wide, bared and tan. Dark hair still messy from sleep.

Her heart slid right up into her throat.

She swallowed it down, set her coffee mug on the island, and went to the library.

One last bit.

She got what she went there to get, stacked it at the back of the pile she had, and held them all to her chest.

She did not stop again to take more breaths.

She had to do this and do it now, or she wouldn't.

So she moved quickly, directly back to the great room, to the doors to the back deck.

The second she opened the door, Stellan twisted in his seat to look at her, and her heart started pounding, her throat closing tight.

He was just so beautiful.

So, so beautiful.

She closed the door behind her and moved toward him, seeing his gaze had dropped to what she was holding against her chest, and his handsome face had changed.

It had frozen.

But his body hadn't.

He got up and moved free of the chair to stand at its side in his burgundy drawstring pants from the night before. His glorious, powerful chest was bare. The waistband of the pants was hanging so low on his hips they were hanging almost negligently, the weight of the drawstring dipping to the point the curves of muscles that formed a V to highlight his pubis were exposed, and the very top of his dark pubic hair peeked over.

Like that, in all his considerable glory, he watched her make her way to him, making that journey the most painful one she'd ever made.

"Darling—" he whispered when she stopped close.

"Don't," she whispered back.

His eyes were burning, and she couldn't stand the heat.

So she pushed the sketchbooks away from her and into his chest.

Instantly, his arms rose and wrapped around them.

Carefully.

Lovingly.

God.

She started trembling as she stared up into beautiful blue eyes that had gone bright with unshed wet.

He didn't know.

He had no idea.

This was touching him deeply.

But Christ, knowing what she knew, what he'd soon find out, it was killing her.

"Come find me when you're done," she said softly. "I want a chance to explain."

It was guttural when he started, "Simone—"

"You might hate me when you have it all."

"I'll never hate you," he whispered.

She shook her head. "Don't say that now. You can't say that now." She dipped her chin to indicate the books. "I can't be around when you read them. But I'll be waiting."

With that, as fast as she could, she turned on her foot and left him.

It would take him a long time, she knew. There were twelve of them, pages sized eighteen-by-twenty-four, seventy sheets.

A lot of life.

A lot of hideousness.

So much ugly.

Now in Stellan's hands.

Even so, she had to prepare so she didn't chicken out during phase two of losing Stellan forever, but before what she gave him made him let her go, she'd help him to understand fully why he needed to so he could be free.

Therefore, she went back up to the bedroom and got her LV cruiser bag.

She took it down to the library, set it on the big, round, frost-blue upholstered ottoman with its carved wood base that was at the center of the four, buttery-caramel-leather, nailhead-framed chairs. Stately. Classy. Inviting.

Stellan.

She left the room. Back in the kitchen, she warmed up her coffee, grabbed her laptop and phone, and headed back, not once looking at Stellan out on the deck.

She settled into a chair and opened up her laptop, logging in, beginning to do some digging on Josh Coates, owner of one-third of the Bolt.

She didn't get very far.

Instead, her mind wandered, and she looked around the room, taking in the interesting ironwork around the cream sheets of glass on the chandelier. The rich, wood, inset shelving with their sconces in between with single, tapered candles in them. The built-in architect's lamps over each set of shelves. The window seat in the wood-framed bay with its thick toss pillows.

The room was big, but it seemed cozy, welcoming, like the rest of the house. It could so easily be overwhelming, austere, intimidating. But it wasn't.

Like Stellan.

At a glance, he was so visibly physically superior, he was daunting.

But the deeper you got inside, the warmth enveloped you, permeating you, drawing you further in, showing you the way home.

She forced her mind back to Coates and kept it there long enough she had to go get herself another cup of coffee. She did and again did not look at Stellan before she headed back to the library.

Sixx had totally given up on Coates, as well as starting to dig into Barclay Richardson and Pete Beardsley, his two partners, her mug was empty, her eyes were aimed and staring vacantly out the window, but even lost to the nothingness she'd forced in her head in order to deal with what was to come, she still sensed his approach.

Therefore she was turned in her chair, but braced, and looking at the door when he came through it.

She couldn't read his expression, but she noted he didn't have the sketchbooks.

"Please don't say anything," she begged quietly.

He stopped just inside the door, opened his mouth, thought better of it, and closed it before walking to the chair beside hers, sitting, and turning her way.

She took him in, seeing his attention was focused entirely on her, but that was all she got from him.

So very Stellan.

When it happened, it would be quick and clean and as painless as he could make it.

Before then, for him, so he could have it all, she had to get through phase two.

She took a deep breath and turned to the cruiser bag, pulling it off the ottoman and placing it on the floor by her feet.

She opened it, reached in, and found the first of the three things in there she wanted to show him.

She pulled it out and held it up for him.

It was a cheap, plastic, small, tatty, stained baby doll.

"Dad gave me this," she said, staring at it, remembering it wasn't in much better condition years ago when her father had given it to her. "I loved it when he first gave it to me. It was the first toy I ever got. The only toy I ever had."

Her voice faded away as the memories returned, but she put effort into pulling herself back to the present, not getting sucked into and therefore lost to the past.

This effort was easy.

She'd had plenty of practice.

"I played with it all the time." She turned her gaze to Stellan. "Until Mom was in a bad mood one day when I was playing with it, so she told me Dad had taken it right out of the hands of a little girl whose father owed them money." She drew in breath, letting it out saying, "I didn't play with it after that."

Stellan said nothing, his face was still expressionless, but his gaze never left her.

"I was six," she whispered, and she watched his tall, lean body jerk.

And there it was.

Stellan never missed *anything*.

"I had to . . . I had to . . ." Sixx swallowed. "I had to create her so she'd protect me. It didn't start that night they died. I'd been Sixx half my life by then."

"May I talk?" he requested quietly.

"Can I finish first?" she asked back.

Slowly, he nodded.

Sixx set the doll on the ottoman and reached into the bag.

She pulled out a cheap, stuffed crocodile.

Staring at it, she shared, "My uncle won this for me. At the State Fair. He took me and my friends. The ones he killed. He won it for me before he won ones for them. I knew why, even then. I knew. It made it seem normal, the sweet, handsome, kind uncle taking his niece and her friends to the State Fair, throwing balls into holes to get his niece a stuffed crocodile. Then going the extra mile so they didn't feel left out and winning ones for them too."

She looked again to Stellan.

"But it was his excuse. He was trying to impress them. Draw them in. Doing stupid shit, such stupid, stupid *shit*, a man his age winning prizes at a fair for girls he wanted to fuck. After it happened, I would tell myself he never grew up. He was good-looking and always had been. The girls dripping off him in high school. He talked about it all the time, how he was the big man, about those good old days that were all about parties and pot and pussy. But as you get older, that has to translate to something more, or the girls won't keep coming around. And he was nothing. He was a loser and a dealer and a cheat, and his life carried on being about parties and pot and pussy, with the addition of more drugs and dealing them, and that was worse. So he had nothing. Was nothing. And he was left to target the girls who could be won over by cheap stuffed animals earned at a carnival game."

She put the crocodile on the ottoman and again spoke to it.

"That's just an excuse though, I understand that. An excuse for what he was, what he did. He was just evil. In his early forties, seducing sixteen-and seventeen-year-olds. Getting them high. Hooking them on drugs." Her voice dropped to a whisper. "There were no excuses. He was just a monster, and the only way he was not was that he never touched me. Not even when he was drunk or high. But I almost wish he had. I almost wished he'd gotten from me what the monster in him needed so he wouldn't have hurt anyone else. But I had to protect Simone. So I was sure to stay well away when the danger lurked. She had to remain safe. It was the only thing I had. The only thing I could do. I sacrificed friends to it, trying to be normal, to give Simone a chance at something good in her life. I sacrificed friends to keep her safe. But at least I did that. At least she was safe from him. He never touched her, and to make that so, he never touched me."

"Sweetheart—"

He said no more when she reached into the bag and pulled out a folded-over double frame.

She opened it.

"Corny," she muttered, staring at the pictures. "And sick."

She took in what she'd seen thousands of times.

One side, a bride and groom. The groom was in clean blue jeans and a crisp, ironed white shirt, his long, dark hair tamed in a ponytail at the back. The bride was wearing a tacky, shiny satin, cheap, white, strapless dress with a peplum and a too-short and too-tight skirt, hair teased out huge, face made up in Vegas-showgirl-with-a-palsy.

They were making out like they really needed to get a room.

The other side of the frame, a picture of two hands together, the woman's on top of the man's. It was akin to those traditional photos taken at traditional weddings, but on the ring fingers were bulky silver rings in which were etched in black the word HITCHED.

It might have been cute, if it wasn't them.

But it was them.

So it wasn't.

Not looking at him, she handed the frame to Stellan.

"He was a user," she said when he took it. "Coke mainly. She wasn't. She was the brains of the operation. He wasn't her husband, the father of her child. He was her lackey. She used him as an enforcer. A bag man. A delivery boy. An available cock. I was a mistake, and she told me so, more than once. Looking back, I see that I was the only thing she gave him, because when they found out she was pregnant, she wanted to get rid of me, he wanted to keep me, and she wanted to keep him at heel. So she had me so she could use me to keep him where she wanted him."

She looked up at him, then her eyes again dropped to the frame in Stellan's hands that he wasn't looking at because he was looking at her.

And she kept talking.

"I don't know what went on between the time those pictures were taken and when I came around. He looked happy in that photo. But she always looked like that. Vulgar and common and mean. They're kissing, but I know them. I can see the looks on their faces and read them. He looked like he had the rest of his life in front of him and was looking forward to facing it with the woman in his arms. She looked like she was ready for him to get on with it and give her an orgasm. It never changed. For the rest of their lives, it never changed. He hoped. He dreamed. She used and schemed."

She realized she was wringing her hands in her lap and stopped doing that.

But she didn't stop speaking.

"He loved me. He was a mess and he was an addict and he was under her thumb so he wasn't good at looking after me." She closed her eyes tight and turned them back to Stellan, opening them. "So Sixx did her best to look out for him too." She shook her head. "It wasn't what you might think. The trauma of what happened in that room didn't split me in two. I had been that way for a long time. What I couldn't handle about what happened in that room was that he died for me, instead of the way it was supposed to go for Sixx. That happening the other way around."

She vaguely noted he looked ill, as he would do with all this filth exposed, when he asked softly, "Can I speak now, sweetheart?"

But it was like he didn't say a word.

She kept going.

"I did those things, in the sketchbook, to prove I was better than her. Not much better, but I didn't ruin lives for a living. I have skills. I'm good at what I do. I was in demand. I had respect. I did them because I had this . . . this weird sense of invincibility. Like I survived that room, and I had to test life to see if that feeling was real. I did them because that was who I was, that was what *they* made, and I didn't think there could be anything else. And if that was the life I was born to lead, I was going to best it, best *her*. I did those things because it was all I knew, and I was scared of breaking free and how that would affect me, harm me, affect Simone, harm her. I did them because I constantly had to take risks to keep sharp so I could keep Simone safe. I did them because that was just . . . it was just . . ." she choked out the last word, "*me*."

"And each act you deemed unworthy scarred you," he noted quietly.

She gave a jerky nod. "You see this Sixx, but she hides the real me. It's a disguise. The Sixx in my books is the real me."

He nodded once, but his was firm, not jerky. "And I'm assuming, to escape the anger and blame that dogged you due to your uncle's activities, you left school the minute you turned eighteen, never earning your diploma or GED. However, you had to survive, feed yourself, and there were a variety of things you could have done, including going into the family business. You did not. You used your network of contacts to hire yourself out for anything *but* that. Illegal activities to be sure, aiding and abetting in the background, but never committing any felonies you masterminded for your own ends or your own gains."

"Now it's you who's making excuses, Stellan," she whispered.

"When you speak to me in that tone, darling, especially when we're talking about something this important, this intense, you call me 'baby.'"

Sixx sat up straight and blinked.

"And I'm not making excuses," he went on to declare. "I'm pointing out realities."

"Did you *read* my sketchbooks?" she asked dubiously.

"Every page, every word. It was the honor I expected it to be, from the minute I knew they existed. They moved me, they touched me, they filled me with anger as well as fear. But they didn't surprise me, and they absolutely did not repulse me."

"That's impossible to believe," she breathed.

"How?" he asked, not expecting an answer. He immediately went on, "Do you think I, or anyone else who knows you, would have preferred you were the spunky girl who got your GED, went to beauty school, and set up shop doing hair? No. Because that wasn't the route you took to the you we all know and want in our lives. Would you be more worthy of the people who care about you if you fought and scratched to get your diploma and then a law degree and worked at that firm where you work now, except doing it as an attorney? No again, for the same reasons."

"Stellan, I—"

He lifted his hand with his palm facing her way and shook his head, interrupting her.

"You can speak until you pass out, Simone, but you forget. I know you, and I knew you before I made my move to claim you. Perhaps I didn't know it in the depth and completeness I know it now, but that makes no difference to me. It's speculation, but I would wager it's accurate that you did not wander into Aryas's life randomly, and he did not offer to train you as a Dominatrix out of the kindness of his heart and his driving bent to offer nurture and care to everyone who partakes of kink. Even though, if he could, he would. He's just realistic enough to know he can't, and he does what he can for our kind. But instead, he met you through other means, and he doesn't give a damn what brought you to him. He's just glad you came into his life."

He was right about that and more, she hadn't thought about it like that.

However.

"But Stellan—"

"I'm in love with you, Simone."

She clamped her mouth shut, and her body locked.

Stellan kept at her.

"I know myself, and I don't give a fuck if it sounds full of conceit, it's the damned truth that I know the kind of woman who would be worthy of me, and she is not simply beautiful. She is not simply intelligent. She is also not simply stylish. Or brave. Or protective. Or amusing. She would not have to be well travelled or well read or have the love and adoration of scores of friends and family. She would have to be *all* this, perhaps without the scores of friends and family. For her it would be no family and a handful of friends. And I know this is the woman worthy of me because she's *you*."

Sixx didn't move. She didn't because she couldn't.

She also didn't because she didn't know what to say, to do, to *think*.

It wasn't as if she didn't know already that Stellan had fallen for her.

It just never occurred to her he'd share that with her in words.

And further, the reasons *why*.

He carried on, "And if you say you're not worthy of me, if you say it's not safe to love you, then right now I'm demanding another month on our deal, and you will give it to me. If it takes longer, I'll demand another month and another and another. And I will be perfectly fine if you never truly believe, and those months turn to years and those years turn to decades and you die in your sleep at a very old age, but do it lying beside me."

It was then the first tear slid down her cheek.

It did not go unnoticed.

"Darling," he whispered.

"I thought you'd read my books and ask me to leave," she whispered back.

"Sweetheart, reading those books only made me more determined

to make you stay. Frankly, your strength and determination and au-
dacity and will to survive and nurturing spirit to the child you've
kept safe and alive inside made me wonder if I was worthy of *you*."

And it was then the second tear fell.

The third followed it, and there was no stopping them, or the
sob that tore up her throat and out between her lips.

And then she was up and immediately down, Stellan sitting in
the chair where she'd been, Sixx in his lap, curled close in his arms.

"I-I-I'm sorry," she blubbered, trying and failing to breathe
deep, her voice cracking as she continued, "I'll p-pull it together.
P-p-promise."

"Why?" he asked.

Why?

The hero never falls apart.

The hero *always* stays together.

Remains strong.

"Because—"

"Be strong for the world, darling, if that's what you need to be.
But here, with me, you can be whatever you care to be."

That just made her cry harder, shove closer, her body rocking
deeper with her sobs.

Stellan held her tight against him, stroking the nape of her neck
with his fingers while she did it.

Eventually, the tears subsided, and Sixx just sat there, curled in
his arms, sniffling.

"Can I ask you for something, sweetheart?" he requested.

He could ask her for anything, and she'd fight, steal and die to
give it to him.

"Sure," she answered.

When she did, his arms gave her a squeeze, and she knew she'd
amused him because she knew he knew the understatement that word
represented.

She'd fight, steal and die for an opportunity to keep giving that
to him too.

But his tone was grave when he said gently, "I want to take those things to the garbage bin."

She pulled her face out of his throat and looked at him.

"If you're not ready," he continued quickly, "that's understandable. But I want you to think about it."

"I only let her out . . . for you."

His head twitched.

"She was only safe to come out . . . for you," Sixx went on.

His expression changed, growing fierce as his hands moved to frame her face.

"Now she's me," she told him. "We're together. The idea of that petrified me. But she came out, and I didn't even notice. That's how safe we were with you."

A growl rose in his throat, but she didn't stop speaking.

"I was terrified of you. My dad, I couldn't keep him safe. I knew I couldn't look after two people I loved. I'd already learned that. I lost him, but I found a way to survive. I knew the same wouldn't be true if I lost you."

Something flickered deep in his eyes, and he began, "Simone—"

"If you want to throw those things away," she talked over him, "then do it."

"You have to be ready to let go."

"I was ready the second you grabbed my chin at the side of the gladiator pit. I just didn't realize it then, baby."

His gaze took in her face as his lips rumbled, "Fuck, I need to fuck you."

She shifted in his lap and whispered, "Do it."

"Not with that shit in this room."

She pressed her lips together.

Stellan surged up, taking his feet, putting her on hers.

"Do you want to take them, or shall I?" he asked, staring down at the stuff on the ottoman like someone had smeared his gorgeous piece of furniture with feces.

"Do you actually know where the trash bins are?" she teased.

He turned to her. "Darling, as deeply as I love your sense of humor, I must inform you this moment is one that, although I expect they'll be very rare, you must know I can't fully appreciate you being amusing."

She pressed her lips together.

His eyes narrowed on them.

Okay, her man was not feeling like lightening the mood.

So noted.

But she felt like she could climb Camelback Mountain in a single bound and then leap directly through the sky, straight to the stars.

He bent, grabbed the doll, which he handed to her, the crocodile, something he also handed to her, and the frame, which he kept.

It was lucky she tucked the two things in her arm because he then took her free hand and pulled her out of the room.

It appeared he really *didn't* know where the trash bins were, considering they were lined up against the wall in the garage by the door, but he guided her toward the great room.

Through it.

Out the door.

She opened her mouth to share he was going the wrong way, but closed it when he led her to the recessed seating area around which were white-padded, built-in, backed benches. In the middle there was a fire pit.

He took her right down and stopped them at the pit's side.

"I'll be back," he murmured, turned, and strode up the two steps to his built-in barbeque area.

He opened a drawer and came back with a long grill lighter.

He went to the side of the pit, turned a silver key, flicked the lighter, and a wave of heat came with the blaze of fire that shot from the lava rock.

Stellan then tossed the lighter to the pad on a bench and moved back to her side.

"I take it the garbage isn't a permanent enough solution for you," she quipped.

He leveled his eyes on her.

Right.

Still not the time to be amusing.

"Go, darling, crocodile first," he ordered.

Yes.

It wasn't time to be amusing.

She turned her gaze to the fire.

It was probably over a hundred degrees outside, but somehow the heat of the day mingled with the flame from the fire seemed less like a roasting and more a cleansing.

She tossed the crocodile in.

It went up like a torch.

"Whoa," she mumbled.

"That fucking doll," Stellan, not wasting any time, growled.

She glanced at his stern face and back to the flames.

She tossed the doll in and took a step back as the plastic hair curled into nothing nearly instantly and the plastic face started melting, both searing the air with an acrid scent, and the clothes went up like tinder, so fast, it was almost like they evaporated.

The doll oozed, dripping between the lava rock, the crocodile totally gone, disappeared. And she stood with Stellan at her side and watched as the doll continued to liquefy, vanishing drip by drip.

This morning it's my famous French toast for my baby girl!

"I didn't need French toast, Daddy," she whispered to the blaze. "I didn't need a doll. I needed you to be a father."

Stellan moved closer.

Sixx and Simone, as one at last, stood and stared at the only thing she had that her father had given her as it trickled away.

"We needed you to be a father," she repeated.

Stellan had all the patience in the world now, and the doll was long gone, not a speck of her in sight, before he spoke again.

"Are you ready for the pictures?" he asked gently.

She turned to him and nodded woodenly.

So lost in this bizarre, but powerful, ceremony, she hadn't noticed he'd taken them from the frame.

He handed the paper to her.

So flimsy. Once she threw them in, they'd be gone in seconds.

How odd that something that captured a moment in time that should have been beautiful, emotional, precious—those pictures kept and treasured and handed down so the people in them would never be forgotten—could be so frail.

If there existed a picture of her and Stellan, she'd throw herself into any flame that threatened to erase it from existence.

She tossed the pictures of her parents in like they were completed grocery lists.

And she was right.

They were gone in seconds.

Stellan curled her into his arms, but even as he did, Sixx kept her eyes aimed at the blaze.

"He made you French toast?" he murmured.

"Not often. When he didn't wake up strung out or hungover and was in a good mood."

"I shall never make you French toast," Stellan vowed.

She stared at the flames, then tipped her head back and stared up at him.

Her handsome savior.

Her beautiful healer.

She wasn't the hero of her own story. She also wasn't the villain.

What she was, was one half of a whole.

Just not the half she thought.

The half that fit the other half of him.

She could go on and fight again, stronger, smarter, more power-ful, along the way giving him what he needed to do that in return.

They were the dynamic duo.

"I love French toast," she said softly.

"Have you had anything to eat?" he asked.

Not a chance. The way she spent her morning, if something went down, it would have come right back up.

But suddenly, she was feeling seriously peckish.

"No," she answered.

"Then we're having French toast," he decreed.

He also started to move, his hold on her sharing he was going to take her with him, but she locked her arms around him and he stilled.

"I thought you were going to fuck me," she noted.

"I am. But I haven't eaten either, and since the both of us will be naked for the rest of the day, and active, we need fuel."

She smiled up at him. "Are you going to turn off the fire?"

He sighed, let her go, went to the silver key, turned it, and the fire slowly died.

Her parents and her past were wisps on the wind, ashes.

She felt no loss.

She felt reborn.

At that point, she could have made a joke about ending up in Phoenix.

Looking at Stellan's face, though, she decided . . .

Later.

He came back to her, tossed his arm around her shoulders, and moved her to the steps.

She slid her arm around his waist and walked with him, their hips and legs brushing as they went.

She heard the relaxing fall of water from the feature as they made their way to the house.

"Can we do some of our nakedness and fucking in the pool?" she requested.

"Anything you want, darling," he murmured.

Anything she wanted.

It was the first time he said that that it didn't terrify her.

She felt nothing.

But light.

Clean.

And happy.

STELLAN

After breakfast, while Simone was upstairs getting sunscreen, Stellan moved out to the fire pit to retrieve the frame he'd left there.

He took it through the house, to the garage, and opened up the trash bin that sat next to the recycle bin just beside the back door.

He tossed the frame in.

Then he stared at it.

Reached in.

Retrieved it.

Lifting his arm, with all his strength, he pitched the frame into the bin and the cheap, flimsy wood cracked, the thin glass shattering.

He picked up what remained intact and repeat.

Repeat.

Repeat.

Until there was nothing but bits of detritus.

Only then did he lean into the knuckles of his fists against the wall and look down at his trash, his breaths coming fast, expanding his rib cage, his chest, as he stared at nothing but waste.

But in his mind's eye he saw block after block filled with Simone's graphically depicted, in more ways than one scarred beauty doing terrifying things to survive a dangerous life and save the day again and again for a little girl who had a life of playing with exquisite dolls and miraculous wonders of fanciful tea sets in a room full of ruffles and lace and love.

He also saw Simone staring at him with fear and heartbreak standing on his deck and sitting in his library, thinking he'd set her free after she shared what beat down to the heart of her.

"You goddamned, fucking motherfuckers, creating that beauty and sentencing her to live that life. I hope you're burning in hell," he growled, took one hand, tossed the lid of the bin down and pushed from the wall.

He stared at the door like he wished he could pulverize it with his eyes.

"She's mine now," he told the door. "Nothing vile or putrid is touching her. Never again. Not ever fucking again."

With that, he straightened his shoulders, drew in a deep breath, and walked into his house, his home with Simone, to spend the day with the woman he loved, which would be just a day that would lead into the next, and the next, and the next, all of them where she'd be safe and happy and loved.

Until neither of them were breathing.

nineteen

Domestic Decadance

SIXX

Late the next morning, Sixx walked into Sip and right away spotted Sylvie Creed sitting at one of the tables.

She was very petite, had long, wild, honey-blonde hair, green eyes and a curvy body that Sixx didn't know if it came naturally or from the fact it seemed she was constantly popping out offspring.

One look at her, you would never guess she was the badass spitfire she was.

But regardless of the fact she was an adoring wife and a devoted mother, her level of badassness made Sixx look like a cheerleader.

The second Sixx spotted her, Sylvie caught her eye and lifted her chin as well as her plastic cup of iced coffee, so Sixx knew to go direct to the counter to order her jolt without worrying about setting Sylvie up.

She did that, grabbed it, and walked to her friend, noting Sylvie watching her with growing intensity as she made the short trek through the kickass structure that served coffee and beer, with a limited but delicious menu of food, all of this in a repurposed garage.

From the minute Sylvie discovered it, that was the only place they met.

Not a surprise, it was so totally her vibe, not to mention it was awesome and had some of the best coffee in Phoenix.

"Hey," Sixx greeted as she sat opposite the blonde.

Sylvie stared at her, then asked, "What?"

Sixx was confused. "What, what?"

Sylvie did not exactly elucidate with her, "What's going on?"

"I told you. I have a job that I might—"

"No," Sylvie cut her off. "What's going on with that look on your face?"

Damn.

"Nothing's going on," Sixx lied (yes, yet again to a friend). "I just got a lead on a side job that, if I take it, and it looks like I'm going to take it, I'm going to need someone to go undercover in a sitch where I can't do that."

"That look on your face doesn't say job. It says my girl is gettin' herself some, and that gettin' is a whole lotta *good*."

Stellan didn't miss a thing.

If possible, Sylvie missed less.

"I'm seeing someone," Sixx muttered.

"Say what?" Sylvie almost yelled.

"I'm seeing someone," Sixx snapped. "No big deal."

"Like, someone you aren't tying up?" she asked back, finishing, "Notthatthere'sanythingwrongwiththat."

"People in my world hook up for more than just a hookup, Sylvie," she educated.

"That look on your face says that's the damn truth," Sylvie shot back. "What's his name and how long has this been going on? And warning, your answer better not piss me off seeing as my girl seeing someone means texting that info to *her* girl ahmee*jee*atly, get me?"

"He and I, we've known each other years. But it started only recently. And so you'll be fully informed, we're living together. I moved in with him."

Sylvie's eyes took over her face.

"It's not that big of a deal," Sixx said.

"It's not that big of a deal," Sylvie parroted.

"No," Sixx said sharply, hoping that'd be the end of it.

It wasn't the end of it.

"Heads up, commitment-phobe, moving in is totally that big of a deal."

It took some effort, but Sixx managed not to roll her eyes.

"At least he didn't move in with you. And please, God, tell me he doesn't live in a shittier studio than you used to," Sylvie added.

"His place is . . ." Sixx couldn't help but grin, "really nice."

"Anything is nicer than that squat you used to call home."

"It wasn't that bad," Sixx protested.

"It sucked," Sylvie returned.

Sixx really couldn't argue that.

"So spill," Sylvie pushed. "What's his name?"

She'd find out anyway considering, outside Aryas, Sylvie was the closest thing to a BFF she had in Phoenix—or anywhere—and Stellan simply wasn't going anywhere.

And Sylvie also was a private investigator, so if Sixx didn't spill, she'd go out of her way to learn what she wanted to know.

Sixx decided to save her the effort.

"Stellan," she answered. "Stellan Lange."

She didn't have to say the second part.

On his first name, Sylvie's eyes took over her face again, and she instantly snatched up her cell sitting on the table in front of her, engaged it, poked at it, and hit speakerphone so that Sixx could hear it ring.

"Sylvie—" she started.

"Yo, baby," Tucker Creed's voice said via speakerphone.

"Get *this*, partner," Sylvie crowed. "Sixx is banging *Stellan*, and by *banging* I mean, all-moved-in-domestic-bliss-if-her-face-is-anything-to-go-by bang . . . *ing*."

The good news was that she wouldn't have to introduce Stellan to Sylvie and Tucker through some awkward dinner party or something. Clearly, for whatever reasons that could come about, they already knew him.

"Well, shit," Tucker muttered, sounding amused.

Sixx looked up to the ceiling.

"She's totally loved up," Sylvie declared, and Sixx moved her eyes back to her friend in order to glare at her. "It's coming out of her pores so bad, it's turning *me* on."

"Then finish your meeting quick, baby, and get your ass to me."

"Roger that," Sylvie replied.

"And tell Sixx I'm glad for her," Tucker said. "Stellan's solid."

He could say that again.

"I'm right here," Sixx piped up. "You're on speakerphone so pretty much everyone at Sip knows I'm banging Stellan."

"Glad for you, babe," Tucker repeated, sounding like he was laughing.

Sixx shook her head.

"I gotta get this meeting done so I can get to you and work out this vibe," Sylvie cut in. "Love you, hubs. Later."

"Love you back," Tucker said before Sylvie disconnected.

"Was that necessary?" Sixx asked.

"Totally," Sylvie said through a grin with her straw to her lips before she sucked. After she sucked, she asked, "Do you tie him up?"

"He's a Dom," Sixx sighed.

"Bummer," Sylvie muttered. "I was having visuals of Stellan Lange tied up. I love my man hard, but they were good ones."

Sixx knew how that felt.

"So, he's a Dom, and that's your swing too, so how's that work?" Sylvie asked curiously.

"He ties me up."

Sylvie grinned. "Even better."

"And gives me toys," Sixx went on, not wanting to, but knowing Sylvie wouldn't let it go.

"Yowza," Sylvie said, her eyes dancing. "*Niiiice*," she finished on an exaggerated drawl.

Sixx's brows went up. "Can we talk about work now?"

Sylvie put her drink down, nodding. "Sure. Shoot."

"You know the Bolt?" Sixx asked.

"Yup," Sylvie answered.

Sixx laid out what Carlo told her, watching Sylvie's face get serious while she did.

She concluded that with, "I've done some research on all the partners. Like my guy said, Josh Coates is a flake, but he's as solid of one as you can get as far as I can tell. Barclay Richardson is just straight-up good people, and from what I got after making a few calls this morning to players I know in that scene, he'd lose his mind if he knew this was happening. The last asshole, Pete Beardsley, is just that. An asshole. He's a mess. Got a rap sheet. Petty shit, but it includes possession with the intent to distribute, something that he pleaded out, and soliciting a prostitute, twice. It's primarily his mismanagement that led the Bolt to nearly having to close down before they recruited Richardson to buy in, turn the place around and run it. Which he does. Efficiently. And now it makes a good profit. The three players I talked to report Beardsley is skeevy, most the women, subs and Dommes, stay well away. And they all shared that they think something has been up recently, at least the past couple of months, since he suddenly has a stable of females available to him when no one would touch him."

"So he partakes as well as hires out," Sylvie mumbled.

Sixx nodded. "Apparently. I can't know unless I get in there. My guy is setting up a meet with me and Josh. That's happening this afternoon. But if I take it on, I can't go in like I'd need to. I'm known in the scene. I'd never get this guy to believe I'm ripe for the picking."

"Babe, I want in on this with you," Sylvie said, picking up her coffee, "but this is decaffeinated."

Damn.

"You're knocked up?" Sixx asked.

"Yep," Sylvie answered before sucking back a sip.

"Again?" Sixx queried.

Sylvie swallowed and smiled as angelic a smile as she could, which meant it was naughty . . . but happy. "Yep."

"Happy for you," Sixx said softly, and Sylvie's smile got bigger.

"I am too. Creed acts every time like it's the first time, so he's clomping that big body of his around on air. Jesse wants a baby brother. Rayleigh keeps screaming, '*thithy!*' so I'm feeling where she's going. I don't care. It's another being made of me and Creed, and he or she will be loved, and that's all I need."

Another being made of me and Creed, and he or she will be loved, and that's all I need.

Sixx looked away.

"Serious as shit, sister," Sylvie said quietly, "you and Stellan would make beautiful babies. He's way hot, and you're gorgeous."

She and Stellan had had the day before. It was the most beautiful day of her life. No day could possibly surpass it. She knew that down to her soul.

And it sucked to realize right then that even though they'd successfully navigated that minefield, things might not be just smooth sailing.

Sixx looked back to her friend, cleared her throat, and stated, "We're nowhere near there yet."

"Well, when you are, don't look to me to throw your baby shower. I'll show, if there's alcohol and I'm not pregnant, though I'll also show if I'm pregnant, but only due to hormones making me a sissy wuss. But I won't throw it."

Sixx shot her a grin. "I'll file that in my memory banks."

Sylvie's eyes sparkled, even if they still looked speculative, and then she returned to serious.

"Back to the situation at hand, Creed would lose his mind if I brought the news to him that I was going in undercover as a submissive at a BDSM sex club even if I wasn't pregnant. Seeing as I am, even not showing yet, if I shot that by him, his head might explode."

"That's cool, Sylvie. I'll find another way."

"Sorry, babe. But if you need backup, I'm in. Creed doesn't start trying to put his foot down about me being out in the field until the middle of the second trimester. And you know you always have him."

Sixx nodded, wondering why she hadn't noticed what good friends she had and the length of time she'd had them.

Unless deep into a pregnancy, Sylvie was always down to partner up or have her back, and the same with Tucker, no matter the situation, no questions asked.

She was seeing, somewhat uncomfortably considering how long she'd held her down, how having Simone back was a good thing.

And she was finding, definitely fortunately, with the friends she'd earned, it was a better-late-than-never scenario, not a too-little-too-late one.

Most important, though, was that now she had this understanding, she needed to keep her head out of her ass and take care of what she had a lot better than she'd been doing it.

"I can do legwork outside the club and computer work if you need it," Sylvie offered.

"I'll let you know after my meet with Coates," Sixx replied.

That was when Sylvie blindsided her.

"If it's this good, and I can tell it's good, Sixx, kids only make it better."

Sixx drew in breath and kept trying out this honesty-to-friends thing.

"I didn't have the best of childhoods."

Sylvie leveled her eyes at Sixx in a way that she believed every word that came out of her mouth next.

"I bet Creed and me got you beat. My dad . . . when I can drink again, I'll share what he did to me, to Creed, the lengths he went to keep us apart. And years later, Creed sprinkled Jesse's hair on that motherfucker's grave. We didn't make our boy as a fuck you to my father. But it was a helluva fuck you to my father. And that's the thing, Sixx. In the end, the beauty of it is that you don't need that fuck you. The fact you went on living, finding someone to love who loves you back with everything he is, and making babies is just that, all for you, all you need. It just becomes the beauty of your life. But it doesn't suck either, having that damned fine of a *fuck you.*"

Sixx grinned at her again. "Oddly, for the first time in my life, I'm feeling maternal."

Sylvie burst out laughing.

And Sixx, continuing to explore this sharing business, and finding it also didn't suck, not by a long shot, laughed with her.

Sixx got home that night at a decent hour, having texted Stellan she would so he knew evening plans included both of them together for dinner . . . and whatever came after.

She'd met with Coates, who was a lot more together than she was expecting. Though she got the feeling that having one of his partners providing illegal sex-for-hire services using his meal ticket to do it had scared him straight.

He was also a lover not a fighter, and that love, and respect, extended to women. The mere thought his partner was taking advantage of the fairer sex was visibly nauseating him.

So she took the job, even if the guy could only hand her five hundred bucks in cash, saying, "Promise, Sixx, I'm good for it, and if

I'm right, Clay will back that, and make sure you get your usual fee with any expenses."

Now she just had to figure out how she was going to get what she needed as Mistress Sixx at the Bolt.

It was going to have to be observation and paid informants.

And that last part got expensive.

Not that she didn't have it, or didn't think Coates and his partner would be good for it, just that information acquired like that was usually expensive, but it wasn't always accurate.

Undercover was the only way to go, the optimal play.

She just didn't know who she could recruit to go in.

As she walked down the back hall toward the kitchen, hearing strains of Stellan's favorite light rock station, primarily "Cool Change" by the Little River Band, she felt nerves start to set in.

They were real.

They were happening.

She was in love with him.

He was in love with her.

They had a future.

And it was freaking her out.

In order to handle that, she focused on the fact that Stellan listened to light rock when he was at home. But in his cars, he was all about Sirius's Classic Vinyl and Classic Rewind stations.

He seemed like the kind of guy who would listen to Bach, Chopin, Beethoven, stuff like that.

Little River Band, the Eagles, Fleetwood Mac, Pink Floyd and Led Zepplin would not have been her call.

But she loved that about him.

Fortunately, this was her thought, not her nerves, when she turned the corner and saw him standing at the island, surrounded by the makings of whatever their dinner was going to be.

She stopped as she took him in in his suit trousers, his feet bare, his dress shirt still on, tie gone, shirt open at the throat, vest still in place, shirtsleeves rolled up.

He got her text, came home, got semi-comfortable, and started dinner for them.

And he prepared food exclusively at the island. He used the stove, obviously, and the grill outside. But all prep work happened at the island. Without fail.

She knew that about him.

She knew that later he'd put on jeans, or some lounge pants, or be wearing nothing at all because they'd be making love.

She knew the kind of music he listened to in his house and his cars, and she knew his washcloths in his private bathroom at his office were bright white and that he never put celery in his salads because he hated it and he took his steaks rare (like she did) and his martinis dry (like she did).

She also knew the reasons why he loved her.

And he knew her, down to the deepest part of her that was far more important than the fact she also loved light rock and classic vinyl and dry martinis.

And it just made him love her more.

He turned his head her way.

And yeah.

Right.

He was also so fucking handsome, it was nearly impossible to believe.

His lips tipped up in a welcoming smile.

Yes.

So ... *fucking* ... handsome.

"Hello, darling," he called.

"Hey, baby," she said softly, his head tipped sharply to the side, and she made her way to the island, taking only a slight detour to toss her stuff on the counter bar that delineated the kitchen from the dining area.

He was wiping his hands on a towel and rounding the island toward her when she made it to him.

He threw the towel on the island, watching it go.

Then he turned back to her.

And Sixx sucked in breath at the look she caught in his eyes.

It was good she did. It automatically braced her for when his fingers latched on her hips and she was up, ass planted on the island.

Before she knew it she was pushed back to the island, her head barely missing the ingredients for their meal spread out at the other end. Her red leather miniskirt was shoved up, her panties yanked down her legs, and lifting her head, she just caught Stellan's going down, and she sucked in another breath when he went *down*.

His mouth on her, working her deep, he spread her legs wide and ate her until she came, crying out his name, her fingers fisted in his hair.

She lost purchase on his hair when she was dragged off the counter, put to her high-heel-shod feet, turned roughly, and she felt Stellan's hand working at her ass.

"Baby," she breathed.

"Ass up," he ordered thickly.

She did as told, tipping her ass for him, and he slammed inside.

Her hands flew out in front of her to brace against the counter as her head jerked back, hitting his shoulder, and he stuffed his face in her neck, breathing hard there as he fucked her harder, his hand going down her belly, she knew, toward her clit.

"No," she whispered, catching it at the wrist, trying to stop its path. "I just want to feel you, hear you."

"You're coming again with me, sweetheart," he said against her skin.

"I want—" That got cut off with a moan as his finger found her clit and rolled.

She pushed against her hands to rock into his thrusts and pressed the side of her head to the top of his, his face still buried in her neck, and they panted, she moaned and whimpered, he sighed and grunted, and finally his lips found her ear and he whispered, "Now, Simone," and they both came.

She was shuddering against him in her aftermath when she felt that his arms had wound around her, one at her belly, one at an angle across her chest.

His hand at her shoulder moved to her cheek, turned her head, and she was just able to catch his warm, satisfied eyes before he took her mouth in a gentle, slow, wet kiss.

When he finished it, he stayed close, rubbing his nose against hers, asking quietly, "What were you thinking when you came into the kitchen?"

No hesitation, no prevarication, she gave it to him.

"That I like light rock."

She watched that hit his eyes, reveling in the beauty of knowing he understood exactly what she was saying, before he kissed her again, just as gently, just as wet, but a lot shorter.

When he ended that one, he murmured, "You get cleaned up. I'll make us both a drink."

"I can man a martini shaker, hot stuff," she noted.

His brows went up. "Really?"

"I might need some practice to get to your level, but I'll never get it if you're always taking care of me."

"Darling," he whispered, "that's the point."

Oh, she knew that.

And she loved that about him too.

"Baby," she whispered back, "throw a girl a bone. I gotta have some of that action somehow."

The beauty of *that* as it reached his eyes nearly made her knees buckle.

If they had, since he was holding her up with his arms and his cock still planted inside, it would have been okay.

But she would have lost that look, and she wanted it forever.

"You can make our drinks after you clean up," he allowed.

"Much obliged," she muttered.

He slid out and pulled up his pants before he bent to retrieve her panties.

She pushed her skirt down and took them when he handed them to her.

He did up his trousers as he moved back to his preparation station at the island.

She carried her panties with her as she headed toward the powder room on the first floor.

She also moved while calling, "Hot stuff?"

"Right here."

She looked over her shoulder at him, giving him a small smile. "Just an FYI. I wholeheartedly approve of that brand of welcome home."

He smiled back, and his was not exactly small, but it was roguish. She loved that too.

She hit the powder room. She cleaned up. She slid on her panties.

Then she headed out and kept on her high-heeled black sandals that were made of precisely two straps, one across her toes, one around her ankles, and her blousy white top, because she was comfortable in them, and if Stellan didn't take time to change to see to her, she wasn't going to do it either to see to him.

Thus, she made martinis for her and her man.

They weren't as good as his.

But on sip three, seated at the island, chatting with him as he made dinner, it didn't matter.

It didn't matter on sip one either.

She was home.

And he was home.

And they had nothing but togetherness before they had to separate to take on their days the next morning.

So nothing else mattered.

Later that evening, after drinks and dinner, the pool light was roving through yellow, blue, green and red underneath them as Stellan and Sixx floated on his big, beanbag-esque pool floats.

They each had their own, but their floats were connected since

Stellan had his thigh thrown over hers and his arm twined in hers, his fingers lazily stroking the inside of her forearm.

But it doesn't suck either, having that damned fine of a fuck you.

Sylvie's words came to her, and she almost cackled, lying on a float in the pool of a Phoenician mansion with a gorgeous millionaire, her belly full of an Asian salad made hearty with perfectly cooked flakes of salmon fillet, and a martini that led to two glasses of the best sauvignon blanc she'd ever had.

"You look amused," Stellan noted.

"Life is funny," Sixx replied.

He gave her a soft look. "This would partially explain why you look amused."

She explained more fully. "I never thought about it, and it took too long to realize it, but I bested her a long time ago. But here I am, with you, and this is all for me. It doesn't have shit to do with her. And that's the best of all."

The soft didn't go out of his look, but there was some wary that leaked in, and Sixx could understand that. It probably wasn't easy for him to go from her holding back to her giving it all.

She'd have to get him there.

That was something else she was going to best.

But right then, even though Sixx brought her up, it was cautiously when he continued to do that, asking, "Do you wish she could see all you've become?"

"No. I don't even wish he could see it. I don't really care," she answered candidly.

"I think that's healthy," he said gently.

Carefully on the float, she turned slightly to her side, which meant hooking her leg firmer to his and crunching their floats together.

"Baby, I'm still a mess. It's going to take a while to get used to being just me."

"You'll get there," he murmured.

"Yes. On a pool float. At night. In a pool with a hot guy. Orgasmed up. Liquored up. And great-fooded up."

The wary went out of his expression, and she liked it a lot better when gratification filled it.

"Domestic decadence suits you," he replied.

"It would suit anybody," she returned.

"Only those who earned it."

She gave him a gentle smile. "I didn't earn any of this, Stellan."

"Yes you did."

She stared at him.

"I pay for it, obviously," he continued. "But do you think it meant anything to me before except being a place I enjoyed and felt comfortable being in when I was not at work? I grew up in greater opulence than this. It's meaningless. Until you have it to share with somebody, to give to somebody, someone who appreciates it. Only then does it take on meaning."

He just couldn't be believed, even floating beside her, being all that was Stellan.

Honestly, she couldn't take it.

"God, you really, *seriously* need to stop being so damned awesome," she groused.

He burst out laughing.

She lost her pique, which poorly hid the depth of her emotion, and smiled while she watched.

"Now," he said when his laughter died away, "we've had a great deal of weighty, and I think it's a good idea to have it, process it, but mingle it with a healthy dose of normal. Do you agree?"

She nodded.

"Then there are matters to discuss," he went on.

"Like what?" she asked.

"Like the fact I need to take a business trip to New York. I'll be gone three days. I'd like you to go with me."

Whoa.

"Well—" she started.

"Not for the workdays," Stellan clarified. "I'll be busy with meetings, and I don't expect you to drop everything and take vacation in order to travel with me, and not simply because most of the time I'm there, I can't be with you. But we could leave earlier than my meetings start, spend the weekend there together, and you can fly home Sunday evening as my meetings begin on Monday."

That would definitely work.

And she loved New York.

But more, she loved this indication he didn't think she could drop everything, take off on her job, her responsibilities, simply to be available to him.

She just kept getting more from him.

More love.

And more respect.

"If I have enough notice, I think I can make that work with Joel," she told him.

"Excellent. It's in three weeks."

"I'll talk to Joel tomorrow."

"Lovely, darling."

She smiled at him again, and she wondered if she smiled more that night than she had her whole life.

Maybe.

But who cared?

"Now, on to Ami," he said. "It's fortunate your caseload lightened because Aryas said this Mistress he has chosen for him is ready to meet us at the Club. Tomorrow. Ami is also keen to meet her, considering she's a member of the Honey and trained there. He says even if it doesn't work out for the long term, if she appeals to him, he'll go forward regardless in the hopes it'll be an enjoyable scene. His background checks and interview have been approved. So he's free for tomorrow too. We can ask him to come at a time after we set to meet with her. If you don't like her, we can approach one of the other Mistresses to work him so he won't get nothing from the evening. If you like her, and Ami likes her, Aryas wants us to watch her with him. Although she's working subs with supervision, she hasn't strictly been let out on her own. Does that work for you?"

She had wanted to hit the Bolt tomorrow to start up that investigation.

But Stellan had arranged this, and Ami was a good guy who needed a good Domme in his life, and a good woman, so although women being victimized at a BDSM club took precedence, she'd allow this to delay it.

Though during the day, she'd spend time hitting up some of the folks she knew who frequented the Bolt and could keep their mouths shut but eyes open so she could start gathering information about what was perceived to be happening there.

"I'm in."

"Fabulous," he murmured, unhooking his leg from hers and using their linked arms to pull her float even closer so their heads were lined up.

He leaned in, she leaned in, they touched lips, and it was a testimony to superior floats that both of them didn't go under.

When he broke contact with her lips, he made contact with her eyes.

"You ready to get out?" he asked.

"Is that code for, 'Are you ready to go upstairs so I can fuck you senseless?'"

He grinned. "Yes."

She grinned back. "Then yes."

She braced to make a move off the float and into the water, but his fingers wrapped firm around her wrist, so she focused on him again.

"I am always here to take the heavy," he said softly.

"I know, baby," she replied.

"Never forget," he ordered.

"I promise. I won't."

"Thank you for yesterday."

Now he was being awesome *and* making her want to cry.

"Again, handsome, stop being awesome," she warned instead of deep breathing to control the tears.

"It's important you know what it meant to me," he noted.

"Do you know what it meant to me?" she asked.

"You did not hide that."

"You didn't hide it either."

"Simone, understand me, it's important *to me* to know you know what it meant, you sharing that with me."

She didn't get it.

And as ever, he didn't miss that she didn't.

"It was a gift," he stated. "That's what's important that you understand. Yesterday was a gift. A gift of trust. And there are few gifts more important than that. We've got this lovely calm after a storm. But life does not stay calm. Whatever happens, understand this. Understand this calm is what defines us. Whatever happens, we'll find our way to it again. And more, don't twist what happened yesterday out of what it actually was, how important it was. In other words, never regret giving that to me or question whether you should have shared what you shared. Having you whole means more than my home, my cars, my business, anything. That's what you need to understand should anything ever threaten to split you apart again. You can and always will be Simone to me, and that, all of it, is the gift you gave me yesterday."

She sniffled then snapped, "Seriously, lay off the awesome."

He smiled.

Then he totally laid off the awesome when he lunged from his float into hers.

Obviously, that took them both into the drink, and under.

She came up spluttering . . . in his arms.

"Right, total jerk move," she shared, treading water with her hands on his shoulders.

"You love it," he replied, treading water with his arms around her waist.

"Do you think I could dunk you?" she asked.

"No," he answered.

She put pressure on to try to dunk him.

He was right. Even treading water, he stayed head and shoulders above it.

Major lower body power.

So she tried a different tact.

One hand went to his head to distract him.

The other hand went somewhere else.

Right into his swim shorts.

They both ended up going under.

She also ended up giving him head while he sat on the side of the pool before they dripped their way up to their bed, where they fucked like teenagers then passed out.

Domestic decadence.

Indeed.

twenty

Never

SIXX

On her way home the next evening, after a busy day of firm work and recruiting informants for the job at the Bolt, with only had fifteen minutes to change and freshen up to go out to dinner with Stellan and then to the Club to meet Mistress Naya before hopefully approving her for a scene with Ami, Sixx was psyching herself up to do something she didn't want to do.

But she had to do it because she just had to do it.

Also because she was going to be at the Honey later and there was a chance Leigh would be there, so she needed to do it now.

So, stopped at a stoplight, she scrolled down to Leigh's name, reminded herself that all this sharing and honesty had been good, starting with blurting all she'd blurted out at Susan, and all the dishonesty and denial that had come before it had really not been fun, she hit "go" on her steering wheel to make the call.

It rang three times before she heard, "Sixx, *chérie*, how are you?"

The light turned green, she hit the gas and replied, "Good, Leigh. You?"

"Excellent," Amélie answered.

"Listen, do you have a couple of minutes?" Sixx asked.

"Of course."

"I—"

All right. What did she even say?

Things weren't weird. Leigh had never let them get to that.

She still had to say something.

"Okay, I don't know how to start this but I lied in the Dom Lounge the other night. I needed someone to talk to."

"Oh, sweetheart," Leigh murmured. "What's happening?"

"Nothing . . . now. I mean, my head was messed up. With Stellan and well . . . a lot of stuff. But he and I have . . . we've . . . gotten a few things straight. So things are better."

"Stellan is, as you know, a Dom, Sixx, and as far as I know has never switched, so I'll repeat my offer to introduce you to one who I think might be able to—"

"It's not the switch part," Sixx cut her off to say. "I've always been a switch. I've always known I was a switch. Since training. I just . . . never found the right guy."

Leigh sounded amused when she replied, "I can say with relative certainty you've found the right guy now."

Sixx smiled at her windshield.

"Yeah," she said softly. "That's another part of me wanting to talk to you. I wasn't truthful about that either. Stellan and I are together. *Very* together. And we're both going to work at it to keep that so."

"I'm so pleased," Leigh responded.

"I just . . . I just . . ." How lame was she? "I just wanted you to know all that."

"As pleased as I am that you've phoned me, I hope you know you didn't need to. Your business is your own, Sixx, only unless you want to make it mine. And if you do, it'll be gladly received."

"I know that. I just haven't been very good at taking care of my friends because . . ." God! Why was this so hard? "Life didn't start out great for me, Leigh," she whispered. "Nothing good happened, so when good started happening, finding out who I was and what I liked. Finding Aryas. The Club. The people in it. Stellan. I didn't understand the concept, and I definitely didn't trust it."

"I hate to hear life didn't start out well for you, *chérie*," she said softly.

"I'm not alone with that. It is what it is. Or it was what it was. Now it is what I make it. I can keep letting it influence how I live and the relationships I have. Or I can learn to trust in the good that comes my way and believe that I, well . . . deserve it, I suppose."

"You deserve it," Leigh stated firmly.

"How do you know?" Sixx asked before she could stop herself.

"Well, pointing out the obvious, sweetheart, you made this call, which couldn't have been easy, but it was right."

That wasn't a lot to go on.

But Amélie wasn't done.

"And you went from finding out your nature to learning how to do what you needed to do the correct way, and then you took your time to teach others. Aryas has missed you as a trainer at the Club, Sixx. You were excellent at it. It's voluntary to do that, and you took on a good many Doms. That's a great kindness. And I can say for a fact every Master and Mistress you trained would agree."

Well, there was that.

"And you didn't used to talk much," Leigh went on, "and it's very true you didn't let anyone in too deep, but you listened. You always had all the time in the world to listen, Sixx. People are so busy these days, pushing their opinion and their point of view, their stories and experiences, so many have lost the art of listening, and sometimes, in fact, in a good many cases, you simply need that. You don't need to know what people think of your problems or your life. You just need someone to listen. And that's always been you."

That was true too.

"And Aryas adores you," she continued. "Aryas is the best judge of character I know. And frankly, that was all I needed when I first met you. As ever, it proved to be true."

She turned on her turn signal to hook a right onto 44th, promising in a whisper, "I'm going to be a better friend."

"I'm uncertain how, but if that's a goal, I'm not going to talk you out of it."

"Thank *you* for being a good friend."

"And thank you in return for one of the best compliments I've ever received."

"God," Sixx muttered. "These days it seems like I'm always on the verge of crying, and for years, I hadn't shed a single tear."

"That's a shame," Amélie replied gently. "Tears have a bad rap, and I can't for the life of me figure out why. They're very healing."

"People view them as a weakness," Sixx pointed out.

"People are, I've noticed, quite often very foolish," Leigh returned.

That made Sixx grin while saying, "Too true."

"I'm here for you, Sixx, always," Leigh said.

This was it.

It was time.

She took a deep breath and went for it.

"Simone," she declared.

"I'm sorry?"

"Simone. My name is Simone," Sixx told her. "I'm Sixx, definitely, but that's a nickname I gave myself a long time ago. My real name is Simone."

"Simone," Leigh murmured. "How beautiful."

"Thanks," Sixx whispered.

"No, *ma belle chérie*, thank you."

Sixx hit the turn signal again and swung into the suicide lane to make a left toward Stellan's home. "We're going to the Club to-night. Are you guys going?"

"No, Olly's on duty tonight. So I'll be here waiting for him to return home."

"Right, well, I'll see you there sometime."

"And perhaps in the meantime, we can have lunch."

Sixx grinned again, thinking of Amélie at Sip.

She'd probably dig it.

"We'll set that up. I'll call you when I'm not driving."

"Excellent. Until then . . . Simone."

With Leigh's soft accent, that was almost as beautiful as Stellan saying it.

"Until then, Amélie. Speak soon."

"We will. Goodbye, sweetheart."

" 'Bye, Leigh."

They hung up.

Sixx drove home.

And she parked in her bay next to Stellan's Maserati, now under the illusion that sharing and honesty paved the road to good things.

And damned proud of herself for keeping her head firmly *out* of her ass.

"Gordon's cup for Mistress Sixx, a vodka martini for me," Stellan ordered from the server at their booth approximately one-point-two-five minutes after they'd slid their asses into it.

"Isn't it gladiator night?" she asked her man as the server walked away.

Stellan turned to her. "That was last week. However, Ami wasn't participating."

"I know, but how did we miss that?"

Stellan grinned. "It's next week, and Ami *will* be participating. So we'll make a point to go. And I'll make a point to ink each event into my calendar whether your commanding Ami or not."

She actually felt her eyes sparkle at him as she leaned her tits into his arm.

"That'd be appreciated, baby," she murmured.

He bent in, twisting his neck to touch his lips to hers.

She suspected her eyes were sparking more after that.

However, when he straightened away, Sixx blinked into the bar.

This was because Aryas was leading a woman to their booth who was dazzling.

No.

Astounding.

So much so, without thought, out of the side of her mouth, what she had no idea was comically, she muttered, "Text Ami right now and tell him we got a hot one for him."

She couldn't tear her eyes off the woman coming their way, so she didn't see, she just felt it, as Stellan turned his amused smile from her to the direction she was looking.

"I think when he arrives in half an hour, he'll discover that himself," he did not mutter out of the side of his mouth.

What he did do was slide out of the booth.

"Stellan, my man," Aryas greeted on a handshake. "Sixx, beautiful," he said to her on a dip of his chin. Then he put his hand on the small of the back of the tall, lush, exotic beauty beside him. "This is Naya."

Naya smiled a white smile behind deep berry lips, this radiating out of a face whose skin tone and bone structure Sixx could not call—Polynesian, perhaps—but it was bottom-line *stunning.*

Sixx took her in as Stellan took her hand in greeting, and there was a lot of her to take in.

She was tall, for one. And built, for another. She was also wearing an exquisitely draped, long-sleeved aqua dress that highlighted her amazing coloring and thick, long, dark hair. The dress fit like a glove, had a plunging vee neckline, a ruched waistline that made her hourglass figure go straight from gorgeous to bombshell, and interesting flat ruffles down the front that a slit up the middle disappeared behind, so the dress was beyond flirtatious, straight to coquettish.

On sight, Sixx loved her for Ami.

Upon witnessing that sultry but open and friendly smile, Sixx adored her for Ami.

After Sixx murmured her greeting and Naya gracefully slid into the booth, Sixx would do a voodoo dance of good luck to make her personality come close to her extortionate beauty so she'd be worthy of Ami.

"Thank you for meeting me," she said with an accent Sixx again couldn't place, while Stellan slid in beside her and Aryas beside Naya.

"Thank you for meeting us," Sixx replied. "And do you mind if I ask where you're from?"

She inclined her head regally. "French Polynesia, originally. Though I lived in France for about five years growing up before moving here to America when I was seventeen, then living between New York, Paris, London and Milan for a number of years."

Jet-setter.

Which might mean she had money, which might mean if she and Ami took to each other, the gladiator pit would continue to be all kinds of interesting.

Nice.

Stellan and Sixx's drinks were served, Aryas and Naya ordered their own, and the server moved away.

Naya aimed her big, brown eyes over prominent, rounded cheekbones and back to Sixx.

"I understand you own this male I'll be using tonight," she remarked.

"Yes," Sixx confirmed.

Naya looked to Stellan with a not-surprising, huge amount of interest, then to Sixx.

"Not Stellan," Sixx shared. "He's *my* Master."

Aryas cleared his throat.

Loudly.

Sixx narrowed her eyes at him to see him fighting laughter.

Therefore her eyes narrowed further.

Naya looked to Aryas and asked, "I'm sorry. Is this done? A sub owning a sub?"

"Mistress Sixx is a switch," Stellan put in smoothly.

"Ah," Naya murmured. "I see."

"Though, it isn't unheard of for a Dom to allow a slave to play at will with another slave," Stellan shared.

"I'm not sure I would will this," Naya replied to Stellan before turning her attention back to Sixx. "I prefer single-partner play. Aryas has introduced me to multiple, but I didn't fancy it."

Strike another one for a move to approve.

"What, particularly, didn't you fancy?" Sixx asked.

"My style of play, the way I prefer it, rather, is that my attentions aren't divided. The connection feels deeper to me that way. But more, anytime there's another presence in the room, a sub's attention can get caught by something else, and I'm afraid I'm too selfish to wish my subs thinking of or focused on anything but me."

Great answer.

"Sixx is known for her multiple-partner play," Aryas put in at this point, causing Sixx to give him another narrow-eyed look.

"I'm sorry," Naya said quickly. "I mean no offense."

"I'm out of that phase," Sixx told her silkily, deciding against kicking Aryas in the shin because at her angle, she might hit Naya.

It helped cool her temper that at this point, Stellan wound a possessive arm around her shoulders.

But then again, that would always be helpful in whatever situation.

"As with all life, but especially this life, it really is to each their own, no?" Naya said.

"Absolutely," Sixx replied on a smile.

"I . . . may I ask about your sub?" she queried.

"Of course," Sixx said.

"He's experienced?"

Sixx nodded.

Naya bit her so-full-it-was-poofy lower lip.

"He knows you're in training, Naya," Sixx told her quietly.

"I have only recently been left to my own devices, if supervised. But there's so much trust needed. It can be . . ." She seemed at a loss for words. "Intimidating."

"Well, if Ami agrees to share a scene with you tonight, which I have a feeling he'll jump at the chance to do," Sixx started, "then it's the perfect match. He's an excellent sub, communicates very well, has few hard limits and performs beautifully."

Naya shifted ever-so-slightly in her seat.

Sixx grinned gleefully and leaned across the table. "And wait until you see him. He's a *gladiator*."

Naya also leaned across the table, her naturally wide eyes even wider. "As in, he fights for his Mistress?"

Sixx nodded. "It's *spectacular*."

Stellan's hand came to rest on the small of her back.

At his unspoken command, she sat back and looked to him.

He looked amused, and he looked edgy.

Interesting.

When she turned back to Naya, she saw something had clouded her face.

She didn't have to ask after it when Naya said, "So he fights for you."

"If claimed by another, he'll fight for her, if she can afford to buy his place in the ring," Sixx told her.

"I see," Naya murmured.

"And I know the owners of the pit," she continued. "So if you decide to claim him, and want him to fight, if the fee is too hefty, since Ami enjoys it, and I would suspect any Mistress he would allow to claim him would too, I'm sure an arrangement could be made to keep him there."

Another choking noise from Aryas just as Stellan let out a soft chuckle.

"This shouldn't be an issue," Naya declared. "I'm a retired model." Of course she was.

"My career was relatively . . . successful," she carried on humbly, not needing to share that was likely a huge understatement. "And I'm now the creative director for an online fashion magazine that's become quite popular."

And she was hitting all the highs.

But if there was one she might miss, it would be the biggest one, and for Sixx it loomed over the table like a suffocating shroud.

"Considering you're finishing training, I can imagine you're keen to have a variety of experiences with a variety of different subs," Sixx noted leadingly.

Only for Naya to shake her head.

She also squared her shoulders.

"As it is out there in the other world, I understand so it will be here. But I never found a man out there because something was missing. Now I know what I was missing. I also know if I ever found a man who I would want to be a part of my life, he would need to take his place in *this* part of my life. So like everybody, I'm looking for somebody. I just have learned, even if it will still take some searching, I can only find him in the right places."

"If you fall for Ami, I'm *so totally* claiming your bridal shower," Sixx blurted, only for a beautiful blush to strike Naya's cheeks and her eyes to get big again.

She'd started it, she might as well just go with it.

"It'll have a whips and chains theme," she joked.

"I don't yet know how to use a whip. But they don't really do much for me. I prefer switches. And paddles," Naya replied. "Though I've grown rather adept with ropes and chains."

Sixx smiled hugely.

Naya took that in and tipped her head absolutely and beguilingly coquettishly to the side. "Can I take that as approval?"

Naya's and Aryas's drinks came as Sixx replied, "Completely and totally."

Naya returned Sixx's huge smile.

"A Mistress meeting of the minds," Aryas muttered.

Stellan lifted his martini Aryas's way, saying, "Well-chosen, my friend."

"I should go into business with this matchmaker shit," Aryas replied, glanced between Sixx and Stellan and said, "Oh wait . . ."

Everyone in the booth laughed, and then everyone engaged in small talk for the next twenty minutes—small talk that proved Naya was just as lovely as she seemed—before Stellan's mouth came to her ear.

"Darling, Ami has arrived, and he awaits your verdict," he whispered there.

She looked to her man, then to the hunting ground, saw Ami in it, standing leaning a forearm on top of one of the high tables there with a glass of beer in front of him, wearing a suit and looking totally fuckable.

His gaze was on her.

"Will you excuse me, baby?" she murmured to Stellan.

Stellan slid out of his seat and took her fingers curled around his hand to help her out.

Always class, her Stellan.

She gave him a look of gratitude before she moved across the hunting ground to Ami's table.

She barely rocked to a halt before he rumbled, "I'm . . . fucking . . . *in.*"

Sixx nearly burst out laughing.

"So I take it you saw Mistress Naya."

He raised his brows.

That she was taking as a "yes."

"All right, my gladiator. Let's get this show on the road."

He just emitted a low growl.

And again she was fighting laughter.

She turned and walked back to the table to see both Stellan and Aryas out of the booth with Naya sliding out.

Sixx went to Naya, suddenly nervous.

Ami was in. Ami was hot. Ami was built. Ami was a great sub. And Ami was a good guy.

But he might not be everyone's cup of tea.

"Naya?" she called while Naya looked at her feet as she took them at the side of the booth.

She raised those big browns, and they were flashing.

"That's him?" she asked.

"Yes," Sixx answered.

"Can I start now?" she asked.

And yet again, Sixx held back her laughter, but her next, "Yes," was shaking.

"Brilliant," Naya said on a sharp nod.

She then moved away.

"I'll have our drinks refreshed, then we can make our way to the observation room," Stellan murmured and moved to the bar.

Aryas shifted in beside her as Naya oozed her way, with rounded hips swaying, toward the door to the playrooms, her head turned, her eyes locked on Ami, and Ami prowled toward her.

"So Stellan's your Master, eh?" Aryas asked at her side.

Sixx kept her eyes on the couple as Naya stopped at the door, and Ami reached around her to open it for her.

Both did this without breaking eye contact.

Superb.

"Shut up, Aryas."

"You're happy," Aryas declared, and as Naya and Ami had disappeared, she turned to him.

"Shut . . . *up*, Aryas."

"I'm so fucking happy you found your happy, I'd kiss you if I didn't think Stellan would take my head off for it."

"He knows we're friends."

"Babe, you did not see his face when you were talking about your gladiator. Careful there, my beauty. You got a man on your hands who is not into sharing, and you let a Dom claim you who happens also to be that man, and that magnifies that kind of shit about ten million times."

Good Lord.

She was offended.

Actually *offended*.

"I'd never be untrue to Stellan."

"I figure that. I figure he knows that. It won't matter dick. Man like that will piss on his patch as a matter of course, even if he lived alone on an island. If something *really* matters, there'll be hell to pay. My advice is you take that in, beautiful, because when it comes to you, there's a lot of ways that could go south."

In some ways, what he was saying was obvious.

In others, she had no idea what he was talking about.

"I'm in love with him, Ary, and he is with me," she shared. "So that kind of thing doesn't factor."

Aryas looked stunned.

That look didn't last long before it melted to elated.

Then he muttered, "Fuck it."

After that, he wrapped his hand around the back of her head, pulled her in, and kissed her forehead.

Holy God.

When he moved back, she snapped, "You're totally stepping all over my rep."

"Baby, Mistress Sixx is dead, now long live *the queen*."

She kept snapping. "You'd be annoying if you weren't so damned sweet and I didn't like you so much."

He grinned at her, touched her nose with a finger, and lumbered away.

She let out a hefty sigh.

Stellan materialized by her side, and she jumped.

She turned to him.

He handed her a fresh drink, asking, "What was that?"

"Aryas *totally* disrespecting Mistress Sixx," she answered.

"Darling, you do know everyone in this room knows I tie you up and do very naughty things to you," Stellan noted carefully.

"Whatever," she muttered.

It was his eyes that were sparkling then as he offered an arm. "Shall we go watch Naya do very naughty things to Ami?"

She wrapped her fingers around his elbow. "Sure."

He shook his head at her, then moved them toward the doors.

When they were out of earshot of everyone, if not eyeshot, he asked, "Have you a clue how much I adore you?"

She looked up at him as he slid out of her hold to open the door. "Yes," she whispered.

His face got soft. "Good."

He indicated the opened doorway with his head.

Sixx moved through, stopped on the other side, and waited to take her man's arm so they could watch an extraordinarily beautiful woman do very naughty things to an amazingly good-looking man.

My, my, *my*.

"I think it's safe to say she's a natural," Stellan murmured at her side.

Sixx would very much agree.

She'd tabled him.

Christ, like a champ.

That *and* chained him to the wall.

Ami's thick neck was in an iron band attached to the wall. His big fists were attached to the wall at his wrists. And his long legs were up, spread wide and cocked, braces above his knees attached to chains attached to the wall holding his massive thighs wide and relatively stationary, cuffs around his ankles, also chained to the wall, spreading his calves wider.

His bare ass was at the very edge of the table.

And his cock, balls and ass cheeks were covered with dried drips of aqua-blue wax.

Naya *was* coquettish.

She'd been flirting with him all night.

In a kickass, Mistress-with-an-edge kind of way.

Her body was covered in a teddy, the entire front panel a complicated pattern of see-through, delicate aqua lace, the arms of the three-quarter sleeves stretch-aqua netting leading to a band of lace below her elbows. The vee at the front was deep, the lace at the bottom cut high to expose hipbones.

She'd kept on her high-heeled silver sandals, her hair was down and bounding around her shoulders and her ample chest. She also had refreshed her berry lipstick repeatedly, doing this after leaving it staining Ami at his neck, nipples, inner thighs, balls and cock.

The woman was already a master Mistress with restraints and wax.

And it was not her beauty or her body that had Ami's complete attention.

He was so deep in the zone for her, the world was gone, and Naya and what she'd do to him next, but mostly how much he wanted whatever that was, were the only things on his mind.

And what she intended to do to him next made Sixx lock herself firmly in one of the four comfortable armchairs Aryas had set in the observation room that was outside a one-sided window that took up the entire wall.

Her mouth was watering.

And her nipples were tingling.

Naya was approaching him with a large cock.

Ami's own cock was so huge and swollen, it was nearly purple, and they heard his chains rattle through the open speakers as she approached him with that phallus.

"He's going to come," Sixx whispered.

"He'll hold," Stellan whispered back.

Okay then . . .

Sixx was going to come just watching.

God.

"Zzzzsss," they heard Naya make the sexy sound she made often when she was calming Ami as she approached between his legs. "You're with me, no?" she asked.

His head bobbed against the wall.

Oh yes.

He was *totally* with her.

In a somewhat surprising move, she trailed the head of the phallus over his balls, his cock, up his boxed abs, between his pecs, up his throat, his chin.

"Open," she bid.

My.

My.

My.

"Well played," Stellan murmured.

He could say that again.

Ami opened.

Naya slid the cock inside his mouth.

Damn.

"Suck, *mon guerrier*," she ordered.

He sucked, hard.

Holy hell.

"I like this very much," Naya cooed to her chained sub.

Taking his attention at his mouth, and with her eyes on him as he sucked cock, he missed what else she was up to, and his entire big body bucked so hard Sixx worried the chains would tear out of the wall when she drove two fingers up his ass.

"I'm inside you everywhere, Ami," she purred, fucking his mouth and his ass. "Do you like your Mistress inside you?"

His head bobbed again.

"Yes, you do," she decreed in a playful tone.

And then in a move so swift Sixx nearly missed it, if not the culmination of it, the cock was out of his mouth, and she was driving it up his ass.

His chest pounded out, his long legs cranked wide, and his mouth opened on a roar that began unintelligibly and ended in "Yes, Mistress, fuck me, take me, goddamn *fuck*."

Sixx had also missed that Naya had lubed her fingers, so he was primed to take that cock.

But he was primed in more ways than one.

And he was going to be more primed.

Naya wrapped her elegant hand around his dick and started pumping, the wax drips peeling off, slithering to the floor.

"Beg for more, *mon guerrier*," she ordered.

"Fuck, yeah, more, Mistress. Take my ass. Fist my junk. Fuck me, *fuck me*."

It was the first time her inexperience shone through, or perhaps the show was just too good for her to carry on, but she ended it in Sixx's estimation far too soon as Naya drove the cock home, grabbed tight to his balls, squeezed and commanded. "Come immediately."

With zero delay, on a thundering cry, Ami's cum jetted up his chest, his hands in fists, his neck straining, his body pumped so huge, every vein that could pop had, and his legs jacked so wide, the pain of the pull down his inner thighs had to be immense.

"More, Mistress," he grunted, still shooting. "More. Squeeze me. Pump me. *Fuck me*."

She went back to the cock and did the best she could with only two hands until there was nothing but weak spurts of milky fluid coming from the tip of his cock, his huge body convulsing before it went slack.

Naya did not cease, though her movements at cock and ass had slowed, gone gentle, when she asked softly and with the reverence her sub's performance demanded, "I would like to keep going, Ami. How do you feel?"

He could barely focus on her, but he managed it as he managed to growl, "I . . . am . . . yours."

And that was all she could take.

Sixx shot out of her seat.

"Darling?" Stellan called.

She reached down, grabbed his hand, tugged him out of his seat and pulled him out of the observation room.

"We shouldn't leave, Simone," Stellan told the back of her head.

She didn't listen.

She dragged him to the Dom Lounge, into it, right to her locker.

"Sweetheart," he murmured.

She punched in the combination, yanked the locker open and looked up at him.

"Please be quiet," she whispered.

His eyes roamed her face.

Then he dipped his chin to her.

God, she loved . . . this . . . *man*.

She reached into the locker, felt around, found the two things she wanted, and she knew Stellan had to see them when she pulled them out.

He said nothing as she slammed the locker closed, grabbed his hand, and lugged him out of the Dom Lounge.

He still said nothing when she took him to the doors, four of them, that stood close together, thankfully close to the Dom Lounge.

The isolation rooms.

They were called this because they were no bigger than a very small closet.

And with the lights out, they were completely dark.

Aryas had other isolation play at the Honey, namely tanks of water you could put a sub in to do things to them.

These smaller rooms were different. Constricted space. No light. No sound. So dark, some Doms wore night vision goggles to play with their subs in them (and the cameras in the room definitely had night vision).

This was not what Sixx wanted.

She looked at the panels outside the rooms, found three were unoccupied, and opened the door to one.

She immediately hit the switch that told the control room it was occupied.

She tugged Stellan in.

The light was on, she kept it on, and she and Stellan were everywhere since the entirety of the small space was mirrored. Even the ceiling. This, obviously, for other types of play, not isolation.

"Jacket off," she ordered.

She was not looking at him, but she could feel his eyes on her even as she felt him shrug off his jacket.

He dropped it to the ground.

"Face the back wall. Open your shirt," she commanded shortly. "Completely."

No hesitation, Stellan did it.

She positioned behind him, reached around and undid his trousers.

"Legs wide," she kept at him.

He planted his legs wide as she yanked his pants down, glorying in watching through the mirror as his thick, hard, handsome cock sprung free.

She also saw he had his shirt open, it was hanging loose, exposing an inch of skin from throat to cock.

"Hands to the mirror."

Stellan put his hands to the mirror.

She lubed the large vibrator, tossed the tube to the ground, and looked over his shoulder into the mirror, right into his burning, penetrating, dark blue eyes.

"It's not him. It's you," she told him, her voice shaking with emotion.

He dipped his chin again.

"I need it," she stated.

"Then take it," he replied, curt, sharp, like a dare.

Like an order.

Eyes to his, she turned the vibrator all the way to high, positioned it at his ass, and drove it deep.

His breath came out in a hiss, his head slammed back, and the muscles and veins in his neck jumped out.

He righted his head and caught her eyes.

"Fuck me," he growled.

Sixx did—hard, long, deep strokes, reaching around to his front to clamp onto his cock and fist it, pumping brutally.

He moved with her, fucking her hand, fucking his own ass, his noises and hers bouncing around the room, pounding into them, everything she was giving him, he was taking, he was giving, in the mirrors, everywhere she could see.

And through it all, he held her gaze until he couldn't anymore, his jaw hard, his face set in stone, his head hitched back.

"Come, baby," she whispered.

He blew, his long, lean body jerking violently, his cum gushing all over the floor.

Yes.

Yes.

Scalp to toe, she quivered in ecstasy.

He was twitching in her hold as she milked the last drops from him.

And then she had no hold on him at all.

She was back against the mirror in front of him, his hand wrapped tight around her throat, his other hand jerking up the body-hugging skirt of the gray leather dress she was wearing.

It didn't go as far as he needed, but it didn't matter. In a close squeeze, he dove into her panties at the front and rubbed her clit brutally, pushing back hard, diving two fingers in deep, finger fucking her, pulling out and going back at her clit with his face not an inch from hers, his breaths heavy on her lips, hers on his, as she stared desperately into his eyes.

"Please," she whispered.

"Please what?" he bit off.

"Please, Master, let me come."

He shoved his hand between her legs back, fucking her with long, deep strokes of his fingers.

God, she was going to lose it.

"Please," she begged.

His fingers at her throat slid up to her cheek, pushing her head to the side, his face came down, and he latched onto her neck with his teeth, biting her so hard she was sure he'd broken skin before he clipped, "Come."

He latched on again with his teeth, and she jerked against his hold as she came viciously into his hand.

The aftershocks were nearly as extreme as the orgasm had been. Which meant by the time she started coming down, she hadn't felt it that he was stroking her pussy like it was a pet and laving at her neck like it was an ice cream cone.

She lifted her hands and caught his face, pulling it up and away so she could gain his eyes.

He cupped her pussy.

She shared like a chant. "It wasn't him, baby. It wasn't him. It was about you."

"Darling," he gently squeezed between her legs and lifted a hand to cover his mark at her neck. "Calm."

Instantly, her racing heart and rasping breath began to settle.

"Didn't I tell you the other night we were learning this part of our lives?" he asked.

She stared up at him and said nothing.

"Didn't I?" he pushed.

Sixx nodded, because he had.

"Something I've already learned that I'll share now is that outside of the gladiator pit, if Ami is not claimed tonight by Naya, which I think we can both agree that he has been, I cannot allow your attention to toys."

"Oh . . . kay," she said slowly.

"You're very much mine, Simone, in all ways, and I thought I could share that way in order to give you something you need, but I was wrong."

She pressed her lips together.

So Aryas was right.

Damn.

"You can watch," he told her. "If with me, like tonight. But you cannot touch. And you cannot command. Not ever again."

Oh . . .

Shit.

"But you're my Simone, darling," he said gently. "Not my slave, my *Simone.* Even as I've already claimed that of you, I didn't fully understand the difference, but I do now."

"Can you . . . will you share that with me?" she requested.

He smiled a soft smile.

Thank God he was smiling.

Then he spoke.

"I will not be your sub, sweetheart. I will not be whipped and fucked with your heel or commanded to suck cock, real or inanimate. I would give that to you if I had it in me, and I must admit, I love you enough, I want you to have everything you desire, so I've considered it."

It was beautiful that he actually considered it.

More beautiful why.

Before she could form that into words to share that with him, he kept going.

"But you can use me, Simone," he stated, and her belly curled into itself. "I'll allow you to use your Master to get what you need, but you must understand, once you do, you'll give him what he needs in return however he takes it from you. I can imagine that's not entirely understood. We'll need to keep playing to find where the limits are, for you and for me. We already found one limit for me, though neither of us understood it at the time. That being I have you in our bed, as my lover and as my sub. However, you do not take me there. But what you needed tonight, obviously, I gladly will give. I can imagine being restrained by you would be highly enjoyable. Beyond that, we shall see."

"Do you know I adore you?" she whispered, thinking that was another huge gift he would treasure more than her trust.

"I already know that."

She blinked.

He grinned.

"I know you know, but I never told you," she said in an odd voice, like a child's, weak and wounded.

"You told me Sunday."

She did?

"I did?"

"When we were in the library. You said, 'I knew I couldn't look after two people I loved. I'd already learned that. I lost him but I found a way to survive. I knew the same wouldn't be true if I lost you.' I took that as an avowal of love, my sweet darling, and obviously, I was correct."

Holy God.

That might be verbatim.

He remembered it *verbatim*.

"Is that . . . verbatim?" she asked for confirmation.

"I have a very good memory, especially when I'm remembering something that means everything to me."

Lord.

Was this how it was, falling in love when it was safe? When it was real?

Every day, you just dropped deeper?

And the feeling was just . . .

Splendor.

"Okay," she whispered. "Then do you know how much?"

"I hope I have a fair idea," he whispered back.

"It's a lot," she said.

"Thank goodness," he replied.

"You did it," she told him.

"What?" he asked.

"And I love it."

"What?" he repeated.

"You've made me believe in happy."

His face clouded with thunder, and his lips rumbled, "Get that skirt up, darling. If you don't, I'll do it, and I fear I'll rip the seams."

Without delay, taking some effort, stretching the leather probably irreparably, she shimmied the skirt up.

He yanked her panties down, wrapped an arm around her waist, and hauled her up.

He pressed her to the mirror and planted her on his rigid cock.

She framed his beautiful face with her hands and breathed, "*Yes.*"

"Reach around, darling, turn the vibrations down. I don't want to come too soon," he murmured his order.

But her eyes got big at it.

"It's still inside you?"

"It's you inside me, and we're not done, so of course."

He then started fucking her as she reached around and turned the vibrations down.

"The cameras are on, the staff will have seen what I did to you," she reminded him warily.

"If you have not learned about me that I do not give a single fuck what anyone thinks of me, you'll learn it now. But it's more, darling. We shall play here, Simone, all the beauty we have on display, however that comes about, and I not only don't care people will see, I want to rub it in their faces."

Yes.

That was what falling in love with was when it was safe and real.

An endless drop of amazing.

"We should get back to observing," she whispered.

"I'll make this quick."

"Shame," she said against his lips.

He kissed her.

After a while, she came.

A short while later, he came.

After that, they made out in a little mirrored room that smelled of sex and had cum all over the floor.

It was the most romantic moment of her life.

They disengaged, straightened their clothes, went to the Dom Lounge to clean up and tidy up, and put away the toy and lube.

Then they went back to the observation room.

It was clear Naya was in a certain mood and equally clear Ami had some stamina.

Sixx came two more times that night with Stellan's hand up her skirt.

He came once more, with his woman curled on the floor between his legs, sucking him off.

It was a long session.

Thank God.

When Naya was curled around Ami (who was seated on a spanking bench), stroking his bald head, his neck, his shoulders, aftercare he didn't appear to need, but he definitely appeared to like, Stellan texted Aryas to share if Naya and Ami needed observation again, he should call on Stellan and Sixx.

It was not a surprise that they got a return text before they arrived home to be at the Honey for observation the next night.

So Ami might get his own happy.

Naya too.

Since he'd given it to her to read the text, she returned Stellan's phone to him as he coasted the Tesla into his garage bay while she said, "Sometimes the world does not suck."

"New goal," he murmured. "I showed her happy, now to show her a world where most of the time it doesn't suck."

As he powered down the car, she turned her head to him and snapped. "Stop making me happi*er.*"

Stellan looked to her, smiling.

And then he replied.

"Never."

twenty-one

Too Easy

STELLAN

The next morning, Stellan was leaning against the kitchen counter, sipping coffee, listening to M babble, when Simone came down to join them.

He took in her sweet look aimed his way before he turned to pour her a cup of coffee. He then gave her the mug, as well as a quick peck on the lips, before he watched Simone swallow her vitamins with orange juice as she listened to M babble. He continued to observe the two, intermittently interjecting, throughout breakfast.

And through one of these interjections, she promised to go to someplace called Mood during their trip to New York to buy a carrier bag for one of M's daughters who was a fan of some television show, and while at this place, bewilderingly vowed to pet a dog.

Simone had gone off to gather the things she needed to take on the day, and Stellan was putting his coffee mug into the sink when M sidled close.

"These past few days . . ." she began, hesitated, and went on, "she seems much changed. We . . . do we have her?"

Stellan nodded and smiled down at her. "We do. But it wasn't without a fair amount of difficulty, sweetheart. And that difficulty was all experienced by her. She seems to be coping well. Though I don't think it'd be good to let down our guard."

M nodded. "Celebrate victories, large and small, but don't allow them to fool you into believing you've reached the ultimate goal."

"Precisely."

She nodded shortly. "We will persevere."

"I knew I could count on you."

She gave him a beaming smile.

Some minutes later, when he and Simone were walking down the hall to the garage, she told him, "I've got a job on tonight, but since Ami and Naya aren't set to start until ten thirty, I think I'll be good. I might have to meet you at the Honey though."

They'd stopped at the driver's side door of her Cayenne. "That'll be fine, darling. Dinner?"

"Can we meet up and grab a quick bite somewhere?"

"Absolutely."

She grinned up at him, got on her toes, touched her lips to his, and he stepped back as she got in her car.

He was moving to his as she pulled out but looked her way as she tooted her horn in a final farewell.

He was chuckling as he raised his hand in a short wave, and she waited to catch that before she hit the remote to send the garage door going down.

Stellan got in his Tesla, thinking that Simone was giving him every indication she was right there with him. She'd combined her two selves, giving them both not only to him, but as far as he could tell, to everyone. She'd given him her sketchbooks and beyond, she'd given him her past, which offered him her trust. She'd professed her love to him. And once they got through the tough parts, through it all, she seemed . . . fine. Good. Happy.

Fucking perfect.

He backed out of his garage, and once he cleared it, hit the remote, and watched the door go down, he was thinking that his Simone thought she was strong, invincible, a superhero.

But thought this murmuring, "It was too easy. Way too easy."

Stellan was a man who didn't expect the other shoe to drop.

He prepared for it.

And he sensed it would.

Though he couldn't know that it would happen so quickly.

It was late afternoon when the intercom built into Stellan's desk buzzed.

He hit the button to open communications to Susan, saying, "Yes?"

"There's a man named Branch Dillinger here to see you."

Stellan's eyes went right to his door as a heavy feeling settled low in his gut.

He did not consider the fact Dillinger was in Susan's office without forewarning, and he didn't consider this because it was Dillinger. He probably opened the security stanchions with his mind.

"Send him in," he ordered.

Her voice dropped. "Do I have to?"

In any other circumstances, this would make him smile. It could not be lost on anyone, no matter their gender, that Branch Dillinger was a superior specimen of male.

And Susan, even happily married and entrenched firmly in building a family, had not lost her skills as a connoisseur in this area.

However, Dillinger might be the Operating Manager of Aryas's clubs, but he used to be something else entirely. The exact definition of that very few people knew, and Stellan was not one of those people. Further, he suspected even Evangeline, Dillinger's lover, didn't fully know.

That was the kind of man Dillinger was.

He was obviously and almost aggressively good-looking.

He was also stone-cold and exuded danger so palpably a normal man might catch himself flinching simply in the man's presence.

The only warmth Stellan had ever seen from him was toward Evangeline. And it was steady, true, without fail the polar opposite of his normal demeanor.

She was the only one who received that, bar none. He might be able to rein in his menace to show respect or regard, but Evangeline was the only being for which Dillinger showed emotion.

And for her, there was a good deal of it.

Though, rather shockingly, Leenie had shared he was enamored with their little dog.

That Stellan would have to see to believe.

"You do," he told Susan.

"Damn," she muttered, and he heard the click that shared she'd closed communications.

Stellan got up from his desk and was halfway across his office when Susan opened his door, ushering Dillinger through.

It was rumored he was good friends with Amélie's Olly, something else Stellan would have to see to believe.

But the two men couldn't be more different.

Olly was enormous, had a football lineman's body, dark blond hair and a boy-next-door handsomeness.

Dillinger was tall and viciously lean, not to the point he was slim, to the point the definition of the muscles in his body shared he had the power to perpetrate vicious things. He had black hair. And he had ice-blue eyes that Stellan had experienced nothing coming from but chilling cold and even more chillingly astute assessment.

Susan was giving his back view a top-to-toe before she caught Stellan's gaze—and his look—gave him a cheeky grin, and shut the door.

"Lange," Dillinger greeted as they stopped at each other.

Stellan offered his hand to the man. "Dillinger."

They shook and separated.

"Would you like a seat?" he asked.

Dillinger barely spared a glance at the two backless chairs in front of Stellan's desk before his attention came back to Stellan.

"I'm not sure I'll be here that long," he answered.

Interesting response.

"Obviously, this is a surprise," Stellan noted.

"Yeah," Dillinger muttered, and Stellan watched with fascination as he lifted his hand, bowed his head, wrapped his fingers around the back of his neck and appeared to give it an uneasy squeeze before he dropped his hand and looked back at Stellan. "I shoulda called. I've got your number. But I didn't know how to play this, so I asked Angie and she said face-to-face was the way to go."

Angie.

What he called Evangeline.

He was the only one who called her that.

That in and of itself, with the man he gave the world, shared just how deeply his feelings went for his woman.

And their current meeting was full of surprises considering whatever he was there to discuss, he'd first asked Leenie's advice.

"Perhaps you should just get on with it," Stellan invited.

Dillinger looked direct into his eyes, and Stellan fought a shiver.

"It's rampant, you're with Sixx," he declared.

"This is true," Stellan confirmed.

"Right," he muttered, drew breath in through his nose and kept direct eye contact. "What's not rampant is that you shut down her extracurricular activities. But that's been brought to my attention."

Stellan, not entirely relaxed, felt his body string taut.

"You two tight?" Dillinger queried quietly.

"Unbreakable," Stellan said with firm determination.

"Okay then, not my business, but you shutting down those activities, with what they were and her rep out there, that says to me she doesn't know you made that play. Who she is, if she wanted to end that, she'd not get her boyfriend to do it for her."

Stellan didn't reply.

Dillinger didn't need one.

"I get why you made that play. The company she keeps isn't good, and she's got a sweet gig with that law firm. They get wind of that shit, could fuck that up for her. She gets a job that goes bad, other worse shit can get fucked up."

"These are all things I know," Stellan said low.

"She know you went that way?"

Stellan remained silent, though that was an answer, and Dillinger read it correctly.

"None of my business, but man to man, when she finds out, that might not go good for you."

Stellan again didn't reply.

But this, he feared, was the other shoe that was going to drop.

He needed to talk to her about it. He needed to get them through that important part of how her life needed to change.

He hadn't because he was concerned she was too fragile after all she'd given him on Sunday. He wanted her to feel safe. To have time to enjoy the calm that had settled in after that storm.

But perhaps he should reconsider waiting.

Dillinger nodded brusquely. "Right, what you don't know is that she just took a job lookin' into something going down at the Bolt. She spent yesterday recruiting informants to keep an eye on the activities of one of the three partners. Word travels, this word is so far relatively tight, but it still traveled to me."

Stellan drew in breath, turned his head, and looked out his wall of windows.

"I don't know what's happening," Dillinger continued. "I don't have a lot of time on my hands to poke around either. Which sucks since one of the other three partners is a buddy of mine. And if I had to make a blind take on what's happening, I know which of the other two partners is doing fucked-up shit. I know with the kind of guy he is that it's probably seriously fucked up. And I know he's not gonna take kindly to someone, especially, Lange, it's important to say, some *woman* sticking her nose in."

I've got a job on tonight, but since Ami and Naya aren't set to start until ten thirty, I think I'll be good. I might have to meet you at the Honey though.

He did not tell her about all of his business.

They had, of course, only been together for three and a half weeks, *very* together for only two and a half of those, but all of those weeks had been enlightening and eventful.

That said, she had not shared the job she had on was extra-curricular to her paid employment.

It could be read she was keeping that from him.

He'd give her the benefit of the doubt that they simply had just not yet gone there as they were learning about each other and there were other, far more important issues to tackle that took precedence.

However, it was disappointing. He wished they had more time to settle in. But it seemed his earlier thoughts were correct.

It was time to go there.

"I didn't think this was something I should get into on the phone," Dillinger carried on, and Stellan looked back at him. "And it's uncool I blindsided you with it. But I only found out an hour ago, and after talking with Angie, we both thought I shouldn't sit on it and should tell you straight away."

"It's appreciated," Stellan replied. "And speaking of Leenie, does she know to keep this quiet?"

Dillinger nodded. "Yeah. Though I really can't keep shit that might or might not be goin' down in Barclay's club from him, Lange. He's my next visit. And I've already started wheels in motion to find out what's happening, and if it turns out to be a situation, sort it."

With this information, Stellan made a decision.

"That's understandable and commendable," Stellan told him. "If it was my business and a friend knew something, I'd be angry he didn't let me know. However, I'd ask that neither you, nor your friend, intervene with Sixx. I need to handle this with her."

Dillinger nodded again, muttering, "I get that too. Not my place, but gotta say, careful with how you handle that."

He wasn't sure that "careful" was the right play.

He didn't share that with Dillinger.

He said, "Again, I very much appreciate you sharing this."

"Not a problem," Dillinger replied and again looked right in Stellan's eyes before he said in a cautious tone, "It's tough to break the habit. It starts as a job. Earning a buck. For some people, it can become a high. That work for the firm, it might not do it for her, brother. It's vanilla when it's clear your woman in a lot of ways needs the spice. I'd say, because it's true, we need someone skilled at the Honey, so we could throw her more work on background checks I deem need to go deeper. But my guess would be that wouldn't be much better. Bottom line, she's gotta break the habit, Lange. And she'll never be able to lose that rush. She's gotta keep it. It's just gotta come from somewhere else."

"Is this spoken from experience?" he asked.

Dillinger didn't lose hold on Stellan's eyes, and he delivered another shock by sharing openly, "It doesn't suck, washing off the filth, finding your way to clean, or as clean as you can get since that shit seeps in down to the soul, and that's something that you can never get out. But if that's the only thing you had to make you feel alive, something has to replace it, and that something has to be real, Lange. Tangible. And solid. Or it's never gonna take hold."

Stellan was now seeing why Dillinger gave nothing (until recently, and very recently for Stellan) to anyone . . . but Evangeline.

"Then no worries, Branch. I have that part covered."

Dillinger jerked up his chin. "If you need backup with this, or she does, however you're gonna play that, I'm in town for a while and will do my best to carve out time to give it to you two. If you need anything else that might have to do with code, chords or surveillance, got a bud who's moved to town with a variety of skills and an attention deficit disorder. He works better when he has fifty things on the go. And whatever that asshole partner of Barclay's has got goin', my man will have no problem helping fuck it up. In fact, he's the wheels I right now have in motion."

"So you'll be offering these services to Barclay?" Stellan asked.

"Absolutely," Dillinger answered.

"Can you ask Barclay to give Sixx a wide berth while I handle her?" Stellan went on.

"Absolutely," Dillinger repeated.

"Again, appreciated."

They shook hands again, and Stellan walked him to the door.

Dillinger stopped at it in a way that Stellan didn't open it.

"By the way," he began, "Angie wants you guys over for dinner. She's offered up my chicken enchiladas. I'll try to talk her into making her spaghetti. That shit is fucking amazing. Either way, she'll have my ass if I don't leave here with your promise we'll be setting something up."

Stellan's lips quirked at his wording.

Dillinger shook his head and shocked Stellan yet again when his cold eyes lit with humor and more openness came out of his mouth

"Brother, you were the talk of the control room last night, coming all over the floor for Sixx. Don't think you can hand me shit for having a Mistress who owns my ass."

Stellan lifted his brows. "Did I hand you shit?"

Another something moved through Dillinger's eyes that was not chilly in the slightest.

Solidarity.

"Told you you'd enjoy the dark side," he said low.

Stellan did not get into the differences of what they had and who they were in the scene.

He didn't because he was not the kind of man who didn't take advantage of every opportunity, especially the important ones.

Having a friend in Branch Dillinger was such a thing. Not only because of what Stellan sensed he was, and the skills that came with that, but because he was Evangeline's, and Stellan cared a great deal for Dillinger's woman.

And also because Stellan had learned in his life you could trust few, but those few you could trust were worth anything.

And last, because Stellan had sensed from the first time he met him, under all that cold, whatever his reasons, he hid the fact he was a good man.

So if Dillinger was moved to give his trust, Stellan knew he could return that unreservedly.

"Is Leenie partial to restraint?" Stellan asked.

"She seriously rocks that shit."

Stellan smiled.

"I've seen your woman work," Dillinger shared. "Hand her the ropes, brother, but after you hand her a whip. You'll visit another world and won't wanna leave."

"We'll see," Stellan murmured amusedly.

"I bet," Dillinger murmured back and then stunned Stellan again by lifting a hand and clapping him on the shoulder. "Later, brother."

"Goodbye, Branch, and thank you again."

Dillinger opened the door and Stellan followed him through, but he stopped two steps out and watched as Dillinger dipped his chin to Susan before he sauntered through the outer door.

When he turned his attention to his assistant, she was staring at that door.

She must have felt Stellan's regard because she turned to him and declared, "If you tell Harry I drooled, you'll lose your ability to make children."

Stellan shook his head at her, went into his office, closed himself in, walked to his desk, sat down, and picked up his phone.

He scrolled to a number he used frequently, deciding not to go with Sylvie or Tucker Creed as both were friends and would sometimes partner with Simone.

He hit the green button and put the phone to his ear.

"Mr. Lange?" the man answered.

"I want everything you can get on the owners of the Bolt," he ordered. "And I want it fast."

"On it."

Stellan disconnected, gazed out his windows for long moments.

Then he went back to work.

twenty-two

Pixies and Warlords

SIXX

At nine o'clock that night, Sixx, definitely kitted out as Mistress Sixx, sat at a small, round table on the elevated platform that spanned a set of high, stool-less tables that disappeared where they led to a dancefloor that was flanked in the back corners with two large bars.

The Bolt.

The music was loud and thumping. The lights were flashing. The bodies were heaving. There was a smell of booze, sweat and sex in the air.

And Sixx was taking it in wearing skintight, zip-at-the-back, low-riding, black leather pants and a close-fitting, low cut, cropped leather vest, which meant she showed some skin at her tits, hips, back and belly. On her feet were platform black pumps with a scary-high, pencil heel. From her ears dangled long, black tassel earrings.

And around her neck was her rose gold choker.

She was out of sorts.

She should feel in her element. Seemingly on the prowl at a sex club. Something she'd done innumerable times before.

It should have felt natural.

It didn't.

It felt like something was missing.

Not the Sixx part of Simone "Sixx" Marchesa being fully out, taking over, her other half protected, but that not being the case anymore. The child in her had now grown up, and because of Stellan was safe anywhere.

Even there.

Because that world was a part of her, just like it was for Sixx.

It was that she wasn't there with her Master, and it felt wrong.

"You're not here to play," she muttered to herself. "It's just a fucking job."

And it was a good one. Not doing something for the likes of Fred Carvelo, who she was going to need to scrape off.

That kind of thing didn't enter the life she had with Stellan.

But still.

That something was missing.

And it was important.

She'd stationed herself at a table at the front of the club, dead center, with a view to the entire area.

The position was out there, visible, but also secluded. The tables were not the scene.

The dancefloor was the scene.

And the rooms beyond the heavy curtains over the two doors wedged between dancefloor and bar on either side at the back of the club were *the scene*.

But Sixx wasn't there for the scene.

She turned her attention to the length of elevated platform to her left, all the way down at the far end.

It was in shadows, as she was, but frequently lit with the flashing club lights that strobed the floor.

Pete Beardsley sat there, lounged back like he was the king of all he surveyed, a sub on her knees between his feet, her body twisted and her head not visible in a way that Sixx had a good idea how her mouth was engaged.

But his relatively decent-looking face did not register ecstasy or even pleasure, and this both enraged and sickened Sixx.

His sub was holding his balls, or his cock, in her mouth. If the latter, probably instructed to keep it hard, nothing else.

That was something Stellan would require of her.

And this was what enraged Sixx.

Because the woman at his feet was more than likely not there because she trusted her Dom with her heart or simply her kink.

But because her Dom had her fix, and it wasn't a sexual one, and she needed it.

That was *not* the life.

Submissiveness was *not* subjugation.

And that perversion of Sixx's way of life right there on display instead of being spoken of as a possibility made it hard for Sixx to keep her seat rather than make her way on her heels across the platform and show that asshole how it felt to be sexually coerced in a way you very much did not like.

On this thought, a trio of bodies strolled across the front of Sixx's table.

Two hulking warlords trailed by a pretty pixie wearing a short skirt, a laced, lime-green corset and matching gossamer wings.

Sixx caught the movement of the pixie's hand.

Even if she hadn't, the woman was one of Sixx's recruits. Her name was Molly, and those two warlords were her Doms. They all lived together and apparently learned very well how to share seeing as they did it in the scene and in life.

As Sixx watched them go, she made a mental note to discuss scholarships to the gladiator pit with Stellan.

Because both those dudes would rock it, and Sixx didn't know the cost of the buy-in, but if it was hefty, she could tell by the decent but not luxury car Molly had, not to mention the streetwear, shoes and handbag she'd sported when Sixx had met with her about the Bolt job, that they probably were not rolling in it.

She also made a mental note to request Stellan do a night of slumming when she knew Molly and her warlords were at each other. Stellan was absolutely not into roleplay or costumes, and neither was Sixx, but she had a feeling he'd find that trio at the very least interesting, and she herself wanted to see how that all worked out in play.

She looked down at the table to see a square of white against the black tabletop.

A note.

She picked it up, opened it, and read the words, *Station 7—back left—paid play—wait for an escort.*

She folded it, tucked it in her cleavage, and studied the dance-floor, ignoring a preening male sub who was shaking his ass her way.

Seriously, she had to bring Stellan here and give these folks the news that Mistress Sixx was out of commission.

Another time.

She turned her head and saw pixie and her warlords were cozied up at a table three tables down, both men with backs to the wall, Molly with her ass in one of their laps, his arm around her, her fore-head tucked into the side of his neck, her legs thrown over the lap of her other guy, but akimbo.

Those wings were going to get crushed.

The other guy had his hands full. One up his pixie's short, lime-green skirt, the other she couldn't see, but she could tell by its move-ments he was fisting his boy's cock.

But his gaze was aimed her way.

When Sixx had recruited her, Molly had shared her men were not fans of what was going on, and they'd offered to take her back when she was in the club.

She didn't need it, but from the note, the look and head mo-tions this guy was giving her, he wanted her to chill while he took care of his pussy and his meat before she went in.

Nice, but unnecessary.

Unfortunately, since she had to leave in an hour, that night was only reconnaissance. She wasn't going to make any moves.

Further, that wasn't the job she'd been hired to do.

Get the evidence, give it to Josh, he'd take it to Barclay Rich-ardson, and they'd do whatever it was they were going to do.

Still, she might slip up and have to hand someone his ass.

She was unpredictable that way.

In a case like that, it was always good to have backup.

Just, you know, should anyone try to intervene.

Not to mention, anything could happen, and if backup was on offer . . .

Especially from a tall, seriously built warlord.

Therefore, she found herself dipping her chin to the warlord and turning away, wondering what would happen if she told Stellan about this job. He knew she took things on outside the firm. But this one, he'd have a particular response. She was in no doubt he'd find it as offensive as she did, and he'd want something done about it.

Though she might have learned the hard way he could take care of himself, he was still a businessman—not an investigator, not a fixer, not of this part of her life, this part of the world, and maybe that was also what she missed, since they shared everything else, but this was still the great divide.

Sixx put these thoughts of out her mind and gave the dance-floor a good scan, trying to differentiate players, possibly identify the girls Beardsley was using, or, if luck turned her way, witness a solicitation.

Nothing doing.

She turned her head again to the mystical creatures and sighed when she saw her boy was up, his back now to her. He was still fully clothed, but it didn't take close observation to know who'd drawn what straw that night since his boy was now being force-fed cock.

Damn it, she didn't have a lot of time, and her self-appointed backup needed to quit fucking around, literally, or she was going in alone.

On that thought, she stood and moved their way.

When she got close and rounded them, she saw Molly was in-volved, back to the seated man's thighs, mouth full of balls as warlord-sub-for-the-night got his face fucked and warlord-Dom-for-the-night did the face fucking.

Warlord Dom turned his head and frowned down at her.

Yep.

So seriously gladiator material.

"Respect, my man, but I got shit to do," she told him. "You want to get your rocks off, have at it, but I have to go in."

He looked down at the handful of hair he was holding, grunted in a deep baritone that thrummed even through Sixx, "Swallow," then thrust hard, let out a low groan, and jerked a couple of times.

With no further ado, he pulled out and freed himself from the lips latched around his balls, doing this casually, before he tucked himself into his brown suede warlord breeches.

"Keep him hard," he told Molly. "I want him in pain when I come up his ass later."

"Yes, my sire," she murmured, sliding off the guy's lap to curl between his legs and gobble down his now exposed, impressively massive, distended cock that Sixx saw was trussed tight with a thin, leather cord at the base and around his balls, tethering them and separating them.

This meaning it would be impossible for him to come, all this making his handsome, needy face *pained*, handsome and needier when Molly started up on him.

Those wings fluttered very prettily when a pixie gave a blowjob. Nice.

Dom-for-the-night warlord jerked his chin up at her.

Guess in alpha-warlord speak that meant he was ready to rumble.

She moved away, and he fell in step at her side as she tried to remember which of the names she knew the two of them had was his.

It was Diesel, who Molly also referred to as D, or Maddox.

She was thinking Diesel.

"Nice bite," he remarked over the music.

She grinned.

She loved wearing Stellan's mark.

"Nice work back there," she said, also over the music.

"He'll make me pay," he replied.

"Bet that's a fun game," she noted.

"My boy's got a monster cock."

"I saw that."

"And he fucks like a freight train and can shoot such a huge load I can taste it in my throat for a week."

Totally had to bring Stellan to watch that.

Like he read her mind, he shared, "Obviously we do audiences. But you wanna get in there, that's Molly's call. Owning goes three ways, but a woman gets her hand on our cocks or our asses, only Molly can call that play."

How sweet.

"I'm taken."

He looked down at her with heavy brows raised.

She didn't expound.

She stated, "We're not exactly incognito with this shit. Like you just said, you're owned, and my man and me are out, you might not have heard, but others have. So it's not exactly a natural thing, you and me taking a stroll."

"Straight up, you're Mistress Sixx, you got a man but you're out on your own, that'll be understood. And you're Mistress Sixx, even though I'm owned and everyone knows it, no one would question if me or my boy are offered a shot for you to work us over that we'd want it, and it wouldn't be a surprise Molly gave permission. So you're covered."

That was a nice compliment.

However.

"I'm not going to work you," she hesitated and tried out, "D."

He gave a brisk nod.

So Diesel it was.

"Givin' the impression of feelin' me out works too," he said.

She hoped so.

Although Beardsley could have no idea she was on his case, in an uncertain situation she'd learned taking precautions every step of the way, though tedious, was essential.

One of the reasons she'd accepted backup.

She and D skirted the dancefloor, and he threw aside the heavy black curtain to expose the door to the play area for her and held it back as he opened that door.

She went in and felt his big body follow her in his heavy, leather riding boots. A big body that, as well as the breeches and boots, at the shoulders with the ragged ends over his pecs were covered with hides that were banded to his wide chest with buckled leather straps.

The play area of the Bolt was very different from the Honey.

The Honey had a comb of connecting hallways with varyingly-equipped rooms, mostly uniform in size, some smaller, like the isolation room Stellan and she'd been in the night before, and some larger, for multipartner or audience play and demonstrations. They all had at least one glass wall so members in the hallways could watch, with the option for the Dom, if they wanted, to lower the white, opaque blind to silhouette the proceedings, or the blackout blinds, for private play.

Membership fees covered a variety of things, including cleanup. So any bodily fluids spilled, unless the Dom required their sub to take care of it, was seen to by staff.

The only additional charge was receiving a monthly bill for the drinks you consumed at the bar. The staff kept track, and the charges were steep, since you were not expected to do anything as common as take out money to tip while enjoying a beverage in the hunting ground or the social room. But also, Aryas paid his staff handsomely, expecting a certain level of service as well as varied duties performed. So yearly membership, guest passes and bar tabs were set at exclusive levels.

The Bolt, you paid at the bar. The background checks were relatively thorough, but not invasive (as the Honey's were). Guest passes were a hefty fee and required a weeklong wait for the check to go through. But yearly membership fees were nowhere near the Honey's.

It showed right there in that large space.

The Bolt had a central, open, communal play area that was sectioned off with stations made obvious by the equipment in them or low partition walls. Bodily fluids outside the natural excretion of sweat were not allowed to be expelled, so every exposed cock she saw was covered in a condom. There were discrete but copious posts providing bleached white hand towels, boxes of large wet wipes and industrial-sized bottles of antibacterial gel.

There were also DMs, or Dungeon Masters, roaming the space, which was not surveilled by copious cameras due to the cost, though there were cameras, just not many of them. DMs kept an eye on the action, making sure Dominants didn't get out of hand or too in the zone to be at one with their sub. Each DM had on a bright red polo-shirt that had a white lightning bolt stitched over the left chest and a big, white DM emblazoned on the back.

Sixx clocked three of them in that space, which was probably one above necessary. There was a lot of activity. It still said Barclay Richardson liked to take care of his players.

Separated by a wide passageway, all around the outer walls were rooms with varying themes and equipment and glass walls facing the common area. If a Dom wanted privacy, vertical blinds could be pulled over the windows, though Sixx knew the sliding glass doors had no locks seeing as the DM had to have access for regular check-ins. You had to reserve these rooms and pay extra for them above and beyond membership, per use.

As no Dominants or submissives were allowed to play unsupervised at the Honey unless they'd passed the rigorous checks, the intrusive interview and were either referenced in with the experience Aryas required or trained under Aryas's program, DMs did not roam the halls there. But every square inch was monitored by cameras, and that action was recorded.

As Sixx surveyed the scenes playing out, she saw a lot of talent.

She and D also got a lot of looks.

She ignored them, and with some judicious touches to the small of her back, D led her to, and slowed their going by, what had to be station seven.

She felt her lips had thinned by the time they passed it and knew D's mood when he mumbled a deep and displeased, "Unh-hunh, that shit ain't right."

"She's barely conscious," Sixx mumbled back.

"Yup."

"How many times has she been branded?" she asked.

"Too many," D answered. "And word, branding only happens with Clay's approval, and he's stingy with that shit. Though there's three DMs, if they get on schedule together, you can bet Clay's not around, because all kinds of shit goes down where Clay would lose his fuckin' *mind*."

"Are those DMs on tonight?" she asked.

"Nope. Just one of them. Not the gang. Means Clay's probably in the house."

"Where's Josh in this mess?" she inquired as they made their slow turn to go down the other long passageway between open play area and closed playrooms.

"Wasn't here, but heard there was a bust-up between Josh and Pete. And it was public. No other details to that but noted since word got 'round about that sitch, blood's bad between them and stayed that way."

It seemed her stroll with D had been more useful than she expected.

"How many girls, do you know?" she queried.

"I'd say five, but I'm not allowed in the women's restroom. We'd have to ask Molly her take on that shit since they do their duty then get their reward and go right there to use."

"Beardsley doesn't pay them?"

"Not seen any cash exchange hands but have seen dope do it. A lot."

Sixx was again enraged.

Forced service as a sex-for-hire worker was bad enough, but they were *for hire*.

It shouldn't be happening at all, but since it was, at least they should get paid since Beardsley had to be, considering he needed the money to buy the dope. He wasn't doing it to be a drug fairy.

So he was pocketing the proceeds.

Motherfucker.

"Did you book a private space to finish off your boy, and does it have a view to station seven?" she asked.

"Planned a long night for him, Mistress. Wanted his balls blue before I took Mad and Molly home and fucked him full of my cum while he eats our pixie until she screams."

"That would be blue-*er*," she muttered as they finished their stroll at the opposite door and stopped.

Sixx shifted back into a shadowy area between door to dance-floor and the last playroom, where there was a dark hall that led to something, probably a storage closet or cleaning cupboard.

She heard the grin in his voice and looked up and saw it on his tanned, rugged face when he replied, "Mm-hmm. But you want, I'll go to the front, see if they got a station that we can take and put on a show for visiting Mistress Sixx, hopefully in a place you can keep an eye on that action."

This was actually an excellent suggestion, providing a different kind of cover for her to be at the Bolt when she had no intention to play at the Bolt, and if she kept coming just to hang, something she'd never done, that might be noticed.

It also would open her sphere of observation, giving her an excuse to be where the action was happening so she could keep an eye on what was done to the girls, and as a Domme in attendance, since the DMs were obviously not doing it, stop it if it hit extremes.

However, thinking on it, that night, she might not have the time.

"I wouldn't want to mess with your plans."

He gave a truncated bow, head bent splendidly, and if he were her sub, she'd reward him for such a lovely show. "Be an honor to blow inside him for the viewing pleasure of Mistress Sixx."

Although that would be fun to watch, only if Stellan was around.

How times had changed.

She drew in breath, stared unseeing at the scene and tried to figure out what time it was.

"How often do you kids come and play?" she asked.

"Mad's not a big fan of waiting for payback, so he'll be buried up my ass tomorrow night, among other things."

She nodded and peered across the expanse but couldn't see into station seven.

Tomorrow night.

That would have to work for her.

"So regardless of the DMs, shit goes down. It just gets more extreme when Barclay isn't here but the gang of three are," she remarked in order to confirm.

"Yup. Always a girl gettin' herself used, not in a good way, and always one stationed between Pete's legs, latched onto his junk. Serious as shit, Mistress, it's a wonder he hasn't shriveled up. He's always shoved up in moist. But just to say, he doesn't keep the whole stable available every night. In twos and threes. Probably easier for him not to get caught, he doesn't have tons of action happening all over the joint."

Sixx nodded again.

So Beardsley was a relatively smart motherfucker.

He was still a motherfucker.

"But, of course, the straight-up dealing happens nonstop," D noted.

She focused more fully on him. "Straight-up dealing?"

He nodded but looked surprised. "You didn't know?" When Sixx indicated she didn't with a movement of her head, D continued, "The dude's full-on a dealer. Smack. Crack. Blow. X. Meth. He's all-purpose. The convenience store of narcotics."

"Is he open about this?"

D shook his head. "When Mad and me started noticing shit going down, we started noticing other shit. Safe to say, he's more out about sellin' pussy than he is dope. Which is weird 'cause Clay'd get way more pissed about the pussy, though he would *not* be a fan of the dope. That said, if he's nailed by law enforcement, right or wrong, it's fact he'd be more fucked peddling drugs."

This was bigger than she suspected.

Definitely her stroll with D was a worthwhile use of time. Molly told her they knew something was up and were not real happy about it, but she hadn't shared this in depth.

Then again, Diesel or Maddox, depending on whose turn it was to be in charge, had more opportunity to keep an eye on things. Molly was probably mostly otherwise engaged.

"Back the way we came, big man," she said. "Slow. I want another look at that girl. Then we walk up the platform by Beardsley. I want a closer look at him too. And if you're up for it, we'll start our show tonight, make it look like a tryout. But I'll probably need to be leaving in half an hour. We'll reconvene tomorrow, you tell me the time the girls start working."

"Uh, at opening?" he asked in order to answer. "They service one after another and it doesn't end 'til closing time."

Lord God.

"More than one john a night in an intense BDSM scene?" she asked.

"Yup," he answered. "Like, three or four."

Damn.

"Like they have appointments?" she queried.

"Seen some recruiting on the dancefloor, but yeah. Like that."

This was not good.

"So this is why you haven't seen money exchange hands," she guessed. "It happens before the johns get here."

He shrugged massive shoulders. "Maybe. Probably. Maybe the shit on the dancefloor happens if there's an open spot."

"Fabulous," she muttered.

She was going to have to watch Beardsley closer if the deals were struck off-premises.

Or hope for a fucking open slot.

Damn.

It was time to pull in Sylvie and/or Tucker.

D had been positioned hiding her from view, but he moved out, and they made their trek back, slower, with D walking closer, Mistress and player having come to an arrangement, intimacy being established.

The guy was good. Good enough, in her renewed self, she'd think of calling on him to partner up on jobs if she needed it. A little bit of training would undoubtedly be warranted, but he was proving he was a natural.

And obviously he'd be good at taking orders.

Out of the play area, D escorted her up the steps to the platform on Beardsley's side, and since he was at the table at the very top, her eyes were on him before she made it there.

His attention was on the dancefloor, but sensing movement, it came to her and D, primarily her.

He wasn't a big guy, but he wasn't small. He took care of his body, which was a minus. She'd taken down men bigger than him, but they hadn't been in shape. The in-shape ones, if the situation got physical, you had to be quick, smart, careful and have no problem punching throats, gouging eyes or torqueing the fuck out of gonads.

Though without a lot of effort, Diesel or Maddox could more than likely twist that cocksucker into a pretzel.

Yes.

She was going to keep those boys around.

Domme to Dom, it cost her, but as they passed Beardsley, she tipped her chin down in a show of respect, like she would catching the eye of any Master or Mistress.

His lip curled in a sneer that was supposed to be a smile, and he returned the gesture.

They were well on their way back to complete D's tribe of three when she heard D mutter, "Need a shower?"

Oh yes.

She liked this guy.

So she let him hear her quiet laugh.

When they arrived back at his partners, he said gently, "Bag of tricks, baby," and Molly immediately disengaged from Maddox's engorged cock, eliciting a lovely sound that was half groan, half sigh of relief.

D made a show of getting a chair for Sixx and setting it so she had an unobstructed view of the club and the action they'd be enjoying on the shadowy platform.

Although the shadows were carefully constructed to offer enough lighting to see even when the club lights weren't dancing their way, but plenty of dark to hide certain things; this was another difference between the Honey and the Bolt.

Subs might get played with in booths in the hunting ground at the Honey, but requisite to the club's rules, whatever happened to them could not be open to any eyes. You might be able to tell by an expression on a sub's face, but that was it.

Beardsley, the trio, and a couple of Masters watching their subs rub up against each other on the dancefloor from mid-platform opposite Beardsley were the only folks up on high. So it wasn't very populated. But even though they probably did it to be stationed close to her, it was clear the comfortable way the trio settled into play there, and no staff came to intervene, that something like that wasn't unusual.

After she was seated, while bent double to seat himself, D shot her a wolfish grin.

"Time to play," he said.

She allowed her lips to tip up.

He reached to the side, caught his boy by the back of his thick neck, and shoved him to all fours on the floor in front of him.

D then bent forward and with practiced hands had the man's suede breeches down over his sculpted ass in no time.

"Legs wide, Mad, thighs tight against that suede," D told him. "You know the drill."

Maddox instantly adjusted his position as told.

Molly, standing at the ready at D's side with a dark green velvet bag opened for him, offered it up.

D reached in, felt around, pulled out a wide plug, muttered, "Get the remote, baby," and then, without lube, shoved it up the ass in front of him.

The resounding grunt coming from the floor made Sixx out-and-out smile and catch D's eyes.

"I take it you like payback," she remarked as D lifted his big, booted feet and rested them on the back of the man in front of him while he took the remote from Molly.

He hit it, a groan floated up as D's boots jerked, and he wasn't the one jerking them, and D grinned audaciously at Sixx.

"You're gonna get fucked, Mistress, only way to go is raw." He looked to his feet. "Am I right, Mad?"

"Yeah, D," Maddox growled.

"How blue are those balls, bro?" D asked.

"You could get to the fucking-me-raw part anytime, my man."

D slid his big, white smile Sixx's way. "I think Mad and me have different definitions of when 'anytime' should be. Too bad you're gonna miss that action, Mistress. My boy here likes his big daddy's cock. Almost more than I like his. But God didn't grant me the ex-tra inches, so I gotta go at him with all sorts of endurance and get creative."

Sixx had no doubt he had the skills to achieve all of that and again smiled back.

"How hard you gonna go at me tomorrow, boy?" D asked the man under his boots.

"Am I sleeping with your cock up my ass?" Maddox asked back.

D dug the heel of his boot into the guy's shoulder as the mis-chievous Dom took a hike and D's baritone came out like a slow roll of warning thunder. "What's that you say?"

"Am I sleeping with your cock up my ass, big daddy?" Maddox amended.

D took his boots off his man's back, leaned down, reached in and obviously gave some balls a hefty squeeze because Maddox's head stretched well back, his attractive lips parted in a silent groan. "That's how you talk to your big daddy, boy," he educated quietly.

Though Sixx was in little doubt he needed to do that. This crew had been together for so long, especially with an audience, Maddox bought just that because he wanted it . . . bad.

His sub's needs communicated to him, D then hit the zone.

"You like this?" he asked gently.

"Yeah," Maddox answered, and Sixx guessed at ball massage.

D reached deeper, and Sixx knew he was now stroking cock, and Lord, if he wanted to make certain that anyone who was watching would know they were pulling out the stops to put on a show for Mistress Sixx, he was certainly succeeding.

"How about this?" D queried.

"More, my man," Maddox begged, his hips beginning to hump fist.

"You'll get more," D promised. "You gonna like sleeping with my cock up your ass?"

"Always. Love your meat up my ass, Diesel."

"Yeah," D grunted, jacking him faster, and a low noise rumbled up Maddox's throat, his head still back. "Jack that fist, my monster, keep that head back. I like your back arched for me."

Maddox started fucking the fist wrapped around his dick.

D handed the remote to Molly and went in two-handed, and Sixx couldn't see, but she figured he was working cock and balls and knew it was good by the permanent wince, white teeth sunk into full lower lip and the hissing, labored breathing of the man on his hands and knees.

"Fuck me, but I like to watch that ass moving," D muttered reverently, eyes locked on his man's ass. "So damned pretty, all plugged and shit. Almost as pretty as it looks when it's full of my cock." He kept his attention on the swinging, carved buttocks in front of him as he asked, "How 'bout you, Molly baby? You like to watch your Mad's ass move while he jacks your D's fist?"

"I love it, sire," Molly breathed, pressed tits to shoulder at D's back, watching.

"Better plugged or full of me?" D queried.

"Full of you, D," she whispered worshipfully. "Always love to watch you inside my Mad. But you're right, it sure is pretty right now."

"Gonna come up there tonight," D shared. "Use that ass good. Shoot load after load inside my boy."

"Fuck," Maddox hissed, his hips moving savagely now.

"I can't wait," Molly said excitedly.

"My boy's gonna sleep plugged with my cock and full of my cum," D went on.

"God, *fuck*," Maddox grunted.

"Though he's gonna fall asleep inside you, my sweet pixie," D kept at it.

"*Shit*," Maddox ground out.

"Lovely," Molly whispered.

"Faster," D commanded.

"*Christ*," Maddox bit, giving his Master what he'd ordered and suffering gloriously for it.

"My dick is twitching, waiting to get all up in there," D told him.

"Take my ass now, D." Maddox's grating voice was low and ragged.

"No, my monster. Want you on your back, locked to your bars spread wide first time I fuck that ass tonight," D informed him.

Nice visual.

Seriously.

"Fucking *fuck*," Maddox panted.

Apparently, Maddox agreed.

Then again, he probably had repeatedly experienced the real thing, so there you go.

"Though second time, you suck me hard again, do it good and ask nice, I'll fuck you on all fours," D offered.

"I'll ask nice," Maddox clipped out his vow.

D kept up the torture. "You won't be coming though. Not until you come with me for time number three. How you want to take my cock that time, monster?"

"Shit, fuck, *Jesus*," Maddox grunted.

D leaned into him and Maddox emitted a long, low, pained groan. More ball action.

"Was that an answer?" he asked.

"Any way you wanna fuck me," Maddox forced out.

"Any way I wanna fuck you, what?" D pushed.

"Any way you wanna fuck me, big daddy."

"Say it like I like it, monster," D bit off.

"Any way you wanna take your boy's ass, big daddy. I'll take it. I'll love it. I'll beg for your cum."

"Nice," D murmured, leaning back but keeping at him. "Now answer my fuckin' question," D ordered. "How hard you gonna go at me tomorrow night, Mad?"

"How hard do you want it, D?"

"Stop," D growled and Maddox impressively immediately quit moving, except his chest, which was heaving. Then his big body began trembling as D started stroking, slow and so deep, his whole upper body went up and down with it. "How much do I like this monster?"

"You love it," Maddox pushed out.

"And you know I like it when you fuck me hard and blow so goddamned deep," D murmured. "Gonna earn that good, my monster. Gonna earn payback that's gonna blow my mind. You're gonna bury that huge dick so far up me, I'll feel that motherfucker in my chest." He ceased his stroking. "How do these feel?" he asked, and Maddox grunted.

Ball squeeze.

"Ready to explode," Maddox answered.

"Make 'em feel better by sucking them sweet while I fuck our little pixie later."

"Thank fuck," Maddox breathed out.

"Though they'll still be bound."

"Jesus," Maddox groaned.

The balls let go, the plug pulled out, D set it in the indent of Maddox's spine, drove two fingers inside and immediately commenced stroking deep.

"Need to fuck those," Maddox grunted.

"Be my guest," D invited.

Maddox rolled into his finger fucking.

"Now, ask you one more time," D said. "How fuckin' hard are you gonna go at me tomorrow night, boy?"

"Make you beg me to split you in two," Maddox rumbled.

D turned to Sixx, straight back to cheeky, and cocked a cheerful brow. "Something for you to look forward to."

She shook her head at him but did it thinking she seriously liked this guy.

"So you're big daddy now," she noted. "Tomorrow night," she tipped her head to the man on the floor, "what're you going to be to him?"

D grinned his impertinent grin. "His boy," he answered. "And Mistress girl, wait until you see me be boy to this big monster daddy and his huge cock. I rock that shit."

"He does," Molly put in. "But Mad will probably shake it up. He always does."

Sixx looked to Molly. "How?"

She smiled huge. "It'll probably be straight M/M tomorrow, with a little F thrown in for me. But when Mad goes at D like that, he knows I like it best to watch, and they take care of me after. Mad's old school. He likes it straight up. Fucking and pain. So he likes D's ass real red before he fucks it. And God, D's dick trussed up the way Mad does him? It's so, *so* pretty, all hard and red and thick. If I'm good, Mad lets me suck D off while he's spanking him. So it . . . is gonna be . . . *epic.*" Her smile got bigger as she carried on, "But tonight's awesome too. I love it when D gets creative. And I'm sorry it sounds like you can't come home with us, because he's just warming up."

Just warming up?

"And tonight's special," Molly carried on. "They just do the war-lord and hides and breeches thing for me. They aren't really into it. But it's super sweet they gave it to me tonight. It's been a while."

Damn, they must love her to put on the breeches and hides.

Seriously, Sixx liked all three of these guys.

And she really wanted to introduce Stellan to them.

They might dig his playroom, and he might dig whatever antics they dreamed up.

"You gonna spank me tomorrow night, my monster?" D asked the man between his legs quietly, taking Sixx out of her mini-reverie.

"So fuckin' hard, D," Mad grunted, still fucking his own ass while taking a finger fucking. "When I'm up your ass, you'll feel me hit before I take you to the root."

"Something else for me to look forward to," D mumbled, with-drew his fingers from ass, his hand from cock, re-inserted the plug, replaced his boots on his human footstool, looked up at Molly, and his strong-featured face got soft as he twisted, reached back a brawny arm, and hooked her at the waist, murmuring gently, "Come here, baby. D's cock needs some of your sweet pussy. Face your Maddox. He's gonna be getting some of your loving attention."

"As you wish, sire," she murmured, beyond ready, she was right in there (and Sixx didn't blame her), throwing a leg over his lap to straddle him, facing out.

Wardrobe adjustments were made, bodily adjustments were made, and on a cute sigh, Molly slid D's thick, hard, divinely veined cock up her veiled-by-her-skirt pussy.

It was then Sixx noted he might not have the extra inches, but he made up for it with additional girth.

Yowza.

"Just sit on it, honey, but give Mad some of your extra-special loving."

She bent forward, kissed Maddox's ass cheek then took hold of the plug and slowly and rhythmically fucked him while she reached around to stroke his cock.

Another groan from below before a tender, "Thank you, my pixie."

"That's it," D cooed approvingly as well as adoringly, gliding one hand up from her belly to cup her breast over her corset, the other one headed downward and dove under her skirt.

Figuring the headliner event was over, at least deciding it was for her, Sixx reached behind her back, pulled her phone out of the waistband of her pants, brought it forward and looked at the time.

She had fifteen minutes.

She turned her attention to Beardsley.

His head was bent to look down at his lap, and she couldn't see his expression but his arm was moving and she knew he was done with cock holding. He was forcing out a blowjob.

"Give me a couple bounces, baby," she heard D whisper.

Sixx looked to the crowd, giving it another scan, and this time honing in on one girl who was exceptionally thin, barely dressed, and definitely spacy. A girl who had not been there earlier. She danced by herself, and as Sixx watched, a man approached her, and she smiled vaguely, though she clearly wanted it to be coyly.

Her lips moved, and the man jerked back, gave her a stone-faced look, shook his head once and moved away.

She watched him go like it was all the same to her and then got lost in the music again.

Pay to play, he wasn't down with that . . . *next.*

Sixx wished she had time to fashion an approach and question that guy about what had just gone down without freaking him out she might be a cop, but she unfortunately didn't. Though she studied him closely as he shifted through the crowd so she could clock him if he was there the next night and maybe make an approach.

She couldn't spot another girl who might be in that game, and she hadn't noticed anyone other than the girl in station seven in the play area.

D had said twos and threes.

Apparently, tonight it was threes.

"Up and fuck that," she heard D command and looked back to them.

Maddox was up on his knees between D's spread legs, Molly could be seen riding D behind him, her wings aflutter, even as she was grasping Maddox's big dick and he was fucking her fist.

Sixx's eyes went around the action to D, who probably liked an audience but was now all about the two people between his legs.

"I'm hitting the ladies' room then I'm out," she told him.

"Cool," he grunted.

"Contact me about a time tomorrow," she told him.

"Guess what, Mad?" D asked roughly. "In case you didn't pick up on it, you get to return the favor for Mistress Sixx tomorrow night."

"Fuck . . ." Maddox puffed out, his black eyes so glazed, he was so getting off on what was being done to him, she wasn't sure he was actually replying to D when he said, "*Yeah.*"

She got up, shoving her phone back in her waistband.

"Thanks for the time and the show. You all do brilliant work. Look forward to tomorrow night. Later," she muttered.

"Pleasure," D groaned, then, "Faster, baby, *bounce.*"

Molly bounced and shot Sixx a happy, zoned-out, turned-on, sexed-up grin, which seriously, all that meat all hers to watch fuck and to get fucked with, sweet and adoring too, Sixx wouldn't blame her if she looked like that permanently.

She moved away from the trio.

She did a sweep of the ladies' room, which was shared by female Dommes and subs. It was not a thing like the Dom Lounge at the Honey, far more utilitarian, but did have a small rest area with lockers. The whole place also had nothing in it but a couple of women refreshing makeup.

Time to meet Stellan at the Honey, but not enough time to meet him at home and go together.

She texted him on her way out that she had to meet him there, and it wasn't the loud club music that was the reason she didn't hear it, even though it sounded right over her head.

It was the fact that it was up in the soundproofed office with the window overlooking the club where the beep signaled that her text had been delivered.

Sixx was somewhat surprised when Stellan wasn't in the observation room at the Honey when she arrived.

He'd replied to her text, **On my way, X**, and their home was closer to the Honey than the Bolt was.

She was a worried and about to text him again when her phone binged.

Held up. There soon. X

She let out a sigh of relief and left the room to get them drinks.

On the way in she'd seen Naya and Ami, who were seated at a booth in a way that conveyed it was definitely a getting-to-know you session. Therefore she hadn't interrupted. She'd just caught their eyes before she'd gone back to the observation room of the playroom they'd be using in order to meet up with Stellan.

By the time she returned after ordering drinks to be delivered, the couple was in the playroom, seeing to preliminaries.

And it would seem it was Sixx's night to view inspiration because it would appear that Naya had been emboldened by Ami's response the night before.

She was taking them somewhere deeper, maybe even darker, and Sixx's attention peaked.

She was sitting forward in her armchair, not because it was intriguing, though it was, but because she needed to be ready to intervene if Naya took Ami to a place he didn't want to be but was too into her or too much of a guy to stop it.

The door opened, and she turned her head to see Stellan enter wearing his usual-for-the-Club suit, looking dashing, hot and utterly bangable.

He closed the door behind him, glanced at her, looked to the window and hummed, "Mm," as he moved her way.

She tipped her head back.

When he arrived at her chair, Stellan took her invitation, bending and touching his lips to hers before his eyes dropped to her collar and warmed. He lifted a finger to touch the gold at her throat lightly in a weird way that seemed more doting than his normal doting, and she knew he liked her collared, before seating himself beside her. He reached for the drink that was sitting on the table on his other side and leveled his gaze on the window.

"That's interesting," he remarked before taking a sip.

She looked back to the scene where Ami was roped bent over the end of a spanking bench. His arms were trussed from the tops of his biceps to his wrists at his back in what could only be described as a work of art, not near the work of a trainee, the ropes and knots also spanning his beefy thighs.

He'd been ordered to don a modified jock strap that bound his waist and under his buttocks but was open at the front, the elastic only surrounding his privates, not obscuring them. More rope was tied around his balls, and tight knots bound the length of his hard shaft.

He'd been collared, like last night with thick iron, a rope from a hoop at the back tied to the rope binding his wrists, this holding his head back, and stretching his arms up.

It was clear Naya had gone shopping after last night's festivities, because up his ass, she'd tailed him with what Sixx could only describe as a warrior's tail.

The plug had been substantial. The tail was black and looked scaly, it was shortish and curled up in a perfect arc, the flared, dragon-like tip of it pointing at the small of his back.

And last, he was gagged by a pair of aqua, stretch-lace panties that overextended his cheeks and tied at the hook on the back of his collar.

Naya was currently cooing over him, running oiled hands over his body, his bindings, lightly fucking his ass with his tail, massaging his swollen, trussed balls, and often circling a finger what had to be maddeningly around the tip of his cock.

"She didn't wait long to put him to the test," Stellan observed.

"I'm concerned," Sixx told him.

She looked Stellan's way and saw him studying the scene closely before he said, "Ami appears to be relatively comfortable, or as comfortable as one can be that way, and enjoying it."

"Ami might let her drag him barefoot across broken glass with that tail up his ass and a leash around his cock and balls that she's pulling at . . . *hard*."

Stellan turned to her. "You know, that *is* the place we're supposed to get them to, darling."

"They've had one scene, and she isn't out of training."

An unmistakable noise came, followed by a different one, and they both turned to the windows with Stellan noting, "The soft sell is over."

He was correct, considering Naya was switching Ami's ass, outer, back and inner thighs. And she didn't lie. She was adept with a switch.

They had a side view of him, and with each blow they heard a garbled groan from Ami and saw the flinch around his eyes.

But it could not be missed that after she really got going, his cock was straining its bounds, and it didn't take long before his control snapped and he started humping the air, his hips slamming against the bench, his dick tied up in a way release was out of the question.

It had to be agony.

And very visibly, it was also ecstasy.

Uncontrolled muffled words started to come from behind aqua panties, and Naya went at him viciously with the switch, making Sixx tense in her seat in preparation to move in and give Naya warning she was taking it too far before Naya stopped suddenly. She dropped her whip and jerked him up further with a hand under his chin so his chest was off the bench. She straddled it and shoved his face in her pussy.

"Calm, *mon guerrier*," she purred. "And no eating."

Ami's torso heaved, and she stroked his bald head.

"I think she has it in hand," Stellan drawled.

Sixx reached out and took a drink.

When she set it back, she found Stellan's hand and wrapped her fingers around.

His curled instantly into hers.

"What held you up?" she asked.

"Something unforeseen," he murmured before he took another sip of his own drink and set it aside. He turned his gaze to her. "Did you get your job sorted?"

It was on the tip of her tongue to tell him about it, but she had a feeling if he knew about the warlords and their backup, he might not be a fan.

And it was just too . . . sordid to touch the likes of Stellan.

The bad business was also happening relatively openly, and Sixx had a feeling with some time and legwork she'd have the evidence Josh and Barclay needed in pretty short order.

And then it would be over.

"Not really," she answered. "I'll have to keep at it tomorrow night."

"Ah." He looked back to the window.

She played with his fingers, wondering if she'd made the right decision and instead should share.

"Just your tongue. That's it, my sweet slave, that's it," Sixx heard Naya say as she turned her attention back to the scene.

The panties were around Ami's neck, and Naya had his head in her hands, guiding it up and down between her legs.

Stellan disengaged their fingers but only to glide his down her inner arm.

"Would you like to ride my hand while she works him?" he offered.

"I'm not there yet, baby. I was a little too freaked with where she was going."

She felt his gaze, so she looked to him to see him openly surprised.

She shot him a jaunty grin. "You with me now, I'm sure I'll get here."

"Zip open your pants, darling. If I want access, I don't want to have to ask."

She kept grinning at him as she leaned forward and did as ordered.

He studied her with an odd expression she couldn't quite place before his fingers captured hers again when they were free. They curled around her hand, which he brought to his lips.

"Love you," she whispered, watching and feeling those beautiful lips against her skin, remembering another time he'd had those lips to her fingers, glad she'd had both times, and hoping there would be more.

"And I you," he replied, his eyes warming, which was not odd at all.

They both turned to the scene, watched Naya allow limited head to be given to her before she shoved him deep, pressed up into his face deeper, and demanded it all with no breathers until she had an incredibly attractive and openly intense orgasm.

She then pushed him up to his knees, removed the spanking bench, slipped the knots on his cock so the ropes fell away, but not the ones from the base and his balls, and got down on all fours in front of him. Reaching between her legs to guide him in, she ordered him to fuck her.

Watching his reddened ass filled with that awesome tail bunching and releasing with his thrusts, his craggy, handsome face a mask of pain and pleasure as he fucked bound and tailed without hope of release, Sixx muttered, "I might need those fingers now, baby."

Stellan let her hand go and relocated his, replying, "And I'm here to oblige, my darling."

Arms bound behind his back, Ami fucked Naya to another orgasm while Stellan fingered Sixx to her own.

After, Naya unbound the root of his dick and his balls, strapped on a substantial phallus, turned Ami toward the windows, relieved him of his tail, and Stellan shoved Sixx's hand down his pants so she could give him a handjob while Naya fucked Ami to a splendidly thunderous orgasm during which he offered his Mistress a highly impressive load. One she wasn't quite happy with, however, so she squeezed his balls and jacked his dick through several violent aftershocks with reciprocal jets of cum.

Through this, Sixx used her other hand to pull out Stellan's handkerchief from his trouser pocket and covered the head of his cock with it before she put her fingers to his cheek and turned him to look at her so she could watch his face as she finished stroking him to climax.

Ami and Naya were something.

But she'd take Stellan's quiet climax from a handjob delivered by her any day of the week.

When he'd recovered, they kissed soft and wet before Stellan took the handkerchief from her, straightened his trousers, and shoved it back in his pocket. Sixx leaned sideways, dropping her head to his shoulder and looking back to the window.

Naya had pushed Ami down to his forehead on the floor, and she was still fucking his ass, though now slow and steady, rather than as she'd gone at him.

Still in training or no, ex-model or no, it must be said, the woman could fuck like a marine.

"Thank me, my handsome slave," she ordered softly, even tenderly, definitely affectionately.

Intense, explosive scene, getting-to-know-you session in a booth prior.

This held promise.

And that made Sixx happy.

"Thank you, Mistress," he said roughly and immediately.

"Your offering was substantial but shall we try that again?" Naya asked, still fucking his ass.

Sixx grinned when Ami answered, "Abso-fucking-lutely, my Mistress."

"It's very soon in our acquaintance, *mon guerrier*, but I'd like you to think about fighting for me at the gladiator games."

"It would be my honor, my Mistress."

"I'll expect you to fight wearing your tail," she told him.

"Whatever you desire."

"And fuck with it when you win for me."

"Your pleasure is mine."

"Tuesday's going to be fantastic," Sixx declared.

Stellan chuckled.

"You deserve a reward," Naya told Ami, not ceasing in taking his ass, and Sixx knew she'd positioned him like that, facing the window, forehead to the floor, so that her observers could better enjoy the ongoing show.

Kind of her.

"I'm thinking suspension," Naya stated musingly. "Facedown. Arms like that. Calves cocked. Legs spread wide. Parallel to the floor. But I'll release your head. You look so lovely in ropes, and I'm sure you'll enjoy watching your cock jet for me while you watch me disappear inside you."

"Fuck yeah," Ami growled.

Suspending that behemoth with ropes?

Definitely, Naya had been emboldened.

"It seems we're going to have another long night," Stellan noted.

Sixx lifted away from his shoulder and looked at him. "Do you have more handkerchiefs?"

He shook his head.

"So I guess I'll have to use my mouth."

Stellan's hand darted out.

He caught her chin, pulled her close . . .

And right before he kissed her, he smiled.

When he was done, he didn't pull away.

He ordered, "Pants off, darling. Me first."

Sixx didn't make her Master wait.

twenty-three

Ceaselessly

SIXX

The next morning, hands over hers pressed into the wall over the headboard, Stellan fucked Sixx from behind on their knees.

He kept one of her hands against the wall, took the other one, shoved it between her legs and used her finger to manipulate her clit.

Sixx moaned.

"Come," he growled into her neck.

Sixx came.

Stellan waited her out.

Then he came.

He was buried inside her, cupping their hands between her legs, fingers spread around their connection, and licking and sucking at his mark on her neck after they both came down.

His lips slid up to her ear. "You wore your collar last night."

Her lips tipped up, and that could be heard in her, "Yes."

"Did you do that for me?"

She blinked at the wall, confused at the question.

Because it was an obvious yes. That piece of jewelry had totally taken on a certain significance.

And he knew that.

He kissed her neck and went back to her ear, expounding, "To have me with you?"

It sounded like that was important to him, as of course it would be.

And she hadn't thought about it, but like she subconsciously put it on for him the first time, knowing what she'd be up to last night, she'd done it again . . . to have him with her.

"Yes," she whispered.

He slid out and moved off the bed.

Sixx turned her head to watch him go, surprised, considering he usually arranged her comfortably, if she wasn't that way already, when they were done. And often, if he was leaving the bed for good, he'd take her with him.

She fell to her hip on the mattress, dragging the sheet up to her lap, staring at where he'd disappeared through the arch to the bathroom, feeling something funny happening in her stomach.

He sauntered back in, naked, glorious and carrying three black velvet bags with long, dangling, silken black tassels.

His eyes were on her all the way and didn't leave her even as he sat at the edge of the bed and tossed the bags unceremoniously in her lap.

They were surprisingly heavy-*ish*.

"I had those made for you," he declared abruptly. "And as I very much appreciate your chic style, I would wish to do nothing to interfere with it. However, whenever one of them matches an outfit you put together, I want you to wear it. And anytime we're playing or at the Club, you'll have one on."

She watched him while he said this, then looked down at the bags in her lap.

"Open them," he ordered.

Sixx reached to one and tugged the drawstring open.

"In time, I'll have more made in different styles so you'll have a choice, and you'll wear my collar every day."

She upended the bag and felt the cold, heavy gold against her hand.

It was a choker just like the one she had, exactly, except unlike hers, which was costume, she knew by the weight it was pure gold.

"Holy God," she whispered.

"The other two are the same. One in platinum. The other is real rose gold."

She lifted her head to look at him.

"Stellan, I can't . . . this is—"

He looked direct in her eyes. "You're mine, and I want this communicated ceaselessly."

She loved that.

She'd totally go with that.

But . . .

"These had to be expensive," she noted. "And custom made?"

"Darling, look around you," he returned. "I think I can afford it."

"No one's ever given me something this . . . *amazing*," she whispered.

He leaned into her, brushed his lips against hers, pulled back and stared again into her eyes.

"Now, they have," he decreed, pushed from the bed and stated, "M will be here soon, and I have an early meeting. It's time to shower."

Sixx watched him again disappear through the archway and looked down at her lap.

She undid the two remaining bags and withdrew the platinum and rose gold chokers.

They were crazy gorgeous.

But the way Stellan had given them to her . . .

Maybe he didn't want to make a big deal of it. Maybe he thought, the first substantial gift he'd given her (or gifts plural, that didn't include when he gave her a gladiator, of course), he didn't want her to feel uncomfortable. He surely had to know no one had given her anything close to this in meaning and expense, and with what they were and who she was to him, it meant something, she have them and perhaps he simply wanted her to accept them without any drama.

That had to be it.

Though she couldn't help but think that it wasn't.

She couldn't help but think that offering her something that startlingly lovely should have had more fanfare. Even a wee bit.

But maybe that wasn't Stellan. She hadn't learned this side of him yet.

And seriously, she thought as she fingered the glittering treasure in her hands, she shouldn't be complaining.

Sixx walked down to breakfast in an olive-green suede tank, tan short-shorts and nude suede, high-heeled sandals, with her rose gold choker at her neck.

"*Hola, mija!*" M cried.

"Hey, M," Sixx replied.

After giving M a smile, she watched closely as Stellan did as he always did.

He made her a cup of coffee.

He brought it to her as she was downing vitamins with grape juice.

"Ami texted this morning. He'll be here shortly," he shared.

She stared up at him in surprise. "He will?"

"He needs to speak with you, darling. For obvious reasons."

Oh.

Right.

"It really isn't necessary. I get it," she pointed out the obvious.

"This isn't Ami's way. The relationship was short but meaningful. Regardless, he would not show that disrespect," Stellan replied.

It still wasn't necessary, but she nodded.

"I told him you're rather busy so he said he'd come immediately. It shouldn't take long."

"I have time," Sixx said.

"Breakfast!" M announced.

Sixx was almost done with her scrambled eggs, bacon, refried beans and tortillas when the doorbell rang.

"I'll get it," M declared, bustling toward the door.

"M maybe shouldn't be around when this goes down," Sixx pointed out when the lady was out of earshot.

"You can take him to the library. The front room. My study. This house is your house. Have this conversation wherever you wish," Stellan returned offhandedly.

"You're not going to be there with me?" she asked, again surprised.

He turned from his plate to her. "There's no need. You are very taken. It appears if he isn't yet, he's going to be. My presence is unnecessary."

She loved the trust, smiled that to him, and bent in to kiss his jaw.

"Ami is here," M announced, and Sixx and Stellan turned on their stools to see him trailing in behind M.

"I interrupted your breakfast," Ami said, clearly not liking that idea.

"It's cool," Sixx replied, sliding off her stool.

"Would you like some?" M offered.

"No, ma'am, I'm good," Ami declined.

Stellan came off his stool. They greeted and shook hands, then Ami turned to Sixx.

"This won't take long," he told her. "Then I'll leave you to your morning."

She nodded and lifted an arm to the hall, inviting, "Let's go chat."

He shifted to the side to allow her to pass him, and she did, deciding to take him to Stellan's study because she thought of the library as "their place" considering what happened in it, and the front room might seem too formal, even if it wasn't decorated that way.

She led him there, turned to him when they were both inside, and started things.

"You really didn't have to do this," she said. "Not only was I there watching when you gave yourself to her," she shot him a big smile, "I set that up."

He bowed his head briefly and lifted it. "I know, Sixx. But you owned me. You worked me. I performed for you. I liked it. It meant something to me. I think it meant something to you. It wouldn't be right if I didn't do this."

"It meant something to me, definitely," she agreed softly.

"So I had to do this."

The smile she gave him then was gentler. "You're a very chivalrous sub."

Finally, he smiled back at her. "I have a feeling I'm gonna need to be."

She laughed quietly. "Oh yes. I think you've got a bit of a princess on your hands."

Ami chuckled through saying, "This man is not complaining."

"I noticed that," she teased and tilted her head to the side. "I witnessed the naked stuff went over pretty well. How'd the conversation in the booth go?" she asked.

"I'm taking her out tonight."

Sixx's eyes got big and happy. "A date?"

He nodded. "Yeah."

"She seems very sweet," Sixx noted.

"She's great. Out of the scene, she's great," he confirmed, then grinned a particular kind of grin. "In the scene . . . *shit*."

"I was worried last night would be too much for you," Sixx admitted.

He shook his head. "We talked about it beforehand. She was hinting at things, things I could tell she was too wired to try. I told her to let loose. We had a hand signal when I was gagged and obviously a safe word when I wasn't. Anyway, I'm into that, I like to be pushed. The further, the better. It's just that the Domme has to be skilled at giving it for it to work for me."

"She appears to be a natural."

"She said she's always been nervous in scenes so has sucked at it," he declared.

Sixx was stunned. "Really?"

"That was why that Aryas guy was keen to set us up. She wasn't connecting. But also, last night after, when we talked through the play, I think none of the subs she trained on were a big enough challenge for her. She needs to go deep to get the big payoff, and if she isn't feeling it, she's not gonna be able to do that. But I think she was worried she'd break a sub, so she didn't even try, and holding back was frustrating her." That particular grin returned. "She's not feeling so frustrated anymore."

Sixx gave him her own brand of particular grin. "You two seem to have had a meeting of the minds very quickly."

"Yeah, and I'm looking forward to keep working on that."

"This makes me happy, Ami," she told him with open honesty.

"I'm glad, Sixx, and that's another reason I came. I wanted to thank you in person for giving a shit enough to set this up. Even if it doesn't work out, the sex has been the best I've had in freakin' years, no offense, but when you had me, you couldn't go that deep."

"I get it," she promised.

"And she is really not hard to look at."

That made Sixx burst out laughing.

"Very true," she said through it. When she stopped, she told him, "Stellan is really the man behind this magic. He's the one who talked to Aryas for you."

"I already thanked him, but my guess is you were behind that."

She couldn't disagree, so she just inclined her head.

He got closer, and his voice dipped lower. "You've been great, Sixx. Thanks."

"Honest to God, it was my pleasure. And you haven't seen the last of me. I'll be pitside on Tuesday, enjoying you winning for your princess."

"Awesome," he muttered on a smile.

Was she going to do what she was thinking about doing?

Well . . .

Fuck it.

She went in and gave him a hug.

It felt amazingly good when Ami's long arms wound around her and he hugged her back.

They separated, and she looked up at him. "Maybe I should take some krav maga classes."

"I know a guy if you want that."

She laughed again as they headed out. Stellan met them in the kitchen and walked with her to guide Ami to the front door.

Ami gave her another hug, shook Stellan's hand, said, "See you all Tuesday, hope to give you a good show," on a teasing smile, then he headed to his SUV in the drive.

Sixx wrapped both hands around Stellan's elbow as they walked back, sharing, "He and Naya have a date tonight."

"Excellent," Stellan murmured.

They moved inside, he closed the door, and she looked up at him to see he was leading her forward, looking lost in thought.

"You okay?" she asked.

He turned his gaze to her.

"Perfect," he answered before he immediately turned to face forward again.

He looked it, then again, he always looked perfect.

He even acted it, mostly.

But for some reason, Sixx thought he was lying.

Sixx was on her way to the Bolt for the evening's festivities when the music died and the cab filled with ring tones.

She looked at the dash and took the call.

"Hey, Tucker," she greeted.

"Hey, Sixx. Have a minute?" he asked.

She was hoping this was good news.

She'd touched base with the other two members of the Bolt she'd recruited to keep an eye on things, but they'd had nothing for her outside of what she'd seen herself last night.

And that day Sixx had to do firm work during the day, so she wasn't free to follow Beardsley around everywhere. Therefore she'd contacted Sylvie and Tucker, and they had work, but Tucker said he could get free in the late afternoon, try to hunt Beardsley down, and if he found him, watch him.

If Beardsley was meeting with clients, maybe Tucker would see him.

And maybe Tucker *had* seen him.

"Definitely," she answered.

"Got good news," he shared.

Fabulous.

"What's that?"

"Saw some money exchange hands between your guy and another guy. Got pictures. I'm gonna text them to you after this call. I wanted to get into his pad, but I couldn't hit it and keep a tail on him. Can't do it tonight either. Family time."

"Right, no problem. And fantastic about the pictures."

"You see the guy in them tonight with a girl, that's two-plus-two and it equals pimp," he said. "It could be a drug buy, but it was only cash handed over, no product."

So hopefully, it was about a girl.

"Brilliant," Sixx replied.

"You able to hack into his machine?" he asked.

"No. My guess is he turns it off when he's not using it, and I haven't had the time to keep trying."

"If he keeps a schedule of this shit and he's smart, he'd keep that offline anyway," Tucker said. "But if this guy in the picture doesn't come in tonight, I'll try to squeeze a break and enter in tomorrow and see what I can find."

"If I have the chance to hit that before you, I'll let you know. Keep me in your loop."

"Will do. Gotta go. I'll send the pix. Later," Tucker said.

"Later, and thanks, Tucker."

"Pleasure."

He disconnected.

Minutes later, she heard a beep that said she had a text. Stopped at a stoplight, she grabbed her phone and studied the five pictures Tucker sent, expanding them so she could get a good recall of the face of the man meeting with Beardsley.

She was ten minutes away from the Bolt when another call came in.

The number was local, but unknown.

She hit the button to connect anyway.

"Sixx," she greeted.

"Hey, Mistress girl," D's baritone filled her cab.

"Hey," she returned, finding herself smiling, probably because this guy was solid, he was funny, he was full of personality, he treated his sub like gold and he didn't like women getting fucked over. "How did last night go?"

"Woman, it sucks part of me hopes you don't get the goods on your man tonight so you can see our act reach fruition. Last night was *off the chain*. Mad is moving like a caged tiger, he's so ready to get down to business. And Molly's super-pumped you're going to be here tonight. She thinks playing for you as an audience is where it's at. Love my girl, so I take no offense I did all the work and my babe gives me zero credit."

Through her continuing smile, Sixx replied, "I very much appreciated all your efforts, D."

"Word," he grunted. "We're here. Mad is getting drinks. What you want?" he asked.

"Do they have martini glasses?" she asked back.

"Fuck knows," he replied. "I drink beer. Maddox drinks beer.

And when Mol's feelin' fancy, she drinks strawberry daiquiris and shit."

She laughed, not finding any of that a surprise.

"Gin martini, dry with olives."

"Classed-up Mistress. I dig. We'll be at our table. See you soon for fun and games."

With that, he was gone.

And Sixx drove the rest of the way also feeling it slightly sucked that she'd have to have eyes everywhere, and not just on whatever show Maddox was intent to give that night.

It was more.

Stellan wasn't with her, and that definitely sucked.

Therefore Sixx decided, if this went on further than that night, she was going to let him in on it.

She wasn't sure it was prudent to have him around when she was working. But it was high time he knew what she was doing, precisely where she was doing it, and to give him the choice if he wanted to be in attendance for some of the action or not. He could definitely take care of himself in the unlikely event he'd have to. She wasn't going to invite him to hang with her every time she was out on a job. But this had to do with the part of their lives that brought them together.

This was different.

She parked in the Bolt's parking lot, and it was relatively early for the scene, just before nine at night, but it was already filling up.

She hit the reception desk, paid for her guest pass, and since her background check was on file and current, like the night before, she got through the process quickly.

She headed into the club, lights flashing, music blaring, and up the steps to see the trio seated at the table where they'd played last night.

Before moving their way, she took a long pause to check the dancefloor, the platform, the bars, to see if she could spot the man in the pictures, the dude who got turned off the night before or any of the girls.

No going.

Though Beardsley was stationed at his table with a woman between his legs.

God, she'd said not word one to the man, and she wanted to hand him his ass.

She did another scan before she headed to the Shiny Happy *Ménage À Trois* Tribe.

Sixx had marginally known the men prior to last night, but she had connected more fully with Molly at the Bolt because she was sweet, outgoing and a chatterbox.

However, walking up to them, for the first time, she fully took them in.

As noted, Diesel and Maddox were large. Maddox more compact, and shorter, but he was definitely burly. At maybe two or three inches taller than Maddox, Diesel's muscle could only be described as hulking.

Maddox had pitch-black hair, thick and wavy, onyx eyes, olive skin, a defined body liberally furred, including a thick bush around his cock that was impressive. He'd had pitch stubble last night but clearly he'd not only been gifted with significantly endowed man parts, he also had more than his fair share of testosterone in those big balls of his because today that stubble could better be described as a full beard.

Diesel had sandy-brown hair, longish and appealingly messy, and blue eyes under thick red-brown eyebrows. He was also stubbly, but not by much, and when she'd seen him naked in scenes before, she'd noted he had russet scatterings of body hair at chest, legs and forearms.

It wasn't a shocker why Holly liked playing pixie. She was petite, slender, but long-legged, and had a wild mane of auburn hair that went nearly down to her waist at the back in curls and waves that were layered and dipped to the middle in a V, probably to keep the weight manageable.

And tonight, as she approached, Sixx noted that the warlord theme was gone.

Maddox was wearing a black, short-sleeved Henley that, when Sixx got close, she saw since his free arm was thrown wide around the back of a chair, he actually had to snip at the inside seams of the sleeves so it didn't cut off his circulation at his bulky biceps. He'd paired this with a thick, black belt with a low-hanging end strap, faded jeans and motorcycle boots.

Diesel was in a lightweight, white, long-sleeve shirt, untucked, also faded jeans with the addition of what looked like natural fraying from age at the thighs and knees and brown cowboy boots.

Molly looked adorable in a very low cut denim dress, with that cut going all the way down to a high waist that led to a flouncy, full, but short skirt. The dress was held up by denim cords that went through loops at the tips of the bodice and over her shoulders. Her hair was piled high in a messy bunch on her head with lots of tendrils floating around her neck and chest.

And as she sat on a chair between her men, leaned into Maddox with his arm around her shoulders, her legs lifted and draped over Diesel's thigh, she looked alarmingly spaced out.

"Is Molly okay?" Sixx asked when she stopped at the group.

Diesel shot her one of those impertinent grins he should consider patenting.

"Seems I earned an interesting night," he shared. "My service has started, and so Molly doesn't feel left out while Mad goes at me, Mad ordered it, and we ate her out and fucked her before we left. She came six times."

"Seven," Molly mumbled.

"Sorry, baby," D murmured and shot another grin at Sixx. "Seven."

Maddox reached out with his free arm, lifted the chair he'd had that arm draped around, angled it toward their tribe, and then slammed it down before moving his reach to the table and pushing a martini glass toward her.

The warlord gear might be gone, but the warlord vibe clearly remained, at least in communication style. Sixx read that particularly as *Sit* as well as *Drink*.

She sat.

"Got any news?" Maddox rumbled.

"Yes," she told him and pulled her phone out of her cleavage.

For her part, she was Mistress Sixx again, wearing a strapless, black leather bustier that was just a band of material that swelled up higher above her breasts, but dipped slightly lower at her back. She wore this with a matching pencil skirt with a high slit up the front, her platinum choker, her diamond studs, and a pair of black and silver, stiletto-heeled sandals.

She didn't carry a purse at clubs unless she could lock it up somewhere.

So that meant phone, keyfob and card wallet had to have a place against skin under leather.

And she was adept at that.

She pulled up her texts and turned the phone out to the trio with the best picture Tucker had taken, zoomed out.

The men leaned forward to study it, and since Molly was attached to them, she came with.

"Got someone helping me on the legwork with this, and he got photos of money changing hands," she informed them. "You guys will be busy, but I have to keep an eye out for this one. If he comes, odds are, the pay in that photo is for play. I need to get a shot of him here so I can put that together for Josh and Barclay."

The men nodded, and both immediately turned eyes to the club like they were looking for the guy.

Yes. She could maybe partner up with both of them in future.

Molly stared at the picture looking mildly skeeved out.

"Went back earlier, set up our room," Maddox mutely boomed, which apparently was his normal talking voice, not just his getting-jacked-and-good voice, though it sounded even more attractive when he was the latter. "Had a look around. Two girls already being given the business. Not that guy," he bobbed his head toward the phone that Sixx had lowered. "And the three asshole DMs are on."

"So Barclay isn't here tonight," she surmised.

"My guess, no," Maddox replied. "And shit will undoubtedly go extreme. Molly says she'll keep an eye with you while we're back there."

She shook her head. "Especially with those three DMs on, this has to look natural. You guys doing your thing with me an invited observer. I can't risk Beardsley being tipped Josh has moved forward with doing something about his shit. Don't worry. I'm good at observing without appearing to do it."

Maddox jerked up his chin.

D muttered, "Gotcha."

"So business as usual," she told them.

Maddox stared at her like he wanted to burn holes through her with his eyes.

D grinned his grin.

A couple of somebodies wanted to get the party started.

"Just so you know, if I have to move, I *will* move," she asserted, "to get a shot. If this guy is a john, I need a picture of him. But also if shit is going down that's out of line. Even if the DMs don't stop it, it's a Dom's responsibility to step in when play is out of hand. No one will question it. But like any club, if it's serious extreme without true consent or it's breaking rules, it will be investigated."

The trio nodded as one, well, in a way. Maddox just jerked up his chin again.

"One thing," Maddox pushed out like a grunt.

"Yes?" Sixx asked.

"I'm on for you tonight. I'm workin' my boy, but we're all in this with you, Sixx. So Diesel knows how it might go down. Something happens, you need meat at your back, you tap in and I'm there." His full lips spread in a slow, striking, nasty-awesome smile that promised interesting things for D's future. "If I need to take care of business with you, D can wait."

"Word," D murmured, his blue eyes dancing even in the dark.

"Thanks, boys. A six-pack as payback for when this is over seems lame so we'll negotiate something appropriate when this crap is done," Sixx replied.

"Babe, trust us, no payback necessary," Maddox declared. "You hadn't approached our woman, we were talking about doin' something anyway."

"And straight up," D added. "Last night, even on the job, you made lovin' more fun, and I'm guessing we'll get that tonight too, even if you have to go off and deal with a fuckwad."

She lifted her drink to them in a salute while it cemented in her mind she liked these guys.

All of them.

She took a sip.

"Can I ask a favor, though?" Maddox requested.

"Shoot," Sixx invited.

Maddox didn't hesitate, indicating the glass in her hand with another nod of his head.

"Suck that back and quick, Mistress Sixx. I got ass to fuck."

twenty-four

Inspired

SIXX

"Stations six and seven, right beside each other," Molly whispered to her as they moved through the sliding glass door to the room the trio had booked for the evening.

They'd made a good request for space. Sixx surveyed the area and the two mostly serviceable but comfortable-looking armchairs that had been set side-to-side at a slight angle to the room. With Sixx sitting in the outside one, she'd have direct visual on all of station six and most of station seven.

She nodded to Molly, murmuring, "Thanks, babe," as Maddox ordered, "Boots off. Shirt open and on. Edge of the vault. Jeans to thighs."

Molly gave her a bright-eyed, excited smile and moved to the small seating area.

Sixx carried the remains in her martini glass there and settled in.

From there, she watched D saunter casually to the narrow end of a padded vault, undoing the buttons on his shirt as he moved, not exactly appearing like he was chomping at the bit, not wasting any time either.

"How often do you guys play?" Sixx asked Molly as she watched Diesel.

"At the Bolt, if life schedules work, twice a week. And if it happens, it has to be twice a week, one after the other," she answered, and Sixx looked to her. "One night for D to go at Mad. One night for Mad to have D." Molly grinned at her. "We have fun at home, but Bolt nights usually go all night, so we don't do it very often or we wouldn't get a lot of sleep."

Sixx grinned back and turned her attention again to D.

He'd made it to the vault, had his shirt undone and was bent to pull off his boots and socks. When he did, he tossed them away. He then worked the jeans, pulling them down over the molded rounds of a superior ass, widening his stance so they caught on his bulky thighs. Positioned, he rested his hands on the vault.

He was at an angle to her, but she mostly had his back, and his cock apparently was hard, so lifted. In other words she couldn't see it. But his heavy sac was full and high. He was hung that way beautifully.

Though what he was not was trussed. At least not at his balls.

But it appeared he'd come prepared.

As in, pre-lubed. Liberally.

Probably a good call.

Maddox was bent over a new bag of tricks, this one a large, black duffel on the floor beside Molly's chair.

Sixx looked back to D to see his head turned to look over his shoulder at Maddox. He must have felt her attention because he looked to her and winked.

Okay, maybe in a totally-platonic-if-you-didn't-count-watching-him-participate-in-kinky-sex kind of way, she was thinking she loved this guy.

She tipped her lips up at him and then looked away, taking this golden opportunity when nothing was happening to fake-offhandedly glance around the outside playroom space.

As she did, she took in the emaciated, glassy-eyed girl getting almost vanilla worked by a shortish man with a beer belly in station six. She also saw a girl whose face was obstructed giving a blowjob in station seven. Last, she clocked two of the three DMs, getting a good look at them for future tattling.

"Bud, you know that ain't right," Maddox growled, and Sixx turned her attention back to the vault.

Doing so, she caught Maddox shoving a hand into D's back forcefully, driving him to his forearms on the vault.

He ran a hand over the ass now extended to him.

"There it is," he murmured.

He took his hand from D's ass and calmly tossed the tail of D's shirt up so it was folded over around his shoulder blades, leaving the rest of his back bare.

"There it is," Maddox murmured a repeat, his tone different, and Sixx sensed Molly, whose sexed-out vibe had been very slowly retreating, go instantly alert.

She also noted D was no longer cool and laidback, though anticipatory.

His ass and thighs had both visibly tensed.

"Oh my," Molly whispered.

"What?" Sixx whispered back.

"I should have known," Molly kept whispering.

"What?" Sixx repeated, also still whispering.

Molly spared her but a brief glance, saying, "It's going to be an *awesome* night."

Sixx looked back at the vault to see Maddox running his hands slowly over the exposed skin on D's body, back, ribs, sides, ass, crack, outer thighs, inner thighs. He stopped cupping balls.

"Mad," D said quietly, warily.

"You bought it, bro," Maddox said gently, massaging those balls.

"Fuck," D hissed.

"Awesome," Molly breathed.

Sixx didn't understand what was happening, and she watched closely to see if she could get a lock on it when Maddox went in with both hands between D's thighs, stroking cock, massaging balls, and getting low so he could run the edge of his teeth over one cheek of Diesel's ass.

Diesel's head bent back.

He liked it like that.

Maddox must have sensed the move because in his position now at the back of D's thigh he surely couldn't see it, but he still growled, "You bow that head when your Master's at you, motherfucker."

D bowed his head.

Lord God.

So pretty.

Maddox spent some time coddling and caressing his boy's exposed flesh with hands, fingertips, lips, teeth and tongue, and Sixx found this was not good because it *was* good, and it would be expected she'd want to watch it. This meaning she might not have times to look away and search for picture man, take stock of the DMs, or keep track of what was happening in stations six and seven.

She got a shot when Maddox moved away from a slightly trembling but otherwise unmoving D and headed toward the bag.

When she looked, she saw no change in players in those stations and no extreme play, but she did manage to see the third DM and give him a good assessment, fortunately without him noticing.

It was the crack and grunt that brought her attention back to the vault.

Maddox was off to D's side, wielding a long, thick, leather strap and doing it with no small amount of skill, landing blows on buttocks, thighs, and on Diesel's lower back.

D's ass jumped with each strike, and Maddox wasn't feeling stingy, going at him until D had no choice to be up on his toes and was visibly gritting his teeth.

He was also visibly harder, his thick, veined cock hanging lower so Sixx could see it because of the weight.

It got to be too much, and his head automatically shot back, which made Maddox start to move in, dropping the strap. With quick, expert hands, he undid his belt and yanked it free of its loops so fast, the end cracked the air like a whip when it was free. He folded it once, twice.

Putting a hand to the back of D's head, shoving it face first into the vault, Maddox slapped Diesel's ass with quick whacks of the folded-over belt, rumbling, "Where's that head belong?"

"Bowed, Maddox," D grunted through more blows.

Maddox didn't relent. "You feel heat in that fine ass?"

"Fuck yeah," D groaned.

"Guess what, Diesel?" Maddox let out in what was his version of a purr, which was more of a rolling grumble. "You made me wait to blow, but you're comin' with me every time tonight. I'm gonna make you blow," *sharp crack*, "and blow," *brutal crack*, "and *blow*," *vicious crack*.

"Fuck," D bit off.

The belt hit the floor, Maddox clipped out, "Molly, baby, condom," as he worked his jeans in preparation for literally starting the festivities off with a bang. He positioned right behind his boy, wrapped his massive, now-freed dick with a hand, aimed it, and slammed in.

D's entire torso came up to hands in the vault, head thrown back, veins pounding out in his neck as a low roar pumped from his throat.

"You got your monster," Maddox taunted, jacking into him so brutally, the heavy vault was rocking. "Now take my dick and *bow your goddamned head, motherfucker.*"

D bowed his head, and with jaw hard and pulsing, took a brutal fucking as Molly moved in and handed Maddox a condom without the wrapping.

He took it, jerked his head to her, she went in and he bent down and gave her a deep, wet kiss as he kept hammering ass.

When he let her mouth go, she gave him a sweet smile that he took in with warm eyes before he turned back to Diesel, slipped a hand around the front, expertly rolled a condom on D's now-engorged, bouncing cock, then Maddox planted his hand in D's back, shoving him chest to vault.

"Fuck yeah," D murmured, starting to pound back into his fucking.

Maddox slowed his roll but kept stroking deep, with D now meeting him, Maddox's hands moving to his hips. "You love this monster?"

"Love it, Maddox," Diesel huffed.

"Only my boy can take that kinda heat. Only my fuckin' boy can take me to the root." He slid in fully. "How you like that, D? How much does my boy love being full of his monster?"

"Keep fucking me with it," D pushed out.

A punishing thrust sent a powerful grunt driving up D's throat, his head jerking back, but he bent it again immediately.

"That an answer?" Maddox demanded.

"I love it, Maddox. You know I fuckin' love taking that monster."

Maddox pulled out to the tip and teased, working his hips so D only got a couple of inches.

"*That* monster?" Maddox queried.

"*My* monster, Mad. Want it back. Keep taking my ass."

"Can't wait for my cum, can you, D? How bad you want me to blow in you?"

"Bad, Maddox, shit, *fuck*." Diesel's hips were writhing, seeking attention. "Fuck me, give me my monster, your cum, give it, my man, blow inside me."

"How hard you gonna take me?"

"As hard as you can fuck me."

"How hard you *wanna* take me?"

"Hard, Maddox, deep."

"You know better than that, D. *How hard you want your monster up your ass?*"

It was guttural with need when D begged, "Fuck me raw, Mad. Please. *Christ.* Fuck me so hard, I feel like you're gonna split me in two."

"Damn straight," Maddox grunted, got down to business again, shockingly having been holding back, now giving Diesel what he asked for. Pistoning inside him spectacularly, savagely, but this time reaching around and jacking D's cock, words disappeared as low, glorious male noises of effort, excitement and carnality filled the air.

It was when Maddox was jacking with one hand, holding D down to take it with his other hand planted firm in D's back when finally Maddox groaned, "Want my cum?"

"Fuck yeah," D growled.

"Take it," Maddox ordered.

"Give it," D returned thickly.

They both gave it, both of them coming near simultaneously, Maddox's orgasm tipping D's, and thunder filled the room with the low, masculine snarls of their climaxes.

Maddox could not be recovered, and D definitely wasn't, when he pulled out to D's surprised, aftershocks-jolting-his-body-muted grunt.

He smacked Diesel's ass sharply and ordered, "Take your position for your spanking."

With an expert eye, Sixx took in the state of red at D's ass, thighs and back and wondered if a spanking was wise.

"Keep the jeans," Maddox said as an afterthought, now standing at the duffel where he was accepting a wetted, sage-green hand towel that Molly was offering him out of a Ziploc bag.

Still fully dressed with his massive cock exposed through an open fly, he bathed his dick with it as D, jeans hiked up but undone and held up with a hand at the front, moved to a padded kneeling bench sitting beside a straight-back chair.

He did this without looking at her or Molly, which Sixx found odd after that wink.

He'd gotten what he wanted, what he obviously enjoyed, thoroughly. He told her he was aiming for it, actually crowed about earning it.

The non—eye contact was concerning.

But since he wasn't giving it, it wasn't her place as an invited observer to players who knew each other and their style of play far, far better than her to push it to make sure all was okay.

Regardless, nothing extreme had gone down. It was a vicious but magnificent fucking, but he obviously liked it like that, so she couldn't imagine there was a problem.

Maybe D went into his head in a scene. Most subs did. It was just that D going there this quickly when he was so full of swaggering confidence surprised her. She thought it'd take a whole lot more to break a switch, but still a Dom who was now subbing like Diesel.

At this opportunity of a lull in the action, Sixx sucked back the rest of her martini, put the glass on the floor by her chair, got up and moved to lean against the window, this affording her a better view into station seven.

Things were getting more serious in both rooms. Play was going deep, but not out of bounds.

Though she found it disquieting that a DM now had stationed

himself at the wall between the two rooms, and he didn't seem ready to move anytime soon.

Worse, he'd caught her movement and also caught her eye.

Shit.

She lifted her chin.

He glared at her.

Asshole.

She turned her attention back to the room to see Maddox now seated in the chair and pushing D down, chest to thighs. D's jeans were again over his ass, his shirt again hiked up to his shoulders.

Molly was there too, crouched and reaching between D's legs, switching out condoms, her touch making her man's ass and thighs twitch.

"How you doin', bro?" Maddox asked.

"Fuckin great, Mad," D ground out.

Sixx watched as Maddox smoothed a palm down over spine, reaching the end, curving in and taking hold of his boy with two fingers planted deep up his ass. He lifted him slightly in this hold to D gusting out a cut-off grunt, then settling him back down.

Oh yes.

Payback was a bitch.

"There you are, all ready for big monster daddy," Maddox taunted good-naturedly.

"Fuck you," D replied.

"Not until tomorrow, bud," Maddox returned.

He then landed a relatively tame smack on one cheek of D's ass that, even tame, set D to jumping. But then Maddox massaged it, apparently roughly, because him going at that deeply striped flesh with those long, powerful fingers set D squirming.

"Gonna be all up in here a lot tonight," Maddox carried on conversationally. Smacked Diesel's other cheek and massaged that. "So tomorrow night I'm thinkin' I'll be in the mood to allow you to have a go at me."

With that, not giving D a chance to reply, a spanking commenced. And outside of the fact Maddox had more power than most behind his blows, and D was already significantly welted, but the low, gruff noises he was making and the way he was rubbing his hardening dick against Maddox's jeans-clad thigh any chance he got said he liked it, it was standard enough play.

So Sixx pretended her mind was wandering.

She turned back to the windows and scanned the entire space. Taking time to watch the DMs at work, not seeing them doing anything amiss. Taking in players. Looking to see if she could find the guy who got propositioned last night. Or the one in the pictures. But keeping her attention off where the paid play was happening, so if the DM that was still there thought her nosy, he would think it was generally.

She'd heard the spanking had stopped and Maddox had given some other orders, but she didn't look back because she saw Beardsley walking along the passageway at the opposite side of the central play area.

She kept her eyes on him, not giving a fuck if the DMs caught her, and watched him go straight to the one standing outside the stations.

They had a few words without Beardsley even looking into the rooms where his girls were getting worked.

But Sixx did.

All copacetic, if you didn't count the fact it was for the most part nonconsensual and in all parts totally illegal.

She let out an impatient breath and was sure to look away before Beardsley broke it off with his DM and headed down the passageway outside their room.

She turned back to the play and saw D off his kneeling bench but still on his knees, shirt on but again yanked up his back, jeans at his thighs, now in front of Maddox, offering his man a fantastic view, and that man was taking it in. Diesel was bent between

Maddox's spread legs, hands to the sides of his man's hips, sucking big dick.

After avoiding her gaze earlier, Sixx surveyed Diesel closely and with an expert eye.

Maddox had a fistful of D's hair, his other hand tight on the back of his neck, and he was obviously physically controlling the action. But D's eyes were closed, and he gave every appearance he got off sucking cock, not only through his expression but from the rigid state of the meat hanging heavy between his spread legs, which were bound by denim.

While Sixx watched, those blue eyes opened. They looked up at Maddox with something deep and abiding that suddenly stirred Sixx, not sexually, but in a warm way. This was before D's eyes flashed, like an unspoken dare, which bought him Maddox forcing Diesel to take him deeper and do it faster, Diesel groaning, his eyes closing again, this time with open rapture, arching his back, tipping his ass, his fingers clenching into his man's hips.

Yes.

He was definitely all right.

Sixx headed back to her chair by Molly.

After she was seated, Molly asked quietly, "Anything going?"

Sixx kept watching a fabulous blowjob, particularly appreciating Diesel's hollowed-out cheeks, and answered, "Nope."

"I really hope we can stop this guy, and soon," Molly told her. "We were all totally freaked out, in a good way, that you turned out to be a private investigator, and Mad and D were stoked you let them in on this job. It's been really bothering them. They didn't wanna look like dicks and go straight to Clay if what they thought was happening wasn't happening. In the beginning, though, I think Mad was worried that Clay and Josh might be in on it. They were thinking of blowing off the club, even if it would mean we'd lose the money for membership, since they don't do refunds. It was after we realized Clay wasn't around when the extreme stuff happened, or kinda hasn't been around a lot at all recently, that they figured Pete and Josh were acting alone. Then we heard Josh and Pete had that fight, so we figured Josh wasn't thinking good thoughts either. That's when they were going to move in. They even talked about tipping off the cops. But then you called, and it sure made them happy somebody was gonna do something."

Even if Sixx didn't already know it, that sealed it.

These were good people.

"Some coincidences are good ones," Sixx told her.

"Yeah," she agreed.

"Baby, come here," Maddox called while forcing himself out of D's mouth by pushing him up to his knees.

Molly gave Sixx bright eyes while getting out of her seat, whispering, "Yay."

She moved toward the action.

Sixx's attention moved out of the room.

And it was then she saw the girl in station six was alone, the guy was gone. She had a robe on and her head bent to her phone.

The DM was still outside those stations.

But the girl was not putting on street clothes or even BDSM gear, and she wasn't exiting the room.

Guess she had to do her full schedule before she got her fix.

Shit.

"Yeah, take her there, motherfucker," Maddox grunted, and Sixx looked back to them.

Molly was now seated in the chair, D's arms curved around her hips, his face shoved up under her raised skirt between her legs, his activities there and his situation muffling his noises, his ass again getting fucked by his man.

"Took your cum three times last night, D," Maddox told him. "Slept with your cock up my ass, my cock buried in our baby's pussy. But you wouldn't let me fuck her. You took my ass all night long to keep your dick hard, making me hard, but you didn't let me fuck our girl," he recounted. "All goddamned night long, in service to you, takin' your cock," he said, definitely at that precise moment getting his back. "Woke up with you up my ass, you didn't release my service, only then did you let me fuck our Molly, but only with you jacking inside me, and I went to work with fresh cum up my ass."

D grunted unintelligibly.

Molly moaned.

Maddox reached around and started stroking D's swollen, low-hanging dick. "Tonight, boy, you're gonna sleep with your monster in your mouth and you're gonna keep it hard. All night."

D groaned, and his hips jerked back into cock.

He liked it like that too.

"But Molly?" Maddox kept at him. "She's gonna be strapped in, D. Strapped in and buried deep. All night, you're gonna take our sweet Molly, and what she's got for you, she's *never* not hard."

D's arms pulsed around Molly's hips and she whimpered, at what was happening or in anticipation of what was going to happen or both.

It didn't really matter. It all worked spectacularly.

"Your service in the morning will start with me on my back, you on your knees between my legs, bent in service to your Master, blowin' your man, takin' my cum down your throat with Molly fucking you up the ass," Maddox shared.

D's body spasmed.

"Yeah, my man, I know. You love takin' us at both ends," Maddox rumbled approvingly. "But that isn't it, motherfucker. I'm gonna eat breakfast and suck your cock, and I figure that'll get me hard again, so *you'll* be starting the day with fresh cum buried deep."

The one-upmanship was seriously something.

Maddox then got down to business, had his shit tight, and not long after, Sixx found herself witness to a three-way simultaneous orgasm.

Exceptional.

After a short recovery, D was pulled up to sit on his man's cock while Molly straightened her skirt and moved in to her men. First, she made out with D. Then, with his face stuffed in her tits, over his shoulder, she made out with Maddox.

"Almost the best taste in the world," Maddox whispered when they were done. "Tasting you from him in my mouth. Only thing better, having you right against my tongue."

"Love you, Mady," she replied.

"Love you too, baby."

She pulled back and cupped D's dazed face. "Love you, my D."

"Love you too, my Molly," he muttered, seeming to be attempting, but failing at focusing on her.

You could still tell he meant it because he didn't fail at sounding sweet.

Molly took the used condom from D and dealt with it before she moved back to the chairs.

During this time, Sixx ascertained station six was still vacant of a new client, and things were culminating in station seven before Molly collapsed in the chair beside her.

Sixx turned to her.

"You good?" Sixx asked a stupid question with a knowing grin.

"Best ever," Molly mumbled with a goofy smile, eyes aimed to her men. But her face was soft, not just sated from coming, but with something more emotional. "And I'm gonna get better," she finished quietly.

Sixx looked instantly to the boys.

My, my, my.

D was still sitting on his boy's dick, jeans still tight at his splayed thighs, his shirt Maddox had spread open so it was almost hanging off his broad shoulders to expose the muscled magnificence of him fully, from corded throat to thick thighs.

Maddox's arms were around him, one rough thumb rubbing a nipple, one veined hand sliding over boxed abs.

"Maddox," D muttered, looking away from Molly and Sixx, gaze aimed at the floor.

"Sit on your monster and hush," Maddox whispered affectionately, now stroking the area around D's glistening, still-partially-hard cock, an area which Sixx belatedly noted had been shaved.

Maddox was in that same thought process.

"Like you smooth," he murmured.

D said nothing.

"When you were up inside me last night, D, loved feeling that smooth against me every time you filled me," Maddox kept going.

D remained silent, but his throat convulsed with a forced swallow.

"Gonna keep you smooth," Maddox went on.

"Right," D said low, but terse.

"Like you got this, tie you, shave you, blow you, eat you, fuck you," Maddox kept at him.

D was silent, but his big body shook with a faint tremble.

He'd gotten off on that.

"I like how you work me, love my boy's ingenuity, but you're gonna stay shaved for me because we both know who's Master."

Whoa.

That was news.

Dayum.

D didn't reply.

Maddox swept a hand up D's chest.

"Love this body," he murmured.

Suddenly, what was happening outside that room disappeared, and Sixx's attention was riveted to the players.

"Maddox," D whispered.

Maddox pulsed up, and D's rugged, guarded face smoothed out, that's how much he liked it.

Though it was more.

It was how much he loved being intimately connected to the man who held one half of his heart.

"In a minute, I'm gonna pull out of this sweet ass, and you're gonna go to the table and spread yourself out for me like you know I like it."

"Mad—"

"Then I'm gonna do you," Maddox veritably cooed into D's ear, his voice now a gorgeous rough velvet. "Fuck yeah, my D. I'm gonna *do you*. With you laid out for your Master, your Maddox, I'm gonna take my time with that body. Then I'm gonna fuck you and jack you, looking at this fuckin' beautiful goddamned body, that's all..." he tweaked a nipple, making D twitch on his cock, "*fuckin'*" he cupped D's balls tenderly and on a slight squeeze finished, "*mine.*"

D's ass cheeks clenched his man's cock as he swallowed down a groan.

Maddox put hands to D's hips and gently pushed him up. "Go, baby. And take off the jeans. But leave the shirt. You know how I like it spread open for me."

Head bowed, D got to his feet and dropped his jeans on the way to a padded-top, double-wide, wood-based table, climbing up. He lay on his back, cocking a heavy leg high and dropping it to the side, the other leg bent only slightly, also falling to the side, pulling his shirt open to expose himself full body from throat to shoulders to feet.

Serious as all hell, that view was resplendent.

Diesel stared at the ceiling, his chest rising and falling deeply, and Sixx knew that kind of breathing.

It came from the fact he wanted what was coming so bad he couldn't stand it.

And he was terrified of it.

Maddox had also gotten up and disrobed fully, exposing his magnificent, attractively hairy body, before he headed toward the table.

Molly leaned into Sixx. "They're both bi," she said in a very low voice that Sixx knew she didn't want the boys to hear.

But the men wouldn't hear. They were in a new zone, *the* zone, the best there was.

Or Maddox was.

Diesel...

Well, Sixx had a feeling Maddox would get him there.

At least she hoped so.

But Sixx had no idea why Molly was sharing such obvious information.

"Mad is at peace with it. Gets off on it. Says he's got the best of both worlds. All worlds, actually, since he takes it and gives it. D, he loves us both, but the at peace part? Not so much," Molly continued.

Sixx looked to her, startled.

He wore hides. He worked Maddox openly, cheerfully, expertly.

And he was subbing magnificently.

How could he not be at peace with his sexuality?

Whoa.

Well, apparently that explained why he didn't look Sixx's and Molly's way during play.

Molly shook her head, looking suddenly sad. "At home. At the club. It's all good. We're ... what we have ... it's so, *so* good, Mistress Sixx. I mean, they fight. I fight with Mad or D, mostly Mad, he can be so bossy. But we've been together so long, we're just there, so that doesn't happen so much anymore." She flipped a hand indicating the world at large. "It's out there."

She trailed off, seemed to get lost in melancholy thoughts, came back to the room and continued speaking.

"My D works road construction. All those guys talking about tagging ass and calling gays faggots and all that horrible, dreadful stuff, every day, all day long. It gets in his head. But mostly it stems from the fact that his parents are jerks and his dad says stuff like that all the time. Talking smack about movie stars who are out, just stuff like that. They think Mad is our roommate. And sometimes I wish he'd bend D over the couch, take his pants down and fuck him hard right in front of them. Not so they'll get it. I don't care if they get it. They're awful. They don't deserve D, or me, or Maddox. But so they'll go away and *stay away*. I want it to be like when my folks are around, or Mad's. They might not totally get it, but they love us all and want us in their lives, feel lucky to have one extra instead of what they would have if we weren't who we are to each other. So when they're around, it's amazing. D's folks, I don't want to say it, but they earned it. I feel actual hate."

She looked to the table, back at Sixx, and gave her more heavy.

"They never kiss just to kiss. They kiss me all the time, as you can see. Not each other. They say it's respect for me. And I think they're trying to be sweet, but it's silly. And just an excuse. They're like that though. Here, in the club, they never display me. They might eat me or fuck me or make me suck them, but they never show the private parts of my body. They own it, and that's their prerogative, and they're both crazy possessive. I let Mistresses work them, never them working subs. But Mistresses they want, I let it happen when they want it. Not often. She has to be special. Like you. They'd never let another Dom touch me. I don't mind at all. They're so totally enough for me. But that's how they are, both of them. Bottom line, I think it's gentlemanly."

"I noticed that about them," Sixx responded equally quietly.

She nodded and kept talking.

"But Maddox *nor* Diesel ever take anyone else's cock. Not *ever*. Mad suggested it once, I think because he was pissed Diesel holds back, and D lost his mind. Worst fight they ever had. I thought it would break us up. But Maddox figured it out then. He got it. Diesel's response said it all. To Maddox. To me. Not to D. Still, they don't kiss, unless I ask them to when one of them is fucking me and the other is watching. The minute their lips touch, though, they go at it. It makes me sad. Sad for my Maddox. Sad for my D."

"Oh, honey," Sixx whispered, hearing all this, sad for *all* of them.

"I should have known the way D worked Mad last night, Mad would go with this. You're not getting the D he expected you to get. Usually, Mad works him, and D's still cocky. In your face. He loves getting fucked and taking it hard and doesn't mind anyone in the life knowing it. It's like a challenge to him, like it proves he's really *a man* when you can see he is, he doesn't have to prove that to anybody. Even when Maddox is inside him, he's spurring him on to *really* go at him. Bring the pain. Take him rough."

Another hand flip and she kept going.

"This. For him. It's the most difficult for D to take. And it's probably worse for him, you here. They both really like you. Respect you. But in D's head, as crazy as it is since he doesn't feel the same about Mad or anyone else, he's gonna be thinking you'll think less of him, like his folks would. Like the guys on his crew would. But this work, what Mad's gonna be doing, it's my favorite. Diesel's too, but he won't admit it. Mad will ask me for permission to kiss him. Just wait, Mistress. It's beautiful."

Sixx nodded, glancing at the table and immediately looking back to Molly, because what was happening on that table was public, but excruciatingly private.

"He loves it. D. What he did to Mad last night," Molly carried on. "Because he loves it but more, he loves how much Maddox gets off on it. He's always trying to take him higher and higher. Saying that, he knows the further he pushes Mad, the closer he comes to Maddox giving him this as payback. And subconsciously, this is where he's hoping it will go."

She took in a breath, leaned slightly closer, and kept going.

"Maddox is our Master. He lets D Dom me because D needs that, it's the way he is, hetero-speaking, and Mad loves me and Diesel. But D works Mad because Mad gets off on it, and knows D does too, so Mad lets him. But Mad owns D. You could probably tell last night that all that was a run-up to what's happening here, and D knows it. Mad is not about creativity. He's hardcore and uncomplicated. Fuck. Come. Fuck harder. Come harder. But when it's just us, Mad always makes love to me. And when it's just D and me, he always makes love to me. It's only times like now Maddox gets to make love to Diesel. Even when they go at each other at home, not at play, D needs it rough. Like Mad taking him that way somehow is twisted in his head that he's *taking* it and Diesel isn't *giving* it. Though D, he gets in the zone a lot, like he's in another world, another life, and he makes love to Maddox, and Mad and me don't say anything because we don't want to bring D's attention to it. If we did, it might make him stop."

Sixx chanced a look at the table and saw an enraptured face with a black beard sucking a cock he adored with D's back arched so Sixx couldn't see his face, but his long fingers were buried tenderly in Maddox's dark hair.

"See how beautiful they are?" Molly murmured, tone filled with marvel.

"I see," Sixx agreed.

Molly fell silent.

Sixx watched Maddox release D's cock, lave affection on his balls while he stroked his man's dick with his hand, nibbling and licking the skin all around his privates, then he went back to business, this time deep throating.

D's ass clenched on a low, long groan, and he started gently fucking Maddox's face.

Maddox buried two fingers up Diesel's ass, earning another groan, and openly, blissfully took his face-fucking while he tenderly stroked inside.

God.

Very beautiful.

Sixx swallowed and decided to take that time to give them privacy, doing it to force her attention away, definitely not think about how sad all this suddenly was, remind herself why she was there and check out the scene.

Luck finally struck because the girl in station seven was outside of the room, standing with the DM, wearing platforms, a pleather miniskirt and halter, hair mussed, clumsily fisting what the DM was handing off to her.

Sixx honed in but was too far away to see what it was. However the fact that they were trying to be covert about it meant that it was something to be covert about.

Dope.

So the DMs passed it off, which meant maybe they also helped with the dealing.

She was so totally tattling.

The girl skedaddled, probably beelining it to the ladies' loo.

Before Sixx got caught watching, she turned back to the room to find Maddox now up on splayed knees that cradled Diesel's hips. He was inside D, who was still on his back, both his legs now cocked high and opened wide, spread out for his man. Maddox was stroking D's cock and lovingly fucking his ass.

He turned his head to Molly.

"Baby?" he called.

"Of course," she said dotingly.

Maddox needed no further encouragement, took ass, stroked cock, bent in, and devoured D's mouth.

For his part, D caught him at the back of the neck in a tight hold and kept him there, undulating his hips to meet the thrusts he was taking, to deepen the strokes at his cock as they kissed like the lovers they were.

Molly was so right.

It was beautiful.

Things started to get critical, going faster, harder, deeper, and Maddox broke the kiss so both of them could breathe, but he didn't go very far away.

"Yeah, baby?" he whispered.

"Yeah, Mad," D whispered back.

Yes.

Beautiful.

Maddox moved to slow, smooth, thorough strokes, obviously wanting to draw out the experience, give himself more, give D more.

"Love your ass." D arched into him and Maddox groaned, pulling hard on his man's dick. "Love this cock."

Unfortunately, this tripped something in Diesel. His hand, still at Maddox's neck, suddenly fisted in his hair, and Sixx sensed the change immediately.

And automatically mourned it.

Maddox sure didn't miss it.

"Need it rough?" he asked instantly.

"Yeah," D grunted.

"My boy need to submit?" Maddox went on.

"Fuck yeah," D groaned.

Abruptly, Maddox straightened and looked down at D, placing his hands on the insides of his knees, spreading him impossibly wider.

With no choice, D's ass tilted up with the move, and a sound of pained hunger rocketed from his chest as Maddox started pumping in harder.

"You gonna submit?" Maddox asked, his thrusts now fast and going wild.

"If you make me," Diesel dared.

Maddox pulled out, flipped D violently, hauled up his hips, and bumped his thighs wide with a knee. With him in position, Maddox slammed up his ass, mounting him fully by curving over his back, hand curled around the back of D's neck and staying there, forcing him face down to the table, pounding into him.

"Yeah?" he bit off.

"Yeah," D pushed out.

Sixx thought the loss of what they'd had was wretched.

She also thought Maddox giving it up because Diesel needed him to was an amazing display of love.

"Who's up inside you?" Maddox demanded.

"You, Maddox."

Maddox started pummeling, each drive forcing a grunt from D. "Who?"

"Master. My Master's taking my ass."

"You like him up there?"

"Yeah. Fuck yeah."

"You need him up there?"

"Oh yeah, *fuck yeah*, need that monster cock."

"Whose cock?" Maddox demanded.

"Your cock."

Maddox started seriously pistoning, and Diesel's grunts started grating.

"Whose cock, goddammit?" Maddox pushed.

"My Master's cock. My ass needs my Master's cock. *I* need my Master's cock."

"So you submit?" Maddox asked.

"I submit, Mad."

"Then submit, D. Beg your Master to fuck your ass," Maddox ordered, even though he hadn't stopped doing just that.

"Take my ass. *Fuck it.* Fuck *me.* Please, Master, don't fucking stop. Keep goddamned *fucking me.*"

"Stay down, motherfucker," Mad ordered, put a hand into the table for leverage, the hand at D's neck he moved to his cock, and he jacked him and kept fucking him entirely differently than he'd been doing.

Sixx looked to Molly, who felt her gaze and gave Sixx her own.

"Still totes hot," she said softly. "But sad. Though it was nice having it while it lasted."

She was "totes" right.

"Up," Maddox ordered, gaining both women's eyes. "Hands behind your head."

D complied.

Maddox hauled him around so they had D's impressive front, not the men at their sides, doing this still connected, which was an awe-inspiring feat.

Maddox latched on to the dick and balls bobbing in front of him and went at them, pulling and squeezing both ruthlessly.

"*Christ*, yeah," D exploded, starting to move violently, meeting the thrusts at his ass.

"You know you're taking a huge-ass plug, keeping my cum inside you, wearing that home for me."

D just grunted and kept doing it.

"You gave me three loads last night, you take this one, we're done here. When I get you home, D, I'm bending you over the kitchen table at my seat, so I can think of having your ass there, full of me, while I eat, and I'll give you one more load. Now bow your fucking head when you're taking me."

D bowed his head, groaning, "I need to come, man."

"You're not gonna come."

"I need to come, Maddox."

"You're," deep, slow, brutal stroke that jolted D's entire body, "gonna," another, "*hold.*"

Back to pistoning.

"Fuck me," D growled.

"That's what I'm doin', my man."

"Condom," D bit out.

"No. You're gonna shoot for Molly. You're gonna give our girl your cum. We'll clean up after."

"Mad—"

"Take your monster. You love it. Take it."

"*Maddox—*"

"Tell me you love it."

"I love it," D grated, now bucking sadistically into the thrusts he was taking.

"Tell me you love my cock deep up your ass," Maddox commanded.

"I love your cock deep up my ass. Fuck *yeah*, I love it buried deep," D rasped out. "Fuck, Maddox, I need to *blow.*"

"Take it and hold."

"*Christ.*"

"Take it and *hold.*"

"Fuck, baby," D begged. "*Let me blow.*"

Maddox fucked a "baby" out of his man.

Sixx almost smiled.

And that did it.

"Take . . . my . . . *load,*" Maddox's last word was a groan as he blew and so he had to force out a coarse, "Go."

Maddox moved with him as D came fully up on his knees and arched madly, buttocks clenching his man so hard up his ass, through his orgasmic groans, Maddox's throat exploded with a harsh grunt. His head hiked back while D shouted out his climax, Maddox's unceasing hands pulling at him and squeezing him, and Diesel shot cum across the table phenomenally as they both experienced exquisite release.

Now that she was taking vitamins, Sixx needed to find out what these boys took. Whatever it was packed a punch.

Yowza.

They shook with their aftershocks, chests moving deeply, and the comedown took a while before Maddox slid a tender hand up D's chest, around to his back, where he shoved him down, face to the table, and kept stroking up his ass, now slowly.

It was then it hit Sixx that Maddox had given D everything Diesel had forced him to promise to give the night before.

Which was everything Diesel wanted to take.

He might not be creative, but God, he loved his man.

"Molly, baby, bring me Diesel's plug," Maddox ordered softly.

"Okay," she murmured.

Maddox looked down to D.

"Good?" he asked.

"Yeah, man," Diesel replied.

"Had a chance to think of payback?"

"Mind's been somewhat occupied, bro. So not yet, but it's gonna rock your world."

Maddox chuckled, still moving inside D, looking down at the man before him with a gentle face and love in his black eyes, something Sixx had not seen him give Diesel openly, except that sadly short time they were making love.

Then Maddox took his shot.

"You know I live for two things, this ass and her pussy."

There was a hesitation, a tightening of D's body, before he whispered, "I know, buddy."

He said no more, and because he didn't, the new look on Maddox's face tore at Sixx's heart.

God, they were killing her.

Molly arrived with the plug.

Maddox took it, and she sat on the edge of the table, running her fingers through D's hair, which caused him to turn his head and look up at her, keeping his position bowed in front of his Master, probably not cognizant of all that said, especially Maddox still moving inside him, claiming what was his in a moment of calm.

D gave Molly a grin.

"Hey, gorgeous," he said gently.

"Hey, my D," she replied, gazing at him adoringly.

Maddox pulled out, D's thighs tightened when he took his plug, and then Maddox slapped D's ass, giving him permission to be at ease. "Get dressed, my man, time for a drink, recuperation, and I'm back at you at home."

Diesel, Sixx noticed, gave Molly a hard kiss, not Maddox, and he didn't look at Sixx at all as he climbed off the table and headed to his jeans.

Molly set about cleaning up her man's cum.

Sixx rose from her chair and aimed her eyes out the window at nothing, giving them privacy to get themselves sorted.

Maddox caught her attention after he'd yanked on his jeans and started to move with shirt and boots in his hand toward Sixx, stopping close, looking at her and asking her like he didn't care about her answer.

"Work for you?"

Not willing herself to do it, but glad she did, she lifted her hand, laid it lightly on his chest and stared right into his eyes.

"Inspired," she whispered.

He glared at her for a beat before his black eyes melted. He lifted his free hand, curled his fingers around the back of hers at his chest, squeezed them lightly, dipped his chin then let her go.

Her hand dropped, and Maddox moved away.

Apparently aftercare was Molly's territory because she was leaning so heavily into D, both arms around his middle, his arm slung across her shoulders as they made their way to Sixx after D got dressed and Maddox had packed them up that it looked like she was holding him up.

D met her eyes like a dare. "Told you I'd buy it."

"You could give a class on taking an ass thrashing," she quipped. "In a variety of ways."

His eyes—weirdly cold and remote for the man she'd known somewhat meaningfully if only briefly, but had come to like a great deal—roamed her face.

Fortunately, he found what he needed there, his lips quirked in a shadow of his impudent grin, and he said, "Your last martini was on Mad. Your next is on me."

"How about my round?" she asked.

D looked genuinely offended.

"A woman buy a drink?" he queried, like that concept was foreign to him, foreign and repulsive.

"I do have money," she replied.

"That doesn't happen on our watch," Maddox chimed in, joining them, fingers curled around the duffel.

Their . . .

Watch?

"Oh for God's sake," Sixx snapped.

"Just give in. Seriously. Or we'll be standing here all night, and I need a daiquiri," Molly declared.

Before Sixx could reply, Maddox growled, gaze aimed over her shoulder, "Fuck. It's our guy."

Sixx whirled, looked into station seven . . .

And there he was.

The man in Tucker's pictures.

"Molly, baby, hit the bar," Diesel ordered. "Now."

Molly scooted, going directly to the sliding glass door and through it.

Sixx pulled her phone out of her cleavage, engaged it and the camera.

She turned back to the men.

"Ready, boys?"

"Fuck yeah," Diesel said.

Maddox had eyes to the window but jerked up his chin. "Let's roll."

twenty-five

Especially in This House

SIXX

In Sixx's experience, when you were going to be doing something someone might not want you to do, you didn't fuck around.

You just did it before they got the chance to try and stop you.

But you went in prepared that they might try and stop you so you could stop them from doing that.

So with the boys at her back, Sixx strolled right up to station seven like she owned the joint, phone raised, camera at the ready.

The DM clocked them before they got there, obviously, and went on alert.

Sixx ignored him, moved wide of him when they got close, and continued to ignore him when he clipped, "No cameras in the play area."

Apparently ready to rumble after worrying about this situation for as long as they had, although Sixx said nothing, D growled, "Fuck off."

The DM shifted her way, stupidly keeping his focus on Sixx. "I said no fucking cameras."

She got off a shot.

His hand darted out toward her phone as she got off another one.

He didn't catch hold but instead was slammed back to the glass, two big fists in his polo crunched at his chest by Diesel.

"What the fuck!" she heard shouted angrily, by a male voice off to her other side that was too close for her liking, as the DM tussled with D and yelled, "Get off me, man!"

Sixx kept taking shots of the man in station seven, who was now looking out the windows at her with big eyes, the girl with him blinking hazily at the action outside. At the same time she heard male noises at her side and knew Maddox had engaged another DM.

She let the boys do their work and decided to be thorough. If Barclay hadn't noticed, he needed to become aware of the state of the girls working for his partner. So she took several steps wide to the left, firing off shots of the still-berobed girl in station six, withered and wasted (the latter in more ways than one—seriously, the girl in room seven looked relatively healthy whereas this one was totally strung out, carried too many brands, and was scored all over with the scarred remains of blood play) and waiting for her next trick.

"Sixx, watch it!" Maddox grunted, obviously still grappling.

Sixx whirled just before a hand grabbed for her phone, but she did it prepared. Since her arm was already raised, she cocked it higher and let fly with her elbow, striking him hard in the side of the neck.

DM number three made a surprised noise of pain and stumbled back a step but unfortunately recovered quickly and moved quicker.

Catching her wrist, he twisted the skin in his hand in an effort to bring on enough pain for her to drop the phone (he failed) at the same time he jerked her so her body slammed into his.

Getting her there, he demanded viciously right in her face, "Give me that fuckin' phone."

People thought wearing high heels made you vulnerable.

It did only if you didn't know how to use them.

Sixx knew how to use them.

Therefore she lifted a leg and put all her weight into bringing her stiletto down on the top of his foot.

She thought she felt bone crunching.

He let her go as a wounded, enraged yowl came from his throat, and he bent toward his foot.

She was about to make a move to incapacitate him when they were joined by another party.

And who that party was shocked Sixx into immobility.

The yowl truncated when DM number three was slammed chest first against glass, his cheek violently crunched against the window because Stellan's hand was wrapped around the side of his head.

Stellan stepped back, taking the guy with him, turning him, and without delay, taking his head in both hands, he slammed the guy's facedown into his raised knee.

The man grunted as his legs gave out, and Stellan switched holds.

Letting his head go while clenching a fist in his shirt, he held him steady for a succession of blows to the face, each precisely aimed at his cheekbone, the second splitting the skin, the third opening it wider, the fourth sending blood spatter spitting out, the fifth insult to injury, the sixth making it a miracle the guy was remaining conscious.

His head lolling, Stellan let him go, and he floated to the floor.

He straightened from him and didn't look at a stunned Sixx.

But where he aimed his eyes nudged Sixx out of her stasis, making her pivot toward the noises she was hearing behind her.

The DM Diesel smacked to the glass was in a fetal position on the floor, out of commission, moaning and cradling his junk.

Maddox had a chokehold on DM number two, immobilizing him.

But one of the DMs must have alerted Beardsley because he'd entered the fray and engaged Diesel, and now Diesel was going to town on him.

"That's it," Maddox snarled his encouragement. "Fuck him up, bro."

Diesel didn't really need the encouragement, and he was proving Sixx's assessment of last night true.

He could easily twist the guy into a pretzel.

If he wanted to.

He clearly didn't want to.

He wanted to beat the snot out of him.

Guess that myth of fighters preparing for a bout by not allowing sexual release in order to conserve strength was just that. A myth. Diesel had blown repeatedly very recently, yet he was, no other way to put it, *fucking the guy up.*

Sixx had just started to turn to Stellan to ask what the hell he was doing there when a deep voice boomed, *"Stand down!"*

She looked to her right and got shock number two of the evening.

Branch Dillinger was standing there, stony-faced (as usual), hot (as usual) and looking pissed (not as usual, he usually didn't look anything but bored, uninterested or unfriendly).

Behind him stood Josh Coates next to a dark-haired, mildly attractive man of average height and enraged expression who she knew from her research was Barclay Richardson, and a tall, built black man who might be in the top six (now seven—in order: Stellan, Diesel, Aryas, Maddox, Olly, Branch, and that guy) of the handsomest men she'd ever seen.

Diesel pushed Beardsley off, sending him careening into a partition wall then falling flat on his ass, dripping blood from lip, nose and a cut over his eye.

With a nasty shove at the back of his head, Maddox sent DM number two staggering his way, and Maddox must have done some damage before the chokehold because the dude could barely keep himself up. He ended on a knee and both hands, for some reason Sixx suspected was Maddox's doing, his other leg dragging behind him, a few feet away from Beardsley.

"Join your colleagues," Stellan murmured in a voice very like him, silky, calm and articulate, but he did it dragging the stupefied DM number three he'd beat to hell over to his compatriots, dropping him close and stepping away.

DM number one was trying to get to his feet, but Diesel wasn't a fan of that so he planted a cowboy boot in his ass and sent him lurching into the group on the floor of the passageway.

Barclay Richardson at this point stepped over a pair of legs on the floor, walked between Sixx and D without looking at either of them, and slid open the door to station seven, moving to stand in it.

Sixx turned and saw the girl now seemed more alert, so she was also now freaked.

But the john looked terrified.

"Your pimp is out of business," Barclay said in a low, infuriated voice, his gaze aimed at the man. "After I deal with this nightmare, I'm calling the cops. So my suggestion is, get out of my house and do it fast. And my requirement is, do not ever come back."

The guy took off quickly, though he had to slow and suck his gut in to glide sideways by Barclay, who did not move except to turn his head to stare him down as he went. But once free of the door, he raced down the passageway.

Barclay then looked to the girl, and his tone was far more gentle, but still ticked.

"I'm sorry you're in this situation. If you need help getting clean, come to the front desk and ask for Clay. If that isn't something you're ready for, fine. But now I need to ask you to get anything you have here and get gone. I won't call the police on you. But as I told that man, I'm going to be calling the police. So I suggest you leave, do it quickly, and unless you come at some other time for help, please don't come back. I can't have you doing what you do here. Any of it," he told her.

She nodded and moved to where a bulky black purse sat on the floor in the corner.

Barclay moved out of the doorway, eyes to Dillinger.

"This one?" he asked, pointing to station six.

Dillinger nodded.

Sixx looked that way to see the girl now out of her robe and dressed in street clothes in the doorway, cradling her purse in her hands.

"I heard you, buddy," she said quietly to Barclay before she ske-daddled on scuffed, high-heeled red pumps down the passageway.

Barclay turned to Diesel and Maddox. "Can I ask you boys to help me and my boys get these assholes up to my office?"

"Absolutely," Maddox rumbled.

He and D moved toward the body pile.

Barclay turned his attention beyond them, so Sixx did too.

There were two DMs there, in polos and everything, both who had not yet been on that night, though one of them had been on last night.

"You're on duty," Barclay told him.

Not that there was anything to be on duty to do at that present moment. All the players in the play areas had ceased their play and were watching, including some who had gathered around and others who were standing at the windows and open sliding doors of the rooms.

But Sixx thought this, as well the DMs being ready to take over, and Dillinger, that black dude and Stellan there, meant they'd some-how had this takedown planned. Before she and D and Maddox had made their move, they'd had this planned and ready to be executed.

It was just that Sixx, Maddox and Diesel had forced their move. But . . .

How?

And why was Stellan involved?

She looked to her man.

He was in his casualwear, linen shirt, sleeves rolled up to under his elbows, hem untucked, faded jeans, a pair of smart but casual brown suede oxfords on his feet.

"Baby, what are you——?" she started.

He shifted cold eyes to her, and witnessing that look in them, she shut her mouth.

"Not now," he said low.

He turned and moved behind the men who were manhandling their human take down the passageway, and she noted both Maddox and Diesel, each with hands curled in the back collars of shirts, looking at her.

Baby? Diesel mouthed, his brows high, his gaze shifting back and forth between Sixx and the in-motion Stellan.

"D, focus," Maddox ordered, and D did that, shoving a stumbling DM in front of him, following the others down the passageway.

Sixx watched them go, feeling ice start to invade her veins.

Not now.

She looked high around the room.

There weren't many cameras, but a couple of them were roving.

As well as remotely movable.

She located the one aimed directly into the room she'd been in with the trio.

He'd been watching.

Not now.

But why?

Why was he there?

Why had he been watching?

He couldn't possibly think . . .

She shoved her phone in her cleavage, turned her attention to the now-empty passageway, and hustled down it, through the door, around the dancefloor, and to the reception area where she knew the narrow flight of steps behind the front desk led up to the management office.

It was all clear except a receptionist and a bouncer against the wall by the door.

She headed to the stairs.

"You can't go up there," the receptionist called.

"Stop me," she replied, not strolling but running up the stairs.

At the top, she opened the door and went through.

She found herself in large room filled with bizarre, slouchy furniture that looked like huge, partially molded pillows. It also had a large desk that probably was once stately but now was chipped and nicked all around the edges. And the four men they'd caught were on their knees on the floor in front of the desk, Barclay behind it, Josh off to the side.

Stellan was across the room, standing in front of some windows with a view to the club. He stood next to Dillinger and the black man.

D and Maddox were off to the side, just in from the door.

Stellan spared her barely a glance when she came in, though Dillinger gave her a good long look, the black guy gave her a lips-twitching assessing one, and she noted Coates gave her a scarily apologetic one.

She moved to stand with D and Maddox.

"Mistress girl, serious as shit, is that your boy?" D asked under his breath when she got there.

"He's my Master," Sixx replied, also quietly.

Diesel *and* Maddox's brows shot high.

But she looked right into Diesel's eyes.

"I'm a switch," she told him.

Diesel stared.

Maddox did too.

Then D grinned.

Maddox did too.

"Obviously, you're fired."

The words took Sixx's attention back to what was happening at the desk.

Barclay was talking to the three DMs.

"The shit in your lockers has been searched, left where it is, but you can consider it confiscated, including the dope. Doesn't matter what you left in them, you're not getting any of it back because once you leave, I'm not seeing any of your asses again, and not only because you're imminently going to be arrested."

There was shuffling around on knees, and the heavy air got heavier.

That said they'd found a lot of illegal substances in the lockers.

"Needless to say, you aren't getting your final paychecks," Barclay told them. "Vacation will not be paid out. References will obviously not be given. But if you manage to get your asses clear of this mess and think to fuck with me or Josh, don't. Trust me. As you can see, I have good friends. Now pull your pockets out."

No one moved.

Dillinger and the black dude, which triggered D and Maddox, all took a step toward the quartet.

"*Now!*" Barclay bellowed.

The DMs emptied their pockets.

"You too," Barclay demanded of Beardsley.

"Fuck you," Beardsley snapped.

Sixx didn't even catch how he got there. She just saw that suddenly, Dillinger was on Beardsley, bent over him, shoving his cheek viciously to the carpet with a single hand on the back of his neck. Beardsley's labored breaths could be heard trying to power out.

Impressive.

With icy calm, Dillinger stated, "He asked you to empty your pockets."

Moving awkwardly since Dillinger didn't release him, Beardsley complied.

Not surprisingly, of the four of him, old Pete had the most dope.

After he did as instructed, Dillinger let him go and stepped back.

Sixx took that opportunity to look at Stellan, who was standing with his arms crossed on his chest, studying Pete Beardsley like he was a particularly grotesque specimen pinned to a board.

Josh moved forward, ignored the number of little packets of white powder and money clips filled with bills scattering the floor in front of the men, and took up only keyrings. The rest of their possessions he left on the floor.

Josh twisted off what were probably keys to locks somewhere at the Bolt, and once these were freed, he tossed the keyrings randomly to the floor at his side.

Barclay kept talking.

"Josh and I gave you our trust. We needed you to hold that sacred, especially in this house, where the people in it need to understand you, above all others, have their backs. And you sold junk to pollute their bodies and just..." he started losing it, leaning forward, "*sold bodies.*"

It looked like he had to force himself to lean back, visibly deep-breathed, got his shit tight, and only then carried on.

"You disgust me. I can barely fuckin' look at you. The state of those girls..." He trailed off, deep-breathed again, then went on, focusing on DM one, the guy who was keeping guard on the rooms. "And you. Standing there. Standing right outside those rooms, letting them be used. How can you fuckin' sleep? How can you even look at your own face in the mirror?"

The guy opened his mouth to say something, but Barclay wasn't interested.

"Josh is right now making a call," Barclay shared, and he wasn't lying.

Josh had moved to a corner and had his phone to his ear.

"He's phoning the police," Barclay continued, setting the room to wired, but he was opening a drawer in the desk, moving casually like he didn't feel the vibe.

Using a white handkerchief he had in the drawer, he pulled out a heavily used black notebook and tossed it on the desk. He also pulled out two large money rolls and tossed them to the desk. And last, he pulled out a short stack of eight-by-ten, black-and-white pictures, and they slid across the desk.

The revelation of all this made Beardsley look even less happy.

Sixx couldn't see all of the photos, but what she could see was what she'd already seen the likes of in the pictures on her phone that Tucker took. Snaps of Beardsley out and about in Phoenix being given bills.

And there it was.

It appeared someone had been on the job, and they had a lot more time for it than her.

"My man here," Barclay said, nodding toward Stellan, Dillinger and the black guy, "is good with facial recognition shit. Those pictures correspond with a lot of footage in stations six and seven, Pete. And he's gone the extra mile, matched it all up."

Beardsley, and Sixx, looked to the men standing by the windows, and the black dude raised his hand.

"That would be me," he said boastfully, having his own merry grin that was quite like D's, and just as appealing.

"By matching, I mean those men who you've met to take money from the last few days to men using your girls the last few nights," Barclay shared, and got all attention back to him. "We're handing it and all footage we have of those rooms to the cops when they get here. They're also getting this book, which matches girls to johns to times to rooms. This money. And those pictures. The drugs will be self-explanatory. And from what we've got here. And what we found in those boys' lockers. And what Branch left in your house for the cops to find. With all that, you're not gonna plea out of an intent to distribute this time, asshole. And just so you know, my man here also rigged this room, and all of this is being recorded."

Beardsley's bruised jaw was working, but he didn't speak.

"Now here," Barclay said, putting his hand in his pocket and pulling something out.

He clapped it on the desk in front of him and slid it over with just one finger.

When he lifted that finger away, Sixx saw it was a penny.

"And here," Barclay carried on, sliding some papers that had been on the desk across it, toward Beardsley.

He also picked up a pen and put it on top of the papers.

"That's your buyout of the club," Barclay shared.

A penny.

Nice touch.

Sixx grinned as she heard D and Maddox both fail at swallowing back chuckles.

"Fuck what you say," Beardsley sneered.

"Sign it," Barclay demanded.

"No fuckin' way," Beardsley snapped.

Barclay slapped a hand on the desk, leaned into it and shouted, "Sign it, motherfucker!"

"You gonna have one of your pieces of meat make me?" Beardsley asked.

"No." Barclay leaned back. "If you don't take that penny and sign those papers, I'm going to sue you for every fucking thing I can get an attorney to sue you for in civil court for what you've used our club to do. And I've spoken to an attorney, Pete. Josh and I have a variety of grounds for a suit. So you won't just be facing jail time for distribution of narcotics and pandering. In the end, I'll have the damned club anyway, but I'll also have everything else you own. So save yourself at least some hassle, asshole. And sign the goddamned papers."

Beardsley glared at him.

"That kind offer is off the table the minute either one of us walk out of this room. I have all night," Barclay told him. "But you don't."

After a little more glaring, Beardsley moved to get up but thought twice when Dillinger murmured, "Keep your knees."

He shot a scowl at Dillinger, reached out, grabbed the pen, flipped a page, and signed a line.

"Lucky I have a number of witnesses," Barclay muttered.

Beardsley tossed the pen moronically, sending it skidding across the desk to land on the floor opposite, like it was going to hurt Barclay to remember it was there eventually and pick it up.

The room descended into silence until Barclay asked his ex-partner, "Do you have anything to say?"

"Just fuck you," Beardsley spat.

"Anything other than that," Barclay invited.

"And fuck Josh," Beardsley added.

"Is that all?" Barclay asked.

"Got him," he jerked his head backward to Maddox, Diesel and Sixx, "on assault."

"I'm sorry, didn't I tell you?" Barclay asked. "When I heard what was happening, I hired Maddox and D as undercover security. They know you and your boys were under suspicion and were instructed to keep you under their watch and act if needed, with force if necessary. The altercation was also filmed, and you were clearly the aggressor. D was just doing his job."

Sixx looked to D.

He was grinning, felt her eyes, turned his to her and shook his head almost imperceptibly, once.

So Barclay was lying.

He did it well.

When Beardsley fell silent, Barclay looked to Sixx.

"Ms. Marchesa. Thank you for participating in this investigation. After the imminent situation is dealt with, we'll settle your fee and reimburse expenses. I'll be in touch."

She decided not to share she hadn't exactly earned that fee since someone else did a whole load of the work. Though she and her crew did get their man, in a way, not to the extent the police were going to have their *men* due to what appeared to be Dillinger and his buddy horning in.

Instead she just lifted her chin slightly and said nothing.

Josh was back at the desk. Barclay shot him a glance, then moved it through the room.

"I think we're done here," he said.

Dillinger and the black guy were settled in and didn't move, so as Sixx had guessed, they'd done the legwork and would be talking to the cops.

Stellan did move.

He did it sauntering across the office right to the door.

"Hey," Sixx called, moving to him.

He stopped at the door and looked down at her.

"We'll speak at home."

With nothing more, he opened the door and moved through it, leaving her behind.

Leaving her behind.

Her first thought was to run after him.

Her second thought was that if she did, once she caught him, she might do something really stupid.

Because it was clear he was pissed.

But she was working.

Sure, it was in a sex club.

But *she was working*.

So why, exactly, would he be pissed? Act that way? *Treat* her that way? Cold. Remote. Like he was a frustrated parent dealing with a wayward child.

Not now.

We'll speak at home.

Fuck . . .

That.

Sixx looked to Josh, and he scrunched his face at her in apology, telling her he knew in whatever way her man was on board in this situation that her man was on board but Josh hadn't told her when he should have told her that her man was on board.

In other words, before Stellan got pissed at her.

She decided not to broach that now, or maybe ever. Josh had enough to deal with.

She just nodded to him then hit the door, yanking it open angrily and stomping out.

She heard big bodies clomping down behind her, and when she hit the reception area, Maddox caught her elbow.

She whirled on him.

He held on.

"That okay?" he asked, meaning Stellan.

"Is everything all right?" Molly called, rushing into reception toward them.

"It's all cool," D told her, stretching an arm out her way, an invitation Molly didn't hesitate to accept, burrowing under it and right into him as he curled it around her shoulders.

"Is it?" Maddox asked Sixx quietly, regaining her attention.

"I don't know," she replied. "I'll find out when I get home."

Maddox let her go, but continued studying her.

"Your dude is some serious good-lookin', and he's as classed-up as you are, when he isn't busting some asshole's face in," Diesel declared. "But, Sixx, babe, you're the fuckin' shit. The way you marched up with your phone all good to go. No offense to my Molly here," he gave her a squeeze, "or my boy who'd just pumped a huge load outta me and into me," he tipped his head to Maddox, "but I got hard, watchin' you do that. And I think I mighta even popped a bead of precum at your move with the stiletto. Man's got a woman like you in his bed, whatever's buzzin' him, he'll get over it."

She wasn't sure if he'd have to.

It might be her that had to get over it.

"Wow, Sixx, you did all that?" Molly asked, her eyes huge.

"She was the shit," Maddox mini-boomed.

"You're right, D. It'll be fine," Sixx stated, hoping it was the truth.

Molly looked among the group.

"What's going on?" she asked.

"It's all good, baby. All cool. But the cops are gonna be here in a minute, so we might wanna head out," Maddox said, then turned right back to Sixx. "Walk you to your car."

"I'll be fine," she assured.

"Walk you to your car," he repeated firmly.

She rolled her eyes, caught Molly grinning like only a woman in a man like D's hold with a man like Maddox also in her life could do.

"Let's go," Sixx said.

They headed out, hearing sirens.

They were halfway across the parking lot when the first cop car came in, not hot. They knew they had their men. Once parked, they cut the siren immediately.

Molly was still in D's hold as they walked, and she was looking over her shoulder at the squad.

"So it's all over?" she asked.

"Yup, apparently Clay was tipped off before Sixx got in there because he had all sorts of badasses workin' it," D shared, curling her closer.

"So the bad guys are gonna pay," Molly said.

"All on their knees in Clay's office waiting for the police to arrive, I'd say yeah," Maddox muttered.

"You guys look okay," she noted as Sixx stopped them at the back of her Cayenne. "Is everyone okay?"

"Everyone standing here is. Sixx's man showed and fucked someone up and D fucked a couple of them up," Maddox recounted. "But we're good."

"Mad got some of that action," Diesel put in.

"And I missed it all," Molly pouted and looked at Sixx. "Including meeting your man."

She hadn't missed anything.

Stellan was not in the mood for introductions.

"You won't miss what comes next, baby," Maddox said in his brand of purr before he turned heated eyes to D. "Bro, fresh cum plugged up your ass, balls drained dry, you still laid that motherfucker *out*."

Diesel's patented grin was out full force and aimed at his man. "Brother, you're the one who put in the effort, I just took it, and it didn't seem to me you had any problem taking care of business."

"Plans have changed, my man," Maddox informed him. "We get home, don't expect to sleep. After that show, I'm feeling benevolent. And pumped. So big daddy is getting it how he likes it and taking his monster *all fuckin'* night long."

"Yippee," Molly whispered.

D turned to Sixx. "I'm thinkin' I might have to call off work tomorrow."

"No thinkin' about it, D. Straight up, I'm gonna fuck you 'til you can't move," Maddox promised.

"Can I suck my D while you take his ass, Mady?" Molly requested.

Maddox turned doting eyes to his woman. "Baby, you can latch on in the truck, if that trips your trigger."

"Right on," Diesel growled.

"We should let Sixx go and get home," Molly said excitedly, trigger apparently tripped.

The trio turned to Sixx.

Then before she knew it was going to happen, she had her face stuffed in Maddox's chest with his hand squeezing the back of her neck, feeling his chest rumble even as she heard, "Sixx, pleasure." He pulled her away by her neck and looked down at her. "You ever want a show, let us know, we'll pull you up a chair. You ever want a good meal, D can't cook worth crap, but me and Mol got our shit tight in the kitchen. You're welcome at our table, and we'd only invite you for the good stuff."

"Well, hey . . ." Sixx muttered awkwardly. "Thanks."

Maddox smiled down at her and let her go.

Molly moved right in, giving her a hug, pressing her cheek tight to Sixx's shoulder, saying, "What Mad said. Totally." She pulled away but didn't let go, tipping her head back to look up at Sixx. "You're awesome, and I hope you don't become a stranger."

Sixx hoped that too, cupped Molly's cheek and told her so.

"I won't, honey."

Molly smiled radiantly and invited, "When you come over, bring your guy."

That would remain to be seen.

Sixx just smiled.

When she let go, she was engulfed in a Diesel hug.

"He'll be good. You're right," he whispered in her ear. "It'll be fine. He'd be a fuckin' fool if he doesn't work whatever's up his ass out and make that so."

He lifted his head but also didn't let go.

"Thanks," she whispered in reply.

He tipped his head to the side and teased, "Switch, hunh?"

She shook her head but forced a smile.

He started to let go, but she caught him by fisting her fingers in the sides of his shirt.

D focused again on her, raising his brows.

"Thanks for the show."

He shot her his grin. "For you, anytime."

She pressed in at his sides. "It was beautiful, D."

He tensed and his face froze.

He got her.

"Beautiful," she repeated.

He began to pull away, but she didn't let go.

"An honor to watch, Diesel. You're a lucky man. And they're lucky too."

"Know that," he grunted.

"I know you do," she said gently, let him go, but he lingered, looking into her eyes.

He did this for several long beats.

"Beautiful?" he whispered, like that was something he wanted to believe, badly, but couldn't.

"Unbelievably," she told him the truth.

It sadly didn't take long before he shook it off, jerked up his chin and moved away.

When he did, he avoided Maddox and Molly's eyes.

Molly's followed her D.

Maddox was staring at Sixx.

He lifted his forefinger to his temple, flicked it out to her as a salute and they all shifted away, moving slowly as an attached group, Molly in between her two men, their arms around her, hers around them, toward a big, white truck parked opposite her Cayenne, several cars down, both men glancing back repeatedly.

Off-duty, inaudible warlord speak for *Get in your fucking car.*

Sixx moved and got in her car.

She started it up, stared at the lights of her dash, took a breath, two, backed out of her spot and noted that the trio's truck was backed out, *well* out, out enough to give her room to pull out in front of them, but idling behind her, waiting for her to motor.

She saw Maddox behind the wheel.

Diesel was in the passenger seat.

Molly couldn't be seen.

At least that made her smile.

She rounded the empty cop cars that now totaled two, stopped at the entrance to the club, looked left, looked right, looked left again and turned right.

Thus, she headed home.

twenty-six

For As Long As I Live

SIXX

The second Sixx hit the kitchen, she thought it was a good sign that there was a filled, chilled martini glass with three fat olives on a silver pick in it sitting on the end of the bar.

She thought it was a bad sign that only the switches that illuminated spotlighting on Stellan's artwork and the pendants hanging over the bar had been hit, meaning the great room was very dimly lit.

However, she could see Stellan standing at one of the French doors, staring at the lights rotating colors in the pool, a glass of Scotch in his hand.

Her heels had made sounds on the tile, sharing her approach, but he didn't look at her.

So she stopped at the end of the bar.

She didn't touch the drink.

She called, "Apparently, you're pissed."

"That seemed like quite an intense scene you were a part of," he noted toward the pool.

She knew he was possessive of her, he'd made that clear.

But considering the situation, Sixx still had to hold her anger in check as she returned, "As you obviously watched it, you're aware I was only an observer."

"Very true," he murmured.

He said nothing more.

She gave him a shot, but he didn't take it.

So she remarked, "I don't know this particular Stellan. Do you need to brood for a while to get over your bullshit? Or are you expecting me to beg you to share what your problem is so I can beg for forgiveness I'm not certain you're due?"

That made him turn his head to her.

"Be careful, Simone," he warned.

"Why?" she asked immediately.

"You were involved in a situation that included drug dealers and pimps. I would think that you, of all people, would be aware of the kind of element those activities attract."

"Your point?" she prompted.

He turned his body toward her but didn't make a move to her.

"It's dangerous," he stated. "Any one of those men you grappled with tonight could have had guns. Knives."

"They didn't."

"They could have, and you walked right up to one of them armed with a phone."

Okay, she had to concede that.

Though, not verbally.

"How did you know I was there?"

"Branch heard through however Branch hears things that you took that job. He shared it with me."

Dillinger did . . .

What?

"Why did he share it with you?"

"He was concerned about the company you're keeping, and not just Barclay's partner, but in all of your extracurricular activities. He spoke with Leenie about what he should do, and he came to me."

"So *Evangeline* told him to share his concerns with you?"

"Yes," he confirmed.

Sixx had to take in a breath so as not to get sidetracked with additional anger at the sisterhood doing what the sisterhood often did in a way that was so integrated in society's mindset, most of the time they did it without noticing they were doing it.

Underestimating a sister.

Especially when she was engaged in doing something that stereotypically was the purview of a man.

If Branch was worried about her, as a colleague (of sorts), he should have come to her.

Being a man and maybe not getting it, if he didn't know the right way to go with that and asked his woman, straight up, *Evangeline* should have advised him to approach her.

Not Stellan.

However, at this moment, she could not get bogged down with that.

There was enough bogging down the room.

It was very unfortunate Stellan carried on.

"Branch was aware that I'd already spoken with Carvelo, Rodrigo, and their like and shared with them that you no longer were available to provide services to them. As this job was outside that breed of client, and thus I had not talked to whoever offered it to you, he was concerned you'd put yourself in another dangerous situation, knew I'd already acted to keep you *out* of such situations, so he came to me."

Learning this news, Sixx stood there, staring at the man she loved, breathing heavily.

When Stellan spoke next, his tone was no longer remote, but warm and gentle.

"You seem to either be in denial of their existence, or have taught yourself to ignore them, or have forced yourself with that exceptionally willful mind of yours to forget them. But I enjoy your body daily, and your gunshot wounds are not lost on me, darling. They're a constant reminder of that life you used to lead. A constant reminder that if you keep leading it, one day you might not come home to me."

Okay.

Right.

Sixx looked down to her drink, reached out a hand, picked it up, and brought the chilled gin to her lips.

She took a sip.

She then studied the oil from the olives skimming the surface.

She took another sip.

And she did all of this reminding herself, she was an adult.

She was in a relationship.

She'd never been in a relationship.

But now she was.

So she had to handle this.

As an adult.

Facts:

She was in love with this man.

He was in love with her.

She wanted a future with him.

He wanted a future with her.

So she could not lose her mind, say something stupid or do something stupid.

He had valid points.

They were bullshit, but perhaps he didn't know that.

She had to keep herself together and explain that to him. Calmly.

She took one last sip, put the drink down, and looked to him, having to regain her control because he was watching her, but he was still all the way across the damned room, berating his wayward girlfriend.

She drew in another breath and wished she hadn't set the drink aside.

"First," she started softly. "You began with me observing Maddox and Diesel's scene. Do you have an issue with that?"

"I can't imagine how you could ask that," he replied. "You were in a room with two men having sex without me there."

"I was on a job."

"It's trite to turn the tables, Simone, but it's also effective. To that end, I must ask how you would feel if, unknown to you, I was in a room watching women have sex?"

Fuck.

Another point.

"It was a job, Stellan."

"I understand you wish me to get there with you, Simone, but that excuse does not wash. The only reason I'm not infuriated by that particular part of this scenario is that you wore my collar. Both nights. So at least you were thinking of me."

She worked hard, and fortunately mostly succeeded, in keeping the exasperation out of her, "Of course I was thinking of you. I'm always thinking of you."

"I'm afraid I'm not convinced of that at this present time."

"It was a—"

"Repeating it doesn't make me understand it."

"Don't interrupt me, honey," she said quietly.

Stellan held her gaze but said no more.

"As I was going to say. It was a job. A good one. An important one. One I had to take. The situation in question was happening at the Bolt. I went there last night for reconnaissance purposes. I have a paying job. Responsibilities to my employer and this was outside that. I couldn't give all my attention to it, but it was important, and with what was happening in that club, it was pressing. What was happening there could not stand. I recruited informants, but that's never the best scenario when you're gathering information, especially when you need solid evidence. I had to go in. I had utterly no intention of observing any scene outside perhaps strolling past one."

When she paused and he didn't speak, she was relieved to learn he was the kind of man he had proved himself to be in the past, even if they hadn't exactly had a situation quite like this.

In other words, a man who would listen to what she had to say. She carried on.

"You did not get to meet them before you left, Molly, Diesel and Maddox. But I've known Molly for some time. She's sweet and friendly and has her head together. I recruited her. Her two Doms, Diesel and Maddox, had noticed what was going down and offered to assist, at first, mostly to take my back because as you could see, they're skilled at that. In the natural course of things, it became clear that going undercover as an observer of one of their scenes would put me in a better position to be at the Bolt for reasons that wouldn't be questioned, place me there for longer when I was not going to play and allow me to keep a much closer eye on things."

Regrettably, Stellan had something to say to that.

"You watched two of their scenes, Simone. You sat and watched the big one work the dark one on all fours on the platform last night," he pointed out.

He'd been there last night.

She took up her drink again, staring into it as she calmed herself before she took another sip.

She set it down and noted, "So that was why I beat you to the Honey last night."

"Yes," he confirmed immediately.

"You're right. I misspoke. I watched two of their scenes," she said tightly. "Last night was supposed to look like a tryout."

"It succeeded," Stellan shared. "And the only reason I wasn't infuriated last night was because you were obviously not moved by their performance because you didn't want me to service you at Naya and Ami's scene until their display, witnessed with me, moved you to have that need. For you, what Diesel was doing to Maddox, or whichever one is which, would normally be quite affecting. Last night, it did not seem to have that effect."

"That happens *when I'm working*," she stressed. "And I'll add, when you're not there."

He took a sip of his drink but said nothing.

"I was not there to get my rocks off, Stellan. I wasn't there to get my Mistress on. I would never do either of those without you with me. Not ever. I did not participate. I did not touch. I did not command. I used their scene to keep an eye on the stations Beardsley was utilizing and to get a take on the DMs that were in his pocket. That said, with full disclosure, which I would have told you regardless because I'd very much like you to meet all three, but also what I learned of them is troubling me and I'd want to talk it out with you. Molly is incredibly lovely and there's a deep, emotional issue the trio is enduring with Diesel. So I cannot tell you I was not moved when that came out in their scene. Diesel isn't comfortable with one side of his bi nature, and it doesn't often get to where Maddox was able to take him tonight. It was an honor to witness that, even as Molly explained what was happening, so it also felt like watching something tragic. But the bottom line is, Stellan, as important as that is to those three, all of that is an aside to what I was doing there. This is my job. It's what I do. It's what I'm good at. And you have to trust me to do it *without* intervening."

He opened his mouth, but she lifted her hand.

"Please, let me finish," she requested.

He inclined his head.

"You may choose not to believe me," she continued. "But as I was driving there tonight, I made the decision that if this investigation went further than tonight, I would share it with you and invite you to be a part of it in terms of being with me at the Bolt. Molly, Diesel and Maddox don't do other Doms, but they were impatient for something to be done about the situation, so they might have allowed you to observe as well if it facilitated that. They might not have, and I could have figured something else out. But I was going to give you that choice. Now as you decide whether or not to believe me, I'll point out, if I had not had you on my mind, if I did not want to have you there with me in the way I could, I would not have worn your collar."

"Point taken, Simone," he said quietly.

Good.

But they weren't done.

"As for Carvelo, Rodrigo, and the rest, you may also choose not to believe me, but I'd also decided, although I'd done it very recently, I still had made the decision that they no longer had a part in my life. It's mostly due to you. I want a future with you, and they don't belong in a life that includes something as beautiful as you."

His face began to shift to warm as he started, "Simone—"

"*But*," she said forcefully, cutting him off, "it also has to do with me. It's been pointed out to me, also very recently, that the reasons I did all of that at all no longer factor. I don't need to best my mother. I don't need to survive in that world when she did not. I don't need to inhabit that world at all. So I was going to scrape it off."

"I'm delighted to hear that, sweetheart."

She was glad he was.

They still weren't done.

"What is not okay, Stellan, is having my boyfriend phone around town and warn assholes off me. That's archaic and frankly ridiculous."

"I did it at a time when you weren't letting me in, Simone," he explained. "You weren't taking care of yourself. You weren't opening up to me, to the people who care about you, definitely not to yourself."

"Stellan, I absolutely understand the impetus. It's still not acceptable. If you had issues, you should have talked to me about them."

"Darling, if you'll remember, I tried. That wasn't somewhere you would go. We had a deal. A month for me to try to break through. And I made moves I don't regret to make sure you came home to me every night of that month, and then on, so I could *break through* and, when I did, *have a future with you.*"

"Okay. I get that. But are you getting me?" she pushed.

"I am," he replied.

"So, we're understood. This is my work. I can assure you that I'm limiting it to legal activities, of a sort, but I think you understand me. But the concerns you have you need have no more. You can also not intervene."

"I love that you would commit so fully to the mission you had these past few days because of what that mission was," he returned. "For, as I hope you know, I very much agree what was happening at the Bolt was deeply offensive and had to be stopped. That said, I hesitate to inform you of this, my darling, but I feel it's vital that it's said. You are not a superhero."

She stared at him.

Stellan kept talking.

"You cannot always save the day, the terrified, broken child inside. The junkie prostitutes having their bodies abused. The lonely sub who's looking for a Mistress who can meet his needs who is also a woman with whom he can share his life. The rich, successful, but stupidly stubborn Dom who's fallen in love with a remarkable woman that for some reason he will not allow himself to have."

Sixx couldn't stop staring at him.

"You are flesh and blood," he whispered. "Capable of being harmed and hurt and worse. I love you, Simone. I want a future with you. I want to live my life beside you. I want to make children with you. What I don't want to do is live that life terrified of losing you."

"You won't lose me," she whispered back.

She jumped when the Scotch glass shattered against the wall.

After that, she stepped back, in utter shock, witnessing Stellan Lange totally lose his cool.

"*You walked up to that man armed with a phone!*"

Damn.

There it was.

He wasn't pissed.

He'd been scared.

She'd scared him.

He'd loved his sister, she'd been harmed and hurt and worse, and he'd lost her.

She hated that. *Hated it.*

But in this instance it was vital for him to understand . . .

She was not his sister.

"I had backup, baby," she said soothingly.

"You have two gunshot wounds, Simone." He walked to the dining room table and slammed his fist into the top of it twice. "*Two.*"

God.

Her man.

He really loved her.

"I did research on these people, honey," she said calmingly. "I talked to regulars at the club about all the players. I've been there before. I did a thorough walkthrough last night. I spent the scene with D and Maddox assessing those DMs—"

"You are not fucking understanding me," he bit out. "One got his hand on you."

"I had that situation under control."

"He *touched* you, and he was twice your size."

"Stellan, honey, I can handle myself."

He looked away, dragging his hands through his hair, muttering, "Jesus Christ."

"Baby, you need to trust I know how to do my job. It's my *job*. You need to trust in me that I can do it," she said.

He turned back to her. "In all my life, in truth, to the soul, right now, there are two beings who are breathing, only two, Simone, who I love. Who it would rip me apart if I lost. But only one that if I lost her, it would fucking *destroy* me. And that one *is you*."

"I don't have a hero complex, honey."

"I read your sketchbooks."

"That was for Simone."

"You *are* Simone."

"I know."

His chest moved with his deep breaths.

"We needed to have this conversation," she said. "It's important we get to the right place here, baby."

"And when we have children?" he asked. "Will you do these things when you're a mother?"

"I think you know Sylvie Creed."

He looked to the pool, and a muscle jerked up his cheek.

He knew Sylvie.

She was a fabulous mother.

And she was a kickass investigator.

"Actually, first we need to get past the when-we-have-children part," she tried to joke.

He turned his head and locked eyes on her.

"You're having my children," he growled.

"Okay, honey. How many do you want?" she whispered.

"Get over here."

She decided to cross the great divide. Her man was emotional. He'd had a shock that night.

Apparently, even Stellan Lange had times he needed to be soothed.

So she went there.

She nearly stumbled when he yanked her to him the minute she was within reach, slamming her close and holding her closer.

Sixx wrapped her arms tight around her man.

She let him hold her, assuring himself she was right there, in his arms, breathing, okay.

Then she set about assuring him of other things.

"Right here, right now, I promise never to take unnecessary risks. I promise to do my research and always be cautious and prepared. In my work for Joel, it's rare there's danger, but if there is, I promise I won't go in ill-equipped in any way or without backup. There will be no occasion where I will go gung ho. Above all I will do everything in my power to come home to you, safe and sound, every night, Stellan, for as long as I live."

With every word she spoke, his arms squeezed tighter and tighter so she was nearly wheezing when he was done.

He got what he needed out of that hug because he took the pressure off but didn't let her go.

He rested his cheek on the top of her head and murmured, "I shouldn't have called Carvelo."

No, he shouldn't have.

She didn't confirm.

She just said, "It's done. We're past it."

"Or Rodrigo."

She grinned against his chest. "Okay, baby, I get it."

Stellan held her and she held on.

Eventually, quietly, she promised, "The stuff I did to get those scars, Stellan, I vow to you. It's done."

"All right, darling."

She let out a big breath.

"You might want to know, Susan tried to warn me about interfering with your work," he shared.

Sixx didn't know her well (yet), but she had a feeling Susan was the kind of woman who would have learned about the Bolt job and taken her concerns direct to Sixx.

"She's pretty awesome," Sixx muttered.

"Yes," he agreed.

"It was righteous that Barclay made Beardsley sell his share in the club for a penny," she remarked, tipping her head back.

Stellan lifted his to look down into her eyes.

"In getting to know him, I've noted that Barclay is 'righteous' in a number of ways. To say he was beside himself about what was happening is an understatement. Branch had to physically pull him off that Josh character when he admitted he'd suspected something was going on for weeks and he hadn't shared."

"But how could he have not known before?" Sixx asked a question she'd had since the beginning. "Everyone thinks this Barclay guy is awesome, but in one night, the state of those girls, it was obvious."

"Apparently Barclay has recently met a woman who he's become rather fond of, and they spend quite a bit of time together," Stellan explained. "Also apparently, Josh has been lax on holding up his end of the partnership, but he respects Barclay and appreciates what he's done for the club, which is Josh's livelihood. So, to give Barclay time to be with his woman, and simply to give him a break since it seems he's been running the club mostly singlehandedly for years, Josh told Barclay he could take a step back, and Josh would step in. Barclay agreed, continuing to do the books, supervise the bars and stocks of liquor, but gave up night management to Josh so his evenings would be free, and unfortunately handed staff scheduling to Beardsley."

"And thus Beardsley took advantage of that change in circumstances," she murmured.

Stellan nodded. "Further to that, although it's costly, as a precaution, Barclay keeps security footage backed up for six months before he records over it. Branch's colleague assessed it, and it appears the prostitution situation is relatively new and has only been going on for around three months. It did not escape Josh for very long, and he shared he confronted Beardsley about it repeatedly, being rebuffed. Getting increasingly panicked about it, this culminated in a nasty public argument that set him to finding an outside source to assist him in proving what he sensed to be true, this giving him the ammunition to go to Barclay so they could handle it effectively. Not an altogether wise strategy, but he was trying to do the right thing."

No, not wise, but at least it ended up getting sorted.

"The dealing, however," Stellan continued, "through Beardsley and via the DMs who were working that side job, has been going on much longer, right under the noses of Barclay and Josh, who were both unaware until last night."

"Why didn't any of the members report anything?" she asked, deciding also to ask the trio the same thing, because they knew it was happening and they didn't say anything either.

Maybe she'd bring it up when she went over to their place for dinner.

"Drugs are rampant everywhere, Simone," Stellan pointed out. "And the people dealing them, and doing them, tend to be careful about other people catching them. But I would say it's more, especially in an environment like that. What people do is their business, and not your own. Reporting decadent behavior, even illegal behavior, isn't exactly a part of our way of life. In this instance, that could be debated right or wrong. But I can understand why members would simply let it be."

That made sense.

He was right, it was debatable, but it made sense.

Stellan carried on, "That said, it would seem to me Beardsley was gaining confidence his sideline moneymaking schemes would continue to fly under radar, considering he'd been able to deal drugs in his establishment for a long time without his partners' knowledge or consent, recruiting others to expand the operation, all without getting caught. However, I suspect it's easier to hide a drug deal than it is a young woman being marked with the Chinese symbols for 'Darren' in one of his club's playrooms."

She felt her eyes get big. "Someone marked one of those girls with his name?"

"Apparently."

"How do you know that?"

"Branch's colleague was able to track down a young woman who worked for Beardsley for a while and decided it wasn't to her taste. She shared about the whole operation, the drugs, the DMs, the clients, the extremes."

Whoa.

That guy worked fast.

Totally impressive.

"Is Branch's colleague that black guy there tonight?" she asked.

"Yes."

"Did you meet him?"

"Are you asking me that because it's clear he's highly skilled, efficient, fast and effective, and he might be useful to you in some capacity in the future, or are you asking me that because you wish to invite him to our next dinner party?"

She smiled up at him. "Our next dinner party?"

"He's not in the life, so the next *party* we have, he probably would be uncomfortable. But it's apparent you're expanding the number of people you share time with, and I have a home fit for entertaining. So yes, our next dinner party. And Cam would be an excellent candidate. He's an interesting man, very funny and has the miraculous ability to shovel huge amounts of shit Branch Dillinger's way, and Branch takes it. It's fascinating."

Dillinger was not the kind of guy who took *any* shit, so that would be.

"It sounds like, except for you getting increasingly pissed at me, you had an interesting couple of evenings," she noted cautiously, not wanting to take him back if he wasn't entirely over what they just went through.

"I would hazard to say yours were more interesting." He tipped his head to the side. "Which one is the dark one?"

"Maddox."

"The man fucks like a machine."

Sixx smiled up at him again.

"I didn't have a good view, but it also appears he can take it like a champ," he remarked.

She cuddled closer. "He's a very experienced switch."

Stellan drew her closer. "Get any pointers?"

"I was working, baby," she murmured.

"Mm," he hummed, bending and touching his nose to hers.

Okay, so he was over what they went through.

Good knowing he was a man who could not only talk through important issues, and do it while listening, but also get over it.

No.

That was excellent.

When he pulled away, he didn't go very far.

"Do you wish to observe them again?" he asked quietly.

"I don't know. They really like having me around. We definitely connected in a way I don't think I've ever really had with anybody."

Stellan looked wary at that, so Sixx rushed to assure him.

"I mean in a friendship way, baby. Seriously, they all hugged me before we parted tonight, and D assured me whatever was bothering you would be okay. But as for their play, it seems very intimate, and like I said they don't do male Doms, and if you can't be there it wouldn't be any fun. I do know I'd like to get to know them all better and introduce them to you."

"We'll do that, and if it goes to that place, perhaps they'll enjoy doing their thing in our playroom for you to enjoy, and if they're not comfortable having me around while they do, I can keep myself entertained elsewhere, and we can all share a drink after they're done."

That was a surprising offer, for a variety of reasons.

She was only going to question one.

"You're going to keep your playroom?"

"Considering you don't have the option to meet certain needs in our bed, and we've found it useful for other things, I think it would be foolish to dismantle it."

Nice.

"Agreed," she replied, pressing closer.

"Darling," he said on a squeeze. "If you were not wishing me to do that, it's your playroom too, so you simply need to say. This is your home, and what happens in it and to it needs to be a joint decision."

"I will, in future," she promised.

"Two," he stated firmly.

And confusingly.

"Sorry?"

"Two."

"Two what?"

"I want two children."

Sixx froze in his arms.

He gathered her closer to his warmth. "Darling—"

"I need . . . we're just going to need . . ." She blew out a breath. "When you held Crosby, you were so . . . *Stellan,* but with a baby in your arms. It was awesome. It was gorgeous. It made me feel wonderful things. And terrifying ones. But you were just all that's *you,* with a baby. How did you do that?"

"No one knows how to handle a baby until they actually handle one, sweetheart."

Well, she'd handled one that night too, and the kid just wanted his "Steyan."

She didn't remind him of that.

She said, "Okay."

"And no one knows how to be a parent until they become one."

That was true and it made sense.

She nodded.

"We've been together only weeks," he declared.

"I know."

"I don't intend to attempt to impregnate you tomorrow."

She grinned at him and relaxed in his arms. "I know."

"We can work up to that."

Well, that was a relief.

"Is this normal?" she asked.

Now he looked confused. "Is what normal?"

"Things like we have getting so deep in only weeks," she explained.

The confusion left his handsome face and tenderness entered it. "As you know, honey, I'm not only not terribly concerned with normal, I avoid it vehemently."

That almost made her laugh because not only did she know that very well, it was part of why she loved him so much.

"I do know that," she confirmed.

"And we haven't been together for mere weeks. We've been *living together* for mere weeks. In relationship terms, I would suspect that's more like being together for three months. In terms of a relationship with you, it's more like three years."

She smiled up at him even as she swatted his shoulder in fake indignation.

He grinned down at her with humor, but the grin changed to just warm and sweet when he went on, "And you forget, I knew you and you knew me in a variety of ways prior to this starting, darling. I am not a young impetuous man, and you're not eighteen. We both know at this juncture in our lives what we want and thus knew when we found it. So I wouldn't concern myself with time, Simone, just feelings."

As ever, her wise Stellan had all the answers.

"So, we're learning a lot about each other tonight," she remarked. "You're even more protective than I knew and have an impressive right hook. We both need to be more forthcoming about our activities. We're going to have a variety of parties. I'm good at my job but absolutely do not intend to take unnecessary risks while doing it. You want to be a father, and I'm down with that . . . probably. And when you're angry with me, you still make me drinks. Did I miss anything?"

His lips were twitching when he answered, "Not that I can tell."

"Do you think Ami and Naya had a good date tonight?" she asked.

"I think Naya is getting vanilla fucked to within an inch of her life tonight."

Her body started shaking with laughter, and her voice was shaking with it when she shared, "When they got home, Maddox was going back at Diesel too."

His brows hiked up. "The big one can take more?"

"Molly says they go all night. But Maddox was turned way the hell on with Diesel beating the crap out of Beardsley, and he's top Dom, so I'm not sure D has a choice."

"He won't be able to walk tomorrow," Stellan murmured.

"I'm not certain he cares."

Stellan gave her a certain look. "So everyone we know is fucking . . . but us."

"I'm not sure *everyone* we know is fucking," she teased.

"Darling, excepting M, but including Susan and Harry, who have a very active sex life, and I will not share the excruciatingly painful reasons I know that, or details of the same, everyone we know is likely fucking, or has already gotten fucked."

She got up on her toes, sliding her hands up his back.

"Well, we better catch up," she muttered, her eyes falling to his beautiful lips.

"Agreed," those lips said.

Then he used them to kiss her.

And he didn't stop as he started walking her around the dining room table.

Sixx broke it off, still walking backward because she was compelled to do so since she was in Stellan's arms and he was moving forward.

"Honey," she whispered.

"If you intend to say anything that will delay me getting inside you, please save it. We can talk after."

"I just wanted to thank you for listening, talking tonight through, being cool, and being so easy to love."

Immediately, she was whipped around, lifted up, and found herself planted ass to the dining room table.

She then found herself gasping when she felt Stellan's hand up her skirt, and in a blink she was divested of her panties.

"Okay, you *really* don't want to delay, do you?" she breathed.

His response was to yank up her skirt.

But he didn't even have to make that response. His face was dark, and his eyes were burning.

She read him.

She lifted a hand, hooked it around the back of his neck and pulled him to her.

His mouth against hers, his hands spreading her legs, he whispered, "Darling."

"If you intend to say anything that will delay you getting inside me, save it."

She felt his hand now working his jeans.

"I just wanted to tell you I hope you know how much I love you."

She didn't smile. She didn't simper. She didn't whimper.

She pulled her man's mouth to hers and kissed him.

Hard.

Stellan slid inside and fucked her.

Sweet.

(And hard.)

And they joined the ranks of the fucking.

The perfect end to their evening.

And Sixx wouldn't think about it then, her mind being on other things.

But she would think about it later.

And in that later she would realize why she no longer needed to take risks for whatever reasons she'd taken them.

Because she'd taken the greatest risk of all.

And bested the fuck out of that bastard.

epilogue

The King and His Queen

SIXX

Tuesday night, Sixx sat in her throne by the gladiator pit beside Stellan, looking across to the thrones at the curve on the opposite side.

Naya was sitting there in a bright fuchsia, wraparound dress with a halter bodice made of a delicate ruffle that curved around her neck and flirted at her cleavage. The skirt was opened, showing a goodly amount of beautiful brown skin of shapely legs that shone like they'd been oiled. These legs led down to a pair of utterly stunning, silver, high-heeled sandals that glittered in the overhead lights of the stadium.

Her head was up, regal, but her eyes were cast down at her feet where her warrior was fucking the gladiator he'd just defeated soundly for his princess. Ami's ass bunched around the warrior dragon's tail proudly planted inside that he'd worn strolling in and throughout the bout.

Their eyes were locked as he fucked for her, and her glossy lips were parted, showing her gladiator how much she enjoyed it.

Although it was a tremendously entertaining performance, Sixx's eyes wandered to exactly opposite where she and Stellan were sitting, to where Amélie sat in a throne next to Evangeline.

They were turned toward the action, Evangeline so far as twisted in her seat and leaning on the arm of her chair to take it in, her face rapt with interest to Leigh's much more dignified expression. She just wore a cat's smile.

Both their men were elsewhere that evening.

But both the women were clearly enjoying their girls' night out.

As if feeling her regard, Leigh looked to her, seeing her beside Stellan, holding hands, and that cat's smile became a different kind of smile.

Sixx returned it.

It was then she saw that Leenie had turned to look at them too, but she was looking at Stellan.

She suddenly lifted her hand, and Sixx didn't know much American Sign Language, but she did know the alphabet, and Leenie spelled out the word *fool* with her hand and pointed at Stellan.

She was smiling madly.

But Sixx felt her brows snap together as her hand, which Stellan was holding, got a squeeze.

She turned to him with her mouth moving. "Why did Leenie just call you a fool?"

"I once accused her of being a fool in love," he answered unperturbedly. "She's returning that favor."

Well.

Okay then.

She smiled at him.

His eyes dropped to it as his hand brought up hers. He rubbed her knuckles against his lower lip, and she watched that far more avidly than she'd watched any of what she'd been treated to that pleasurable evening.

"Having a good night?" he asked.

She studied him. Then she looked between their thrones to the bleachers right behind them that were elevated enough to see over the backs of the chairs to give a full view.

Sitting right behind them, one, two, three, were Maddox, Molly and Diesel.

She'd figured out what she could give them to thank them for all they'd done.

When she'd made the offer, they'd turned it down, but they hadn't turned down those tickets.

Sensing her attention, Molly tore her engrossed eyes from Ami and Naya, looked down to Sixx and immediately lifted up both hands formed in thumbs-up positions, pumping them in front of her as a happy smile beamed out of her face.

Her men, always attuned to their Molly, noted her movements, and both took their absorbed attention from the festivities, gave it to their woman, then transferred it to Sixx.

D, of course, gave her one of his cheeky grins and added a wink.

When she took in Maddox, he mouthed the word *Nice* in a way, even mouthed, she knew was drawled and underlined in spirit with his mini-boom.

The trio turned their attention back to Ami, and Sixx turned hers back to her man, only then answering his question.

"I'm happy."

At that, his hand snaked out, he caught her head, pulled it to him, and took her mouth, thrusting his tongue inside, powerfully claiming what he had no reason to claim seeing as it was all very much *his*.

There was an unmistakable roar right before a roar from the crowd, and Stellan broke their kiss so they could give their attention back to Ami and Naya.

Ami was arched magnificently into the ass he was climaxing into, his head thrown back, the cords of his muscles popping in his neck.

His spine had barely relaxed when Naya shouted a majestic, "Come to me!"

And without delay, Ami pulled out, got to his feet, put a bare one in the back of his opponent, taking him down to his belly (to another cheer from the crowd), but he didn't stand on him.

He stood astride him as he bent to his Mistress. Grasping either side of her neck in his hands, he pulled her up from her seat, not fully, but her ass was absolutely no longer to throne, and she was suspended by his hold on her neck and her hands in the arms of the chair.

In that position, he consumed her mouth in a voracious kiss that had the crowd going wild and proved beyond doubt that their date had gone very, *very* well.

"Mistress Sixx saves the day," Stellan whispered in her ear.

She turned to him, and he adjusted his head so she could catch his eyes. "I love you."

Those eyes went soft. "And I you."

"Warning, if you keep it up this way, you're going to get sick of hearing me say that," she shared.

"Never," he whispered.

"Kiss me, Master," she whispered back.

He did, and he did it for some time.

When he finally released her, the crowd had calmed down because Ami was gone, Naya was no longer seated on her throne, and the action had lulled, waiting for the next gladiators to duel.

"Totally getting you a dragon's tail, bro," she heard Maddox growl from behind them.

"Totally getting *you* one, my man," D returned.

"You're both totally getting one," Molly declared. "When you play with your pixie at home, you're now gonna be my *dragon* warlords."

"Word," D agreed, sounding keen.

Maddox said nothing.

Sixx grinned, then turned immediately to Stellan, leaned in, and opened her mouth.

"Darling, please," he murmured before she could say anything. "Allow yourself to bask in the glory victorious of your last amazing feat," he indicated Naya's empty seat with an inclined head, "before jumping right into another one."

Since that night at the Bolt, she'd fully shared about her experience with the trio.

"They're so happy, and they're so good together, but if someone can get through to D, they could be *more* happy—" she started softly so the trio wouldn't overhear.

"Make a deal?" he asked, brows raised.

She grinned again. "Sure."

"One week. Hang up your cape for one week. Then you can dig into fixing all the problems of your precious *ménage*."

"Thanks, baby," she said to agree. "But I don't wear a cape. I wear leather."

His eyes dropped to the bronze leather under her gold choker at her chest.

"And I thank the superhero gods for that."

She burst out laughing.

Stellan kissed her lips while she did it.

Then the next gladiators came in.

And the king and his queen sat in attendance, holding hands, enjoying their evening.

STELLAN

Stellan opened the door to his office and stopped dead.

His first inclination was to clench his teeth so he wouldn't say anything he'd regret.

What happened next made that effort unnecessary.

The dancing, happy eyes of both the women he loved turned to him amid the laughter they were sharing, and one of them greeted through it, "Yo, boss man," while the other one greeted, "Hey, baby."

He moved to the jamb and leaned a shoulder against it, crossing his arms on his chest, aiming his gaze at Susie sitting behind the desk, not at Simone, who was standing in front of it.

"Have I not shared the instruction that you were to inform me when Simone was here?"

"She has her own keycard, Stell. She showed to surprise you to take you out to lunch, the operative word being 'surprise,' and I was just telling her you have a lunch meeting, so we decided we're going to go out together instead."

Stellan pushed from the door, ordering, "Cancel my lunch meeting."

Susan's eyes got big. "Stellan, it's in fifteen minutes."

"Cancel it," he repeated. "I'm having lunch with my assistant and my girlfriend."

"You're negotiating a seven million dollar deal at this meeting," Susan reminded him.

At that, Sixx's eyes got big just as he made it to her and curved an arm around her waist, pulling her body into his.

But he turned his head to Susan. "The deal will still be there when we reschedule the meeting."

"You're annoying," she snapped.

He raised his brows.

She threw up her hands. "How am I going to get all the juicy tidbits of Stellan Lange as boyfriend from Simone with you sitting there?" she demanded to know.

"Precisely," he replied.

Simone laughed softly, and Stellan looked down to her.

"Where shall we go to lunch?" he asked.

"I promise, I would only tell her the parts about such things as you casually throwing thousands of dollars of gold and platinum custom-made jewelry in my lap like you did it every morning before taking your vitamins," she said instead of answering. "I wouldn't have gotten into the sex parts."

"Good," Susan said into their exchange. "I can't handle the sex parts. He already *seems* like a god. I don't need proof he *is* a god."

Simone was laughing again, he felt it against his body, and it gave further indication that when he struck their deal weeks ago he was very unusually woefully unprepared for the ramifications of pulling out all the stops to make Simone Marchesa happy.

In other words, just how doing that would return the feeling.

"Darling, I asked, where would you like to go to lunch?" he repeated.

"Where would you like to go?"

"I'm in the mood for steak."

Her brows rose. "Aren't you always?"

It was resolute when he replied, "Absolutely."

To that, his Simone just smiled.

It was warm.

It was sweet.

It was happy.

That evening, having turned the page on the sketchbook to where Simone had finished her latest story, studying the image on the page, Stellan had a queer sensation he'd never felt before.

As queer as it was, he knew instinctively it was one he'd forever treasure.

The tone of her story had changed significantly.

Through her new association with a mysterious, shadowy man who possessed great powers, it would seem Superhero Sixx had a lock on a miracle cure that was slowly erasing her scars with each good deed she did.

So as she fought to find ways to offer love and succor to the brave soldier through the arms of a beautiful princess . . .

And as she kept her eye on the beneficent business tycoon who was in love with a protégée, but his hesitation meant he might lose her to another man . . .

And as she looked into the demons of a rough but handsome, loving and good-natured man who had the love of a beautiful pixie and the adoration of a powerful warlord . . .

Her scars were fading.

And in that last panel, Superhero Sixx lay naked atop her shadowy savior, her forehead tucked into his neck, her legs straddling his thigh, his face obscured, but her face was not.

Even still scarred, it was the first time she'd depicted her alter-ego's expression as soft, unguarded, and filled with beauty.

Yes, that queer sensation was something he'd forever treasure.

"So, what do you think?"

Sixx was reclined beside him on his chesterfield, pressed to the back of the couch and down his side, her eyes on the sketchpad he held up, braced against his stomach.

His voice was not his own, hoarse and gravelly, this catching her attention as her eyes shot to his when he asked, "Is that how you see us?"

Gently, she answered, "That's how we are."

Fuck.

But he loved her.

"You should publish these, Simone."

Her chin jerked into her neck.

"They're extraordinary," he declared.

"They're my life. And now, yours too."

"No one need know that. No one need know you did them at all. You can publish under a pen name."

"I—"

"They're beautiful. Your talent is unquestionable. They're provocative. They're erotic. They're emotional. You can't help but root for Sixx. And now, as the story turns, root for her and her shadowy lover as she turns from life as a heroic antihero with a chilling, tragic, jaded past to an unadulterated hero with a future filled with hope."

"Stellan—" she whispered.

"Think about it, darling. I know people who publish erotica. They do very limited graphic novels, but I feel they'd jump at a chance at this."

"Someone might know it's you," she told him.

"I don't care," he replied. "But I can't imagine they would. You cloak my face."

"I don't cloak mine."

"Regardless."

"I want you protected."

Of course she did.

She was Simone.

But she'd always be Sixx.

"That's hardly necessary," he said quietly. "Especially not now, no one's seen these but me. Though that's a shame, considering how remarkable they are. But just to say, if anyone were to guess it was me, I would far from care. And not simply because you've cast me as gallant redeemer to your hero. A savior. All-powerful. That's hardly unflattering."

She looked to the pad, mumbling, "I'll think about it."

He used his other arm, which was around her, to give her a squeeze, regaining her attention.

"I hope you truly do."

Her head quirked to the side, and an expression he could not read filtered over her pretty face.

As was becoming her way, Simone did not make him wait or even ask after it.

She gave it to him.

Freely.

"You know, I never thought I'd show these to anybody. Now I'm right here with you while you read them, and I'm honestly considering the idea of sharing them further."

"Does all that worry you?"

"No, I think it's . . . I think it's . . ." She pressed closer and suddenly smiled. "I think it's proof you *are* all-powerful."

Relaxing into her mood, Stellan chuckled.

"Thank you, baby," she whispered.

"My pleasure," he replied. "Even though I don't know why you're expressing gratitude. You giving me the honor of sharing this with me," he lifted the sketchpad to indicate what he was talking about, "deserves the gratitude."

"And *that*," she lifted a finger and put it to his lips, "the fact you'd say something like that, the fact you're that man, is why I'm thanking you."

It was clearly time to move the evening onward.

Therefore, with care, Stellan reached out and set the sketchpad on his coffee table.

After he did that, he turned into his Simone.

And after enjoying something extraordinary that was all Simone, he enjoyed something tremendously extraordinary that was all Simone.

Simone.

SIXX

Sixx got into her Cayenne, looked at the dash, and froze.

On it was propped a female action figurine wearing a fake leather bodysuit, little plastic high-heeled boots, a tiny mask over its eyes, short brown hair on its head, a miniature whip in its hand.

In front of it sat a folded-over note with *Sixx* written on it.

Carefully, she reached out, took hold of the note and unfolded it.

It read:

> *Sixx-*
> *Debt paid.*
> *Not going to miss worrying about your crazy ass.*
> *But I'm going to miss you.*
> *-Your Favorite Asshole*

Carlo.

She looked up and around the parking lot, seeing random people, not seeing Carlo.

As she wouldn't.

But he'd been watching her. He was likely watching her right now.

Thus he knew more than from the fact he hadn't heard from her (undoubtedly looking into it because of that fact) that she was out of commission.

He'd also figured out why.

And he was happy for her.

She grinned at the action figure as she took hold of it.

It was the second doll she'd ever owned.

This one was kickass.

So this one she would keep.

But that wasn't the only reason why.

She bent the doll's legs to sit her on the seat beside Sixx and pulled out her phone.

Next time you're in town, come to dinner and meet my man, she texted Carlo.

She was not surprised when she got no reply.

She did not yearn for any part of her old life.

But seriously . . .

He could be a pain in the ass.

But she was going to miss that guy.

SIMONE

Simone was sitting next to Stellan at the island, having her breakfast and listening to M prattle when Stellan's phone rang.

She looked to him to see him staring at it sitting beside his plate, but her eyes immediately darted to the phone when she saw his brows had drawn together ominously.

She just caught that the screen said HARRY CALLING before he snatched it up and put it to his ear.

"Hello, Harry, how——?" he started, stopped, and shoved back his stool so violently in order to burst out of it, Simone grew still before she jumped off her own stool, her gaze shooting to M who was staring at Stellan, her face now pale.

"Of course," Stellan said on the move. "I'm leaving now. I'll be there as soon as I can."

Simone chased after him.

M chased after Simone.

"Yes, right. Yes. I promise, Harry, I'll be there shortly," Stellan told him, and Simone practically had to run to keep up with his long, agitated strides.

He'd clearly disconnected because he took the phone from his ear.

Before she could ask, he turned his head to look over his shoulder at her, but did it still moving.

"Susan's gone into labor. Harry needs someone to look after Crosby," he shared tersely.

Oh no.

"She's not due——" Simone started.

"For six more weeks," Stellan clipped out, yanking open the door to the garage with such force, it was a wonder he didn't pull it off its hinges.

"I'm coming with you," she said.

"Thank you," he bit off.

She kept hustling after him as she turned back to M.

"We'll be in touch," she said.

M stood in the door she was holding open and nodded.

Stellan practically threw himself in his Tesla.

Simone followed suit.

She let him concentrate as he pulled out and only spoke when they were on the road.

Putting her hand on his thigh, she gave it a squeeze as she said softly, "It's going to be okay."

Stellan made no reply.

He just drove.

STELLAN

Stellan looked to Simone, who was standing in the waiting room with Crosby on her hip and was swinging him around, chattering to him, and he was chattering back like they were carrying on a weighty conversation when they were enumerating his favorite stuffed animals.

Stellan's chest felt like it was filled with quickly drying concrete.

It was the second time in his life when he consciously had to remind himself to breathe.

The first was when he'd opened the door to his own car in his father's garage and realized his sister was dead.

Harry had been sent out of the delivery room due to the fact they'd had to perform surgery. An emergency C-section, for some reason that had been explained, but Stellan was not in the state to grasp, both mother and child were in distress.

However, half an hour ago, Harry had been called to his wife.

They gave no further news, no staff had returned to share any, and they'd not seen Harry since.

Stellan sat still in his chair, which he thought was a miracle considering he was coming out of his skin.

"Who's that?" he heard Simone ask, and he focused on her, saw her head bent toward Crosby still at her hip, but she was pointing at Stellan.

"Steyan!" Crosby yelled.

She pointed to herself. "Who's this?"

"Shimone!"

"That's me." She smiled at him and held him closer, swinging him around. "Shimone."

"Daddy!" Crosby cried.

Simone whipped around, and Stellan's head jerked toward the door as he straightened from his seat.

Harry walked in looking haggard, but not destroyed, and Stellan started breathing slightly easier.

He was with a nurse, but she stopped at the door to the waiting room as Harry strode right up to Simone and gently took his son from her arms.

He pulled him tight to his chest, murmuring, "Hey, son, hey, boy." He drew in a ragged breath. "You've got a baby sister."

Stellan closed his eyes.

"Shishter!" Crosby shouted.

Stellan opened his eyes and watched Harry's come to him.

"She wants you, brother."

Stellan glanced at Simone, fell more deeply in love with her at the soft relief shining from her beautiful face as she kept her gaze on him, but he did this walking directly to the nurse.

"Just follow me," she said.

He did, and he felt she moved far too slowly.

He was taken to the door of a room that, when she stopped at it, and before she could say a word, he pushed straight through.

The nurse did not follow, and she vanished from his mind as he saw a wan Susan lying propped in a hospital bed with a very tiny bundle cuddled to her chest.

Stellan stopped dead at the door, hearing it close behind him, but with the crush of emotion he had not allowed himself to feel landing on him now that he saw them both alive and well, he was unable to move.

Susie's eyes lifted right to him.

"She's fine," she said, sounding how she looked—exhausted. "She's breathing on her own and nursing on her own, which is a relief. They say she'll sleep a lot, and we'll have to help her keep warm. But other than that, she's good. I'm good. We're all good, Stell."

Stellan still didn't move.

Susie kept her gaze locked to him.

"We've named her Silie, honey," she whispered.

It was at that he remained unmoving for an entirely different reason.

Also at that he allowed one.

Just one.

One tear to fall from his eye.

Then he pulled himself out of his inertia, walked direct to her, bent in, and kissed his girl on the forehead. He moved and kissed his new girl on her diminutive but mercifully chubby cheek.

"Hello, Silie," he said quietly.

He heard Susie's soft sob and lifted his head to look at her.

"Sh, no," he murmured. "None of that."

"I really love you, boss man," she said hoarsely.

He looked into her beloved eyes. "And I thank God every day you do."

She swallowed and pulled her bundle closer.

The door opened, and Stellan straightened away to watch Harry walk in.

"Crosby?" Susan asked.

"He's with Sixx. He's good. Excited about his sister," Harry answered, walking to Susan's other side.

He sat on the bed, put a hand to the rump of his daughter and bent close to kiss the lips of his wife.

"We'll bring him in when it's time, then we'll take him home with us and bring him back when it's time," Stellan offered.

"His things—" Susan started.

"It's my understanding Simone is adept at breaking and entering, sweetheart. We'll be fine," he assured.

"What?" Harry asked, confused.

It was only then Stellan found true relief.

Because Susan started laughing.

Hours later, Stellan rounded the chesterfield.

And he stopped dead for the second time that day at what he saw.

Simone, flat on her back, Crosby flat out on her chest . . . and just out.

This was not a surprise.

What was a surprise was that Simone was not also sleeping the sleep of the dead. Woman and boy had been on the go with toys, pool play, the kind of hide-and-seek you could enjoy with a twenty-two-month-old, which happened to be exceptionally loud, and the very messy results of cookie baking from a tub when a toddler was the one forming the batter.

She was always lovely.

Right then she was exquisite.

"Four," she said.

His gaze went from the child on her chest to her eyes.

"Pardon?" he asked.

"Not two. Four. Or at least three."

Staring at her, before Stellan could open a throat that had suddenly closed, M bustled around the couch, tsking, "He should have been in bed an hour ago."

She reached out to Crosby, carefully taking him from Simone as she explained, "He got a baby sister today. We had to celebrate."

M shook her head in silent reprimand, but when her back was to Simone and her gaze came to Stellan, her eyes were dancing.

And bright.

She winked at him.

Then she walked with Crosby to the stairs.

Simone sat up and reached out to the baby monitor on the coffee table, muttering, "Considering the fact we've set up his bedroom in the same house, but still it's in practically another state, probably should figure out how to turn this on."

"Darling?" he called.

She looked up at him. "Yes?"

"I love you."

Her face got soft. "I love you too."

"Warning," he whispered. "If you keep it up this way, you're going to get sick of hearing me say that."

The beauty of the look those words wrought was indescribable.

"Never," she replied.

SIMONE

The bed moved when Stellan joined her in it, rousing her from sleep.

Even if that hadn't happened, he would have roused her considering he claimed her, doing this turning her, pulling her to him, and arranging her mostly on top of his body.

"How was it?" she mumbled sleepily.

"Interesting," he replied.

This caught her attention and cleared some drowsy, forcing her head off his shoulder to peer at his shadowed face in the dark.

"How was it interesting?" she asked.

"Barclay, plus Aryas, co-hosting a bachelor party, darling, how do you think it was interesting?" he asked back.

"Were there strippers?" she continued the interrogation.

"Absolutely not."

"Was there flesh?"

"Absolutely."

The drowsy disappeared, and her hand began to move to find out for herself even as she queried, "Are you turned on?"

"Not . . . exactly."

Her hand stopped on his tight abs.

"What does that mean?" she inquired.

"I don't know. I've never had 'buds,'" he stated. "But I do think one of the cardinal rules to having them is that what happens at a bachelor party stays at the bachelor party."

Unable to stop it, she dropped her head to his chest, and Simone burst out laughing.

Olly and Leigh were getting married the next weekend.

And that night, Stellan had attended Olly's bachelor party.

Actually, he'd been invited to both of them. The first one was given by Olly's best buddy from the firehouse, some guy named Chad.

This one, though, only a certain variety of Olly's brothers were invited to attend.

Since she'd known Olly, he and Stellan had always shared an

affinity. But apparently, when Stellan became involved at the situation at the Bolt, he'd been adopted by the bro crew that included Olly, Barclay and Branch, and they had recruited Aryas along with Stellan.

It wasn't often, but it wasn't rare, that they met for drinks.

Stellan met with them acting like it was somehow under duress.

But Stellan didn't do anything under duress.

He liked them.

He'd even asked Maddox and Diesel to join them.

And they had.

When she stopped chortling, she lifted her head and asked, "Was it sordid?"

"Do you think Aryas would do anything sordid?"

She kept grinning at him through the dark. "Why are you answering my questions with questions?"

"Because I'm trying to communicate to you none of your questions are going to get answered."

That made her burst out laughing too.

"Branch proposed to Leenie last night," he announced.

Simone went still.

"She, obviously, accepted," he carried on.

"Holy God," she breathed.

"In his style, he's warned they'll be having a very low-key ceremony with limited invitations being sent."

"Do you think we'll be invited?"

"As far as I know, Branch holds regard for five people. Olly. Barclay. Cam. Aryas. And me. So unless by 'limited' he meant only him and Leenie will be in attendance, I'd wager . . . yes."

"Cool," she mumbled.

He turned to her so that he was now on her.

"If you're awake . . ." he murmured.

"Did Olly have a good time?" she whispered.

"The man is much loved, that was proved without doubt tonight, so yes, darling, he did," he whispered back.

That was the only question that she needed answered.

She communicated that by sliding her fingers in his hair.

And her Stellan, as ever, missed nothing.

Certainly not that.

"Stellan."

"Simone."

"*Stellan.*"

"Come, Simone."

She came.

Wrapped around him, the spiked heels of her Zanotti sandals digging into his ass, her head shot back, and she shuddered as her pussy clutched him through her release.

His hips moved, stroking inside her, caressing her the only way he could through it and as she came down.

When she was done, she kept her arms locked firm around his shoulders but adjusted her legs so her heels were no longer digging into his flesh.

"You didn't come," she whispered.

"I'll be coming with you sleeved, your silk sashes binding you knees-wide to my bed, those shoes still on but calves bent up and trussed to your thighs, but like now, you'll be wearing nothing else, your face in *my* pillow, my cock up your ass," he growled.

She shivered, impaled on him.

"To do that, you need to untie me," he pointed out thickly, but rationally.

"After I do, should we enjoy a drink before we leave?" she teased.

"You just earned that ass fucking with very red cheeks."

That set her to trembling.

"Simone," he warned.

She kissed him.

He kissed her back.

Then she climbed off, dropping to her feet, and she knew what she was buying when she zipped herself into her skintight cream leather boatneck dress before she moved to her man to release him.

The shades were up on their room at the Honey.

This was at Stellan's decree.

He liked them to show off, when he worked her, when she used him.

Sometimes, however, if it was in her power, she closed them.

Because some moments were just for them.

This night, her work had been inspired.

So she did not.

However the switch Mistress Sixx and the seemingly switch (but not so much) Master Stellan had lost the allure of most the patrons of the Honey, so their audience tonight was thin.

They were more interested in what was happening with Talia and Aryas.

As it went.

And always would.

Happily-ever-afters only remained exciting to the ones living them.

But as she turned to attend to the white ropes that bound her man, she thought it was a shame she had to let him loose.

Her work had been sublime.

She took a mental snapshot to sketch it later before her fingers moved to the web of rope and knots she'd tied up his back, ropes rounding him at waist, ribs, under his bulging shoulder blades and along the sides of his neck as well as at his biceps with a fanciful (and hot) set of doubled-over bindings at his right thigh.

The ropes also led from biceps to wind again and again around his wrists, and from junctures of the riggings from biceps to wrists led ropes that also wound again and again around a ring suspended from the ceiling to which his arms were raised and his fingers curled around.

All this led up from a similar formation at the front that tucked through his legs, embedded in the crease of his beautiful ass up to web at his back.

As she'd noted . . .

It was *inspired*.

She'd had to use him to hold herself up to *use* him since he was on his feet but did not have the use of his arms, and as she untied him, she saw the marks her heels had made in his ass.

She whisked a hand across one.

"That okay, baby?" she whispered.

"I like restraint, as you've discovered. And as with your experimentations with paddles and switches shared, I also enjoy pain. So yes. As those scenes were far more prolonged, this is nothing. However, I liked it understanding I would soon *give it*, so stop concerning yourself with your marks and untie me, darling."

She suppressed a smile and got back to the matter at hand.

When he was fully released, the white rope falling to the floor at his feet, with an arm he swept her against his body and took her mouth in a kiss that left her silly.

"Of all of that, outside having your pussy, and your heels digging deep, I enjoyed the placement of the ropes best, my Simone," he murmured. "So when we get home, I'll be working you after you plug me."

God, she loved it when he was in that mood.

Her legs started shaking so she held on.

"Can you stand?" he asked.

"Maybe," she answered.

"Please try so I can get dressed and we can go home."

She nodded, let him go, managed to stay upright on her own two feet as he moved to his clothes, unconcerned there were members lingering outside the windows.

Watching him, the way he was, all that he was, she thought, seriously.

He was just so . . .

Everything.

Simone stayed where she was and called, "You know I love you," as he pulled on his trousers.

"Yes."

She grinned.

"You know this is totally making my sketchpads," she shared.

"Yes," he repeated simply.

"You better give it to me good at home, honey, so that'll make it too," she urged.

He turned to her, shrugging on his shirt. "Do I ever not?"

She shook her head. "Nope."

His eyes dropped to the rose gold collar at her neck. "You gave a mark, you've earned one. Alas, that means that will eventually have to be removed."

He was buttoning up his shirt when she replied with feeling, "Alas."

His gaze came to her eyes. "Your impudence will also need to be addressed."

"Nothing you're saying is not making me think that you're dressing way too damned slowly."

That was when he smiled his oh-so-special smile.

And started doing his buttons a lot more leisurely.

She crossed her arms on her chest and hitched out a foot.

Catching her stance set those smiling lips to twitching.

"Do you know I love you?" he asked.

"Yes," she answered.

"Good," he murmured, reaching for his tie.

He lifted up his collar.

"For God's sake, Stellan. We're going home. You don't need to knot your tie."

"Get over here, Simone."

She huffed her way over.

The instant she was in arm's reach, he grabbed hold, shoved her against the door and ravaged her mouth.

She was finding it hard to breathe when he lifted his head.

"You'll wait, Simone," he growled.

"Of course, baby," she breathed.

"Mm?" he prompted in that purr of his that slithered so lovingly against her clit.

She arched into him, tightening her arms around his shoulders.

"Of course, my Master," she whispered.

"There's my Simone," he murmured, staying in her hold even as he knotted his damned tie.

But as ever he was right.

His Simone.

There she was.

And always would be.

No longer wondering what it would feel like not to be healed, but you were again whole.

Knowing precisely what it felt like to be healed.

And made whole.

As well as safe.

In love.

Happy.

Knowing she'd have all this . . .

For as long as she was breathing.